Sally of Sefton Grove

Dee Williams

headline

First published in 1995
by HEADLINE BOOK PUBLISHING

First published in paperback in 1995
by HEADLINE BOOK PUBLISHING

20 19 18 17 16 15 14 13 12

ISBN 0 7472 4880 X

Typeset by Keyboard Services, Luton, Beds

Printed and bound in Great Britain by
Clays Ltd, St Ives plc

HEADLINE BOOK PUBLISHING
A division of Hodder Headline PLC
338 Euston Road
London NW1 3BH

This book is dedicated to my two dear Aunt Renes, and also my Auntie Edie, who have been such a help with all their war-time stories.

It is also for my young sister, Christine, whom I mustn't leave out.

I would like to thank Julie Robertshaw of the Imperial War Museum for the invaluable information she supplied me with.

Chapter 1

Sally Fuller bent down and picked up the last of the wilted brown flower petals lying forlornly on the colourful rag rug that had pride of place in front of the hearth. Many years ago Sally had watched her mother sit night after night, patiently pulling strips of cloth through a piece of sacking, gradually transforming it into the rug.

Sally looked at the photograph of her mother on the mantelpiece. It had been taken when she was young and the warm smile and twinkling eyes had never left her.

Although the front room curtains were pulled together, the last rays of May's late evening sunlight were defiantly piercing through chinks in the thin material. Dust hovered and danced in their beams. All the curtains in Sefton Grove were drawn as a sign of respect, for Hilda Fuller had been very well liked by friends and neighbours alike.

Sally wanted to throw back the curtains and open the windows wide to let in the light and fresh air. The wreaths had made the room smell sweet and sickly. She slumped down on to the hard brown Rexine armchair and played with the petals in her hand. Tears slowly ran down her pale cheeks.

Her thoughts went to just a year ago, when, on Johnny's eighth birthday, everybody in Sefton Grove had been happy and had all joined in the street party to celebrate the coronation of King George and Queen Elizabeth. But this year, Johnny had spent his birthday sitting with his mother, holding her hand till the end.

'Mum,' whispered Sally. 'What are we going ter do without yer?'

'Sal, Sal, you all right?' Pete Brent's voice broke into her thoughts. He poked his head round the door, his dark eyes full of concern. Nervously he ran his hand over his slicked-down straight, dark hair. Today he looked more handsome than ever in his dark suit, his starched white collar and black tie such a contrast against his tanned face.

Sally quickly brushed the tears from her cheeks. 'Yes thanks, Pete,' she said, smiling faintly. She didn't have to pretend to him. They had known each other all their lives. Pete, at twenty-one was two years older than Sally, and theirs was an easy and comfortable friendship.

'Yer pop's sitting outside in the yard – 'e's a bit down. 'E said 'e fancies a drink so I'll be off up the Nag's wiv 'im. Yer don't mind, do yer?'

'No, course not. Where's Babs and Johnny?'

'In the yard playing wiv the cat. I'll keep me eye on Pop, and I won't let 'im stay too long.'

'Thanks, Pete.'

'Yer sure you'll be all right?'

Sally nodded.

'I'll call back later.'

The sound of her father's footsteps echoing along the linoed passage stopped. He called out. 'Ready, Pete? Won't be long, Sal.' He didn't come into the front room.

Pete looked round. 'I'll be off now.' He quietly closed the door behind him.

Sally sat back wistfully and thought about her family. Dear Dad – he was going to miss Mum, and her younger sister and brother were very upset at losing their mother.

Babs, like Sally, took after her father in colouring. Her straight dark hair was cut to just below her ears, with a fringe framing her round face. Her dark eyes flashed with every mood. She was slim, and seemed to be all arms and legs. At twelve, she was growing up fast.

Johnny was the quieter of the two. He was sensitive, and a worrier. Pale and skinny, he never looked well, and with his light brown hair and soft green eyes, he took after his mother. His shirt was always hanging out of his trousers, and his socks permanently down in his shoes. Sally could almost hear Mum shouting at him to smarten himself up, 'and pull up those socks.' She would have been proud of him today – he had looked very smart, and had tried hard not to cry as he sat quietly in the carriage behind the hearse, watching the horses' bobbing heads. Their mother's funeral had been a very sad affair.

Sally sighed. What would they do without Mum? How would she manage to do the shopping, washing and ironing, and go to work at the chocolate factory, where she was a packer? Mum had always done everything for them. She had been loving and cheerful, and always found time to listen to them. A tear ran down Sally's cheek. She would be nineteen next month and Mum wouldn't be here to share her birthday.

Then there was Pete. He never made any bones about how ambitious he was. By day he was a stevedore like her dad and they worked in the docks together, but at night and weekends he helped his older brother Reg with the small printing business in the back yard. In between he was taking driving lessons from his uncle, as the next thing he wanted was a car. Sally and Pete had been seeing each other for years, when he wasn't busy. It wasn't romantic like in the films she saw at the pictures, and she knew Pete wasn't in any hurry to get married, but she was quite happy to wait for him.

Sally heard someone pull the key that hung on a piece of string behind the door, through the letter box. She looked up at the clock on the mantel shelf. It couldn't be Pete and Dad back already, it was much too early. She jumped up and threw open the front room door.

''Allo, Sal. All right if I come in fer a bit? I saw Pete and yer dad go out so I knew you'd be on yer own, so as soon as I got the kids down I fought I'd pop in and see if yer wanted a bit o' company.'

To Jessie Walters' surprise, Sally threw her arms round her neck, almost knocking her off balance.

'Oh Jess, I'm so unhappy,' she sobbed.

'Yeah, I 'spect you are. Yer've been frough a lot terday, and yer've bin ever so brave.'

Sally stood back and wiped her eyes. 'I think it's only just beginning to sink in.'

'Yer shouldn't bottle it all up, yer know. D'yer fancy a cuppa tea?'

Sally nodded.

'Well, sit quiet in 'ere, and I'll go and make one.'

Sally didn't argue. Jessie was Sally's only close friend. She had known her all her life. Jessie was a year older than Sally, but they had always lived in Sefton Grove, Rotherhithe, gone off to school together, then worked together at the chocolate factory till Jessie left to have her first baby.

Even though Jessie was expecting when she got married she didn't care about all the talk and had her white wedding. Sally was chief bridesmaid, and they had a super party afterwards. A year after Harry was born, Pat arrived. She was almost two now, and Sally was godmother to both children. It was Sally who had comforted Jessie when her husband, Vic, whom everybody knew was a bit of a philanderer, ran off with a young girl from his work. He was good-looking and everybody was amazed he'd married Jessie, even though she was expecting. To Sally, she would always be Jessie Walters, never Owen. Jessie was a good needlewoman and Sally wasn't surprised when, after her husband left, she took in sewing. Now she made just enough to make ends meet.

Jessie walked in carrying the heavy tray, and kicked the door shut behind her. 'Young Babs said, could they finish orf the last o' the cake?' Without waiting for an answer she went on. 'I told 'em they could – that all right?'

Sally nodded. 'I could 'ave come out in the kitchen, yer know.'

'Yeah, but it's cosy in 'ere. 'Sides, I fink yer wonner be on yer own fer a bit.' Jessie slowly stirred the tea in the brown china teapot. 'That was a nice service 'e gave yer mum. Did yer wonner bit o' cake?'

Sally shook her head. 'No, thanks. Are the kids all right?'

Jessie smiled and patted the back of her fair wispy hair. Her smile lit up her full face, making her striking blue eyes almost disappear. Jessie had inclined to put on a little weight since having the children. 'It's finishing up all the bits they leave. Me dad can't stand wasted food,' she always told Sally.

'Yeah, they're fast asleep. I fink Mum was bit upset she 'ad ter look after 'em this afternoon, but I told 'er it was 'er or me what went to the funeral, and I won.' Jessie smiled again. Although she and her mother had had their differences, she had stood by Jessie and would do anything for her and her kids, and Jessie thought the world of her mum. 'The flowers were really nice. I fink the wreaf the Grove got was nice. D'yer know, everybody put sumfink in.' She poured the tea and handed the cup to Sally. 'I was surprised ter see Pete took the afternoon orf, wiv 'im always ser worried about money.'

'Dad says there ain't a lot of ships in at the moment, and the foreman said it was all right.'

'Still, 'e didn't git paid.'

'Well, 'e wouldn't anyway if 'e'd bin sent 'ome.'

'No, course not. 'Ere, Sal, will this make any difference ter you and Pete?'

'Why? What d'yer mean?'

'Well, will yer be gitting married soon?'

'Don't think so. Besides I've got ter think about Dad and Babs and Johnny now, and anyway, Pete wants ter get a car.'

Jessie sat back. 'Oh yeah, I forgot. Don't 'e wonner git married?'

'Jessie Walters, I've told yer before, Pete and me are friends. What is the 'urry ter git married?'

'OK, keep yer 'air on. By the way, me and Mum was wondering what yer gonner do about the shopping and washing?'

'I dunno.'

'If yer like, we could do it for yer.'

'I couldn't let you—'

'I ain't saying we'd do it fer nuffink. We fought if we charged yer, yer wouldn't be under no obligation – and,' she smiled, 'that way I'd be earning meself a few extra bob on top of me sewing. Anyway, 'ave a word wiv yer dad.'

'Thanks, Jess. There's so much ter think of now. D'yer know, I can't believe Mum's gone.'

'Yeah, well, it'll take time. She was a good woman. It seems all wrong someone like 'er should go when there's that cow-son of an 'usband o' mine still living, and sniffing around any bit o' skirt that'll give 'im the time o' day.' Jessie's face was full of hate.

'Still, in some ways it's just as well 'e went off,' said Sally. 'Just think of all the kids yer might 'ave finished up with.'

'That's what Mum says. Good job 'e ain't interested in the kids, ovverwise 'e'd be back. Then 'e'd git me fist in 'is face, and Gawd knows what Mum and Dad would do ter 'im.' She laughed. 'I bet 'e'd 'ave a job walking after.'

Jessie stayed until it was time to get back to her children. Sally was sorry to see her go. A long evening stretched ahead of her now that Babs and Johnny had gone to bed. She was sitting in the kitchen alone, reading when her father opened the door.

''Allo, Dad. Pete with you?'

'No, 'e went on 'ome. All right then, gel?' he asked slumping heavily in his old wooden armchair. He suddenly looked old and drawn.

'Yes, thanks. What about you?'

Stan leant back. 'Can't say I feel anyfink. I feel sorta numb.'

'Oh Dad . . .'

He took his tobacco tin from his coat pocket, staring at it as he turned it over and over, almost as if seeing it for the first time. With his head still bent, he said softly, 'I'm gonner miss 'Ilda. Yer know, Sal, I loved yer mum.'

Sally choked back a sob. She had never heard her dad say anything like that before. 'We all did,' she whispered.

He opened the tin and carefully rolled a cigarette. After lighting it he sat back and silently blew the smoke in the air.

'Dad, Jessie said she'd do some shopping fer us, and a bit of the washing as well.'

He sat up. 'I ain't taking no charity, gel, we'll manage somehow.'

'Dad, it won't be charity. We're gonner pay 'er.'

'That's all right then. Don't want people ter feel sorry fer us.'

He sat back again and closed his eyes. The only sound that filled the air was the ticking of the wooden clock on the mantelpiece. When it chimed eleven he opened his eyes and sat forward, and with his finger and thumb put the cigarette out, letting the tobacco fall on to the clean hearth. 'I fink I'll be orf now. You coming up?'

'In a minute. D'yer want a cuppa cocoa?'

'No, fanks.' He stood up. 'Don't stay down 'ere too long. Remember yer got ter git up fer work in the morning.'

'I'll be up soon, I promise.' She kissed his cheek. 'Good night, Dad.'

Sally stretched out her legs, clad in her best black silk stockings. She put her feet on the brass fender hoping she wouldn't have to wear these stockings again, even though they'd cost her three and eleven. She didn't like black.

'I'll 'ave ter stop Dad doing that now I 'ave ter keep it clean,' she said to herself, looking at the mess her father had made in the hearth.

Her mother had always kept the fender well polished,

and with the range black-leaded and the hearth whitened, it was always pleasing to the eye. She had been constantly busy and bustling about, proud of her home and her family, forever cleaning and cooking. Even when the General Strike was on they hadn't gone without, not like some round here. Sally could just about remember that time when her dad was out of work. Babs had been only a baby. Sally sighed. She knew she had a lot to live up to.

Tiger, the cat, jumped on her lap. She gently fondled what was left of his right ear. He'd lost most of it in one of his many fights. As she tenderly ran her fingers over his soft black fur he purred contentedly. Tears slowly ran down Sally's face. Her mother, who had died of pneumonia, had always been a fighter, and Sally loved to hear her talk about the marches she went on when she was a young suffragette. Why hadn't she put up more of a fight to live? Somehow Sally was almost angry with her mother. She blew her nose. She was being silly, she told herself. Tomorrow was going to have to be a new start.

'And we've all got ter learn ter manage without yer, Mum,' she whispered.

Chapter 2

The last Friday in June 1938 was Sally's nineteenth birthday. Only six weeks had passed since the funeral but the family was beginning to settle down to a new routine without their mother, although they missed her dreadfully the whole time. Jessie and her mum were taking a lot of the chores off Sally, which meant she could just about cope with the house and her job and still go to the pictures now and again.

It was a warm pleasant evening, and as Sally hurried home from work she had a spring in her step. Normally she stayed in on a Friday night to have a bath, wash her hair, and listen to Henry Hall's guest night on the wireless, but tonight was different. Tonight Pete was taking her out. He had just passed his driving test, and was borrowing his uncle's car.

She had just come through the arches into Brigg Street, and was wondering excitedly what birthday present Pete could have bought her when she heard Vera Brent, one of Pete's twin sisters, calling her name. Sally turned and waited until Vera caught her up.

''Allo, Sal,' she puffed.

''Allo, Vera. You on yer own?'

'Yeah, me mate's waiting fer 'er boyfriend. You're in a bit of an 'urry.'

'Pete's taking me out in yer uncle's car tonight. It's me birthday.'

'Oh yeah, 'e did say. 'Appy birfday.'

'Thanks. I'm ever so excited about it.'

'I don't fink our Reg is all that pleased about Pete going out ternight. 'E's got a lot o' dance cards to deliver, and wivout Pete, well . . . Our Reg can get very stroppy at times.'

Sally tossed back her dark curls. 'I only 'ave a birthday once a year. Surely Reg can let 'im off this once. Me and Pete don't go out that much.'

'Don't get on yer 'igh 'orse wiv me. I'm only telling you.' Vera ran her hand over her damp forehead, pushing away stray hair from her happy round face. She wore her long hair tied back because of her job at the creamery. 'It's bin a bit warm terday.'

'Sorry. Pete was saying 'e's going to get a car now, then 'e'll be able to deliver the goods a bit quicker.'

'Well, anyfink's got ter be better than waiting around fer a bus wiv a load of parcels, especially in the winter.'

As they walked past the arches that ran all along Brigg Street, Sally screwed up her nose. 'Cor, those coalies' horses smell worse than ever terday.'

'It's this warm weather – makes 'em stink ter 'igh 'eaven,' laughed Vera, holding her nose.

High above them the steam engines chuffed and puffed, sounding their whistles as they rattled along to their destinations, but the girls didn't notice; it was part of their lives. Day and night the banging of the trains hitting the buffers as they were shunted into the sidings filled the air, but nobody really heard them.

A lot of the arches were bricked up at the back and had doors on the front. They were dry, and used for many purposes apart from stabling horses. There were a couple of blokes who mended cars, and some of the lorry and van drivers garaged their motors there. Not all of the uses were legal. Pete had told Sally that a card school often met there, and Tommy Tanner, the bookies' runner, and his dad did a lot of their wheeling and dealing in one of the lock-ups.

'Where yer going ternight?' asked Vera.

'Dunno.'

'I've used Lena's complimentaries this week, so 'e won't be taking yer ter the pictures.'

Sally didn't often go to the pictures with Pete, not when he was busy with the printing, despite Vera's twin, Lena, being an usherette with a regular supply of complimentary tickets.

'D'yer think 'e might take yer to the dogs?'

'I 'ope not.'

''E nearly always goes to New Cross on a Friday night.'

'Well 'e's not going ternight.'

They left the cobbles of Brigg Street and turned into Sefton Grove, with its row of back-to-back houses, and closets out in the yard behind. Some of the houses looked smart, with clean lace curtains at the window and gleaming white doorsteps, while others were dirty and run down. The landlord didn't do a lot to keep them looking nice, and a few years ago he was very reluctant about them having electricity. But in the end he agreed, and Sally was thrilled as it meant they could have one of the latest wireless sets and not have to worry about changing the accumulator.

'Well, 'ave a good time ternight,' said Vera, crossing the road and waving goodbye.

Pete's house was next to Jim's sweet shop, then came Tamar Street, cutting the Grove in half on that side; Florrie's grocers was on the other corner. At the top end of Sefton Grove, looking very grand with its ornate windows and brightly painted front, was the pub, the Nag's Head. On the other corner was the newsagent's.

Sally walked on. She could see Mr Slater sitting on his window sill at number forty, and guessed his dog, Bess, was at his side. He was a nice old man. He wore his still-dark hair parted in the middle, and with his thin pencil moustache and bow tie, he always looked very dapper. He had been wounded in the war and walked with a stick. He wasn't married, and talk was, that was because of his sister, whom he lived with. She was supposed to have sent his young lady packing. Miss Slater was thin, with sharp features and a voice to match. Jessie's mum always reckoned it was never being married had made Miss Slater nervy and skinny. 'Born ter be spinsters, some women are,' she'd often say.

Mr Slater was talking to his mate, old Fred, who lived in Tamar Street, but spent most of his time with Mr Slater since his wife died a few years ago. They were drinking partners and probably waiting for the Nag's to open. Every Friday and Saturday night everybody heard them come home, usually singing their heads off. The neighbours wondered what Mr Slater's sister said to him, but they never found out. They reckoned the only time Fred was good company was when he drowned his sorrows, as he was always moaning about some illness he thought he had.

‘’Allo, gel,’ said Mr Slater. ‘All right then?’

‘Yes, thanks. Hello, Fred,’ said Sally, smiling. She dare not ask him how he felt.

‘’Allo, love. ’Ow d’yer like this wevver? Bit too warm fer me – plays me back up sumfink chronic.’

‘’Eard Pete’s passed ’is driving test then.’ Mr Slater gave her a wink and smiled as he leant forward on the handle of his walking stick. ‘When’s ’e gonner git a car ter take yer out?’

‘We’re going out in his uncle’s car ternight. Mustn’t stop. Bye.’ She hurried on, and as she pushed open the front door of number sixty-eight she noticed the brass knocker could do with a clean.

The sound of shouting came up the passageway. It was Babs having a go at Johnny again. Sally went to the kitchen door. ‘Now what’re you two arguing about?’

‘It’s ’im. ’E wet ’is bed again last night, and didn’t tell anyone about it, and when Jessie brought the clean sheets in, she ’ad a go at me. She said I should ’ave known about it. I told ’er I ain’t ’is keeper, dirty little devil.’ She stormed out into the yard.

Sally sighed. Johnny had become very withdrawn since their mother died and the bed-wetting had started then, too.

‘Oh Johnny, why didn’t yer tell me, or at least take the wet sheets off the bed? Look, if Jess is good enough ter change the sheets and do the washing, yer should tell ’er. How many times ’ave yer wet the bed this week?’

‘Only once. I’m ever ser sorry, Sal.’ He hung his head and his hair fell forward over his eyes. ‘I didn’t mean ter.’ Slowly his shoulders began shaking. ‘Babs said she’d tell the kids at school,’ he sniffed, his voice soft and sorrowful.

Sally pulled him close. 'Come on now, no tears. I'll 'ave a word with Babs. She won't tell the other kids.'

He buried his head in her chest. 'I don't 'alf miss Mum,' he sobbed.

'We all do, Johnny,' said Sally tenderly. 'We all do. But Mum wouldn't want us ter cry for ever. We've all got ter get on with our lives. Now come on, dry those eyes. Remember it's me birthday, and I don't want tears on me birthday.'

Tears streaked his dirty face, but he managed a smile. 'Sorry, Sal. Did yer like the present me and Babs got yer?'

'They're lovely, and I'll wear 'em tonight. They'll look real smart with me frock.' Johnny and Babs had given her a pair of pearl earrings, which Sally knew her dad had paid for. 'Dad'll be in soon.' She looked up at the clock. 'I tell yer what, why don't you go up the road and meet 'im. It's Friday, pay day, and if yer lucky 'e might even give yer 'apenny fer some sweets.'

Johnny's face lit up. 'D'yer fink so?' He sniffed and wiped his nose on the sleeve of his shirt.

'Go on, be off with yer.'

Sally waited till she heard him slam the front door before she went out to Babs.

'Babs, yer mustn't keep on to Johnny. 'E gets very upset about this bed-wetting.'

'Yeah, I know. But 'e should tell us – Jessie wasn't 'alf mad.'

'I'll go and 'ave a word with 'er a bit later on. Johnny's very sensitive, and he's still very upset over Mum.'

'So am I, but I don't pee the bed.'

'No, I know.' Sally half turned to go. 'By the way, he's worried you'll tell the other kids – you won't, will you?'

Babs' smile lit up her round face. 'Na, course not.'

From her expression, Sally wasn't so sure. 'Come on in and 'elp me lay the table. Dad'll be in soon.'

'What's fer tea?'

'I'll pop round the corner fer some fish and chips.'

'That ain't much on yer birfday,' said Babs sadly.

'I know, but we ain't got Mum ter make a cake.'

Babs followed her sister into the kitchen. 'I 'ope I get a cake on my birfday.'

'You'll 'ave ter wait and see. 'Sides, yours is a long way off.'

'You going out ternight?'

'Yes, I told yer.'

'But what about our bath?'

'I'll see ter it tomorrow.'

'Can I go out and play with Connie after tea, then?'

'See what Dad says.'

Babs smiled. ''E don't mind me going out, but I don't want Johnny 'anging round.'

'Well, yer have ter see ter 'im if Dad goes up the pub.'

'No I won't. 'E can put 'imself ter bed.'

Sally wasn't going to argue with her, but she wasn't keen on Babs going out to play with Connie Downs. Her two older sisters had a bit of a reputation, and they could have a bad influence on Connie. Once Sally had caught Babs with rouge on her face.

But Sally's worries were put aside when her dad came home from work carrying a small cake. Sally was surprised, and very pleased.

'It ain't got no candles, gel, but we couldn't let yer birfday go wivout a cake.'

Tears filled her eyes, and she kissed his cheek. 'Thanks,

Dad,' she whispered. 'I'd better dish the fish and chips up, before they get cold,' and she hurried into the scullery.

After they'd finished tea, Sally went upstairs to the bedroom she now had to share with Babs to get ready for her outing with Pete. She didn't like sharing, but Babs was getting too old to sleep in Johnny's room, and since the bed-wetting she refused even to go in there, saying it stank. Sally sat on the bed. Poor Johnny, what could she do about it? The front door slammed shut and the window rattled – that must be Babs going out.

She looked at the watch Pete had bought her for Christmas. She sighed. Pete had been her only boyfriend, she loved him, but whenever she talked about getting married or even engaged he changed the subject. He always said he wasn't in any great hurry and wanted a nice place of their own before they settled down – and that would have to come after he got a car. Sally wondered how could she leave her dad now.

She smiled at the box of chocolates on top of the dressing table her Dad had given her. Even though she packed slabs of chocolate all day, she was pleased to have a whole box. She would wait till the kids were in bed and her dad up the pub before opening them. So far, she had done very well this birthday, what with the earrings and a nightdress case Jessie had made her.

Pete arrived promptly at seven.

''Appy birfday, Sal,' he said, kissing her cheek when she opened the front door. 'Yer ready then?'

'Come in, I'll just get me bag.'

Pete stood in the passage. 'I got yer this.' He handed her a small brown paper bag. ''Ope yer like it.'

Sally smiled as she opened the bag and took out a small

jeweller's box. She blushed and looked at him, but felt a little disappointed when she opened it and found a brooch inside.

'Don't yer like it?'

She quickly recovered and lightly kissed his cheek. 'Yes, yes, I do, it's lovely. Thank you, Pete.'

'Lena got it for me. She 'ad one and I thought yer'd like it.'

'I'll just pin it on me frock.'

'Ready then?'

'Yes.' She patted the brooch with its blue stones. 'Bye, Dad,' she yelled down the passage.

She felt like a queen when she stepped on to the wide running board of Pete's uncle's car. 'I feel ever ser grand,' she said, looking round, hoping some of the neighbours were watching her get inside the large black car.

'Why, yer daft 'apporth, yer bin in it before,' said Pete, walking round to the front, waving the starting handle. He pushed back his trilby and began cranking the car.

'Yes. I know, but not on our own.' Her voice was drowned as the engine burst into life.

'Right, gel, off we go then,' said Pete, grinning broadly as he slipped behind the wheel.

They drove out of Sefton Grove and Sally caught sight of Jessie coming down the road and frantically waved at her. Then she sat back in the soft green leather seat, feeling wonderful. 'Where're we off to?'

'I thought we'd 'ave a run out Crystal Palace way, but I've got ter drop these off first.' Pete nodded towards the back seat.

Sally turned, and for the first time noticed two brown paper parcels. 'Where yer got ter take 'em?'

'Only up to old Solly's in Sydenham. They've got a dance on at the end o' next month. 'Ere, d'yer fancy going? It's at the town 'all. I'll print us a couple o' tickets if yer like.'

Sally laughed. 'Ain't they all numbered?'

'Yeah, but old Solly don't mind. 'Sides, I could pick up a bit a business there.'

'All right then. Could yer do one fer Jessie as well?'

'I'll 'ave ter see about that.'

'It was a shame Crystal Palace burning down,' said Sally, her thoughts wandering. 'I wonder if they'll ever rebuild it?'

'Shouldn't fink so. I should 'ave liked ter 'ave seen that fire. I bet it wasn't 'alf a sight.'

'It was on the newsreels. I told you about it, remember? Now they're full of things about Hitler and Germany.'

'Yeah. It could get nasty over there.'

'Yer don't think there'll be a war, do yer?'

'Na,' he laughed. ''Sides, I can't go, got too much ter do, got a lot of dosh ter make yet.'

'Oh you.' Sally nudged his arm. 'Yer always working.'

He turned to look at her. 'No, joking aside, Sal, I wonner make a few quid. I want me own car, and you of all people should know that if there ain't no ships in, then there's no dough. That's why I does all the overtime I can get me 'ands on, and the printing. I like ter 'ave a few bob in me pocket.'

'And if yer don't keep yer eyes on the road, Pete Brent, yer won't be able ter drive this 'ere car, 'cause we'll be all smashed up.'

'You're a right cheerful Charlie, and no mistake. Now I'll only be a tick,' he said, stopping the car. He grabbed the parcels and ran up the steps of Solly's house. They exchanged a few words and he was back down and in the car in a flash.

She laughed, and her heart was full of love for him. 'I wish we could go out tergether more, though,' she said seriously as they moved on.

'I've told yer before, Sal. I know what it's like ter be 'ard up – really 'ard up, that is. To 'ave ter go ter the soup kitchen, and only 'aving one pair o' boots between the three of us, and 'aving ter take fings up ter old Mick's pawn shop. That was the only reason we all joined the Boys' Brigade when we was old enough, ter get a uniform and not 'ave the arse 'anging out our trousers all the time. I tell yer, Sal, that's not fer me, and I never want me mum ter be in that state again. So, all the while I can earn a few extra bob at the bottom of the garden, I will.'

'Thank you fer that fine speech, Mr Brent, but you forgets, I've 'eard it all before. And yer forgot the bit about passing yer scholarship, and yer mum not being able ter afford ter send yer ter grammar school.'

'Don't take the mick.'

'And,' Sally went on with a grin, 'I might add, it ain't a garden, it's a titchy little back yard that yer can't swing a cat round in with that great shed in it.'

It was Pete's turn to laugh. 'I could swing that moth-eaten old cat of yours round in it.'

'You'd better not, otherwise yer'll 'ave all the Fullers after yer.'

He stopped the car near the park. 'Look, I'm shaking in me boots.'

Sally laughed. 'You're daft.'

Pete put his arm round her shoulders. 'I like you, Sal. Yer a good mate.'

Sally kissed his cheek. 'Come on.'

They walked round the lake and watched the kids paddling and sailing their boats. Some of the boats were quite grand, but most of them were home-made.

'I ain't never been 'ere before,' said Sally. 'It's ever so nice.'

'Well, when I've got me car, I'll be able ter take yer ter all sorts o' places.'

She looked up at him and smiled. 'Thanks. I'd like that.'

Throughout July the papers and newsreels were full of the events taking place in Germany.

The week of Solly's dance approached. Sally had decided she wanted a new frock so today being Saturday she was going to take Babs to Peckham Rye shopping. She was in the yard taking in her bit of washing when Jessie came out of the lav.

'You're all dolled up – where're yer going?' she asked, smoothing down her skirt.

'Rye Lane. Fancy coming with us?' asked Sally.

'Who's us?'

'Only me and Babs.'

'I'll ask Mum if she'll keep an eye on the kids. She did say she wasn't going up the pub with Dad any more, or ever again.' She tutted. 'I've 'eard it all before. Needless ter say they've 'ad another row.'

Sally smiled. 'Well, 'urry up if yer coming. We'll be waiting for yer outside.'

In a few minutes Jessie joined them. She had changed her frock, combed her hair, and plastered some lipstick on.

'I'll git out while the going's good,' she said, looking up at the bedroom window. 'Just in case she changes 'er mind.' Jessie's mum moved as the mood took her. She'd said she wouldn't look after Harry and Pat on the night of the dance, so Jessie wasn't going.

When they got off the bus they wandered around, looking in the shops.

'What yer gitting then?' asked Jessie, looking at her reflection in a window and patting her hair.

'I got ter get meself a new frock for next Saturday, and Babs needs a new pair o' shoes – that's if I see a pair cheap enough.'

'I'd like a pair like Connie's got.'

'We'll have ter see about that.'

''Ere, what they all looking at?' Jessie jumped up to look over the heads of a crowd that had gathered in front of a shop window. They were watching a box that had a small screen, flickering. ''Ere, look at this.' She pushed her way to the front with Sally and Babs close behind. 'I ain't seen nuffink like this before,' said Jessie, with her nose pressed against the window.

'It's television,' said a man behind them. 'They reckon every 'ouse will 'ave one one day.'

'What, at fifty guineas a throw? Yer got ter be joking!' someone yelled out.

The crowd laughed.

'Anyway, they only 'ave pictures showing fer a couple o' hours a night,' the man added.

Sally was standing mesmerised at the lady in the long flowing flowery frock and big hat, singing. She couldn't hear her, but watched fascinated at her moving in and out of some white pillars, her organdie gown wafting all around her.

'Ain't it smashing, Sal?' said Babs, her nose pressed against the glass. 'Cor, I'd like ter be rich.'

Sally smiled. So would she.

''Ow do they get them pictures on there like that?' Babs asked her.

'Don't ask me.'

'It's waves,' said the man in the crowd. He seemed to know all about it. 'Comes through the air on waves, like the wireless.'

Sally wasn't any wiser, as the working of the wireless still flummoxed her.

'Look at that frock,' said Jessie. 'I bet yer'd like one just like that fer next Saturday.'

Sally laughed. 'Could yer see me floating around in somethink like that?'

'No, but there ain't no 'arm in wishing.'

'Come on,' said Sally. 'Let's go.'

'Just fink,' said Jessie. 'If yer got one o' them there television sets it'd be like 'aving the pictures in yer own 'ouse.'

Suddenly Babs grabbed Sally's arm. 'Look, Sal,' she whispered. 'There's those Blackshirts again. They frighten me.'

'Don't look at them,' said Sally quickly. 'And walk past 'em. Remember what Dad told us?'

'Bloody Nazis,' said Jessie, as they pushed past the crowd around them.

Some people were listening to the speaker, who was raised on a soapbox, his friends handing out leaflets to the crowd, but most of those gathered were arguing and heckling as the Blackshirt leaders shouted about how good the fatherland was. 'My dad reckons there could be anovver war.'

'Don't say that,' said Sally.

'Well, we 'ave seen some 'orrible fings at the pictures, and if—'

'If there's a war, what will 'appen ter us, Sal?' asked Babs, her voice full of alarm.

'Nothink. Don't listen ter 'er, Babs.' She gave Jessie a withering look.

'I'm only saying, so don't 'ave a go at me.'

'I'm not. It's just that I don't like talking about it.'

'Well, not saying anyfink won't be able ter stop it.'

'No, I know,' said Sally thoughtfully. The idea of war filled her with fear. It was a reality she hoped she'd never have to face.

Chapter 3

Once or twice during the evening of the dance Sally got cross with Pete as he seemed to be spending more time talking to other people than to her.

'I don't know why yer bothered ter bring me,' she said sulkily.

'I told yer before, Sal, I've got ter make contacts if we're going in fer big printing contracts.'

'I wish Jessie could 'ave come. At least then I'd 'ave 'ad a couple of dances, instead of sitting 'ere all night looking like a lemon.'

He kissed her cheek. 'Yer don't look like a lemon. In fact yer look very nice. I like yer frock; blue suits yer.'

Sally smiled. At least he'd noticed her new frock. At that moment the band struck up with 'The Lambeth Walk'.

'Come on, gel, I can do this,' said Pete, pulling her to her feet.

For the rest of the evening they danced and laughed. Sally was happy in Pete's company – that was when he could find the time to be with her. She didn't want to spoil their friendship in any way, yet sometimes she couldn't help wondering if it was ever to become anything more.

It was in October when Pete finally got his car, a blue

Morris 8. It was his pride and joy, and he garaged it along with a few others under the arches.

One bright Sunday morning Sally was helping him clean and polish his baby.

'We spend more time cleaning this thing than going out in it.'

Pete's head shot up. 'It ain't a fing, it's me Betsy.' He ran his hand lovingly over the bonnet.

'We still don't go out in it all that much. I reckon yer think more of that than of me.'

'Don't talk daft, course I don't. 'Sides, we went out in 'er last Sunday afternoon, didn't we?'

She nodded. 'To deliver some club cards.'

Suddenly the sound of hobnail boots, racing along Brigg Street's cobbles, made them look up. Tommy Tanner and his father came rushing past, red-faced and panting. With sparks flying from their soles they disappeared into Rick the coalie's arch.

Shouts of 'Stop them!' came from two policemen as they hurtled round the corner.

'Which way did they go?' one yelled at Pete.

'Who we talking about?'

'Yer know full well. The Tanners.'

'Oh them. Dunno, I wasn't looking.'

'Don't give us that. Yer must 'ave seen 'em. What about you, miss?' the constable panted.

'I was busy – I didn't see.' Sally carried on with her polishing.

The policemen hurried into the arch next to Pete's. After a few minutes they came out and made their way towards the small group that had gathered.

'Come on, one o' yer must 'ave seen 'em.'

There was a low mumbling among the onlookers, but nobody volunteered any information.

''Ere, watch what yer doing,' said Pete, as one of the policemen stepped back, kicking his bucket of water over. The police then made a move towards the doorway of Pete's garage but he was too quick for them and stood barring the way. 'This is my place, and they ain't in there.'

They pushed him to one side and after a few minutes' looking round, they moved on to Rick's.

There was a lot of shouting and swearing, and the crowd could hear that a scuffle had broken out. The horses were neighing, as the banging, crashing and hollering got louder. A few more men joined those outside.

'Someone better go and git Sadie,' said one of the onlookers.

Sally glanced at Pete. 'I'll go,' she said, wiping her hands on a piece of old towel, but before she could move the police came out of Rick's, holding a very dishevelled Tommy and his dad by their coat collars.

One of the constables turned to Pete and Sally, and said, 'Next time I ask yer a question, I expect an answer. I'll remember you two if our paths ever cross again.' They walked up Brigg Street, half pushing and half dragging the two reluctant wrongdoers.

Sally's face went pale.

'Don't worry about them, love. You go and tell Sadie.' Pete gently patted her back.

Sally hurried along to Mrs Tanner, who lived at number twenty Sefton, next door to Babs' friend Connie. Connie had told the Fullers about the noise that came through the thin walls, and how they would listen to the rows and fights that went on in there, and everyone knew the abuse and threats Connie's dad got if he dared to complain. She also told Sally about all the blood-red stains on the walls from where the girls, with their shoes, squashed the bugs as they came through the cracks in the lathe and plaster at night. And if they sat very quiet they would watch the mice creep in through the holes in the skirting. Sally said the Downs family needed a cat like Tiger.

Sally lifted the knocker very carefully with her finger and thumb, and let it drop. It felt greasy and slimy. She shuddered and looked over at the front room window that had a piece of yellowed lace curtain stretched taut across it. When the front door was opened the smell from inside almost took Sally's breath away. It stank of damp and dirt. Everybody knew Sadie never did any housework. The passageway was full of old junk, including a couple of pram wheels, and looked as if it hadn't been swept for years.

'Yeah? Whatcher want?' Sadie was a big woman with a red round face, her dark wiry hair scragged up on top of her head in a kind of bun. Sally involuntarily took a step back.

'It's Tommy and Mr Tanner. The police 'ave just taken 'em in.'

Sadie slowly wiped her hands on the bottom of her faded floral overall. 'Oh yeah, and where was that?'

'The arches.'

'Silly sods got 'emselves in trouble again, and I s'pose they want me ter bail 'em out?' She sniffed and wiped her nose with the bottom of her overall.

'I dunno.'

'I'll just git me coat. Fanks, Sally.'

Fascinated, Sally peered into the dingy passageway, her eyes gradually becoming accustomed to the dark. She watched Sadie waddle away. Sadie had difficulty walking because her legs and feet were so large. When she stood on the rug at the bottom of the stairs, great puffs of dust swirled round her ankles. She took a scruffy black coat with a tatty fur collar from off a large nail that stuck out of the front room door, and after a few attempts at finding the right hole in her sleeve and not going through the lining, she pulled it round herself. There were no buttons left to do up. She bent down and fished under a table that was piled high with all sorts of items, including a stack of yellowed papers, and a vase full of flowers that must have been dead for many months, and pulled out a large black hat decorated with a rose now completely squashed out of shape.

She saw Sally looking at the flowers in the vase and a smile filled her round face. 'Me old man gave me 'em munfs ago. I ain't got the 'eart ter frow 'em out – it's the only flowers 'e's ever give me. 'E was drunk at the time, and I don't s'pose 'e bought 'em, but it was a nice fought.'

She ran her hands over her hair and plonked the hat on top. 'Yer don't 'appen ter know what nick they took 'em to, do yer?' she asked as she pushed a large pearl hatpin through the hat.

Sally shook her head. 'No, sorry.'

'Not ter worry. Old Perc'll tell me. Mind you, I'll kill those cow-sons when I gits me 'ands on 'em fer spoiling the dinner.'

Sally shuddered at the thought of what the kitchen looked like, and the idea of them all sitting eating their dinner made her cringe.

Sadie pushed past her. 'Come on then, gel. Don't stand there all day.'

They walked up to Brigg Street, and Sally was pleased when Sadie went off in the opposite direction, as the smell of dried pee was overpowering.

'I tell yer, Pete,' said Sally, when she rejoined him, 'that place is like a pigsty, and she don't half pong.' she screwed up her nose.

Pete laughed. 'Yeah, but she does look after 'er old man, and young Tommy – more so since 'is big brother, Ted, finished up in the nick. Come on, let's be going, otherwise we'll 'ave Ma shouting 'er 'ead off that I'm late fer dinner.'

Sally grinned. They all knew about Granny Brent, as Pete's mum was known. Sally was glad her dad liked a pint on Sunday morning, and they had to wait till he came home after closing time before they had dinner. The meat was in the oven and should be doing nicely, and Babs was going to put the potatoes in.

As she and Pete wandered back he asked, 'Coming in for a tater?'

'I'll have ter be quick as I've got ter put the veg on.' For years she had gone over to Pete's on a Sunday morning and if the printing business was busy she would help fold club cards and number dance cards, and her reward had always been one of Granny Brent's golden roasted potatoes. Sally couldn't resist them. There was something so deliciously different about them, she was almost drooling at the thought.

Although Mrs Brent wasn't a granny, everyone in Sefton Grove called her that, and liked and admired her for the way she had worked hard and single-handedly brought up her five children after her husband had been killed at the very end of the war.

'Sit yerself down, Sal,' she said when they walked into the kitchen, the mouthwatering smell of the dinner filling their nostrils. 'I've got yer tater ready fer yer.'

'I'll just go out and see what Reg and Danny's up to,' said Pete, going out of the back door.

'The police took Mr Tanner and Tommy away this morning,' Sally called after Granny Brent as she went into the scullery.

She was back immediately. 'No!' she said, plonking on the table a plate with a steaming roast potato on. 'What they done this time?'

'Dunno. I had ter go and get Sadie. 'Ave yer seen the state o' that place? I tell yer, it stinks in there.' Sally cut the potato in half with a fork and blew on it.

''Allo, Sal,' said Pete's sister Lena, coming into the kitchen. She walked over to the mirror that hung over the fireplace, and patted her short bobbed hair. She licked her fingers and twirled the flat curls that rested on her cheeks. Her large brown eyes expressed approval as she quickly took in her appearance. Lena wore a lot of make-up and was tall and willowy, so very different from her dumpy twin, Vera. With her job at the Red Lion cinema, she was always well dressed. 'Dinner gonner be long, Ma?'

'Why?' came back the sharp retort.

'I'm off work this afternoon and I'm going out.'

'Anywhere nice?' asked Sally.

'Don't know yet.' She smiled, her full red lips parting.

'Who's this bloke then?' asked her mother.

'Just someone I met at work.'

'Yer wonner be careful, my girl, going out wiv any old Tom, Dick or 'Arry what buys a ticket fer the pictures. Could be a right dirty old sod.'

Lena pouted. ''E ain't old and 'e ain't dirty. Yer always fink the worse of all me men friends.' She stormed out of the kitchen and they heard her stamp all the way up the stairs.

'She always goes orf like that when I 'as a go about 'er different blokes. I can see 'er finishing up in the family way, the way she carries on.'

Sally just smiled. Everybody knew about Lena's reputation with men, more so since one of the wives came looking for Lena, threatening to tear her hair out. But Granny Brent always protected her flock, and had chased the woman away. Sally would have loved to have seen that fracas, it was the talk of Sefton for days. Poor Vera always said she was frightened to bring a bloke home in case Lena ran off with him.

'Look at the time,' said Sally. 'I must go. Tell Pete I'll see 'im later.' She hurried across to home and, in crossing the road, changed the role of the child for that of mother in her own home. The cooking of Sunday dinner was a part of the new responsibilities she'd perfected over the months, but even so, the table was incomplete without Mum.

As the year was coming to an end, the Fuller family began thinking about Christmas. It was going to be hard without their mother.

Two weeks before the big day, Sally, Babs and Johnny were sitting at the kitchen table making paper chains. The flour-and-water paste was beginning to get low.

'When it's finished put everything in the box and then it's off ter bed,' said Sally.

'Oh, do we 'ave ter?' whined Babs.

Johnny slowly stirred the empty paste dish with his

paintbrush. 'Don't know if I want Christmas wivout Mum,' he said softly.

'Don't talk daft. Yer can't stop it,' said Babs.

'It won't be the same.' He brushed his hair from his eyes.

'It'll be nearly the same,' said Sally, picking up the strips of coloured paper and putting them in the box. 'I know we'll still miss Mum but we've all got ter try.'

'What about a pudding?' asked Babs, obviously thinking more about her stomach. 'You gonner make one?'

'I'm gonner 'ave a go. I found Mum's recipe. I'll 'ave ter make it on Sat'day as it 'as ter boil fer eight hours.'

'You gonner put some thrupenny bits in it?' asked Johnny, cheering up at the thought of food.

'Now would a pudding be a Christmas pudding without 'em?'

Johnny smiled. 'What about a cake?'

'I'm going ter 'ave a go at making one o' them as well.'

'Good.'

Sally ruffled his hair. On the whole he seemed to be a lot happier these days, and had stopped wetting the bed.

'I dunno why I 'ave ter go ter bed the same time as 'im,' said Babs.

'Yer don't. Just go up and get ready. Then yer can come down 'ere and listen ter the wireless for a little while.'

'Yuck, I don't wonner listen ter that muck you like, I'd rather 'ave a read in bed.'

'Please yerself.' Sally pushed the box of paper chains under the dresser and sat in the armchair.

Her thoughts went to her mother and the fun they always had at Christmas with a tree and presents carefully placed underneath. Jessie, her mum and dad, and the kids would come in for tea. Then when it was time for Jessie to put her little ones to bed Sally would go across to the Brents'.

She sighed. The Brents certainly knew how to enjoy themselves. They were a talented family. They could all play the old piano, which they'd got from the Nag's Head years ago when it was being refurbished. It was beer-stained, the notes were yellowed with age and two of them didn't work, but that didn't matter. They could still thump out a good tune on it. Pete could also play the guitar, and Reg was good on his accordion, and Danny, the younger brother, strummed the banjo. There had been some good parties at the Brents' . . .

Sally was dozing when her father returned from the Nag's.

'Sorry, Sal, did I wake yer?'

'That's all right. I should 'ave gone up ages ago. How did yer dominoes go? Did yer win?'

He smiled. 'Yeah. Mind you, old Fred was a bit put out.' He sat down and began undoing his boot laces. 'I dunno how Slater puts up wiv 'im, always moaning.' He took his boots off and sat back, resting his feet on the fender. 'That dog of Slater's got drunk again ternight.'

Sally laughed. 'Who carried 'er 'ome this time?'

'The landlord lent 'em a barra.'

'I bet Miss Slater will 'ave a few words ter say about that.'

Well, at least they won't try ter bury 'er again.'

Sally grinned, remembering the rumpus when Mr Slater thought Bess had died and was going to bury her the next day, only to find her sitting at the end of his bed in the morning wagging her tail.

'Any strangers what puts their pints on the floor ask fer

trouble when that dog's around. Yer should see the way she sidles under the chairs looking fer beer.'

Sally laughed again. 'Sounds like a right old soak ter me.'

Her father paused and suddenly looked serious. 'Sal? 'Ave you and Pete ever talked about gitting married?'

Sally blushed. 'No, not really. Why, what's brought this on?'

'Well, wiv all this talk about a war.'

Sally sat forward. 'Dad, yer don't think . . . ?'

'Wouldn't like ter say. Been 'aving quite a chat about it ternight.'

Sally smiled. She had heard all about the Nag's bar-room politics. They were always trying to put the world to rights.

'I reckon you two should git married. What if 'e gits called up?'

Sally froze. All the things she saw every week on the news at the pictures – it never occurred to her that they could happen here. 'But, Dad, yer don't think . . . ? What about what Mr Chamberlain said? 'E's made an agreement with 'Itler.'

'Yeah, I know. But I still fink you and Pete should git married. Yer don't 'ave ter worry about us, yer know.'

'I'm only nineteen, Dad. 'Ere, you wonner get rid o' me or somethink?'

'Na, course not. It's just that after all the good times me and yer mother 'ad tergevver, well, I'd like ter see yer happy and settled. 'Sides, Pete's a nice bloke.'

Sally smiled. What were their good times? 'And who would look after you and the kids?'

'I dare say we would manage.'

'And where would we live?'

'Dunno.'

'Well I think I'd better wait fer Pete ter ask me first, so don't go poking yer nose in.' She laughed. ''Sides, yer know Pete: 'e's always working, and looking fer ways ter make a bit extra. He might ask you fer a dowry.'

'I should cocoa. 'E'll be gitting a right bargain if 'e snaps you up, and if 'e ain't careful someone else might come along and grab yer.'

'You're only saying that 'cos yer biased.'

Stan stood up and patted the top of her head. 'Yer could say that. I'm going up now.' He kissed her forehead. 'Good night, love.'

Sally sat for a while thinking about what her dad had just said. She would like to marry Pete, she loved him and knew there could never be anyone else in her life. But how could she leave Dad to cope with Babs and Johnny? Now Babs was growing up there were times when she could be very difficult, and what about Johnny? He was just a child. But what if there was a war? Would Pete have to go away?

Chapter 4

Despite her misgivings, Christmas was turning out to be all Sally could have wished for, and the party at Pete's was going great, with plenty of beer, singing and laughing. They were all getting a little drunk.

She fell breathless on to Pete's lap when they finished another knees-up. The Brents' small front room was packed with people Sally had known all her life. For the first time Gwen Holt, Danny's girlfriend, was there to join in the family fun. Everybody knew all about the Holt girls who lived in Tamar Street. There were six of them, and Gwen was the youngest and quietest. She was a thin, mousy-looking girl, with short brown hair and sad-looking eyes, who had always worn hand-me-downs. She was overpowered by her sisters. Some were married but always seemed to be at home with their kids, and Gwen said it was like a madhouse round there.

Sally giggled. 'Look at Danny,' she whispered loudly in Pete's ear, and nodded to a dark corner of the room where Danny and Gwen were locked in each other's arms. ''E can't leave Gwen alone.'

'Silly sod, if 'e ain't careful she'll finish up up the spout. She was trying fer months ter get 'im ter take 'er out. Now it seems she'll do anyfink ter keep 'im. She must think 'e's got a bit o' loot or somefink, and if Mum sees 'is 'ands up 'er blouse, she'll give 'em both what for, and a swipe from one o' mum's 'ands'll send 'im and 'er flying.'

Sally giggled even louder. 'Pity you ain't a bit more romantic.'

Pete almost spat out his beer. 'Yer don't call that romantic, do yer? They're more like a couple o' alley cats. 'Ere, Danny,' he shouted across the room. ''Bout time yer give us a song.'

'Spoilsport,' said Sally.

Danny looked round, sheepish. His face red and his eyes shining. 'Yeah, yeah, all right.'

Gwen quickly straightened her blouse, and blushing, smoothed down her hair.

Danny was certainly very appealing. He had dark hair like Pete, but his eyes were a soft brown. He was the youngest and shortest of the Brent boys and had a round boyish face, and a cheeky grin. He was grinning now as he picked up his banjo and gave them a rendering of 'I'm Leaning on the Lamppost'.

It was the early hours of the morning when, after a lot of struggling to get Granny Brent up the stairs and into bed, the party finally began to break up. Pete said he would see Sally across the road.

'Thanks, Pete,' she said, clinging on to his arm as they staggered to her door. She felt happy and flung her arms round his neck, kissing him long and hard – pleased he responded.

'Pete, let's git married,' she murmured.

'Come on, yer drunk.'

With a silly grin on her face she nodded. 'Yes, and I don't care. I wish you was Danny.'

'Why, d'yer fancy 'im more than me?'

'Course not, but at least 'e shows 'e loves Gwen.'

'Yer don't call that love, do yer?'

'Well, at least 'e makes a fuss of 'er.'

'So that's it: yer want me 'and up yer blouse?'

She nodded again, and her grin widened.

'Come on, Sal, stop being daft. Yer dad wouldn't fank me if I got inside yer drawers.'

Sally giggled, and slowly slid down the front door, coming to rest propped against the paintwork. ''Elp me up. This coconut mat's sticking in me, and it don't 'alf 'urt.'

It was Pete's turn to laugh. 'Come on, Sal, on yer feet,' he said, pulling her up. 'D'yer fink yer'll be able ter git ter bed all right?'

She shook her head. 'No,' she said petulantly. 'You've got ter 'elp me.'

Pete pulled the key through the letter box and opened the door. 'Go on, up ter bed wiv yer. I'll see yer termorrer.' He pushed her through the front door and gently closed it.

In the passage Sally stood upright. 'Well, at least I gave him somethink ter think about,' she said to herself, taking off her shoes and quietly climbing the stairs.

Babs' birthday was on 28 January 1939. Sally was pleased it fell on a Saturday and she could spend all afternoon doing sandwiches and preparing tea for Babs' two friends, Connie Downs and Iris Russell. Sally didn't know Iris. She was a school friend and didn't live around Sefton.

At three o'clock sharp someone was banging the knocker. Babs rushed excitedly to the front door. Sally could hear the girls laughing and giggling all along the passage. The kitchen door flew open and they came in.

Sally felt happy as she watched Babs tear open the paper on her presents, and ooed and aahed with her over the neatly knitted multicoloured scarf.

'That's just what you could do with,' said Sally. 'Did you make it?' she asked Connie.

'Na, me mum did.'

Iris gave Babs a small manicure set. 'I got two fer Christmas,' she said, unperturbed.

Sally could see that they were enjoying themselves. Even Johnny joined in the games. Sally had been very apprehensive as this was Babs' first birthday tea without their mother and knew she had a lot to live up to. She smiled as Babs blew out her candles.

'Make a wish,' shouted her friends.

'I 'ave,' she said, smiling at Sally.

It was such a happy afternoon, a world away from all the talk of war – the kind of day when Sally could believe that wishes really would come true.

The beginning of the year had brought a lot of talk about the air-raid shelters that were going to be delivered to every house in London. One evening Pete and Sally were sitting in her kitchen discussing the news.

'Look, it says 'ere,' said Pete, flicking the newspaper with his finger, 'they're gonner be free ter families earning less than two hundred and fifty pounds a year.'

'Well, that's us,' said Sally. 'I don't think Dad and me earn that much.'

''E does all right if it's been a good year,' said Pete, going back to the paper.

'What about you lot?' asked Sally.

'With all of us at work I don't fink we'll qualify.'

'Still, if Danny gets married he'll be off.'

Pete rested the paper on the table and smiled. 'Yeah, seems funny that the youngest brother might be gitting 'itched first.'

'Where will they live?'

'Dunno. It can't be round 'er place, not wiv all them females. Drive the poor bloke mad. That's why I reckon old Holt kicked the bucket – they drove 'im to it.'

''Ave they set a date yet?'

'Na. I don't fink 'e's in any great 'urry all the while 'e gets 'is oats.'

'Does 'e tell yer that?' asked Sally in amazement.

''E does if we keeps on enough.'

'Poor Danny, you're always teasing 'im. I reckon 'e'll be glad ter get away from you lot. 'E's such a nice-looking bloke. Pity the rest o' you don't look like 'im.' She quickly stood up.

'Yer saucy cow.' Pete grabbed hold of her and pulled her on to his lap.

Sally laughed, looking at him. Suddenly his lips were on hers. She was taken aback. Pete had never kissed her like this before. There had always been a quick peck, and sometimes it had lingered a little longer, but never anything like this. She relaxed as waves of pleasure drifted over her. She didn't want him to stop.

The key being pulled through the letter box caused them to break quickly away.

'That was nice,' she whispered, breathlessly jumping up. 'It's Dad.' She looked in the mirror and quickly ran a handkerchief over her smudged lipstick. 'Yer got lipstick round yer mouth – you'd better wipe it off,' she said over her shoulder.

'I'll go out in the bog and do it.' Pete hurried outside.

'Hello, Dad,' she said, her voice high and unnatural.

'I fought Pete was 'ere.'

''E's just popped out for a jimmy.'

Her father looked at her quizzically.

'Me and Pete 'ave been talking about these air-raid shelters. Will we 'ave one?'

'Dunno. The yard ain't that big. We'll 'ave ter wait and see. 'Allo, son, all right then?' he asked as Pete walked in.

Pete nodded. 'We've bin talking about these shelters.'

'So Sal said. They was saying up the Nag's that a bloke's coming round ter tell us all about 'em and ter measure up. That should be a game when they go into Sadie Tanner's. I wouldn't like ter 'ave a guess at what they've got in their yard.'

They laughed.

'Mrs Downs, Connie's mum, said it looks like a junk yard out there,' said Sally.

'I bet old Sadie'll 'ave a thing or two ter say ter the blokes what puts it in.' Pete stood up. 'Well, I'll be off now. They said we should 'ave that Russian ship in on ternights tide. It's a big 'n.'

''Ope Chalky's foreman on it. Stand a good chance o' being picked if 'e's in charge.'

'They might need a couple o' gangs,' said Pete.

'If it does come ter a showdown I wonder whose side they'll be on?' said Stan, the prospect of war never far from his mind.

'Dunno. Those Ruskies are a funny lot o' buggers. See yer in the morning, Pop.'

'Yeah, OK, son.'

Sally went to the front door with Pete and snuggled into his arms. 'Do I get another kiss like that one?'

'Sal, I've been thinking, if there's gonner be a war I reckon we ought ter think about gitting 'itched.'

'Pete, Pete. D'yer really mean that?'

'Why not? We git on all right tergether, don't we?'

She nodded eagerly.

''Sides, if there is a war I might get called up, and they don't git a lot o' money – but if we was married I might get deferred.'

Sally pushed him away and anger filled her face. 'Is that it? Is that all you think about – money?'

'Course not.'

She opened the front door. 'I think you'd better go. I thought you loved me.'

'I do, Sal. Come on, give us a kiss.' Pete pulled her close and kissed her.

Sally didn't want to respond but her love for him overcame her anger.

'See yer termorrow,' he said when they broke away.

That night Sally lay in bed thinking about what Pete had said. Could they really be facing another war? Would he be called up if there was? Was she being selfish thinking only of herself? She knew Pete loved her, and she hoped they would get married one day, but had it been only the thought of a war that made him mention it this evening?

The end of April was warm, with a cloudless blue sky and the promise of spring in the air. It also brought the first of the Anderson air-raid shelters to Sefton Grove. When Sally turned into the Grove she couldn't believe her eyes. It seemed everybody was out. All the women were standing at their doors, or gathered in tight little groups, talking and laughing. The kids were running around, yelling and screaming. Johnny gave Sally a quick wave then continued with his game of marbles. His mates, like him, had their socks down in their shoes and their shirts hanging out of their trousers. Some of the girls were swinging on a rope around the lamppost, while Babs and Connie were huddled in the Downses' doorway, giggling. Sally hurried on to find Jessie.

'What's going on?' she asked.

Jessie was laughing. 'Oh Sal, yer should 'ave been 'ere.' She was holding young Pat, Harry was playing with a ball at her feet.

Mrs Walters was leaning on the railings that fronted the houses. 'I ain't seen nuffink like it in all me born days. Better than up the pictures,' she said, grinning.

Sally began laughing with them, but she didn't know why.

Granny Brent waddled across the road. ''Allo, Sal. They told yer about the rumpus?'

'No, they ain't, they just keep laughing.'

'It's old Sadie,' said Mrs Walters. 'When those blokes took the first bit of 'er shelter frough ter the back, it seems they dropped it and it crashed right frough the closet door, and the old man was sitting on the bog at the time.'

'Yer should've 'eard the 'ollering,' said Jessie. 'We could 'ear it right up 'ere.'

'Mind you, it could've killed the poor old sod,' said Granny Brent happily.

Jessie's mum sat on the window sill. 'Mrs Downs said old

Tanner was running round the yard wiv 'is trousers down round 'is ankles, and 'e 'adn't buttoned up the back flap of 'is combs, and 'e was showing all 'is arse and yelling and shouting at the blokes. D'yer know, she said the colour of 'is combs 'ad ter be seen ter be believed.' She wiped the tears from her eyes with the bottom of her pinny. 'One o' the fellers, 'e was only young, poor little sod – 'e run out scared stiff. 'E said 'e wasn't going back in there and sat in the lorry. So after a lot o' arm waving and carrying on, Sadie 'ad ter 'elp the ovver bloke. Yer should 'ave seen 'er trying ter 'old these great lumps o' metal.'

Sally too was laughing at that thought.

'You wait till yer see 'em, Sal. Bloody great fings they are,' said Granny Brent.

'Sadie was running and struggling . . .' said Jessie, sitting next to her mother who was also still laughing.

'Where was the old man?' asked Sally.

'Still sitting on the bog, so Mrs Downs reckoned.'

''Ave we got one of 'em?' asked Sally.

'Yeah, I let 'em in,' said Jessie.

'Are they very big?' asked Sally.

'Enormous, and they've got ter be put in the ground. Gawd only knows 'ow they're gonner do that. The ground's as 'ard as a bullet,' said Mrs Walters.

'Who's gonner do the digging?' asked Sally.

'Dunno,' said Mrs Walters, 'but they've give us a bloody great spanner ter bolt the bits tergevver wiv.'

'Well, we ain't 'aving one,' said Granny Brent. 'The boys said they ain't pulling the shed down fer no one.' She folded her arms across her ample bosom.

'But what if—' Sally stopped. There was no point in saying it, as Pete had told her the only way they could get one in the tiny yard was to pull down the shed, and they weren't going to do that as it had the printing press in.

Gradually the groups began to break up and Sally went in to see what was in her yard. She ran her hands over the great lumps of shiny metal, and couldn't believe that these would have to be almost buried in the ground. Surely the government didn't expect people to use them? She went inside and filled the kettle. A cup of tea was more important at that moment.

Jessie's dad, it seemed, had stopped Stan Fuller at the front door and told him the story of Sadie in all its glory. By now Sally was sure it was greatly exaggerated, but he had a good laugh about it, though the size of the shelter rather wiped the smile off his face when he saw it.

'I dunno 'ow they expect us ter dig an 'ole in this yard,' he said, kicking the ground with the toe of his boot.

'It says 'ere,' said Sally, reading the leaflet that was with it, 'that a man's coming round ter tell yer all about it.'

''E better bring a sledge 'ammer wiv 'im,' said her father.

It was later that month that the government announced plans to evacuate from inner London all children and mothers with under-fives, in the event of war. Babs and Johnny came home from school with the forms to fill in.

'Well, I ain't going,' said Babs.

'And if I say yer are, yer are,' said her father, studying the sheets of paper.

'I'll run away,' said Babs.

'Yer better not,' said Sally. 'Yer'll 'ave Johnny ter look after.'

'I don't wonner go,' whined Johnny.

'Yer'll 'ave to if there's a war,' said Sally.

'Yer can't make us,' said Babs.

'The government can,' said their dad. ''Sides, it might only be fer a week or so, and yer might even like it.'

'What about when I'm fourteen, and leave school?'

'We'll 'ave ter wait and see about that.'

'Yer might finish up in the country,' said Sally, 'You'd like that, with lots o' green fields and cows.'

'I won't,' said Babs. 'I don't like cows.'

'I don't like cows eiver,' said Johnny.

Sally looked at them. She didn't want them to go, but if there was a war what choice did she have?

Chapter 5

Sally hurried home from work. Tuesday was one of the evenings Jessie's Mum looked after the kids while Jessie and Sally went to the pictures. When she turned into Sefton Grove it seemed to be full of women, some standing in tight little groups, some at their front doors, while others were wandering back to their houses. In the road two lorries were parked and the kids were running round them, screaming and shouting. The lorries were loaded with parts of the Anderson shelters. Workmen were leaning against them, smoking and deep in conversation.

''Allo, Sal,' said Mr Slater. 'They're 'ere again. They're 'aving a right old game wiv us lot round 'ere, and no mistake.' He bent down and patted Bess's head.

Sally smiled and hurried on. 'Now what's up?' she asked, coming up to Jessie and her mum. 'I thought we'd all got those in this road.' She nodded towards the lorries.

'Yer'll never believe this, Sal, but they're taking 'em away. Seems we can't 'ave these bleeding shelters after all,' said Mrs Walters.

'What?' said Sally, almost in panic. 'Why can't we? What we gonner do if there's a war?'

'We can't 'ave 'em 'cos all the pipes run under the ground at the back, and they can't go deep enough,' said Jessie, very matter-of-fact.

''Ow do they know?' asked Sally.

Jessie and her mum laughed.

'Well, they started up this end,' said Mrs Walters, fussily pulling her floral overall round her, 'in Silly Billy's place. When they started ter dig down, they'd only gone about a foot, so the bloke said, and they 'it the gas pipe and then the next bloke 'it the water main. You should've seen it. The water shot up in the air like a bloody great fountain.'

'Soaked all our washing, it did,' said Jessie. 'And there was poor Billy – running around going spare, 'e was.'

Sally had always felt sorry for Billy. He lived with his invalid mother, who shouted at him a lot. People said he wasn't quite all there because they reckoned she'd tried to get rid of him before he was born. It was supposed to have turned him, and her. Sally never knew where they got that bit of gossip from.

Billy was about thirty, a good man who had never married. He worked as a cellar and bottle man at the Nag's, and all the kids took the mickey out of him because he was slow. He smiled a lot and always passed the time of day with everybody as he shuffled to and from the grocer's or the pub. From outside, the house looked spotless. Billy was always busy, cleaning the step and the windows, but nobody ever went in, and Mrs Billy, as they called her, was never seen out. She sat at the upstairs front room window watching all the goings-on. There wasn't a man in her life, even when they'd moved here about ten years ago. She could walk a little then, but always kept herself to herself, never talking to anybody, which didn't please the people round here. Nobody knew what they lived on – it certainly wasn't Billy's money. Sefton Grove loved a mystery. For years they talked and speculated about Billy and his mother, but now, with time, the novelty had worn off.

'Didn't 'ave any gas or water all morning,' said Mrs Walters.

'Couldn't even pull the chain in the lav,' said Jessie.

'Is it on now?' asked Sally.

'Yeah, fank Gawd. I fink they must've made a fine old mess in Billy's. 'Is mum wasn't 'alf 'aving a go. Yer should 'ave seen the mud on the blokes' boots. Bin walking it in and out all day. I ain't 'alf glad it wasn't our place,' said Mrs Walters.

'So what's gonner 'appen now?' asked Sally.

'They're taking 'em away,' said Jessie.

'What? After all the trouble they 'ad getting 'em through the 'ouse? And the mess they made? Nearly frightened poor Tiger ter death, they did. What we gonner do now?' Sally was getting anxious.

'Looks like we're gonner 'ave brick ones,' said Jessie, picking up Pat from off the ground. 'Come on, it's bed fer you two.'

'Gawd only knows what sort o' mess we're gonner 'ave when they 'as ter take all that concrete and bricks frough. It'll be worse than when the coalman comes.' Mrs Walters was pushing Harry into the house.

'See yer about seven, Sal,' said Jessie, closing the front door.

Sally went to look at the great lumps of metal still sitting in her yard. The men would reach her house soon. She looked round the small yard. Where would they put a brick shelter?

* * *

A week had gone by and Pete was studying the newspapers when Sally walked into Granny Brent's kitchen. She leant over and kissed his cheek.

Without looking up Pete said, 'It says 'ere that blokes under twenty-one are gonner be called up.'

'Well, yer all right then,' said Sally flippantly.

Pete folded the newspaper.

'We going out?' asked Sally.

'Yeah.'

'It's Danny I'm worried about,' said Granny Brent.

'Well I don't fink yer got anyfink ter worry about, Ma,' said Reg, swinging back in his chair. ''E's a Brent and the Brents know how ter look after 'emselves.'

'Watch that chair, yer'll 'ave the bloody legs orf it if yer ain't careful. I 'ope we don't 'ave anovver war,' said his mother, her voice softening. 'I didn't bring you lot up ter 'ave ter go orf and fight the Germans again.'

Sally was getting tired of all this talk about war. 'We going out ternight or not?'

'Yeah, course.' Pete scrambled to his feet. 'See yer later,' he said to his brother and mother.

'Where're we going?' asked Sally.

'D'yer fancy a stroll round the park?'

She laughed. 'Round the park? You want to go round the park?'

'Yeah.'

Sally could see Pete was serious, and for the moment decided not to be cheeky and just go along. 'Me and Jess saw that film *Jezebel* last night.'

'Oh yeah? Any good was it?' he asked casually.

'Smashing. Bette Davis was . . .' Sally stopped as she

could see he wasn't interested. 'Pete, is somethink worrying yer?'

He laughed. 'Na. Come on, race yer ter the gates.'

'What, in these heels?'

When they reached the park they sat on a seat and Pete took out his cigarettes. He lit one for Sally. 'Sal, Danny's gitting married.'

'Well, so what's new?'

''E ain't told Ma yet, and don't forget, 'e's still under age.'

'What, they've fixed a date? Is Gwen – you know?'

'Don't fink so, it's more ter do with this war and being called up.'

'Oh. When they gonner tie the knot then?' asked Sally, drawing long and hard on her cigarette.

'June.'

'What? That's only two months away.'

'I know. That's why I wanted ter come out ternight. 'E's gonner tell Ma.'

Sally laughed. 'She's not gonner be too pleased. Where they gonner live?'

'Seems they've got a couple o' rooms lined up round in Silver Street.'

'That's a right dump round there.'

'She wants a white wedding with bridesmaids and all that stuff.'

'Well, why shouldn't she? I know I will.'

'Sal, what about us?'

Sally looked at him. 'Are yer asking me ter marry you, Pete?'

'Yeah, of course.'

'When did yer 'ave in mind?'

'I reckon we should do it in about August. I could 'ave a week off then. But let Ma git over losing one first.'

'What? But that's only four months away. And where will we live?'

'I reckon we could find some rooms somewhere, and we could do 'em up in me week off.'

'I dunno. It's a bit quick, and I ain't living in Silver Street. 'Sides, I don't fancy leaving Dad just yet.'

'But I fought yer wanted ter git married?'

'I do, but . . . I'll be worried about Dad and the kids.'

''E can't expect yer ter stay wiv 'im for ever.'

''E don't, but . . . let me think about it.'

'Well, don't be too long.'

'Pete, what about all this talk of sending the kids away ter the country? It'll break Dad's 'eart if Babs and Johnny 'ave ter go, and if we get—'

'I dunno, Sal. I really think there could be a war, and the government must think so as well with all the money they're spending. I see we're gonner 'ave gas masks next. I tell yer, Sal, I'm really worried, and I think we should spend some time tergevver.'

'We do, except when yer working.'

'I don't mean that, I mean . . .' With the toe of his boot he ground his cigarette end into the grass. He turned her round to face him. 'Sal, I love yer, and I want us ter get married soon.'

She giggled, and quickly put her hand to her mouth. 'Sorry, Pete, but I ain't used ter yer being all serious like.'

'Well I am serious, deadly serious, and I . . .' He pulled her forward and kissed her.

'Yes please,' she panted when he released her. 'Yes,

please.' She snuggled against him. 'Shall I say somethink ter Dad?'

'Later on, let's wait till Danny's dropped 'is bombshell first. Let Ma git used ter losing one wage packet before she finds out she'll be losing anovver.'

'Will you and Reg still carry on with the printing?'

'I should say so. Don't forget that's where we gets our extra money from. 'Sides Reg wouldn't be none too pleased if we left 'im in the lurch.'

'Cor, it only wants Reg to say 'e's gonner marry Joyce Downs, then yer mum would come down on you lot like a ton of bricks.'

Pete laughed. 'Na, our Reg is too clever for that. 'Sides, she's gotter catch 'im first.'

Sally gave him a playful push. 'Oh you,' She suddenly looked wistful. 'I wonder who Gwen's getting ter make 'er frock?'

'How would I know?'

'I reckon it'll be one of 'er sisters. I'll let Jessie make mine. Oh Pete, I'm ever so excited about it, let's 'ope we can find some decent rooms near by.' She sat up. 'And when you're at yer mum's and doing a bit of overtime, I'll be able to call in on Dad and make sure they're all right.' She snuggled back down again, all thought of a war gone from her mind.

Sally was finding it hard not to say anything to her father, and when Jessie came in the following evening she found it even more difficult to keep her thoughts to herself. But she knew how news flew around here, and she had promised Pete they would wait to deliver it.

'I'm gonner go wiv me kids,' said Jessie, watching Sally

put one flat iron on the stove and pick up the other. Turning it uppermost, she spat on it and it sizzled.

'Where?' asked Sally, miles away.

'Evacuated. Yer know? If the war comes? Cor, bugger me – what's wrong wiv yer?'

'Sorry, Jess, I was concentrating on what I was doing. P'raps it won't 'appen,' said Sally, pressing down hard on her father's shirt.

'Well, I ain't taking no chances. What if 'e bombs us like those poor buggers in Spain?'

Sally winced, remembering how upset they both had been when they saw it on the news at the pictures.

'Do yer think that will 'appen?'

'Me dad reckons it could, and London would be on the top of 'is list. Anyway, I've filled in all me forms.'

'Do yer want ter go?'

'Na, not really, and Mum ain't all that keen on me going. But I reckon it might be nice ter 'ave a trip ter the country, especially if the government's paying. We might even finish up at the seaside. 'Sides, it could do the kids a power o' good.' Jessie sat forward. 'I've been really worried about young 'Arry's chest – 'e can't seem ter shake that cough orf. I can't afford ter take 'im ter the doctor's, so I took 'im round the corner the ovver day ter where they were boiling up the tar ter spread on the road. I made 'im take lots o' deep breaths. Yer should 'ave seen the poor little bugger. 'Is face went all red as 'e coughed 'is 'eart up, but I fink it 'elped.'

Sally carried on ironing. When she couldn't sleep she often heard Harry coughing, along with all the other noises that floated on the night air – the cats fighting, dogs barking, and the people shouting at them to be quiet. On foggy nights, the fog horns of the ships on the Thames boomed out to add to the sound of trains rattling and shunting along the top of Brigg Street.

'You listening ter me?' asked Jessie.

'Course.'

'Didn't look like it. 'Ere, you got somefink on yer mind?'

'No, don't be daft. What would I 'ave on me mind?'

Jessie looked at her suspiciously. 'I dunno.'

Sally wondered if she'd be able to hold out till Pete said it was OK to tell.

By May, Pete and Sally still hadn't told anyone about their plans. How long would they have to wait till Granny Brent got over Danny going?

On Johnny's birthday Sally had some of his friends in for tea. It was a very noisy affair. The following afternoon being a Saturday, all the Fullers went to the cemetery to place a few flowers on their mother's grave. She had been gone a year.

Sally was upset on the way home, and they were all very quiet as they sat in Pete's car.

'Cheer up, love,' said Pete, when they arrived home. 'I'll be over later.' He looked about him. There was no one within ear shot. 'I'm gonner tell yer dad about our plans.'

Sally looked at him, her eyes smarting with the tears she had shed. 'Why today?'

He kissed her cheek. 'Yer look like yer need somethink ter cheer yer up, and ter look forward to. Besides, Ma's all right about Danny now.'

That evening, after Babs and Johnny had gone to bed

and before her Dad went up the pub, Pete asked him if he could marry Sally.

Mr Fuller slapped Pete on the back. 'That's the best bit o' news we've 'ad fer months. When d'yer reckon it'll be then, son?'

Pete looked nervous, which was out of character for him. 'We thought about August.'

'August? Blimey, that's quick.'

'Don't see the point in waiting,' said Sally hastily.

'You ain't . . . ? You know? Are yer?'

'No I ain't, Dad. And I'm gonner 'ave a white wedding, and I'm gonner ask Jess ter make me frock.'

Her father laughed. 'Yer should see yer face.'

Sally blushed. 'Well, I don't want you ter fink me and Pete . . . I'll make a cup a tea.' She rushed out into the scullery.

'I fought we all ought ter go up the Nag's and 'ave a few bevvies ter celebrate,' said Stan when Sally walked back in with the tray of tea.

Sally glanced at Pete. 'If yer like.'

'Pete 'ere was saying yer 'ope ter git a few rooms ter live in?'

'Yes, but I ain't going round Silver Street.'

'That's where young Danny's going, ain't it?'

Sally nodded.

'It's a bit rough round there,' said Pete, 'but Danny seems 'appy enough.'

'When's 'is wedding?' asked Stan.

'Sat'day, June the third at two o'clock, round St Mary's.' He laughed. 'I should know – we printed the cards.'

'Should be a good do wiv all those 'Olt gels. Right old lot, so I've 'eard.'

'Yeah, they do 'ave a few ups and downs,' said Pete.

'As long as they don't cause any trouble at the wedding otherwise yer Mum will give 'em what for,' said Sally.

Pete laughed. 'One swipe from 'er and they'll wonder what 'it 'em.'

When Jess heard about Sally's forthcoming wedding she was thrilled.

'About time too,' she kept saying. 'I knew you two'd get 'itched one day, I just knew it. So that was yer little secret, eh, Sal?'

Within hours of the news breaking she was like a child, rushing in with pictures of wedding dresses.

'D'yer like this one?' she asked, shoving yet another picture under Sally's nose.

'Dunno. It looks nice.'

''Ave yer made up yer mind what sort o' frock yer wants?'

'Not yet.'

'What about material? You 'aving satin?'

'I dunno.'

'Satin's a bugger ter work on, but if that's what yer wants . . . Don't leave it too long, remember I've got ter make it.'

'You don't have . . .' Sally stopped in mid-sentence. The look on Jessie's face told her that only she would be allowed to make this frock.

Chapter 6

Saturday, 3 June 1939 was a glorious day. As Sally crossed the road to go to Pete's she looked up at the clear blue sky hoping it would be like this on her big day in nine weeks' time – Saturday, 5 August. She pushed open the front door, and made her way down the passageway stacked high with crates of beer.

''Allo, Sal,' said Granny Brent. 'You look nice.'

'Thanks, you don't look ser bad yourself. I love yer 'at.'

Granny Brent proudly patted her wide-brimmed navy-blue hat that had a light blue feather draped across the crown. 'Lena 'elped me chose it. I'll 'ave ter wear it ter yours. Can't afford anovver one right away.'

Sally felt hurt. Wouldn't anybody be wearing new things for her wedding? 'P'rhaps we could put a flower or somethink on it, just ter make it look a bit different fer the photos.'

'Yeah, why not? You boys ready yet?' she suddenly yelled up the stairs, making Sally jump.

'Coming, Ma,' said Pete, clattering down, Danny behind him. ''Allo, Sal, I must say yer look very nice.'

'Thanks, Pete, so do you. 'Allo, Danny.' Sally kissed his cheek. 'Nervous?'

'I should say so. Look, me 'ands are all sweaty.' He ran his finger round the inside of his stiff white collar.

'Well, that 'cos yer finking about ternight,' said Pete.

'Don't know why 'e's gitting in a state about it, it ain't nuffink new to 'im,' said Reg, coming to join his brothers.

'Reg,' said his mother sharply, 'we don't want none of that sort o' talk – d'yer 'ear?'

'Yes, Ma.' He shrugged his shoulders.

'Right now, come on, boys. You, Reg, and you, Danny, can 'old me arm. Pete, you walk wiv Sally.'

'Yes, Ma.'

Sally wanted to laugh at all these men, who were head and shoulders taller than their mother, doing as they were told.

All of Sefton Grove came out to wish Danny good luck. Granny Brent was beaming as she walked down the road with her three sons. Vera and Lena were bridesmaids and were going from Gwen's.

In the church everybody turned at the sound of the Wedding March, and Sally was eager to see what Gwen was wearing as she walked down the aisle on her brother-in-law's arm. She looked beautiful in her long white frock, with her three bridesmaids behind, quite transformed from her usual mousy self.

Lena, tall and willowy, looked lovely in the pale-pink figure-hugging frock, a gold-leafed head dress on her neat bobbed hair. Vera, who was dressed the same, had had her hair done, and the fitted frock made her look slimmer. They both gave Sally a slight nod as they passed her. Sally felt pleased they were going to be her bridesmaids too, along with Babs, and that she'd chosen blue for them so that everybody would know they weren't wearing the same frocks. Pete hadn't been able to understand why Sally's bridesmaids couldn't wear what they'd worn for Gwen's wedding and said it was a waste of money, but he'd quickly shut up when he'd seen the expression on Sally's face.

After the service, and photos, and all the usual ribald remarks, it was back to Granny Brent's for the real celebration. Most of the people in Sefton Grove crowded into the house.

The barrels had been set up in the yard, and the beer was being drunk out of all shapes of glasses. Sally noticed Mr Slater and her dad were drinking out of flower vases, while Bess was lapping up the beer out of a basin that had been placed on the ground under the tap to catch the drips.

Sally smiled. 'Hope yer got the wheelbarra ter take Bess 'ome ternight,' she said to Mr Slater.

'Not ter worry, she'll find 'er own way 'ome in the morning.'

It was hot and all the windows had been flung wide open to catch the slightest breeze. The Brent boys were singing and banging out all the latest tunes on the piano and their other instruments, with a good old knees-up in between for good measure. With all the family and guests the house was full, and overflowed into the yard.

By the time it was getting dark, a few of the guests and Bess were slumped outside. Gwen had changed into a smart navy suit, but Danny wasn't making any attempt to leave. They weren't going away, just back to their two rooms in Silver Street.

Sally was sitting outside on the window sill. The heat from the room had been overpowering. Her eyes smarted from the smoke, and the drink was making her head fuzzy.

Suddenly there was a terrific crash from the back yard. The music stopped and the sound of raised voices took over. Sally rushed through the house, and joined the crowd of onlookers. In the middle of everyone was Gwen's eldest sister, Peggy, holding what was left of a flowerpot, a plant and all the earth at her feet.

'I'll give yer chuck that at me, yer cow.' She glared at her younger sister, Ginny, a well-built blonde. Peggy raised her hand to throw the remains of the pot back, but Reg was behind her and took it from her hand.

'That's me best geranium, that is. Bin looking after it fer years,' yelled Granny Brent, pushing through to see what was going on. She bent down and picked up the plant by its roots. 'Who chucked it? I'll kill the cow.'

'It was 'er,' said Peggy, dancing up and down, almost hysterical.

Ginny straightened her skirt. 'Fink yer clever, don't yer, sneaking up on people, bloody peeping Tom.'

'Peeping Tom? Yer got a bloody nerve – 'e's my old man.' She turned and faced the crowd. ''Ere, d'yer know she's bin 'aving it away wiv 'im?' She pointed a bony finger at a weak-looking man who was half hidden behind Ginny. 'Caught 'em out 'ere, I did. Bold as brass, they was. 'E 'ad 'is bloody 'and up 'er skirt. Me own sister! Oh I know it's bin going on fer months. Finks I'm bloody daft, don't yer, yer dirty little cow?'

There were lots of shouts and whistles from the crowd. 'Go on, gel, you tell 'em,' someone yelled out.

Ginny tossed her blonde curls.

Peggy grabbed her by her shoulders and shook her. 'I'll kill yer. I know what's bin going on.'

Ginny pushed her hands away. 'You leave me be, yer

nagging old cow. 'E don't git none from you, so 'e 'as ter go elsewhere.' Smiling at everybody, she patted the back of her hair. 'And I fink 'e's very good at it.'

That remark brought forth another howl of laughter.

'Well, if anybody should know, it's gotter be you,' said another of the Holt sisters. 'Yer gits enough practice.'

'Very funny,' said Ginny. 'I'm going up the pub. Anyone coming wiv me?' She turned to Peggy's husband. 'What about it, Sid?'

Peggy lunged at Ginny and smacked her in the face.

'Oh. Me eye, me eye,' yelled Ginny, holding her eye. 'I'll 'ave a black eye in the morning, you cow.' She threw herself at Peggy but Reg got between them.

'Now come on, gel, we're 'ere ter enjoy ourselves, so why don't yer patch it up?' Reg held on to her arm.

'Patch it up wiv 'er? Yer gotter be joking.' Ginny freed herself from Reg and, tossing back her head, pushed her way through the crowd. 'I'll settle wiv you in the morning,' she called to her sister, over her shoulder.

A great cheer went up.

'Sid's gonner git a bit o' stick ternight, I shouldn't wonder,' Pete said, coming up to Sally.

'Well, 'e 'as been asking fer it, carrying on like that in front of Peggy.'

The crowd began to break up, and Sally could hear Reg on the piano.

'Let's go in, Sal. I tell yer, I was worried ter death when I 'eard that crash. I thought the barrel 'ad gone over.'

Sally gave him a playful push. 'Oh you.'

'I knew this would 'appen,' said Gwen in her little mousy voice, coming to stand next to Sally. 'I wanted me and Danny ter git away 'fore it blew up. That Ginny's been 'anging round Peggy's 'usband fer monfs, and I saw 'em out 'ere kissing.'

Sally wanted to laugh. Everybody knew about Ginny Holt. She said she liked married men as she knew they couldn't get too serious.

Fortunately the fracas didn't stop the party, and it was well into the early hours before it finally broke up.

Sally and Pete stood close together at her door. 'I think Dad enjoyed 'imself ternight,' she said, snuggling even closer. 'Just think, in nine weeks' time it'll be our wedding night.'

Pete kissed her upturned face. 'Yer'll be Mrs Brent then, but Gawd only knows where we're gonner live.'

'Don't worry about that now,' she whispered, and putting her arms round his neck, kissed him long and hard. At this moment she didn't know if she could wait nine weeks to become Mrs Brent.

As the month drew to a close, the talk of the forthcoming evacuation of London children was on everybody's lips. Jessie was looking forward to it and in between making Sally's wedding dress and the bridesmaids' frocks, she was busy altering and making herself and her children new clothes. Johnny and Babs were still arguing with their dad about going away, but when Babs heard Connie Downs was going she didn't seem to mind so much. By now they had all been fitted with gas masks, but every day some new government order or form arrived. Piles of bricks and sand lined Sefton Grove as the brick air-raid shelters were being erected in the back yards. There were the usual moans and complaints from the residents about the mud and dirt being dragged through.

'Blocks out all the sun,' said Sally, when Pete was peering into the dark shelter that had been put up in the Fullers' yard.

Pete laughed. 'When did this yard see the sun?'

'What're you lot gonner do?'

'They reckon the arches is as good as anywhere ter shelter.'

'What, with all those trains going over yer 'ead all night?'

'Still, wiv a bit o' luck we might get some rooms wiv a shelter in the yard – that's of course if it comes to a war.' He put his arm round her slim waist and pulled her close.

'Pete, I'm getting worried. We've only got a few more weeks. We should try and find somewhere ter live soon.'

'I wish we could afford one of these new 'ouses going up in the country.'

'Well, we can't. 'Sides, what about yer job and the printing?'

He smiled. 'Well, we've always got that offer round in Silver Street. Danny said they're not too bad once yer git yer own bits and pieces in there.'

Sally pulled away. 'You ain't really trying, are yer? I think yer wonner live round there.' She walked into the kitchen.

'What's up wiv you?' asked her dad.

'It's 'im.'

Pete shrugged his shoulders.

'What's 'e done?'

'She don't reckon I've tried ter get any rooms.'

''E 'as, Sal. Been out most dinner times.'

'I bet,' she said.

'Look, sit down the pair o' yer. I fink I might be able ter 'elp yer out.'

Sally could see her father was serious, and sat down hard at the kitchen table. Stan and Pete joined her. She stared at her hands as she played with the pulled strands of the green chenille tablecloth.

'I've bin giving this 'ere wedding a lot o' thought. We've only got what – four weeks?'

'Four weeks terday,' said Sally.

'Well, what if yer both lived 'ere?'

Her head shot up. 'What? But 'ow? We ain't—'

'Shut up and let me finish. I reckon young Johnny could go downstairs in the front room. We don't use it that much. Babs could go in 'is room and you two could stay in yours. Well, what d'yer fink?'

Sally sat with her mouth open. She hadn't even given that a thought.

'Well, say sumfink, gel.'

Pete looked at Sally. 'Well, Sal?'

'I dunno. I ain't thought about that.'

'This way yer won't 'ave ter worry about coming round ter see us, and we'd all muck in tergevver, and Pete can still go over the road ter do the printing, and you can still git ter work – well, gel?'

Sally jumped up and threw her arms round her father's neck. 'It's the best present we could 'ave. I didn't want ter leave yer anyway. Now the only difference will be that Pete will be living 'ere. Thanks, Dad.'

Pete shook her father's hand. 'Fanks, Pop. That's great, really great, that's if yer sure I won't be in the way, and Johnny don't mind being down 'ere?'

'Na, don't worry about 'im. 'E won't mind.'

In fact, Johnny and Babs were delighted with the news.

'Fought I might 'ave ter do all the cooking,' said Babs.

Sally laughed.

'And I fought yer might go away and I wouldn't see yer again,' said Johnny.

Sally ruffled his hair. 'Don't talk daft.'

'Sal, if there is a war and we 'ave ter go away, would yer try ter come ter see us?' asked Johnny.

She held him close. 'I will if I can.'

Babs snorted. 'Well, there ain't a war yet, so yer ain't got nuffink ter worry about, 'ave yer? Sal, Jessie wants us ter go in ter try on our frocks.' A smile spread across her round face, lighting up her big brown eyes. 'I fink my frock's smashing, and Connie's ever so jealous 'cos she ain't never been a bridesmaid.'

'She might one day when her sisters get married.'

'Dunno about that. Their mum reckons they'll never find a bloke the way they carry on. What she mean, Sal?' asked Babs.

Sally smiled. 'Don't worry about it. We'll go in to see Jess after tea.'

She couldn't wait to tell Jessie she was going to continue living at home, either. War or not, married life was going to be perfect.

Chapter 7

Sally lay in bed reflecting on her big day. She seemed to have sailed through it, dreamlike, and now all too soon, it was over. Tomorrow she and Pete were going on honeymoon. They had decided to have a few days in a boarding house Solly had recommended at Ramsgate. She was so excited about it.

Getting dressed in the lovely, long white frock Jessie had sewn made her feel like a queen. Babs and the Brent twins had been her bridesmaids and Babs had looked lovely. Sally smiled when she'd caught sight of her preening in front of Connie Downs, showing off her long blue frock.

Her father had spared no expense and the cake, with its silver bells and flowery top, was wonderful. She had felt so proud when she walked down the aisle on Dad's arm. Her only regret was that her mother wasn't there to share the day. Now a tear slowly trickled down her cheek. Her wedding, and the party that spilt out into the street afterwards, would be the talk of Sefton Grove for a few weeks. Everyone had come out to wish them well. She smiled. Despite Sadie Tanner's feet and Mr Slater's bad leg, she could still see them doing the Lambeth Walk in the middle of the road. Mr Slater's singing drifted through the open window. He must be sitting on his window sill. He probably finished up round Fred's when the party broke up. It suddenly went quiet. His sister must have taken him indoors. Sally smiled and wiped away her tear.

Moonlight was shining through the window and, to Sally, everything looked romantic. She glanced across at Pete beside her. He was snoring so she gently turned him over. The party and drink had been too much for him, and as she had helped him to bed she wondered how many other brides didn't do it on their wedding night. If the rest of the Brents ever found out, Pete would be the laughing stock of the family, Sefton Grove and the docks.

Sally grinned to herself. They had waited all these years so another night wouldn't make a lot of difference. However, Jessie would be round first thing in the morning asking questions – if she didn't have a hangover.

She put her lips to Pete's cheek and kissed him. He slowly turned over.

'Sal,' he whispered, putting his arms round her. 'Sal, I'm sorry, gel, if I let yer down.' He pulled her close and kissed her.

Slipping the straps of her new white satin nightie from her shoulders, he gently caressed her breasts. Slowly he moved down her body. She shuddered with excitement and anticipation. Jessie had always told her it was great. 'Pete, yer don't 'ave to, not if yer don't . . .'

He propped himself up on his elbow and kissed her neck. 'Oh Sal, I want to . . . I want to . . .'

She wanted him to as well, so she lay back and let his love flow over her.

The following morning, after all the goodbye hugs and

kisses, the car moved gently through London and into the Kent countryside.

Sally snuggled up to Pete. 'I can't believe we're really married.'

'Well, we are. Just look at all that confetti over the floor.'

Sally giggled. 'We'll 'ave ter get it out. Don't want everybody ter know we've just got married. It was a lovely wedding, better than Danny's.'

He laughed. 'I dunno – we didn't 'ave any punch-ups.'

'Yer mum's hat looked nice with that big rose on it, didn't it?'

'Didn't know they 'ad blue roses.'

'Oh you!'

'Now, you looked smashing.'

'Jess made a good job of those frocks, didn't she?' Sally sank back in the seat. 'Babs looked so grown up.' Her voice dropped to a whisper. 'I wish Mum could 'ave seen us.'

Pete patted her hand. 'Come on, Mrs Brent, we don't want any tears.'

Sally kissed his cheek. 'I'm all right, Pete, honest. I love you.'

He stopped the car, and pulled on the handbrake.

'What is it? What's the matter?' asked Sally, anxiously looking round.

'Nothink.' He pulled her close and kissed her. It was a long passionate kiss. 'I've been dying ter do that all day. I'm sorry about last night, but it turned out all right in the end, didn't it?'

She blushed, nodding.

He kissed her fingers, and then they continued their journey.

The three days they had in Ramsgate were wonderful. The sun shone all day, and they made love at night. Sally didn't want it to end. It wasn't like real life at all, a million miles from Sefton Grove, the air-raid shelters and all the talk of war.

When they had arrived back home the war was still the main talking point, and things seemed to be moving quickly. Her father had told Sally the council were filling sandbags in the park and were looking for volunteers.

Then Babs had brought a letter home from school and Sally reread it several times, unable to believe it: the children in their area were going to be evacuated on Saturday, 2 September.

All week Sally was busy making sure Babs and Johnny had enough clothes packed in their bags for their big adventure.

On Friday evening everybody was very quiet. There weren't any of the usual squabbles over who was going in the bath first.

'Yer never know, yer might finish up in an 'ouse wiv a proper bath,' said Pete.

'I'm all right 'ere,' said Babs solemnly.

'Why do we 'ave ter go away now? The war ain't started yet,' said Johnny.

'It's what the government says,' said Sally. 'Right, up ter bed, you two, I've got a lot ter do.' She was surprised she didn't get any of the usual moans and arguments as they kissed her good night.

'I'll empty the bath for yer, Sal,' said Pete, walking in with the bucket and ladle.

'Thanks.' Sally was ironing the last bits they had to take.

'You going up the dogs ternight?' she asked him when he'd finished emptying the tin bath.

'No, not ternight. Thought yer might like a bit o' company.' He picked up the bath and took it outside.

'But yer always go to the—' she began when he returned.

'Yeah, I know,' interrupted Pete. 'But, well, ternight's a bit different.'

Sally sighed. 'It'll be funny without 'em.'

'Yeah. London'll be strange wivvout any kids.'

'It'll be a lot quieter.' There was a catch in her voice. 'Why don't yer go up the Nag's with Dad?'

'You wonner get rid o' me?'

'No.' She put the iron back on the stove and sat next to him. 'I'm ever ser worried about 'em. Johnny wet the bed again last week. Jess told me not ter say anythink. Poor little devil.' Slowly a tear trickled down her face. 'I don't want 'em ter go, Pete.'

He put his arm round her shoulders and pulled her close. 'It might not be fer long. They could both be back 'ere next week getting under yer feet, then you'll be moaning about 'em.'

It was a weak smile she gave him. 'Let's 'ope so.'

'Yer dad's ever so upset.'

'I know.'

'Shall I write these labels for yer?'

'Ta.'

Pete took the two brown labels and wrote Babs' and Johnny's names and address on them. He put them next to their gas mask boxes. 'I'll make a cuppa tea.'

'Ta.'

They spent the evening under a cloud of gloom, having run out of comforting words to say.

* * *

The following morning Sally was reminded of the story of the Pied Piper as all the children made their way to the school. Charabancs and buses were waiting to take them to the station. The government had taken over all public transport to move these children and mothers out of London and to safety.

Jessie pushed Pat along in her pushchair while her mother held Harry's hand. 'Don't know if I'm ser keen ter go now it's come to it,' said Jess, looking round.

'Well, I wish yer wasn't going,' said her mother. 'Poor little buggers some of 'em. I'd like ter know who's gonner wipe their snotty noses and dirty arses.'

'It might not be fer long,' said Sally as they got nearer the school.

'Christ! Look at this lot! Dunno who got all this sorted out, but they ain't done a bad job,' said Stan, his arm round Johnny.

Johnny was very quiet, he hadn't said much all morning.

'Now, Babs, remember what I told yer. You mustn't be separated from Johnny,' said Sally, fussing with Johnny's coat and making sure his label was facing the right way.

'No, no, I'll remember.'

Sally could see she wasn't taking any notice of her as she looked around for Connie Downs. Suddenly she spotted her and waved frantically.

Connie came racing up. 'Look, all the family's come ter see me orf. It's like going on 'oliday, ain't it? Your lot coming ter the station wiv us?' She was jumping up and down, bursting with infectious happiness and enthusiasm, and right away Babs' mood changed as she linked arms with her very special friend.

The railway station was full. Apart from all the children, there were men in uniform looking for their trains. It was chaotic. The noise from the engines was making it difficult to hear the orders being shouted over the Tannoy.

'Now, Babs, yer will write, won't yer?' Sally asked.

'Course.'

'And you will look after Johnny, won't you, and don't let 'em separate you. You both got to go to the same 'ouse. Are yer listening?'

'Course.'

'And you will tell us if things ain't all right?'

Babs shuffled her feet and looked about her. 'Sal, how many more times yer gonner say all this?'

Sally looked embarrassed. 'Sorry. It's just that I worry about yer.'

'Now come on gel, yer sister's only trying ter protect yer,' said their father.

'Will we miss the war?' asked Johnny softly.

'I shouldn't fink so,' said Pete.

'I don't wonner go, Sal.'

Sally bent down and held him close. 'I'm sorry, love, but it's fer the best. Yer might be 'ome next week.'

'What if we ain't?'

'I tell yer what, as soon as yer get settled, and if it ain't too far away, we'll come down in Pete's car ter see yer.'

'Will yer, Sal? Will yer, Pete, really?'

Pete ruffled the top of Johnny's head. 'Course.'

For the first time since the letter arrived, Johnny's face lit up.

Suddenly their school was being told what platform to go to, and all the children made their way to catch their train to somewhere only the WVS women knew.

Sally kissed Johnny, and then clutched Babs to her. Tears filled Sally's eyes. 'Take care,' she whispered as they parted and were herded through the gates.

Jessie kissed Sally and held her close. 'I'll write when I gits settled somewhere,' she said tearfully.

For all Sally's life Jessie had been next door. Now would she ever see her again? What would happen to them all? Sally said a silent prayer: please don't let there be a war.

Sunday morning was bright and sunny, but to Sally the day was dull and miserable without Babs and Johnny around. Even their bickering would have made her smile. Where were they? Were they safe? What were the people like that they finished up with? Would they ill treat them?

Pete had to go over to his mother's to finish off an order, and the house was very quiet. At eleven o'clock, Sally sat at the kitchen table with her father, listening to the wireless. Mr Chamberlain was telling them that Britain was now at war with Germany. When the broadcast had finished Sally turned off the wireless, but neither she nor her dad moved. For all the rumours of the past weeks, now war had finally come, they were completely stunned by the news. Minutes passed. They didn't speak.

Finally her father rolled a cigarette. 'Well that's it,' he said.

'What's gonner 'appen to us?' asked Sally.

'Dunno.'

'I got ter go and tell Pete.'

'Reckon 'e'll know.'

'Not if they've got the printing press going. You can't 'ear a thing when that's banging away.'

'I'm surprised 'e's still got work.'

'It's dropped off a lot, but they've got ter finish this job,' she said, hurriedly leaving the room.

'Ain't it awful, gel?' Mrs Walters shouted across to her as she reached Granny Brent's front door. 'Christ only knows when I'll see me Jessie and 'er kids again.' She began to cry.

Sally stood wavering. She didn't know whether to comfort Mrs Walters or go and see Pete. She suddenly felt miserable and frightened. When would she see Babs and Johnny again? What was in store for them?

A terrible moaning sound suddenly filled the air. Sally screamed. The door of Granny Brent's burst open and Reg and Pete came rushing out.

'Sally, Sal, 'ave yer 'eard?' Pete clasped her to him.

'Pete, what's that noise?' She pulled away and looked about her, terrified. People were rushing from their houses into the road.

'It's the siren. Quick, git in yer shelter. Go on, Mrs W, git indoors.' Pete was pushing Sally into her doorway and Mrs Walters into hers. 'I'll git Ma.' He rushed back across the road.

'Pete!' yelled Sally.

'Come on, gel. Git in 'ere, quick.' Her father took her arm and pulled her along the passage.

'But Pete . . .'

''E'll be 'ere in a tick.'

They stood in the brick shelter. Pete and Granny Brent soon joined them.

'Well, if we're gonner 'ave a few more o' these going orf,' Stan flicked his thumb over his shoulder, 'we'd better make this place a bit more comfortable.'

Sally screwed up her nose. This was the last place she wanted to make homely. It smelt damp and felt cold.

Suddenly a long clear note filled the air.

'That's the all clear,' said Pete. 'I reckon they was just trying it out.'

'D'yer fink so?' asked Stan.

'Yeah, and I reckon you're right: we should get a few chairs in 'ere, just in case.'

Sally looked at him. Fear was making her heart beat very fast. Air-raid practice, moving chairs into the shelter – where was it all going to end?

Chapter 8

Throughout Sunday, panic stayed with Sally. All day she went about her chores in a dream, unable to get her thoughts off the siren, the war, and her brother and sister. Time and time again tears filled her eyes.

'Look, love, why don't we all go up the Nag's?' said her father after they'd finished tea.

Pete was standing behind him, nodding.

'What if we 'ave another air raid?'

'I told yer, they was just trying it out. It'll be all right.'

'OK then, if yer think it's safe,' she said half-heartedly. 'I'll just nip upstairs and get me coat.'

'I'll get me fags,' said Pete, following her out of the kitchen.

'I'm glad yer said you'd come wiv us,' said Pete. 'Yer dad's really down. I think 'e needs a bit of cheering up.'

'Don't we all?' said Sally.

It was still early when they walked in the Nag's, and there weren't many of the usuals holding up the bar. They were surprised to see Silly Billy sitting in the corner. Sally nodded and smiled.

Billy's grin lit up his podgy face. He gave a little wave.

'Don't see 'im out much,' Sally whispered to Pete.

'It must be the war. Don't encourage 'im ovverwise 'e'll

be over like a shot. What's brought 'im out?' Pete asked Wally, the landlord, quickly inclining his head in Silly Billy's direction.

''E said 'is mum's scared stiff and wouldn't stay upstairs. Poor sod's 'ad ter bring 'er bed down ter the front room. I fink she's bin giving 'im a bit o' stick.'

'Just as well 'e's come out then,' said Stan, walking up to the bar, ''Cos it's a bit quiet in 'ere ternight, Wal.'

'Yeah, bloody 'Itler, ain't it? Reckon this could kill trade. What yer 'aving, Stan?'

'A pint o' usual. Same fer you, Pete?'

'Fanks,' said Pete. 'What about you, Sal?'

'I'll 'ave a shandy.'

''Ave this one on the 'ouse,' said Wally, quickly looking about him.

'Christ!' said Stan. 'That's gotter be a first.'

'Shh, shh. Keep it down.' He looked towards Silly Billy and leant on the bar, smiling. 'Make the most of it. We might be all blown ter kingdom come by next week.'

'You're a right bloody Jonah and no mistake,' said Pete.

Sally sat at a table and fidgeted with her glass. 'Yer don't think he's right, do yer?'

'Take no notice of 'im. 'E's just peeved that everybody ain't come out ter drown their sorrows,' said Pete, sitting next to her.

After a few drinks they relaxed and talked about what bits of furniture they needed to put in the air-raid shelter.

'Got ter put a door on it first,' said Stan, sitting back and rolling a cigarette. 'Those bleeding cats 'ave made it stink to 'igh 'eaven.'

'I'll give yer 'and,' said Pete.

When Fred and Mr Slater walked in the atmosphere was improving. They were quickly followed by Connie Downs' mum and dad with their other two daughters, Joyce and Doreen. Sally wondered if Connie and Babs had finished up together. Sadie Tanner came in to fill her beer jug. She nodded to her neighbours and after drinking the froth off the top of the beer, left. Everybody knew Mr Tanner was back in prison. Shortly after, Reg, Vera and Granny Brent joined them, and when Reg started pounding away on the piano, everyone began singing, and the pub took on a party feel.

Granny Brent was looking at Joyce Downs leaning on the piano. 'Look at 'er, making sheep's eyes at our Reg. Silly cow. I know that lot come out a bottle. She didn't used ter be that colour.'

Joyce Downs, the eldest of the sisters, was flicking back her long blonde hair, and smiling at Reg.

Sally laughed. 'And Reg is lapping it up. That's a nice coat she's got on,' said Sally, admiring the garment slung round Joyce's shoulders.

'Fancy wearing a fur coat this weather. Fur coat and no drawers, I shouldn't wonder.' Granny Brent tutted. 'I'd like ter know 'ow she got that.'

'Probably saved up 'ard fer it,' said Vera. 'I wish I 'ad one like it.'

'Hummh,' said Granny Brent, pulling at the scarf she had round her shoulders. 'And look at that frock. It's so low yer can very nearly see 'er bloody belly button.'

Sally laughed, pleased their thoughts were being taken off the war.

'Ma,' said Vera, laughing with Sally, 'why do yer always think the worst?'

'I know what young gels gits up to.'

Vera winked at Sally. 'Makes yer wonder what she used ter git up to.'

Granny Brent smiled smugly. 'I ain't telling yer.'

Joyce Downs lit a cigarette and passed it to Reg. Sally noted the smug grin on Reg's face as the smoke trailed upwards. Joyce was slim, and with her lovely hair, very attractive. Sally watched her gently sway in time to the music. Many times she'd wished she could dress and do her hair like Joyce. Joyce had told Sally she liked Reg, but couldn't get him to take her out. Which was a pity as Sally would have liked Joyce as part of the family.

'I'm gonner join the ARP termorrer,' said Fred, coming towards them with a pint in his hand.

'Good fer you,' shouted Stan above the noise, and slapped him on the back.

''Ere, watch me pint, and me back. You'll 'ave me laid up fer weeks. By the way, I'll be round termorrer ter make sure yer all got yer black out up, and Gawd 'elp any o' yer if yer got a chink o' light showing.'

'Don't, Fred. Yer making me shake in me shoes,' said Mr Slater.

Sally was laughing with the rest of them, but she knew about the heavy fine they could get if any light was showing.

'What about you, Den?' Stan asked Mr Slater. 'What you gonner do then?'

'Bugger all. I did my bit first time round, so let these youngsters 'ave a go this time.' He waved his arm at Pete and Reg.

Sally looked afraid. She hadn't thought that Pete might have to go.

* * *

At the end of the week Sally had her first letter from Babs. Tears ran down her face as she read the neat handwriting. The address was Worthing.

Dear Dad, Sal, and Pete,

Today is Sunday and we have just heard that the war has started. It's not too bad here. Mrs Good that's the lady we live with said we should write to you right away as she said you must be very worrid about us. She is old but quite nice. She has got two other evacues another brother and sister, the boy is older than me. I don't like him. I wanted Connie to come here but the bossy WVS woman said no. I don't know why miserable cow. Mrs Good aint got no husband and her daughter lives near, she's maried so she's got one.

Me and Johnny have to sleep in the same bed and I don't like that so far he aint wet the bed. But when he does I'll bash him. We are going to school tomorow which is Monday I don't think it's too far away I hope not I don't fancy walking about round here, we might get lost. I think we are near the sea.

Our train ride down here was good, we all mucked about, and the ladys shouted at us to be quiet. We didn't like it when we got here and they put all this powder down inside our frocks, they thought we was lousy what a cheek.

Look after Tiger for me. I hope to see you soon.

With love from your daughter and sister Babs.

PS, Johnny wants to add a bit.

Sal. I dont like it here. I want to come home.

PPS, Dont take no notice of him. Love Babs. XXXX

Sally was having trouble seeing the words through her tears. 'Poor little devils,' she said out loud.

A banging on the knocker brought her back, and she hurried to the door.

'Mrs Walters!' she was surprised to see Jessie's mum standing there. 'Come in. What's wrong?'

Mrs Walters' face broke into a smile. 'I've 'ad a letter from Jessie. Fought yer might like ter see it. It ain't very long, and she ain't very 'appy.'

Sally ushered her down the passage. 'We've 'ad one from Babs. Where did Jess finish up?'

'Dunno. Sounds like some godforsaken place ter me.'

'Fancy a cup o' tea? I'm just making one 'fore Dad and Pete get in.'

'Yeah, all right then, gel.'

'I'll put the kettle on then I'll read Jessie's letter. 'Ere's Babs' letter.' She pushed it over to Mrs Walters.

Jessie's was from a place called Renton in Sussex.

Dear Mum and Dad,

Well we got here at last. All day it took us and I can't say I'm thrilled with it. Can't see me staying here for long. All ready had one move. Do you know they shoved me and the kids in some old boys, it was a right dirty hovel, and they had the bloody cheek to fumigate all of us just cos we come from London. That nearly caused a riot. I had a right go the next morning well I wasn't going to stay there. I'm on a farm now, after a lot of sodding about. The kids like it but the old dear didn't want us. Lets hope this war don't last too long. I miss you Mum.

Love Jessie, Pat and Harry. XXX

PS, Give Sal my love.

Once more tears flowed from Sally's eyes. 'She don't sound very 'appy, does she?' she sniffed, getting up to make the tea.

Mrs Walters wiped her nose. 'Na. Fancy fumigating 'em. Bloody cheek, I calls it. Just 'cos we live in London we ain't all got fleas and bugs.'

'It must be some sort of precaution,' said Sally, but she too was angry about it.

'I'd like ter git me 'ands on that bleeding 'Itler, breaking up families. I can see 'er coming 'ome.' A faint smile lifted her troubled face. 'Still, Babs and Johnny seem ter be all right.'

Sally nodded. 'I 'ope so.' She poured out the tea. 'Now we've got an address I'd like ter go and see 'em.'

'That'll be nice. They'd like that.'

Mrs Walters put her elbows on the table and held the cup to her lips. 'I really miss those kids o' Jessie's.'

'Well, let's 'ope we'll be seeing 'em all soon. In the meantime, I'll write to Jessie as well as Babs and Johnny.'

Most people soon settled down after the announcement of the war, and apart from the kids being away, the only sign of the war was the blackout. Without the kids running around shouting and screaming Sefton Grove seemed uncannily quiet.

Two weeks after the outbreak of the war, Pete came home fuming. 'Seen this?' He threw the newspaper on the table.

'What's wrong?' said Sally.

'They've gorn and rationed petrol.'

'I said they would, didn't I?' said Stan. 'How much yer gitting then, son?'

'For my car it'll be four gallons a month. I'll be able ter do about a hundred and sixty miles.'

''Ow far is it to Worthing?' asked Sally.

''Bout sixty there and back.'

'Can we still go and see the kids next Sunday?' asked Sally, apprehensively.

'Just about. I managed ter put a few gallons by just in case, but I don't know about after that. I've got ter save a bit ter do the printing deliveries.'

'Yer still got work then?' asked Stan.

'For the time being, but I don't know 'ow long it'll last, and I've got ter go out and try ter drum up some extra work from somewhere. Can't 'ave that machine standing idle fer too long.'

It was the Sunday two weeks after Sally had had Babs and Johnny's letter, and Pete was taking Sally and her father to Worthing. It was debatable who was the more excited about seeing the kids again.

'Ain't they gonner be surprised when they see us?' beamed Stan.

Sally smiled. All Pete's hard work had been worth it, when he'd bought the car, but now with petrol being rationed Sally wondered how long these pleasures would last.

'Will it take long ter get there?'

'A couple o' hours. We'll stop a bit later on and 'ave that drop o' tea and the sandwiches yer made.'

The journey was all new ground to Pete, and with all the road signs and directions removed for security reasons he found it difficult to get his bearings. 'According ter me road map we should be near it now.'

'Can't we ask someone?' said Sally, winding down her window.

'D'yer fink they'll tell us?' said her father. 'They might fink we're German spies.'

Sally laughed. 'Now I ask yer, what would a German spy want in Corneal Road, Worthing?'

'Dunno, there might be a big spy ring there,' her father chuckled.

'Shut up, you two, and look out fer the street names,' grumbled Pete.

They seemed to travel round in circles, and finally decided to go into a pub to ask the way.

'Nice drop o' beer down 'ere,' said her father, smacking his lips.

'Yeah, it ain't 'alf bad,' said Pete. 'And we know where ter go now.'

At last they turned into Corneal Road.

'Cor, don't they look posh 'ouses,' said Sally, eagerly sitting forward as they slowly made their way along the road looking at the numbers. Number forty-eight was at the far end.

'Fancy 'em finishing up in a place like this,' said her father.

'Now this is what I call a nice-looking 'ouse,' said Pete,

stopping the car. 'You go and knock, Sal, just ter see if they're in.'

Self-consciously, Sally walked up to the front door and, after knocking, pulled at her skirt and checked her seams were straight. She could hear a scuffle inside, then the door was flung open and Babs stood there open-mouthed.

'Who is it?' a woman's voice came from a room at the end of the passage.

Babs found her voice and screamed out, 'It's me sister! It's me sister!' She then caught sight of Pete and her father behind Sally. 'And me dad!'

Now Johnny was at the door. He flung himself into Sally's outstretched arms, and they both laughed and cried together.

'Dad,' he said. 'And Pete.'

Their father clasped his children to him in a tight little group.

When Sally broke away, she wiped her tears and found herself looking at a woman standing in the passage.

'Hello, I'm Mrs Good.'

Sally was taken back. She wasn't that old, she was about forty.

'Do come in.'

Sally gently pushed Johnny in front of her. Stan quickly pulled his trilby off and, taking Babs' hand, followed Mrs Good. The passage smelt of lavender polish, and the beige patterned lino gleamed. Small colourful mats were at the doors of the two rooms they passed, and at the bottom of the stairs.

'We'll go into the kitchen. It's cosy in there,' said Mrs Good.

The kitchen was bright and uncluttered, not at all like

that in Sefton Grove. Sunlight streamed through a large window. In the middle of the room stood a big round table with a pretty lace cloth over. Placed in the centre of the table was a bowl of flowers. A dark wooden sideboard stood against one wall. Sally quickly noted there were six matching chairs placed evenly round the table.

'This is a very nice room,' she said, trying hard not to be seen to be looking around.

'I was lucky my husband had a good job, and now I have the four little evacuee children, and what the government pays us is very handy. Do sit down.'

They all quickly did as they were told.

'How are yer both?' asked Sally.

'We're all right,' said Babs. 'How's Tiger?'

'Oh your cat,' said Mrs Good. She turned to Sally. 'She's told me all about him.'

''E's all right,' said Sally. 'What about you, Johnny?'

He looked at Mrs Good. 'I'm all right.'

'What about school?' Sally was finding this conversation hard going. It wasn't like her brother and sister to sit so very quiet.

'It's all right.'

'Is it very far away?' asked Pete.

'It's not too far,' said Mrs Good. 'But it isn't just round the corner like I understand they've been used to.'

'We don't come 'ome fer dinner,' said Babs.

'Well, yer didn't after Mum died.'

'I know, but we went inter Jessie's,' said Babs, fidgeting in her chair.

'Look, why don't we all go out fer a walk? I'm sure you can take us ter some nice places. It looks very nice round 'ere,' said Sally, standing up and gathering together her gloves and handbag.

'Is the sea very far?' asked Pete.

'Too far for them to be back in time for tea,' said Mrs Good. 'Remember tea is at four, Barbara.'

Sally sat down with a jolt. She looked across at her father, who sat open-mouthed. Nobody ever called Babs Barbara apart from the teachers at school.

Sally quickly recaptured her composure. 'Don't worry, we'll get 'em back in time.'

'I have to be strict about meal times with four children, otherwise I'd be at their beck and call all day. They'd have me run off my feet if I wasn't strict.'

Sally nodded.

'Don't worry, missis, we'll git 'em back in time,' said their father. His tone was one of relief.

'She seems very nice,' said Sally, as soon as they were out of the door.

'She's all right,' said Johnny half-heartedly. 'But I wonner come 'ome.'

'Don't start on that again, Johnny,' said Babs quickly.

'I don't like it when she makes me eat up all me greens.'

'Well they're good fer yer,' said Sally, smiling. She remembered the times she'd tried to get him to eat things she knew were good for him.

'And she makes us do all the work,' added Johnny.

'I don't believe that,' said Sally.

'We do 'ave ter 'elp 'er,' said Babs.

'Well, that don't 'urt yer,' said their father.

'What's school like?' asked Pete.

'Bit posh,' said Babs. 'The kids round 'ere don't like us evacuees. I told 'em we didn't wonner move down 'ere, away from our own 'ouse.'

'They're big bullies,' said Johnny.

'We're gonner git a gang up and bash 'em one o' these days,' said Babs confidently.

'You mustn't do that,' said Sally in alarm.

'That won't solve anyfink,' said Pete.

Her dad put his arm round Babs' shoulder. 'Yer got ter give 'em a chance ter git used ter yer ways, gel.'

'Well, we don't like 'em.'

'What's that lump under yer frock?' asked Sally, pulling at it.

'It's the elastic in me drawers,' replied Babs, looking embarrassed. 'It got loose so I 'ad ter put some knots in it. Now it's a bit tight and I 'ave a job ter pull 'em up.'

Sally laughed. 'Ain't that Mrs Good got some elastic ter put in 'em?'

'I ain't asked 'er.'

'But she does yer washing and ironing, don't she?'

Babs nodded.

'Well, I would 'ave thought she'd see the state of 'em then.' Sally felt put out. She'd always made sure their clothes were repaired. 'I'll send yer some elastic.' She looked at her watch. 'Look, it's getting on fer four. I think we'd better start making our way back.'

'I don't wonner stay 'ere. Can we come back 'ome wiv you, Sal?' pleaded Johnny.

Sally couldn't look at him, her eyes were full of tears. 'I'm sorry, Johnny.'

He pulled his hand away aggressively. 'Yer don't love us. Yer was glad we got sent away.'

She bent down and held him close. 'I wasn't, Johnny, honest. I didn't want yer ter go.'

He stood stiff, he didn't put his arms round her, but she could feel his tears wet and warm on her neck.

'It's fer the best,' she croaked.

'Come on, love,' said Pete softly, taking her arm. 'They mustn't be late back fer tea.'

Babs was clinging to her father's hand. 'Yer will come and see us again, won't yer?'

'Yeah, course we will.' He pulled Johnny to him. 'Now come on young feller me lad, remember you're the man now, and yer supposed ter be looking after yer sister.'

'She can look after 'erself,' he sniffed.

Sally straightened up. 'Well, if we're gonner 'ave all this fuss every time we come ter see yer. I don't know if we ought ter bother.' Everybody knew she was just putting on a face.

By the time they reached the gate they were very quiet and subdued.

'We better not come in,' said Sally. 'We don't wonner upset Mrs Good.'

'Will yer write?' asked Babs.

'Course I will, and now we know where yer live perhaps next time we can go and see the sea.' Sally was trying to sound cheerful.

'It ain't got no sand, just stones.' Johnny pushed open the gate and banged on the knocker.

'About time,' said Mrs Good. She looked up and suddenly smiled. 'Are you coming in?'

'No thanks, we better be going. Pete don't like driving in the dark with this blackout, and not being allowed proper lights now.' Sally could almost hear Mrs Good sigh with relief.

Once more they kissed, hugged and said their goodbyes. Quickly Johnny disappeared into the house instead of standing at the gate to wave them off. Sally and her father hung out of the car window waving till Babs was out of sight. Then Sally slumped back into the seat and cried.

'Don't take on so, gel,' said her father, gently patting her shoulder. 'They'll be all right.'

Sally blew her nose. 'D'yer think so?'

'Yeah. It's bound ter be strange fer 'em at first.'

'But is that woman looking after 'em all right?'

'Well, they looked clean enough.'

'But what about—'

'Give 'em time,' interrupted Pete.

'They'll settle down, you mark my words,' said her father. 'Then I reckon we'll 'ave a job ter git 'em back 'ome.'

Sally knew that would never happen.

Chapter 9

The following day Sally hurried home from work, eager to tell Granny Brent about Babs and Johnny.

A cup of tea was put in front of her as soon as she sat at the table. 'I'm ever ser worried about 'em. I really can't make out if they're 'appy or not.'

Granny Brent eased herself into the chair next to Sally. She gently patted the back of Sally's hand. 'I shouldn't upset yerself, gel. Kids are funny buggers, they 'ave a way of bouncing back. I bet as soon as yer was out of sight they was larking about as if yer'd never been there.'

'D'yer really think so?'

'Yeah. 'Allo, Vera,' she said, looking up as her daughter walked into the kitchen.

''Allo, Ma, Sal,' said Vera. 'Tea ready, Ma?'

Granny Brent laughed. 'See what I mean? They only fink of their stomachs, and I bet those two toerags o' yours is just the same.'

'Did yer see the kids yesterday?' asked Vera.

Sally nodded.

'They all right then?'

'I think so.'

'Somefink wrong?'

'Johnny's not very happy. 'E wants ter come 'ome, and I'm not sure that woman's looking after 'em properly.'

'Why d'yer say that?' asked Granny Brent.

'Well, Babs didn't 'ave any proper elastic in her drawers, fer one thing.'

Granny Brent laughed. 'Is that all yer got ter worry about?'

'Don't worry about 'em, Sal,' said Vera. 'They'll be all right. Ma, I'm going out ternight.'

'Oh yeah, who wiv?'

Vera looked embarrassed. 'It's a bloke from work. 'E's asked me ter go to the pictures wiv 'im.'

'I'm glad they're open again. I really missed going,' said Sally.

'Yeah, Lena was dead worried about it,' said Granny Brent. 'I told 'er she better start looking fer another job, but 'er boss said they wouldn't be shut fer long.'

'Anyway, Vera, what's this bloke like? Is 'e nice?' Sally asked eagerly.

''E's all right I suppose.'

''E coming 'ere?' asked Granny Brent.

'No, I'm meeting 'im outside.'

'Why's that? Ashamed of us?'

'Don't talk daft, Ma. 'E lives near the Red Lion so it's a bit pointless 'im coming over 'ere fer me.'

'As long as 'e's not married already,' Granny Brent smiled.

'Course 'e ain't. Yer always fink the worst.'

'Is 'e good-looking?' asked Sally.

''E's not bad.' Vera gave a little smirk.

'I bet our Lena'll give 'im the once-over if yer going ter the Red Lion.'

'Good job it's dark in there,' said Sally. She won't be able to see 'im in the dark.'

They laughed.

'Yer, well, that's another reason I won't bring 'im 'ome, you know what Lena's like, she'll 'ave anyfink in trousers.'

'Well yer just 'ave ter make sure you 'ang on to 'im then, that's if 'e's all right and worth 'anging on to,' said Granny Brent.

Vera didn't answer. 'I'll go up and git ready. See yer later, Sal.'

'Let us know what 'e's like,' called Sally after her as she left the room. 'Thanks fer the tea, Ma. I better be going. Pete and Dad will be in soon.'

'All right then, love, and don't yer go worrying about those kids too much. They'll be all right.'

But Sally still wasn't convinced.

That night Sally wrote to Babs and Johnny, asking them all sorts of questions.

Two weeks later she had a reply, and the only reference Babs made to her letter was to say she had received it, and that they had been pleased to see all of them. Sally was very concerned. The letter was very short and precise, and the spelling was correct. There was no PS from Johnny.

'When can we go and see 'em again, Pete?' Sally asked after reading the letter again.

'Dunno. Depends if I've got enough petrol.'

'Well, yer shouldn't 'ave used it ter take that printing out. You could've gone by bus,' snapped Sally.

''Ang on. I was looking for work. Yer know as well as me, Sal, the printing's almost dried up, and we've got ter grab work where we can. 'Sides, petrol ain't cheap now.

They've just gorn and put it up ter one and ninepence 'a'penny a gallon.'

Her father looked up from his newspaper. 'It says 'ere butter and bacon are gonner be rationed next.'

Pete laughed. 'Pity we ain't Jews then.'

'Still, that'll be a lot fairer,' said Sally. 'I was talking ter Florrie in the grocer's and she was saying we've got ter be registered with a shop.' She felt guilty at snapping at Pete when she knew he was doing his best. 'Jessie's mum was telling me there's been some right old rows round the shops when they know there's stuff inside and they won't let 'em 'ave it. They keep it under the counter, yer know.'

'How is Jess, Sal?' asked her father.

'She ain't that good at writing letters so 'er mum don't hear that often, but she's really fed up down there.'

'I can see 'er coming 'ome soon,' said Pete.

Sally looked wistful. She missed Jessie. 'Yeah so can I.'

''Ere, Pete, will young Danny be called up?' asked her dad.

''E reckons so. 'E ain't told Ma yet.'

'She'll go mad,' said Sally.

'Yeah, after losing Dad in the first lot.'

'What will 'appen to Gwen?'

'They git an allowance.'

'But will it pay the rent?'

Pete shrugged his shoulders. 'Dunno. Now the printing's getting 'ard, Reg'll 'ave ter find work soon, or else join up.'

'What's 'e doing now, son?'

'Just scratching around. 'E's thinking o' going in a factory, but I can't see 'im sticking at that – 'e ain't used ter taking orders from a gaffer. Ma was telling me Vera's bloke, Roy, is going in the RAF.'

''E's nice,' said Sally.

'You didn't say you met 'im.' Pete scowled.

'Only got a glimpse of 'im the other night when I came 'ome from the pub. They was outside yer mum's. I told yer, but you wasn't listening, it was the night we was seeing Cissy off, you know Cissy at work.'

'Yeah, yeah, you told me.'

'I hope 'e writes ter Vera.'

'She's worried about 'er job.'

'I fought food stuff was important,' said Stan.

'It depends. I know we're going on war work soon,' said Sally.

'Yeah, well, chocolates ain't gonner end the war,' laughed Pete.

'A lot o' the girls are talking about joining up.'

Pete sat up. ''Ere, you ain't finking o' that, are yer?'

Sally smiled. 'Course not.'

'I should bloody well 'ope not,' said her father. 'What they reckon you'll be doing then?'

'Dunno. The foreman reckons it'll be somethink ter do with soldering from the stuff that's coming in.'

Pete laughed again. 'What, women soldering? That's gotter be good fer a laugh.'

'Well, women will 'ave ter be doing a lot more funny jobs if all the men go away.'

'S'pose they will. Can't see 'em doing fings like unloading ships, though.'

'Or going down coal mines,' said her father. 'What about Reg? Will 'e git called up?'

'Depends how long it lasts,' said Pete.

'Good fing they made you exempt then, ain't it?' said Stan.

'Yeah,' said Pete, 'but don't forget we can be moved anywhere in the country if the ships can't git up the Thames.'

'Why can't they do that?' asked Sally.

'Subs,' said her father. 'They can slip across the North Sea and torpedo the ships.'

'Oh,' said Sally, her mind going back to the start of all this. 'Can we go and see the kids before Christmas then?'

'If we can, but I can't make any promises. Still, we've got a few weeks yet.'

'Only six,' said Sally pensively. 'You can save yer petrol ration fer them can't yer?'

But Pete wouldn't commit himself.

At the beginning of that week, the chocolate factory started doing war work. It seemed to Sally that lately she was out with the girls every Friday evening having a farewell drink with those who were leaving to join up. Although she had never met any of them socially before, it was good to have a night out with them now she didn't have Jessie to go with. She began to enjoy being independent, and looked forward to her Fridays with the girls, even when they didn't always have the excuse of a sendoff.

Although it was hard, dirty work in the factory now, the girls were glad to be helping the war effort. The atmosphere had changed. They were happy, and when they had the odd false alarm, the singsongs in the air-raid shelter kept up their spirits. Many of the men had left, and women were taking over their jobs, just like Sally had said.

Monday was dark and drizzly, which matched Sally's mood as she pulled her collar higher and hurried home from work. She was still cross with Pete from yesterday about not going to see Babs and Johnny. He had used up his petrol allowance, but she wasn't going to let the idea of going down to see them again rest. If he couldn't take her in the car on Sunday, she was going by train. She had to take them their Christmas presents. Christmas, she couldn't believe it, was only three weeks away. It was unimaginable without Babs and Johnny and Jessie around.

It was dry under the arches except for the drip, drip of rain seeping through the concrete, and as she picked her way over the puddles the sound of a man's heavy footsteps running behind her made Sally look round. She could see a shadowy figure coming under the arches. No one else was nearby. She quickened her pace.

As he got nearer he shouted, ''Ang on 'alf a tick, Sal. It's me, Tommy. Tommy Tanner.'

She turned and laughed. 'Yer frightened the daylights out o' me.'

'Sorry, gel. D'yer mind if I walk wiv yer?'

'Course not. How's yer dad?'

''E comes out soon. So does Ted, but 'e's going straight in the army.'

'What about you?'

'I went fer me medical, but it seems I ain't fit enough. Mum was dead pleased about that. 'Ere,' he looked round cautiously. 'Yer knows they're gonner ration sugar soon?'

'About time too. We ain't 'ad any fer weeks. Florrie in the grocer's puts me a bit by now and again, but being at work all day I don't get time to queue up fer things like that.'

Tommy came closer and took hold of her arm. 'Yeah, well, I might be able ter 'elp yer. Yer see, I can git me 'ands on a few pounds – that's if yer interested?'

'I should say so.'

'It's a few pence more, so what d'yer say?'

'How much can I 'ave?'

'Can let yer 'ave four pounds.'

'That'll be great. When?'

'I'll bring it along ternight, OK?'

They had reached his gate. 'OK. See yer later.' Sally's step had a bounce as she walked into the kitchen. Her father and Pete were home before her.

'Git yer wet fings orf, love, tea's made,' said her father. 'You look pleased wiv yerself.'

'Just come along with Tommy Tanner.'

'When's the old man coming out?'

'Soon, but guess what. Tommy's coming up here with some sugar later on.'

'Sugar?' Pete's head shot up. 'Where's 'e got that from?'

'I didn't ask.'

'What's 'e charging yer fer it?' asked her father.

'I didn't ask,' said Sally again, 'but I thought it'll be nice ter 'ave a bit in our tea fer a change.'

There was a knock on the front door. 'I'll go,' said Sally.

When she walked back into the kitchen Tommy Tanner was behind her, a cloth shopping bag tucked under his arm. He quickly pulled off his cap. His brown hair was ruffled, and he looked uncomfortable. His dark, deep-set eyes hastily took in his surroundings. 'Got yer sugar,' he almost whispered as he put the shopping bag on the table and took out four blue bags. 'Might be able ter git yer some more later on, that's if yer wants it.'

Sally gathered up the bags. 'OK, if yer got 'em to spare.'

'How much?' asked her father.

'Sixpence a pound.'

Sally took a breath. 'I'll get me purse.'

''Ere, Tom, any chance of a gallon or two o' petrol? I've used up me month's supply and Sal wants ter go down and see the kids.'

Tommy looked furtive. 'I might be able ter git yer a few gallons. I'll let yer know Sat'day, but keep it under yer 'at.'

Pete smiled. 'Course. Any idea 'ow much?'

'Can't say. I'll let yer know Sat'day.'

Sally reappeared and paid Tommy for the sugar.

'I'll see yer out,' said Pete, going to the door with him. When Pete returned he sat at the table and, putting a heaped spoonful in his tea, asked. 'How much is a pound o' sugar?'

'Thrupence.'

'That's twice the price!' yelled her father. 'The bloody robber!'

Sally laughed. 'Well, we all knows 'e is, but it's nice ter 'ave it, ain't it?'

'I 'ope 'is petrol ain't twice the price,' said Pete.

'Now I've sweetened yer tea, Pete Brent, what's yer temper like?'

'Why, what yer on about?'

'I'm gonner see the kids on Sunday, and if yer don't take me then I'm going on the train. D'yer wonner come with me, Dad?'

'It ain't that I don't wonner take yer. I told yer, Sal, it's the petrol.'

Her father looked uncomfortable as he glanced across at Pete. 'I've left me baccy in me coat pocket. I'll just pop up the passage ter git it.'

'You're a canny cow and no mistake,' said Pete, when Stan had left the room.

Sally turned on him. 'Why?' she asked, looking innocent and opening her big brown eyes wide.

'Yer knows full well I'll take yer if Tommy comes up with the goods, so let's 'ave no more nonsense.'

As she kissed his cheek, her father walked back in the kitchen. 'Pete's going ter take us.'

'Good,' said her father settling down in his chair. 'And, Pete, I'll give yer a few bob towards the petrol.'

Sally was in a happy mood all evening, and when her father and Pete had gone up to bed she sang to herself as she cleared the supper things away. The war had meant she'd had a rise at work, and there was talk they were going to put in a radio. Then her thoughts went to Johnny and Babs. Should she let them come home? She had noticed a few children were back in London, but what if things got bad? She quickly dismissed that thought. She would wait and see how they were when she saw them on Sunday, and if they were really unhappy, well . . .

Later, as she crept in beside Pete, she put her arms round him.

'Christ, yer feet are like blocks of ice.'

'Yer can warm me up if yer like,' she said, snuggling closer.

'Now don't start none o' that, not ternight. I've got ter be up early in the morning.'

'Yer never used ter say that.'

'Well, that was when we first got married. Now turn over and get ter sleep.'

Sally did as she was told and as she hugged the pillow, thought to herself: we've only been married four months and we act like an old married couple. Still, I suppose we're just like everyone else round here.

Chapter 10

It had been freezing cold at the factory all morning and Sally was pleased it was Saturday half-day. The foreman had told them that soon they might be asked to work all day. Pete said he didn't mind as the extra money would come in handy.

As she hurried home Sally was still feeling upset and disappointed that she wouldn't be seeing her brother and sister tomorrow after all. Pete and her father now had to work over the weekend. The ship they were working on had to go out on tomorrow's tide and because of the blackout they couldn't continue through the night. Walking past the arches, Sally wondered if Tommy Tanner would still have the petrol next Saturday. She looked for him, but he wasn't anywhere to be seen. ''Ope 'e ain't bin nicked,' she said to herself.

When she got home she kicked off her shoes and, with her feet on the fender, sat in front of the fire sipping a cup of hot tea. Tiger jumped on her lap. 'You've been a bit neglected lately,' she said, fondling his battered ears. 'I'll try and get yer some scraps when I go ter the butcher later on.' But the thought of going to Jamaica Road and standing in a queue all afternoon in the cold, in the hope of getting something for tea, didn't appeal to her.

Suddenly she sat forward listening. Someone was pulling the key through the letter box. She knew it wouldn't be her dad or Pete. They'd told her they would be late.

She stood up, her heart pounding, as the kitchen door was flung open.

'I 'eard yer come in, so I fought I'd pop round and say 'allo.'

Sally stood with her mouth wide open. She slammed the cup on the table and leapt at Jessie, holding her close. 'When . . . ? Why . . . ?' Tears and laughter were mixed together.

'Got 'ome last night.'

'Why didn't . . . ?'

'I was too bloody tired. Dragging two kids on and orf trains all day ain't easy, poor little devils. I tell yer, Sal, I couldn't stay down there a minute longer.'

'I can't believe it, it's really you.'

'Yes, really me,' said Jessie sitting herself at the table.

'D'yer want a cuppa?' Sally put her hands on the teapot. 'It's still warm.'

'Yeah, why not?'

'It's so good ter see yer again,' said Sally wiping her tears. 'How's the kids?'

'Not ser bad. But honestly, Sal, this 'as been the worst time o' me life. Everyday I said I'd come 'ome.'

'I'm surprised yer took so long.'

'Didn't 'ave the fare, did I?'

'Why didn't yer write and ask?'

'Wouldn't do that, would I?'

'Well, yer 'ere now, so tell me all about it.'

Jessie took a packet of cigarettes out of her overall pocket, lit one, and made herself comfortable.

'When we left 'ere, we finished up in some place in Sussex. The kids was tired and grizzly, and I wasn't in a good mood by then. They took us in ter a big hall and gave us a cuppa tea and a sandwich, and a brown carrier bag with a few tins inside, then they 'ad the bloody cheek ter fumigate us, just cos we come from London. Yer should 'ave 'eard the language from some of the real old cockneys. They turned the air blue. I tell yer some o' those so-called ladies were shocked. Mind you, by the state o' a few o' those old tarts, I reckon they was lousy.'

'Good job Sadie wasn't there. I bet the fleas would've jumped off 'er,' laughed Sally.

Jessie chuckled and stopped to take a long drag on her cigarette. She blew the smoke high into the air. 'Me and the kids was then put in a car by some woman from the WVS and taken to this 'ere cottage. It was getting dark by now, but it looked real pretty from the outside, a bit overgrown but it 'ad nice roses and flowers in the garden. Anyway the old boy wasn't 'ome, so after a lot of mucking about we finished up in the local pub.'

Sally grinned. 'I bet yer liked that?'

'Would 'ave if we'd stayed in the pub, but 'e didn't 'ave no room so 'e put us in the barn out the back. It was pitch-black in there and we only 'ad an oil lamp – no bed just a pile o' straw. Talk about no room at the inn. I know how Mary must o' felt when she finished up in a stable. By now the kids were starving, so the bloke brought us out some food. We 'ad it on a garden table. When 'e left I just sat and cried, I was so miserable.'

'Yer didn't tell yer mum all this?'

'No, I fought it best not to. Didn't want 'er ter worry too much. I didn't git a lot of sleep that night as I was scared stiff of all the creepy-crawlies that was in there, and it rained, and the barn 'ad a tin roof. Talk about noise! The kids was petrified, poor little buggers. When I turned out the light yer couldn't see yer 'and in front o' yer. Black as yer 'at it was. I wasn't 'alf fed up, and dead pleased when it got light.'

'You sat up all night?'

Jessie nodded. 'Got any more tea?'

'Course.' Sally quickly got up and refilled the teapot.

'Next morning the WVS woman came back and took us on to Mr Dwyer's.'

Sally poured out the tea. 'Was that the pretty cottage?'

'Yeah. It looked all right on the outside but inside it was falling ter bits, and filfy dirty, and yer should 'ave seen 'is tatty furniture. 'E didn't 'ave a wife, and said 'e expected me ter look after 'im, and do the cooking and cleaning. Well, I nearly went mad, and that woman 'ad buggered orf before I found out. So ter cut a long story short, I bundled the kids in the pushchair and tied the case on it and trundled down the road. I was coming 'ome. I'd 'ad enough. Those country lanes all look alike, I didn't know where I was going and me bloody feet was killing me – 'ad me new 'igh 'eels on, didn't I? Then some bloke give us a lift in 'is car back ter the pub. He phoned that woman and she came and said she'd found us somewhere else ter stay. She took us ter this farm. When we got there the farmer's wife was standing on the step with 'er arms folded, and she said all posh like, "I don't really want you in my house, but now the war's started I'll have to have evacuees or land girls, and I would have to wait on land girls, but you can look after yourselves."

'I tell yer, Sal, there I was, dirty, tired and fed up – I could 'ave clocked 'er one.'

'But you stayed there?'

'Didn't 'ave a lot o' choice, did I? I was upset when I 'eard the war 'ad started, and I fought I'd better stay away fer the kids sake, but, well, 'as nuffink's 'appened I decided ter come back. I really missed London. Besides, I 'ad ter be back fer Christmas.'

Sally threw her arms round her friend's neck. 'I've really missed you.' Tears filled her eyes.

Jessie brushed a tear from her own cheek. 'Don't, yer'll start me orf again.' She sat back. 'Well, 'ow's married life treating yer then? Expecting yet?'

Sally busied herself clearing the table. 'Course not.'

'Why not?'

'Let's face it, it ain't a good time ter 'ave babies.'

Jessie nudged Sally. 'But Pete's still giving yer plenty o' nights o' passion?'

Sally laughed. 'You know Pete – 'e ain't no Tyrone Power.'

'Still, yer 'appy, though, ain't yer?' There was concern in Jessie's tone.

'Course. But I'm a bit worried about the kids.'

'I was gonner ask about them. Yer said in yer letter they finished up in Worthing. They all right?'

'I dunno. They don't say much in their letters. We went ter see 'em a while back, and Pete's taking me and Dad down there next Sunday. I'm ever ser worried about them.'

'I expect they're all right. Mind you I've 'eard some terrible tales about evacuee kids. Some people are treating 'em like slaves, and doing all sorts of fings to 'em.'

'Thanks, Jess, that's all I need. Look, I've got to go out. Fancy coming with me?'

'I'd better not. Don't wonner leave the kids fer too long, and I've got a lot ter talk about wiv Mum and Dad.'

'Course. I'll see yer termorrer then.'

What Jessie had told Sally about other evacuees upset her, and now she would have to wait another week before she saw Johnny and Babs. Next Sunday couldn't come soon enough.

When her father and Pete came home from work they slumped into the armchairs, tired, dirty and hungry.

'Managed to get some sausages fer tonight,' said Sally. 'Mind you, I 'ad to queue up fer ages. And guess what? Jessie's back 'ome. She's 'ad a terrible time.'

'She got the kids wiv 'er?' asked Pete.

'Yes.'

'Well, I fink it's all wrong, 'er coming back 'ere wiv those kids,' said her father.

'A lot of people 'ave come back,' said Sally, as she laid the table. 'What if Babs and Johnny want ter come back?'

'Well, they ain't. I don't 'old wiv it. There ain't no schools open, fer one fing.'

'But what if they're really unhappy?'

'And what if the Germans come over bombing us and they git killed?'

'Don't say things like that, Dad.'

'Yer father's only being practical,' said Pete. 'Besides, they seemed 'appy enough living in that nice 'ouse.'

'Yes, but are they? Anyway, we'll find out next week.'

'Don't bank on it, Sal.'

'Why?'

'If we git another rush job in—'

'We've got ter be able ter turn 'em round quick,' said her father.

Sally threw the forks on the table. 'I don't believe it. You've not wanted ter go all along. I bet yer dead pleased, ain't yer?'

'Sal, 'ang on. Don't start gitting on yer 'igh 'orse. It ain't Pete's fault. 'Sides, we might not git a ship—'

'Well, I shall go, with or without yer,' she shouted, and stormed out of the room. She stamped all the way up the stairs, threw herself on the bed and burst into uncontrollable sobbing. She was feeling sorry for herself, for Babs and for Johnny, but she was also furious because she couldn't get her own way.

Pete came in, looking bewildered. 'What's up, Sal?'

She didn't answer.

He sat on the bed. 'I dunno what's wrong wiv yer. I said if I can I'll take yer down ter see the kids, but if the work's there – yer knows we've got ter do it. It ain't just fer the money. We could git the sack, and then I'd 'ave ter go in the army.'

Sally sat up, suddenly guilty at being so selfish. She looked away to hide her red eyes. 'It's just I'm so worried about Babs and Johnny,' she whimpered.

He put his arms round her. 'I know, love. Now come on, dry those tears.' He kissed her wet cheek. 'When I see Tommy I'll make sure about the petrol fer next time.'

She threw her arms round his neck and kissed him eagerly and ardently. 'Oh Pete,' she whispered.

He buried his face in her neck and kissed her long and passionately. She lay back on the bed, and as his hand gently ran over her body, she felt like screaming out with pleasure. This is what she wanted – to be loved.

Suddenly Pete sat up. 'Those sausages will be done ter buggery.'

'Don't worry about them. Dad'll look after them,' she whispered and started to take her frock off. 'Come on, Pete. Let's do it now.' She tried to pull him back down.

'Na, leave it out, Sal. Yer dad'll want 'is dinner.'

She sat up. 'I don't believe it.' She angrily buttoned up the front of her frock. 'Pete, yer do love me don't yer?'

'Course I do.'

'But we don't . . . you know, very often.'

'Well, I 'as ter work bloody 'ard.'

'I know.'

'We'll see about it ternight.'

When he'd gone downstairs, Sally looked in the dressing table mirror and tidied her hair. This wasn't how she wanted their marriage to be. She loved him and wanted to be loved, *really* loved. Was being married to Pete going to be like this for the rest of her life?

On Sunday morning after Pete and her father had left for work, Sally sat at the table and smiled to herself. She and Pete had made love last night, but it would have been much more exciting if they'd done it at tea time.

In the afternoon Jessie came in to talk.

'Danny's Gwen up the spout yet?' she asked.

'Not as far as I know. Reg and Danny's in the army. Pete said they're in the same regiment so that's nice fer 'em.'

'Bet Granny Brent didn't fink so.'

'She wasn't very 'appy about 'em going.'

'Can't see Reg knuckling down and taking orders,' said

Jessie. 'Mind you, 'e's a nice-looking bloke. Always fought that Joyce Downs fancied 'im.'

'She did, but Granny Brent always kept 'er at arm's length.'

'Still, 'e can do what 'e likes. After all, 'e's over age.'

'Yeah, but you know Granny Brent.'

Jessie grinned. 'It always makes me laugh the way all those big grown-up blokes take notice of their muvver.'

'Yeah. Vera's got a really nice bloke, Roy 'e's called, ever so good- looking. 'E's in the RAF.'

'You met 'im?'

'Not really, only seen 'im from a distance. Vera's probably worried Lena might whisk 'im away.'

Jessie laughed. 'What does 'e see in 'er?'

'Vera's nice,' Sally protested.

'Yeah, but dead plain. She still at the creamery?'

'No, she works in a factory making uniforms.'

'She gonner marry 'im?'

'I don't know.'

'She's not a bit like 'er sister.'

'Well, Lena's a right flighty bit.'

'She still at the cinema?'

'For the time being. I reckon they'll be calling up all those not on war work soon. Mind you, I'm surprised she ain't volunteered fer the forces. Then she'd be with all the men.'

'She got a bloke yet?'

'Dunno, she don't bring 'em home. Granny Brent reckons they're all married, that's why.'

Jessie laughed. 'Good job me old man's not still around then.'

'D'yer ever 'ear from Vic?'

'Na. Mind you, Dad was saying if 'e gets called up 'e'll 'ave ter tell 'em 'e's married and I might get an allowance. That'd be a right turn up fer the books, wouldn't it? It takes a war fer me ter git a few bob out of 'im.'

Sally laughed. 'You ain't got it yet. He might turn out ter be a conscientious objector.'

'That would be just my luck.'

They sat chatting and drinking tea, Sally telling her about the neighbours and what they were doing. They laughed a lot and to Sally, it was just like old times.

Eventually, Jessie stood up. 'I better be off, got ter git the kids' tea and ready fer bed.' Suddenly she threw her arms round Sally. 'It's good ter be back 'ome.'

Sally swallowed hard and held her close. 'Yer a daft 'apporth. But it's good ter 'ave yer back.'

When Sally arrived home from work on Monday night, her father and Pete were home before her.

'Job finished?' she asked, taking off her hat and coat. 'See yer made the tea. Good, I could just do with a cuppa, then I'll see ter the dinner.'

'Sit down, Sal,' said her father.

His tone made her quickly do as she was told. He looked strained.

'What's the matter?' She looked at Pete. 'What is it?'

Stan handed her a letter. It was written in pencil on paper that had been torn out of a school book. The scrawly writing was familiar. 'It didn't 'ave a stamp on.'

Dear Dad and Sally and Pete,

Please send us some money. We are coming home. You can send it to Connie Downs she lives in the next road. I have wet the bed I cant help it when I does it Mrs Good locks me in a cupboard when I get home from school. She reads all our letters and makes us show what we right to you. I want to come home. Love from your son Johnny. PS, Babs dont know I writ this. XXX.

Sally looked up at her father, tears running down her face. 'What we going ter do?' she whispered. 'We've got ter bring 'em back. I knew they was unhappy.'

As Pete put his arm round her shoulders, she put her head in her hands and cried.

'Come on, love,' said her dad, gently patting her back. 'This won't 'elp 'em.'

'What can we do?' she sobbed.

'I dunno.' Stan sat back in his chair. 'We got ter find out if it's true first.'

'Johnny wouldn't tell me lies.' Sally blew her nose. 'I'll go along to Mrs Downs for Connie's address.'

'You can't send 'em money,' said Pete.

'Why not?' Sally stood up, her eyes flashing with anger.

'They won't know 'ow ter get back 'ere.'

''E's right, Sal. 'Sides, what if Babs don't wonner come 'ome?'

'Course she does. You read what Johnny said. That old cow reads all their letters. No wonder I never get any answers ter me questions. I'll kill 'er when I see 'er. How dare she make 'em unhappy! And she's gitting paid.' Sally was trembling with anger.

'Calm down, love,' said Pete. 'I fink we'd better find out if it's true first. Yer knows how kids exaggerate.'

'But Johnny wouldn't tell me lies,' Sally repeated forcefully. 'I know 'e wouldn't.'

'I don't fink 'e would worry us if it ain't true,' said her father sadly.

'That's what I said. I'll git me coat and go along ter Mrs Downs, I can git a postal order first thing termorrer.'

'Sit down and drink yer tea first, Sal.'

Sally sat down.

'Before yer come in, me and yer dad started talking fings over, and we fink we might take the day orf termorrer.'

'What? Yer can't. What if they sack yer?'

'We ain't got a ship in at the moment, gel.'

'But Dad, yer still 'ave ter go on call.'

'We know that, don't we, but we reckon after we've signed on we'll be sent 'ome, then we can go down ter see 'em.'

'And if fings ain't all right, we'll bring 'em back. I'll go up and see Tommy about the petrol ternight,' added Pete.

'I'm coming with yer termorrer,' said Sally.

'Now what's the point?' said her father as he rolled a cigarette.

'I can't go ter work knowing you two are with Johnny and Babs. 'Sides, I've got a few things ter say ter that Mrs Good, I'll give 'er Good.'

'Now what if Johnny was a bit upset when 'e wrote that?'

'I know Johnny, Pete. 'E wouldn't worry us if it wasn't genuine.'

'She's right, son.'

'Well, that's settled then.'

After they finished tea Pete went and saw Tommy Tanner, who promised he'd get him two gallons of petrol in the morning.

All evening Sally was fidgety.

'Settle down, Sal,' said her father. 'Yer won't make the morning come any quicker by keep looking at the clock.'

She gave him a faint smile. 'No, I know. But I can 'ardly wait ter see the kids.'

Chapter 11

After a sleepless night Sally was up early. She gave her father and Pete their breakfast and contented herself with catching up on the ironing, all the while keeping her eye on the clock. She knew they should be home about nine if they were able to get away from the docks.

It was almost ten when Pete's car drew up outside, and he didn't look very happy. 'I've done a few sandwiches. Did yer get the petrol?' she asked, settling herself in the front seat.

'Yeah, got two gallons. 'E's a bloody robber, Tommy Tanner. D'yer know 'e 'ad the bloody cheek ter charge me five bob a gallon. Bloody five bob! All I 'ope is, what Johnny said is true. If 'e's 'aving us on a wild goose chase 'e'll 'ave me ter answer to. I'll kill 'im.'

'I told yer, son, I'll give yer the money,' said Stan from the back of the car.

'Yeah. Sorry about that, it's just that . . . It just makes me mad, that's all. And another fing: it's the pink petrol they use fer lorries and buses. Gawd only knows where 'e got it from.'

'Will it be all right?'

'Should be if Pete don't git caught wiv it,' said her father.

'You can be fined ever such a lot if yer get caught with stuff from the black market.' Sally looked apprehensive.

'Well, I'll just 'ave ter make sure I don't get found out then, won't I? D'yer know, 'e told me ter filter it through me gas mask.'

'What for?' asked Sally.

'It s'posed ter take all the red dye out.'

'Don't fancy that,' said her father. 'It wouldn't 'alf stink if we 'ad ter use 'em.'

'Don't say things like that, Dad.'

It had gone one o'clock when they turned into Corneal Road. The journey had been very quiet – no laughing about German spies this time.

'I fink I'd better go in and see 'er,' said Stan.

'No, Dad, you wait 'ere.'

'I fink you'd better go, Sal,' said Pete. 'No offence, Pop, but we don't want yer putting yer foot in it, just in case it ain't true.'

'Yeah, I s'pose tact ain't me strong point. But, Sal, mind what yer say,' said her father when they stopped outside the house. 'Let's make sure all what Johnny wrote was right 'fore yer start leading orf.'

She didn't answer as she got out the car and ran up the path. Without hesitating, she banged on the door.

Mrs Good's face was full of surprise when she answered it. 'Why, hello. It's Sally, isn't it? Fancy you coming all this way. The children are at school. You didn't say you were coming.' Her smile was fixed and every sentence was short and clipped.

'We've come ter see Johnny and Babs.' Sally thought it best not to tell her why.

'As I said, they're at school.' The smile didn't change.

'Could yer tell us where it is then?'

'I'm sure you'd be better off waiting for them here.'

'We'd rather see 'em on their own, if yer don't mind.'

'Of course I don't mind, but they don't finish till half-past three.' She looked past Sally towards the car. 'I see your father's here as well. Wouldn't he like to come in for a cup of tea?'

'No, I don't think so. We'd rather just see the kids. So if yer can tell us—'

'I'll just get my coat, then I'll come with you.'

Sally was beginning to get cross. 'Why?' she demanded.

'It will be better than trying to give you directions.' The smile was still there.

'Don't worry, we'll find it. It can't be that far away.' Sally went to turn away.

Mrs Good, still smiling, put her hand out to stop her. 'I think you ought to know Johnny has been a little bit of a naughty boy. He's been wetting the bed just lately. I didn't let them write and tell you. I didn't think it was fair to worry you. Barbara said he's done it before.'

Sally stopped. 'Yes, it was after Mum died. He can't 'elp it. So what did yer do about it?'

'I thought it best if I punished him.'

'So it's true.' Sally tried to keep her temper under control. ''E wrote and told us.'

Mrs Good's face flushed, and the smile disappeared. 'The little devil.'

'So, what did yer do about it?' Sally insisted.

'Well, my mother used to lock my brother in a cupboard when he was naughty.'

'Your mother must 'ave been a wicked old cow, and so are you if that's what yer been doing ter our Johnny.'

Mrs Good looked shocked, and whispered, 'How dare you speak to me like that after I've been good enough to look after them. They're not the easiest of children, you know. I think it's very ungrateful of you.'

'Yer gets paid enough.' Sally didn't wait for an answer. She turned and stormed off down the path, and the front door banged shut.

'What was all that about?' asked Pete, as she got in the car.

'She admits she's shut Johnny in a cupboard.'

'What?' said her father. 'Let me git at 'er, the cow.'

'Now calm down, Pop. Let's find out more about this. Where's the school?' Pete asked Sally.

'She wouldn't tell me. She wanted us ter wait in there fer 'em.' Sally nodded towards the house.

'Did she now? I s'pose that's 'cos she wants ter 'ear what they've got ter say about it. I tell yer, Sal, I'm bloody 'opping mad.' Her father's voice softened. 'I've never 'ad ter lay an 'and on those kids, and I'm buggered if I'm gonner stand by and let someone else 'ave a go at 'em.'

Pete started the car. 'We'll go up ter the shop and ask them where the school is.'

Sally was sure she saw the curtains of number forty-eight move as they drove away.

The local shopkeeper told them how to get to the school and they lost no time driving there. Once again it was Sally who went in, this time to find the headmistress.

The headmistress listened carefully while Sally told her story. 'So yer see, we are all very worried about 'em.'

'Yes, I can understand your anxiety, but you must remember these children are in a very different environment, and some are finding it harder to adjust than others.

Wait here while I have a word with Barbara and John's teachers, and see what they have discovered.' At the door she turned and smiled. 'Children do tend to exaggerate.'

Sally looked out of the window. She hadn't really noticed until now what a bright day it was, the sun straining through clouds that scurried past. This view was so different from in London. Here were trees and open fields, not belching chimneys towering above them. The air smelt fresh and clean. She wondered if she should take the kids away from all this. A smile spread across her face. Jessie certainly didn't like the country.

The headmistress returned. 'Well, I've had a word with both teachers, and it seems Barbara is always getting into trouble with the other children. She hasn't settled in at all well. And John is very quiet and shy. Give them time, I'm sure they'll adapt soon.'

'I'm taking 'em back ter London.' There was no mistaking the firmness in Sally's voice.

The headmistress sat at her desk and looked over her horn-rimmed glasses. 'Do you really think that is very wise?'

'Don't know.' Sally felt she was back at school herself, standing in front of the headmistress, who hadn't asked her to sit down.

'I'm sure the government wouldn't have gone to all the trouble and expense if they didn't think it was best for the children to be out of the cities. Besides, I understand there aren't any schools open in London.'

'Not yet, but they'll 'ave ter open 'em soon. A lot of kids 'ave come back.' Sally was trembling with fear; she had never spoken to anyone in authority like this before in her life.

'What does your father have to say about all this?'

''E agrees. He's outside, with me 'usband in the car.'

'Very well. I still think you are wrong, but if your minds are made up, I'll go and get them.'

Sally followed her out of the room. Did the school want them to go? The headmistress hadn't put up much of a fight. Sally was worried. All the time she kept asking herself if they were doing the right thing.

The expression on Johnny's face put all her fears behind her. He buried his head in her coat and cried. Babs looked bewildered.

'Sal, what yer doing 'ere?'

'We've come ter take yer back 'ome.'

Babs' face broke into a beaming smile. 'That's good. I'll git me fings.' She turned and ran back along the corridor.

'Don't run,' the headmistress's voice boomed out behind her. But Babs didn't take any notice.

''Ave yer left anythink in the classroom, Johnny?' asked Sally.

He nodded. 'I've got ter git me gas mask and books.'

'Well, go and get 'em.'

'And don't run,' came the booming voice again.

Johnny did as he was told.

Outside the tears and smiles were mingled together, as their father held them close.

'Right, in the car,' said Pete. 'Then it's back to Mrs G's fer yer stuff, then 'ome.'

Sally was smiling, but her face changed when they arrived at Mrs Good's. 'You wait 'ere. I'll sort this out.'

She marched up to the house, primed to give Mrs Good a tongue-lashing she would not forget – and then she stopped. She couldn't believe her eyes. On the doorstep were two parcels, and a small case with a note attached: 'This is all they brought with them.'

Sally picked up the parcels, and laughing, took them back to the car. She showed her father the note.

'I'd like ter go in there and give 'er a piece o' me mind.'

'Now what good would that do?' asked Pete.

'It'll make me feel better.'

Pete laughed. 'Come on, leave it be, and let's git on 'ome.'

As they drove home Babs and Johnny told them all about how Mrs Good locked him in the cupboard and made him sleep in wet sheets every night. Then on Saturday he had to wash them. Babs told how they had to polish and clean, and Mrs Good always read their letters and made them write them over and over again if they put anything in them she didn't like.

'Johnny didn't tell yer he'd written then?' said Sally.

'No. Where did yer git the stamp and paper from?' Babs asked her brother.

'Pinched the envelope from teacher's desk, but I couldn't put a stamp on it, and the paper came out me sum book.'

Sally looked behind at her father, laughing as he cuddled them both. She felt like singing she was so happy. They were all together, and with Jessie back as well, this was going to be a lovely Christmas, despite all the shortages.

The start of 1940 was very bleak. It was cold, and queues for food were long. Butter, sugar and bacon were now rationed and Sally was pleased when she heard that meat was going to be next.

'At least we'll get some that way,' she said, reading the newspaper out loud.

Babs and Johnny went out with Jessie and they spent most days queueing, as none of the schools were open. Sally worried about their education but they seemed happy enough.

Sally still had her Friday night out with the girls, and now Jessie came with them. They also went to the pictures, and with the extra money Sally was getting working overtime, things were looking good. It wasn't a happy picture at Granny Brent's, though, when Lena announced she was joining up.

'Gawd only knows what she wants ter go fer,' wailed Granny Brent, burying her head in her apron. 'It's bad enough the boys going, she didn't 'ave ter volunteer. I lost her dad in the first lot. I couldn't bear ter lose any of 'em.' She dabbed her eyes.

'She'll be all right, Ma,' said Pete.

'She won't go where there's fighting,' said Sally.

'No, but me boys will,' howled Granny Brent, burying her head in her apron again.

'Yer still got me around,' said Pete, putting his arm round his mother's heaving shoulders.

'But fer 'ow long?'

Pete shrugged, he couldn't answer that.

One day at the end of January, a week after Babs' birthday, she ran up the passage to meet her sister as she came home from the factory. 'Sal, Sal, guess what. Connie's back. 'Er mum went and got 'er. I fink she's been bashed.'

Sally was shocked. 'Who by?'

'The man she was staying wiv.'

'Didn't 'is wife stop 'im?'

'Na, I fink she was just as bad.'

'Did yer know that when you was in Worthing?'

'Na. She used ter come ter school wiv bruises up 'er leg, but she said she fell over.'

'Didn't the school make enquiries?'

'No.'

'Why didn't yer tell us? We could've looked into it when we was down there.'

'Didn't fink there was anyfink ter worry about. Still, she's back now. Pity she didn't get back in time fer me birfday. I might 'ave got another present.'

A large number of children were drifting back now, and some schools were opening again. The difficulty was finding teachers. A lot of the women had been evacuated with their children, and most of the young men called up.

The war in Europe was not going well. Every night the Fuller family would listen to the wireless, hoping the news would bring them a ray of hope.

Jessie was thrilled when she got her long looked for allowance from the army, and in April she came running into Sally's waving a letter.

'Guess what? 'E wrote ter me.'

'Who?'

'Me old man.'

'No! Why?'

''Ere, read it.' She thrust the letter into Sally's hand.

The letter said how Vic wanted Jess to tell the kids about him, and he was sorry for being such a rotter, and that when he got some leave he would like to come and see her.

'I don't believe it,' said Sally, reading it over again. 'What's 'e after?'

'Dunno.'

'What did yer mum say?'

'Told me ter frow it in the fire.'

'What yer gonner do?'

'Dunno,' said Jessie again.

Sally started giggling. ''Ere, don't yer go getting too friendly, you'll end up with another little Owen.'

'Still, it's nice of 'im ter write.' Jess smiled.

'Yer going ter answer it?'

'I fink so. If 'e goes and gits himself killed, I'll git a widder's pension, and it'll be nice fer the kids if they knows a bit about 'im.'

Sally laughed. 'Yer a callous cow.'

'Well, let's face it, 'E ain't exactly been a model 'usband.'

In May, the weather improved and Sally was seeing more of her neighbours. She would often stop and have a word with Mr Slater, still sitting on his window sill with Bess at his side. Fred now looked very important in his warden's uniform, and a lot happier. Mr Slater said it was because riding around on his bike was good exercise, and even if he did puff, it gave his cheeks a rosy glow.

Sally was worried that Johnny seemed to be getting cheeky. The kids were left on their own for long stretches, and spent a lot of time in the street with their friends. The schools were now open for a few hours a day, but she had no control over what they got up to the rest of the time until she came home from work. Connie Downs and Babs were inseparable, and Sally was a little worried at what they were doing outside school, too. At least Connie's sisters, whose reputations and influence on Babs Sally had worried about last year, had left home. Joyce was in the army, and the other sister, Doreen, had joined the land army.

Sally was on her way home from work one day when she met Joyce Downs.

'You look very smart in your uniform, Joyce,' said Sally.

'Yer, they ain't bad, mind you the drawers leave a lot to be desired. Talk about passion killers. Still I can keep me 'air rolled up under me cap. I was a bit worried I might 'ave to 'ave it cut.'

'How long you 'ome for?'

'I go back tomorrow.' She stopped. 'Sal, do you think you could get me Reg's address, I'd like to drop 'im a line.'

'I could get it off Granny Brent.'

'Oh, that woman. She don't like me.'

'Pr'aps Vera's got it, anyway I'll try, and I'll give it to Connie.'

'Thanks,' Joyce nodded, 'but don't let Granny Brent know.'

'Course not.'

'Our Connie and your Babs stick tergether don't they?'

'Yeah. I'm glad Connie's back 'ome.'

'So's mum, especially now our Doreen's joined the Land Army. Didn't like all 'er flock going. Nice ter talk to yer Sal, see you when I get 'ome again.' She disappeared into her house.

Sally walked on. All around her girls she had known all her life were off doing exciting things. She sighed. What did she want out of life? Was it babies? She and Pete had talked about it, but Pete had made it quite clear that was something they would have to wait for, wartime wasn't a good time for that. She agreed with him in her head, but in her heart felt her life lacked something.

At the end of the month an almighty row broke out when

Lena announced she was going in the WRAF. Granny Brent was beside herself when she told her, and after the first flare up, wouldn't speak to her. Pete was very angry over this and told his mother so. Sally couldn't believe Pete had actually stood up to his mother.

It was the weekend before Lena was going that Danny and Reg came home on leave unexpectedly.

They looked very smart in their uniforms, and when Granny Brent had wiped away her tears of happiness, she asked how long were they home for.

'Only got the weekend, we're between camps,' said Reg.

Granny Brent nodded in a matter-of-fact way but Sally could see she was already counting the precious minutes until she had to say goodbye to them. Sally thought the boys looked tired, but it didn't stop them going along to the Nag's for a party.

The beer was flowing freely when Pete took over the piano from Reg. He was busy filling his glass and Sally managed to get him to one side.

'It's a pity Joyce Downs ain't still on leave,' she said nonchalantly, waiting to see his reaction.

'Yeah, Vera said she's bin 'ome, and she said she's quite a looker now. Bet she looks good in 'er uniform.'

'Yes she does.' Sally paused. 'Reg, d'you like 'er?'

'Yeah, she's a bit of all right,' he said casually.

'She said she'd like to write to you.'

He laughed. 'Did she now? I ain't any good at writing.'

'Well,' said Sally. 'Shall I give 'er your address?'

'Na, I ain't got time ter write.'

He walked away and Sally felt sad. Joyce was good fun and it would have been great if she was part of their family.

* * *

A few months later, Granny Brent told Sally that Gwen was expecting.

'Silly pair o' buggers, what they wonner 'ave a kid fer in this day and age?'

'When's it due?' asked Sally.

''Bout January sometime.'

'You'll be a real Granny then.'

A smile lifted her face. 'Yeah, so I will.'

When Sally told Pete about Gwen's pregnancy he said he still didn't think it was a good idea to have babies now, so any hope Sally had of following in Gwen's footsteps were quickly quashed.

Chapter 12

All through June the papers had been full of the Allies' retreat from Dunkirk. Although the news seemed to be all bad, so far it hadn't really affected any of Sefton Grove's residents, other than those who'd been called up.

With Reg and Danny in the army, the printing business had finished. For weeks Pete had been going round trying to sell the machine and all the type, but so far he had only been offered a pittance for it.

August came in warm and sultry. Every Sunday evening Sally, Pete and her father now went to the Nag's, and tonight, as always, everybody in the bar had been discussing and arguing about the war.

All the way home the discussions had continued. Now Fred had a uniform he felt he knew more than most, much to Mr Slater's annoyance.

Sally lay in bed, happy and content. Earlier, she and Pete had made love.

'I'm a bit worried, Sal, about these planes coming over and bombing the ships in the Channel,' said Pete out of the blue.

'Can't yer forget about the war fer once?'

'No, not if the ships can't git up the Thames.'

She cuddled up to him. 'Come on, Pete, don't spoil a nice evening.'

'Sorry, Sal. Say, d'yer fancy a day out next Sunday?'

'That'll be lovely. Where shall we go?'

'Dunno. It can't be far, I've only got a drop of this month's petrol ration left.' Pete was lying on his back, smoking.

Sally smiled. She pushed herself up on her elbow and gazed down at him. 'That'll be nice.'

'We'll take the kids and Pop, that's if 'e fancies it.'

She ran her fingers down his cheek. 'I do love yer, Pete Brent.' She kissed his cheek.

'Watch it! You'll 'ave me set light ter the sheet.'

Sally lay back and smiled. She was always comparing Pete with her film star hero, Tyrone Power, often wondering what it would be like to be loved by him, to be swept up in his arms and kissed and kissed all over, and have him tell her of his undying love, like he did to his leading ladies . . . but she came back to reality. 'Where shall we go?' she asked.

'Dunno. We'll talk about it. Now let's get some shut-eye.' He stubbed his cigarette out in the ashtray and turned over.

In the middle of the week Pete had a letter from Solly asking about the printing machine. They decided that on Sunday they would go to Sydenham to see him, then on to Crystal Palace.

They woke up to a fine warm day. Johnny and Babs were excited at the idea of having a picnic and sailing Johnny's boat, and chatted nonstop in the car.

'Wish we could 'ave brought Connie,' said Babs.

'Blimey, it's a bit cramped wiv you three in the back as it is,' said her father, looking round proudly at his children. ''Sides, d'yer fink Pete's a taxi?'

Pete didn't look too happy when he came back to the car after calling on Solly.

'Well?' asked Sally eagerly. ''E gonner buy it?'

'Dunno. I'll 'ave ter see what Reg says.' Pete started the car. ''E's only offered a fraction of what it's worth.'

'Yeah, but is it worth anyfink now yer can't git the work?' asked Stan.

'S'pose not. Right kids, let's be off.'

Sally smiled. They were happy and she had no regrets about bringing them back to London. Nowadays, Johnny's bed was always dry.

They finished their sandwiches, and while Johnny and Pete were busy sailing the boat, and Babs and Sally played bat and ball, their father stretched himself out on the grass for a doze. All around them, people were laughing and playing games. Suddenly the distant wailing of the siren brought everyone to a standstill.

'Will we be next?' asked Sally apprehensively.

Over the months they'd heard the air-raid warning going off in the distance, but it didn't always get as far as Rotherhithe.

'Where's the nearest shelter? cried Sally.

'Over there, love,' called out a man as he gathered his children together.

Sally grabbed Johnny's hand and started to run with Babs, Pete and her father at her heels.

'Look,' shouted someone in the crowd.

They all turned and scanned the clear blue sky. In the

distance they could see planes, masses of them, flying about like black birds. They seemed to fill the sky.

'They're Germans,' someone yelled. 'Look, look, and they're our Spitfires.'

Everybody stopped and looked. The sky was being crisscrossed with white vapour trails as the planes weaved in and out, ducking and diving.

There were shouts of, 'Go on, boys, get 'em!'

When a trail of black smoke followed a plane as it spiralled downwards, everyone held their breath, but when someone yelled it was a German, they cheered and clapped excitedly, pointing and laughing. As it was in the distance nobody was afraid.

'Looks like they're over Croydon airfield,' said one knowledgeable man. 'Still, our boys are giving 'em a run fer their money.'

Johnny was jumping up and down. 'I'm gonner be a pilot when I grow up.'

Sally ruffled his hair, amused.

Gradually the planes began to disperse.

'Come on,' said Pete. 'I think we'd better make our way 'ome.'

In the car Johnny didn't stop talking, and his boat was being waved about like a plane. 'This 'as been the best day of me life. Cor, wait till I tell me mates I saw a dogfight. Wish we'd been a bit nearer, then I might 'ave got an empty bullet case.'

Sally smiled, but at the back of her mind she wondered where it was all leading. A dogfight so near to where they'd been picnicking.

That night, when they went up the Nag's, Pete and Stan were full of it. Sally thought they were as bad as Johnny.

For days the papers told of waves of enemy planes being sent over day after day, and how our lads were keeping them at bay.

''Itler's certainly trying ter git to us,' said Pete one evening as he read the papers.

''Ope 'is bombers don't get 'ere,' said Stan.

'Don't say that, Dad.'

'Well 'e's bombing other places. I fink we'd better git some bunk beds in the shelter, just in case. What d'yer fink, Pete?'

'I reckon that's a good idea.'

Some months ago, Stan and Pete had fixed a door on the shelter to keep the cats out. Chairs, beds and an old table had been put inside, a pack of cards and a cribbage board were on the shelf along with the hurricane lamp and candles. But it was pretty basic and Sally hated the idea of sleeping there, quite apart from the danger.

'D'yer think we ought ter send the kids away?' Sally whispered.

'Where to?' asked Pete. 'Couldn't see 'em going back to Mrs G's.'

'I was talking to Mrs Downs in the baker's queue the other Saturday afternoon, and she was saying she's got a relation in Wiltshire. Maybe she could find out what it's like there if we 'ave ter send the kids somewhere safer.'

'I can't see 'em wanting ter go orf again.'

'But, Dad, if Babs was with Connie—'

'Connie going then?'

'She didn't say, but I thought—'

'I can't see Johnny 'aving any of it.'

Sally sat back in her chair and picked up her book. 'But, Dad, what if—'

'Well, if anyfink does 'appen, then at least we'll all go tergevver. I'm going on up ter bed,' said her father, leaving the room.

'Pete, what do you think?' asked Sally.

'Dunno. I've got ter write this letter ter Reg and tell 'im what Solly's offered us fer that machine. I reckon yer dad's right: we ought ter take what we can fer it. You go on up.'

Sally lay for a long while worrying about the future. Did they even have any? Her father's words haunted her.

It was the first Saturday in September, and Sally only had to work till three. She was walking home when she saw Johnny racing up Brigg Street. 'Don't go too far away, tea'll be ready soon.'

'Yer going out ternight, Sal?' he asked breathlessly.

'No. I feel too tired.' Sally had to smile, he looked so scruffy with his shirt hanging out of his trousers, and socks round his ankles, and shoes that were scuffed and looked like they hadn't seen boot polish for weeks. She thought about her mother and how she always shouted at him about his socks.

Babs was sitting outside Connie's house. As soon as she saw Sally she rubbed her hand across her mouth. Sally guessed they had been putting lipstick on. 'Dad and Pete's 'ome,' Babs said.

'That's good, they might 'ave the tea ready,' said Sally hopefully.

'Got the kettle on, gel,' said her father as she walked in. 'Managed ter get a couple o' kippers. Me and Pete saw this queue so we joined it, didn't know what it was for.' He laughed. 'Would 'ave been a right turn up fer the books if it 'ad been fer the baby clinic.'

'Then we might 'ave got some oranges,' said Pete.

Sally was pleased that when they could they all took part in queueing for any food that wasn't on ration. 'I'll get the kids while you do the tea,' said Pete.

They had just finished their kippers when the siren began its wailing. Almost at once the deep, low drone of aircraft overhead filled the air.

'Bloody 'ell. Quick, in the shelter,' said Pete.

As he shut the shelter door the first whistle and thud of a bomb exploding shook the ground. The throbbing of the plane's engines sounded above them.

Babs began to cry. 'I don't like it. We gonner die?'

Bewildered, Sally cuddled Babs close as they sat on the bottom bunk bed, which so far had only been used for the kids to play on. 'Course not,' Sally whispered, but she too was shaking with fear.

'Ma!' said Pete suddenly jumping up. 'I'll 'ave ter go over and get 'er.'

'You can't. You can't go out there,' said Sally in alarm.

'But me ma ain't got a shelter. I can't leave 'er and Vera indoors on their own.' Pete began pacing up and down.

'She's probably gorn in next door's, son,' said Stan. 'Sit yerself down, yer making the kids nervous.'

Pete plonked himself in the chair as another bomb exploded.

'Yer should 'ave thought about yer mum when we was all given shelters.' Sally's voice rose with anger and fear. Pete had put the business first, as usual, and now his mother was paying the price.

'We didn't 'ave the room.'

'Yer should 'ave knocked the bloody shed down then.'

'Couldn't, could we, it was our living.'

'Well, now it could be yer mum dying.'

'Shut it, you two,' said her father.

'Sorry.' Pete sat next to Sally and put his arm round her shoulders. 'I can't 'elp it, Sal. I'm worried about Ma.'

'Course yer are, son. But I bet she'd be over 'ere if she didn't 'ave anywhere else ter go.'

'You're probably right, Pop.'

Everybody went quiet as they listened to more bombs falling.

Sally began to cry silently. She glanced at Pete, his face pale and full of worry. Her father was holding Johnny's head in his lap. Sally and Babs gently rocked back and forth. She didn't want to die.

For hours, which for them seemed a lifetime, they prayed and waited for the long steady note of the all clear. When it finally came they were so relieved that they were still alive.

As soon as the door to the shelter was opened, Tiger raced in. Babs quickly gathered him up.

''E's shaking, 'e's scared stiff,' she said, cuddling him close.

''E ain't the only one,' said her father.

They couldn't believe their eyes when they walked out. Huge columns of thick black smoke rose high in the still air, at times blotting out the early evening sun. Explosions were sending up great showers of sparks, and they were coming from the direction of the River Thames.

'Bloody 'ell,' said Pete.

'Where d'yer think it is?' asked Sally.

'The docks,' said her father. 'Looks like 'e's made a bloody fine mess of it over there. There's a lot o' wood in them warehouses.'

'Was,' said Pete coldly.

'Said all along, didn't I, the dock's a bloody sitting target? They can follow the river fer miles.' Stan was full of anger.

'I'm going over ter Ma,' said Pete. 'Won't be long.'

'Come on inside, Dad. Let's see what sort o' mess we got ter clear up.'

Apart from a few flakes of plaster that had fallen from the ceiling, there wasn't any damage. Sally was surprised to see all the windows were still intact.

'I'll just do this bit o' washing up.'

'Leave it, Sal.' Her father's voice was brusque.

'But why? We always . . .' She stopped and watched him collecting up the few photos they had on display. 'What yer doing that fer?'

'Look, Sal, go upstairs and bring down all the bedding and pillows.'

'But why?'

'With a beacon like that ter guide them Jerry planes, I fink we're in fer a rough night.'

'Yer don't think they'll be back, do yer?'

'What do you fink?'

Sally caught her breath. 'I'll get the kids ter give me 'and.' She hurried from the room.

Standing in her bedroom she looked at her wedding photo. Was it only just over a year ago? Tears filled her eyes. 'This could be our last day on earth,' she said to the picture. 'I don't want to die,' she sobbed. 'Please God, don't let us die.'

'Sal, Sal,' yelled Babs as she stomped up the stairs. 'Dad said we've got ter 'elp yer.'

Sally quickly dried her eyes and blew her nose.

'You bin crying?' asked Babs, coming into the room.

'No, I've got somethink in me eye. Take all yer bedclothes and put 'em in the shelter – and tell Johnny ter do the same.'

Johnny was right behind Babs. 'Great, we're gonner sleep in the shelter ternight.'

Sally gave him a weak smile. To him this was still all a game. 'And yer can take a few games, but not too many, mind. We've all got ter get in, and I expect Granny Brent and Vera will be over as well.'

'Good,' said Babs. 'I like Granny Brent, she makes me laugh. Will she sing all the old songs?'

'You'll 'ave ter wait and see.'

As Sally walked through the kitchen with the bedding in her arms she noticed her father filling her mum's old large black handbag. 'What yer putting in there?'

'All the policies, and a few knick-knacks. Don't wonner lose fings like yer mum's wedding ring and that nice brooch I bought 'er, and I fought I'd put in a couple of photos.'

Once again tears filled Sally's eyes. 'I'll just take this lot out, then I'll come back fer yours.'

Babs and Johnny were laughing and giggling as, laden down with toys and bedclothes, they struggled through the shelter's narrow doorway.

'Put 'em on the chair and I'll sort 'em out.'

'What about Tiger?' asked Babs. 'Can 'e come in?'

'I dunno, you'll 'ave ter ask Dad.'

'I don't want 'im killed.'

'Nobody does,' said Sally looking away.

'What's going on in 'ere?' asked Pete, standing aside to let Babs pass.

'Dad said ter bring the bedding in 'ere.' Sally didn't look up.

'Good idea.'

'Is yer mum all right?'

'Yeah, they went next door, but Ma and Vera said they'd rather come over 'ere ternight. I told 'em yer dad said it's fine.'

Suddenly Sally threw her arms round Pete's neck and, burying her head in his shoulder, she cried.

''Ere, steady on, love.' He gently kissed her cheek. 'Yer dad reckons we all ought ter go up the Nag's, and get a few bevvies in before . . .'

Sally brushed her tears away. 'I'll just finish this. And, Pete, if there's anythink precious yer want ter—'

He held her round the waist. 'I've got everyfink that's precious ter me right 'ere.'

She couldn't believe it. But, when it came to saying what he really felt, why did he have to wait till it could be their last . . .

''Ere yer are, gel,' said her father from the doorway. 'Me bedding and the policy bag, and, Pete, we'd better put a few more chairs in if yer mum's coming over. Then when we've done that, it's all up the Nag's. We'll take the kids with us.'

Pete and Sally followed her father into the house. Everyone had their own private thoughts, but they all tried to put on brave faces.

Chapter 13

'I'll just pop in ter Jess, just ter make sure they're all right,' said Sally, as they left their house.

'I'm going over ter git Ma and Vera,' said Pete.

'Don't be too long, the pair o' yer,' said Stan, taking hold of Babs and Johnny's hands.

Jessie threw her arms round Sally when she walked into their kitchen. 'Oh Sal, ain't it bloody awful? I reckon we're all gonner be killed ternight.'

'Don't be such a Job's comforter, Jess.' Mrs Walters looked worried and strained. 'I said she shouldn't 'ave come back – bringing those kids back ter this.'

'Don't start on that again, Mum. I didn't know this was gonner 'appen, now did I? 'Sides, you wasn't down there.'

Mrs Walters straightened her shoulders. 'I know, but if yer finks more of yerself than yer kids, well, that's up ter you.'

Tears slowly ran down Jessie's cheek. 'Mum, don't say that. I don't fink more of meself than the kids. I love 'em. You know that, don't yer, Sal?'

Sally nodded.

'And I wouldn't let any 'arm come ter 'em,' added Jessie, wiping her eyes on the bottom of her overall. 'I wouldn't 'ave come back . . .' her voice drifted off into a sob.

'I knows that, love. It's just that I'm worried about all of us.' Mrs Walters turned to Sally, her voice unusually soft and calm. 'Bin putting a few bits in the shelter. We're gonner sleep in there ternight.'

'So are we,' said Sally. 'We're going up the Nag's now, d'yer fancy a drink?'

'Na,' said Jessie's dad who had been quietly sitting listening to the conversation. 'Fanks all the same, but I managed ter git a small bottle o' brandy off young Tommy Tanner. Cost a few bob, but I reckon we'll 'ave a few ternight. It'll 'elp us sleep.'

'That's what Dad said.' Sally was trying hard to keep her voice under control.

'Gawd only knows where young Tommy gits all this stuff from,' Mr Walters smiled.

'If yer asks me it's best we don't know,' said his wife, smoothing out a blanket and adding it to the pile of bedclothes stacked on the table.

'I best be off, Dad's waiting,' said Sally. 'See you all in the morning.'

'God willing,' said Mrs Walters as Sally left the room.

At the door Jessie and Sally stood locked in each other's embrace for a few minutes.

'See yer termorrer,' said Jessie, wiping her eyes with the flat of her hand.

Sally could only nod.

She met her family outside the pub, and when they walked in Sally couldn't believe it, half of Sefton Grove seemed to be in there. Everyone was talking at once in very nervous, excited, loud voices. The place was buzzing with the noise and the air thick with tobacco smoke. Nobody was playing the piano, though, this evening.

'Looks like everyone else 'as got the same idea,' said Pete. 'Sit yerself down, Ma. I'll just go and give Pop 'and.'

'What yer gonner 'ave, gel?' asked her father. 'And it better be somefink a bit stronger than a shandy.'

'I'll 'ave a whisky,' said Pete. 'I'll git 'em. I'll git you one as well, Sal.'

She turned up her nose.

'It'll 'elp make yer sleep,' said Granny Brent. 'It's all right us coming in wiv yer ternight?' she asked Sally.

'Course.'

'We 'ad a letter from Lena this morning,' said Vera.

'It's bad enough 'aving the two boys away. She didn't 'ave ter go as well.' said Granny Brent.

'Be fair, Mum. She didn't know this was gonner 'appen, now did she?' said Vera.

'S'pose not.'

'Where is she?' asked Sally.

'Dunno,' said Vera. 'I fink it's up north somewhere.'

'Ain't it bloody awful, gel?' Mrs Tanner came up to them waving her arms, her husband and Tommy in tow. 'Wot we gonner do? Reckon we could all be killed ternight.'

'Yer mustn't talk like that,' said Granny Brent, giving Mrs Tanner a withering look and nodding in the direction of the doorway where Babs and Johnny were standing listening. 'Yer got yer shelter so yer better stay in there ternight.'

'Yeah, I know. That bloody cow-son, sending over them there bombers like that. It shouldn't be allowed, bombing women and children. Yer should see the damage 'e's done ter me 'ouse.'

'You got some damage?' asked Granny Brent in surprise.

'Well, a bit. I still say they ought ter do that 'Itler bloke in.'

'Shut up, yer silly old cow,' said Mr Tanner. 'D'yer fink 'Itler gives a tinker's cuss about women and children?'

'Don't yer tell me ter shut up.'

Mr Tanner took hold of her arm and led her away.

'She ain't very 'appy,' said Tommy. 'The bombing's made 'er best vase fall orf the shelf and it broke. See yer all later.'

Granny Brent laughed. 'I wonder what crawled out of it?'

Mr Slater walked up to them, looking pale and drawn. 'Mind if I join yer?'

'Course not. Sit yerself down,' said Pete, moving along the bench seat. 'You all right?'

'Not too bad.' Bess quickly settled herself at his feet. 'Fred popped in a few minutes ago. 'E said the docks caught it bad.'

'Many killed?' asked Stan.

''E didn't say. 'E looked done in. I reckon they'll 'ave a job on ternight. Me sister's in a bit of a state.' He gave them a weak smile and patted his coat pocket. 'Just got 'er a little bevvy. She don't drink normally, but I reckon she'll enjoy this ternight.'

'She should 'ave come up 'ere, might do 'er good,' said Vera. 'We don't see much of 'er.'

'She ain't very good in company. She was bombed in the first lot, yer know?'

'No I didn't,' said Granny Brent. 'She's never said.'

'Well, she don't say a lot ter anybody. 'Er young man was wiv 'er, but 'e got killed. She was buried with 'im, and she 'eld 'is head till they was rescued.'

Sally was shocked. All the years they had thought Miss Slater was a funny old dear, but nobody ever knew what she'd been through.

'I'm really sorry about that,' said Granny Brent, her voice full of feeling. 'I know how she must feel, 'aving lorst my old man in the first lot.' She took her handkerchief out of the battered black bag she was clutching and blew her nose.

Pete put his arm round his mother's shoulders. 'Drink up, Ma. I'll git another round.'

'Pete, git the kids somefink, and put a drop o' whisky in it. It'll 'elp 'em sleep.'

'We'll make this the last,' said Stan Fuller. 'It's gitting dark, and I reckon 'e'll be over soon.'

On the way home Sally couldn't stop thinking about Miss Slater. No wonder she'd been unhappy.

They had just settled themselves in the shelter when the wailing of the siren filled them with horror. The chatter suddenly ceased. Vera stopped reading to Johnny and looked up. Granny Brent's nimble fingers appeared to move faster than ever, crocheting a pram cover for Gwen's baby.

As the last note faded away the drone of planes overhead could be heard, quickly followed by loud explosions as bombs fell. They were much closer this time. Johnny, his face ashen, was sitting next to Sally. She held him close to comfort him and herself.

Suddenly, a piercing whistle rent the air. Pete shouted 'Get down!' and they all threw themselves face down on the ground. Sally held on to her head as an ear-splitting crack filled the shelter. The blast blew the door open and the flame in the hurricane lamp flickered. Sally felt, as if in slow motion, the floor gently come up and then settle down again. Everyone began to cough and splutter as the shelter filled with dust.

'Dad!' screamed Babs.

'It's all right, love.' He put his arm round her and she buried her head in his chest.

'You all right, Ma?' asked Pete, clambering to his feet and quickly pulling the door shut.

'Yes, son,' came the soft reply.

As the dust settled, Vera started to laugh. It was a quiet, hysterical laugh. 'You should see your faces. They ain't 'alf dirty.'

Even though bombs were still falling, and Sally was frightened, she too couldn't help but laugh, and like Vera, her laughter was mingled with her tears.

'I wonder who copped that lot?' said Granny Brent.

'It sounded real close. I'll look out and see if the 'ouse is still standing,' said Stan.

Pete shook his head. 'I shouldn't. Yer might not be able ter git the door shut in time.'

'Yeah, p'raps yer right, son.' He settled himself back in his chair. 'Come on, you kids, try and git a bit o' shuteye.'

Sally noted how worried and old her father suddenly looked.

'How d'yer expect us ter sleep wiv all this racket going on?' said Babs angrily.

'Why don't yer put them there earplugs in,' suggested Granny Brent.

Johnny took the government-issue brown rubber earplugs from his gas mask box. 'They ain't 'arf funny-looking fings, ain't they?' He held one up. 'What if it gits stuck down me ear?'

'Course it won't, they've been tested,' said Pete.

Johnny stuck them in his ears. 'Can't 'ear a fing,' he said, grinning.

The raid went on for hours. All through the night the noise was deafening. With every new wave of planes, more bombs rained down on them. Every thud of a bomb close by brought the sound of masonry crashing, mixed with the delicate tinkle of falling glass. Their teeth crunched on the dust and soot that seeped through the ill-fitting door, filling their noses and making their mouths dry. Sally was pleased they'd brought in bottles of tea. Even though it was cold, it tasted good. Every now and again, when it went quiet, Sally thought she could hear Granny Brent saying a prayer. She too had been praying hard.

Sally glanced at Johnny, so small and vulnerable, curled up asleep on the bunk bed. Occasionally he jumped when there was a particularly loud bang, but she was surprised he'd managed to drop off at all with the racket going on all around them. Perhaps the whisky and the earplugs were working.

''Ow many more planes 'e gonner send over?' asked Vera.

'Dunno,' said Pete. He looked drawn and tired. 'Try and git some shut-eye. It'll make the morning come quicker.'

'Dunno if I want the morning ter come,' said Granny Brent. 'Gawd only knows what we're gonner find when we gits out – that's if we do git out.'

Babs sat up. 'I wonder if anyone in Sefton's dead?'

Sally had thought she too was asleep. 'Go back to sleep—' Her voice was cut short as another loud explosion rent the air.

'I wonder if I should go out and see if anyone wants any 'elp,' said Pete.

'No!' shouted Sally. 'You ain't going out there.'

'But, Sal—'

'You ain't got a tin 'at. 'Sides, I won't let yer.'

''E's right, Sal,' said her father. 'They might want a bit o' 'elp.'

Tears filled Sally's eyes. 'What if the next one's got our name on it? What then?' She began to cry. 'Please don't go.'

'OK, but calm down,' said Pete.

Babs and Vera dropped off through sheer exhaustion. Granny Brent followed, her gentle snoring comforting. Sally could feel her eyes closing but she tried to keep awake. Then gradually sleep overcame her.

It was the shelter door closing that woke her. She sat up, disorientated. Something was brushing against her legs. Tiger was in the shelter. He hadn't been in last night, much to Babs' annoyance and carrying on when they shut him in the lav. Pete and her father had gone. Where were they? What had happened? Fear filled Sally's head and she quickly stood up. Granny Brent was snoring loudly now. Vera was lying beside Babs, and Johnny was stretched out above them. Sally felt stiff and every bone in her body ached. She suddenly realised it was quiet. There were no planes overhead and no bombs dropping. She wanted to shout out with relief that they were still alive.

Carefully she opened the door. The smell of acrid smoke and burning almost choked her as it caught in her throat. In the early morning gloom she could see Pete and her father leaning against the wall having a cigarette.

'The 'ouse is still 'ere then?' she grinned. She felt like laughing and running round the yard. Jessie's house was still intact, but all the windows of every building around them had gone, and she could just about make out the lace curtains, tattered and torn, hanging limply in the still air.

With the toe of his boot, Pete stubbed his cigarette out. 'The docks is still burning. Reckon it'll take days ter git that out.'

'Indoors is a bit of a mess,' said Stan.

'Yer been in then?' enquired Sally.

'Yeah, just 'ad a quick look.'

'Seems all of Sefton's still standing,' said Pete.

'Is yer mum's place all right?' asked Sally.

'Looks like it.'

''As the all clear gone?'

'Not yet, but we ain't 'ad any o' the bastards over fer about 'alf an hour.'

Sally didn't reprimand her father for his language. 'Is it all right if I 'ave a wee?'

'I should fink so, but be quick,' said Pete.

'Yer don't wonner be blown ter kingdom come wivout yer drawers on,' laughed her father.

As Sally brushed the dirt and dust off the wooden seat of the lavatory, the welcome sound of the all clear filled the air.

When Sally came out, everyone was emerging from the shelter.

'You and Vera 'ad better wait 'ere, Ma,' said Pete.

'And you kids,' said their father.

'Why?' asked Johnny. 'I wonner see if there's any shrapnel about 'fore the other kids git it.'

'You do as yer told,' said Sally. 'It's too dangerous ter go wandering about out 'ere.'

'Watch out fer the broken glass,' said Pete. 'It's everywhere.'

'What's that smell?' asked Sally, gingerly picking her way into the scullery.

'Gas. Don't light any matches,' said her father. 'Go and git the torch.'

Quickly Sally did as she was told. 'Better watch the blackout,' she said, handing it to him.

'Don't talk daft. Wiv all these fires about d'yer fink they're gonner see this little fing?'

'You mind yer don't 'ave old Fred—' As soon as she said it, Sally felt horribly anxious. After last night, what if Fred . . . She was cross with herself for blurting out his name without a thought.

'Bloody 'ell!' yelled her father.

'What is it, Pop?' asked Pete.

'The bloody water pipe's burst. Yer should see the mess.'

'I'll go out front and turn the mains off,' said Pete, hurrying through the kitchen. His movements were accompanied by a string of bad language as he crunched on plaster, stumbling and kicking his way along the passage.

As the sky lightened, more and more people came to stand outside in Sefton Grove. They were unable to believe they were still alive. Sally and Jess ran into each other's arms.

'Yer should see the bloody mess indoors. Still, I expect you're the same,' said Jess.

'As soon as it's light we'll 'ave ter get busy,' said Sally.

They watched a man on his bike stop to talk to those at the far end of the Grove. Then he came straight up to their little group. 'Yer ain't got no water or gas. They've 'ad ter turn it orf cause there's a lot o' mains broke.'

'But we could smell gas,' said Sally.

'That was probably what was in the pipe.'

'And we 'ad water,' said Pete.

'Well, yer ain't got none now.'

'What about a cuppa? I'm dying fer one,' said Granny Brent.

'They're organising a van. The WVS ladies will be round soon.'

'Fank Gawd,' said Mrs Walters. 'Can't do much wivout a cuppa first.'

'Pete, would yer come across wiv Vera and me? Don't fancy going in on me own.'

'Course, Ma.'

'Yer ain't 'alf got a bloody fine mess ter clear up, Sal. Gawd only knows what I'm gonner find indoors.' Granny Brent took Pete's arm and carefully made her way across the road.

In the early morning light the Fullers could see the full extent of the damage.

'Don't look like nuffink structural,' said her father looking up at the roof. 'Got a few tiles missing. 'Ave ter find out what we can cover them holes wiv.'

Pete came over as they stood in the road looking at the sorry state of the houses. 'I'm gonner give Ma and Vera an 'and.'

'Is their place bad?' asked Sally.

''Bout the same.'

'Come on, gel, let's git started.'

Sally followed her father into the kitchen. 'I told yer we should 'ave done this washing up last night,' she said, shaking the dirt and dust from her apron and slipping it over her head. She stood looking at the dirty plates now covered with glass, and plaster that had fallen from the ceiling. 'If we ain't got no water or gas, how am I supposed ter get 'em clean?' Her voice was rising with emotion. 'And look at this. All the bloody soot's come down. It's gonner take for ever ter get this hearth clean again.' She fell to her knees and with tears streaming down her face, grabbed the dustpan and brush and began sweeping wildly. The dirt and soot got down her throat, making her cough.

Her father knelt beside her and held her close. Her tears made streaks down her grubby face.

'Steady on there, gel,' he said, gently patting her back. 'Sod the cleaning. We're still 'ere, and in one piece.' There was a sob in his voice.

'What we gonner do, Dad?' she sobbed.

Johnny and Babs came racing into the kitchen. 'Guess what?' shouted Johnny. 'Someone said the 'Olts' 'ouse in Tamar Street's copped it.'

'What?' Sally leapt to her feet, brushing her tears away with the flat of her dirty hands. 'Is everyone all right?'

'Dunno, we ain't allowed down there. I fink they're digging 'em out now. Got some shrapnel, though. Look.'

'You sure they said the Holts'?'

'Yeah,' said Babs. 'You ain't 'alf got a dirty face, Sal.'

'That's Gwen's mum's,' said Sally to her father. 'I wonder if Gwen would 'ave been round at 'er mum's. She ain't got a shelter in Silver Street. I remember 'er saying the yard ain't big enough and they was going ter 'ave ter go under the arches, or round 'er mum's. What if . . . ? The baby . . .' She sniffed and wiped her nose on the bottom of her apron. 'I'll 'ave ter go and tell Pete.'

'D'yer fink they've all been killed?' said Babs.

'Don't say things like that,' yelled Sally as she ran out of the kitchen.

Her father was right behind her, shouting, 'Go and tell Pete, but don't let 'is mum come round till we've found out 'ow bad it is, and if Gwen is . . .'

Sally wasn't listening. Tears filled her eyes as she ran across the road. Poor Gwen. And what if the baby . . . Poor Granny Brent – her first grandchild.

Chapter 14

When Pete and Sally turned into Tamar Street, her father was already there waiting for them.

'Yer can't git through,' he said.

'I must.' Pete turned to the policeman who stood at the end of the street. 'Let me through. Me brother's wife might be in that lot,' he said, pointing along the road.

'Afraid I can't. It's too dangerous – falling masonry, and they said there could be an unexploded bomb there. Can't let yer through till they say so.' The policeman, his hands clasped firmly behind his back, stood his ground.

'Is anyone killed?' Pete whispered.

'Dunno.'

'Can't we go and 'elp?' asked Stan.

'Sorry, mate. Wait 'ere, a warden'll be along shortly. 'E'll be able ter give yer more information.'

Pete and Sally craned their necks trying to see round the bend in the street.

Suddenly Sally caught sight of Fred and, screaming out his name, waved frantically.

Fred came slowly towards them. He looked bent and tired, his face dirty. His once-smart navy-blue uniform, of which he'd been so very proud, was covered with dirt and white dust. He took off his tin hat and wiped his face with a grey handkerchief. ''Allo, Pete, Sal, Stan. Nasty business, this.'

Pete took his arm. 'Is Gwen all right?'

Fred blew his nose. 'Dunno. The front o' the 'ouse 'as gone. They're still digging round the back trying ter git 'em out the Anderson shelter.'

'*Is* there an unexploded bomb?' asked Sally, her face full of apprehension.

'No. They fought there was, but it turned out ter be an empty shell.'

'Can we 'elp?' asked Stan.

'Yeah, why not? We can do wiv 'as many 'ands as poss. Some of the poor blokes are fit ter drop – been at it all night.'

'What about you, Fred?'

A faint smile lifted his dirty face. 'A bit tired, Stan, but it seems I'm a lot tougher than I fought.'

'Ain't they found anyone yet?' asked Sally.

'No, but they can 'ear 'em. Been banging on the sides of the shelters, so they know we're nearly there.'

Fred had a quick word with the policeman. Then they were allowed to make their way up Tamar Street.

'My 'ouse is still standing,' said Fred. 'It'll want propping up, though. I just 'ope the foundations is good.'

When they reached the Holts', they couldn't get too close because of the wreckage. Sally stood and stared. The fronts of four houses were just a pile of rubble. The upstairs had fallen and blocked the downstairs. Upstairs, a part of every room was uncannily left intact. It was like looking into half a house. Sally felt she was prying into other people's bedrooms, seeing things that only their owners saw. It distressed her that their private possessions were now on show to the world. She could see pictures and photographs, now lopsided but still hanging on the walls. Even a dressing table mirror was left intact and reflecting the sunlight. Beds were made up and one was hanging precariously over the edge of the wreckage. They could hear men shouting and the sound of digging.

'Right, Fred, what can we do?' asked Pete.

'I'll find out.' Fred clambered amongst the debris and disappeared over the hill of rubble.

'Gonner be a job ter git round the back,' said Stan, rubbing his stubbly chin.

'I wonder if the WVS women could come up 'ere with the tea. They could do with it,' said Sally, nodding in the direction of the men.

All at once an ambulance, frantically ringing its bell, came round the corner, followed closely by the tea van.

'They must 'ave 'eard yer, Sal,' said her father with a slight grin.

'Give us a tray and I'll take some over ter the blokes what's digging,' Pete said to the smiling ladies on the van.

'Be careful,' said Sally nervously, as her father and Pete scrambled over the rubble carrying enamel mugs full of hot sweet tea.

Sally could hear Granny Brent shouting at the policeman at the end if the road long before she could see her.

'Bloody cheek! Told me I couldn't come up 'ere,' she said, wobbling towards Sally, fussily pulling at her apron. 'I told 'im 'e better not try and stop me, bloody young whippersnapper. They got anyone out yet?' she added in a whisper.

Sally shook her head. 'Dad and Pete's round the back,

seems like they've been gone fer ages. What state's yer place in?'

''Bout the same as yours inside,' said Granny Brent. 'Did Pete tell yer about the state o' the shed?'

'No. Is it bad?'

'The blast from this little lot's gorn and blown the bloody roof in.' She nodded towards the bombed houses.

The Brents' house backed on to Tamar Street. The bomb had dropped the other side of the road so the houses facing it took the full force of the blast.

'Is the printing machine damaged?' asked Sally.

'Dunno. 'E ain't 'ad time ter clear it away. 'I told 'im 'e should've took the first offer 'e 'ad fer it, but no.'

'Well, you know Pete, always out fer that little bit more.'

'Yeah, but now 'e'll git bugger all if it's damaged.'

'Ma! Sal!' came a voice behind them.

They turned, and hurrying along the road was Gwen, her face ashen.

Sally ran towards her. 'You all right?'

'We fought yer was in there,' said Granny Brent, hugging her daughter-in-law.

'No, but me mum is. 'Ave they got anybody out yet?'

'No,' said Sally.

'D'yer know if anyone's . . . ?'

Sally put her arm round Gwen's shoulder. 'They don't think so. They said they can 'ear 'em banging on the inside of the shelter. Where were yer last night?'

'I was over at me sister's, Blackheath way. I couldn't git back last night and 'ad ter stay till this morning. Been a right game trying ter git over 'ere, I can tell yer. The docks fires are awful. There's a lot o' damage everywhere. There ain't no buses running. The only fing that's working is the underground. A lot o' people slept down there last night.'

'No,' said Granny Brent.

'Can't say I'd fancy that,' said Sally. 'Not sleeping with a lot o' strangers.'

'Look!' suddenly yelled Granny Brent.

They turned towards the houses again and watched a group of men carefully manoeuvre someone towards the ambulance, followed by another group carrying a woman.

'This is the first lot,' said Sally.

'That's Mr and Mrs Cotton, who live next door,' said Gwen.

The Cottons looked dirty and dishevelled but they managed a weak smile to all the onlookers as they were put into the ambulance.

'I reckon that copper's given up,' said Granny Brent, looking at the crowd that had now assembled.

'There wasn't a copper there when I come along,' said Gwen. She looked agitated. 'I 'ope me mum's all right.'

'Look, they've got some more out,' said Sally.

'Mum!' yelled Gwen, scrambling over the pile of wreckage.

'Careful, gel,' called Granny Brent, but Gwen wasn't listening. She threw her arms round her mother's neck and cried.

Her mother and the two sisters who still lived at home were all taken to the hospital and Gwen went with them.

'That was a job an 'alf,' said Pete when he and Stan returned.

'Still, they're all out now,' said Stan, putting his arm round Sally's shoulders. 'Glad we ain't got Andersons, bloody poky 'oles.'

'I'll give Ma 'and,' said Pete, as everyone began to make their way home.

Johnny and his mates started clambering over the debris.

'Be careful, son,' called his father.

The tea van followed them into Sefton Grove and Sally hurried into the kitchen to get the teapot and flask.

'At least now we can 'ave a cuppa. And that lady said they're gonner send round carriers with water in, so that's somethink. We'll 'ave ter fill up all the saucepans. I'll light the fire. It's a good job we've got that ter boil a kettle on.' Sally suddenly stopped, plonking herself at the table, aggressively brushing the dirt and dust off it in front of her. 'Things'll never be the same again.' Tears ran down her face.

'Now come on, gel, don't start that again.'

'But this is only the first night. What about ternight and the next and the next . . . ?'

Her father put his arm round her. 'Now come on, love. Us Fullers are an 'ardy lot – it'll take a lot more than this ter git us down. Now give me 'and gitting all the glass orf the beds. I've got a lot ter do. Got ter see what we can put on the roof, fer one fing, and let's fink what we can put over these winders fer now till I can git enough wood ter board 'em up.'

All day they worked, and by early evening the place looked habitable. Just as they finished, the siren went again. This time Vera and Granny Brent brought Gwen with them. She had nowhere to go – when her mother and sisters were released from hospital they had gone to Blackheath, and there wasn't room for Gwen.

The Fullers' shelter was full. All through the night the sounds of planes, bombs and guns filled the air as its occupants held each other, and prayed, and occasionally tried to sleep. Once again Sally sat quietly wondering if this night would be their last.

On Monday morning they emerged from the shelter, tired, dirty and dishevelled, but still alive.

'Dad, I think we ought ter try and get the kids away,' said Sally, shaking the tablecloth that had once again been covered with plaster. 'I'll be glad when this lot finally comes down.' She looked up at the holes and strips of thin broken wooden lathes that hung from the ceiling. The lamp shade had been smashed and the light bulb hung forlornly on its brown flex.

'I'll git the broom and knock those loose bits off,' said Pete.

'Dad, about the kids?' Sally persisted. Last night had finally made up her mind. However awful Worthing had been, they couldn't go on like this.

'I know – but where can we send 'em to?'

'I dunno. I'll ask Connie's mum what she's gonner do with Connie.'

'D'yer think we ought ter try and git ter the docks this morning?' asked Pete, waving the broom about.

'Pete be careful, you're making more mess,' said Sally. 'Now I've got plaster all in me 'air.'

'I ain't fought about going ter work, son.'

'I reckon we ought ter go and see what's 'appening.'

'Well, we can't do much round 'ere. Might be able ter git a bit o' wood ter put over the front room winder. Don't want any bloody looters gitting in 'ere.'

'What about you, Sal? You going ter work?'

'Dunno. D'yer think the factory's still there?'

'I reckon you'll 'ave ter go and see.'

'I'll ask Jess ter keep an eye on the kids and take 'em in if there's another raid.' She was surprised how matter-of-fact she sounded.

'I'd better go round the garage later and see if me car's still in one piece.' Sally nodded, her mind still on what she was going to do about Babs and Johnny.

Sally first called on Jessie, then set off for Connie's mum's. As Sally walked down Sefton Grove she felt a lump come into her throat. The neat row of houses looked battered. Windows were missing and curtains hung in tattered strips. There were piles of rubble outside every door. Lathes and plaster from ceilings were mixed with glass and broken ornaments, things people had probably treasured for years. Sally remembered her dad stuffing the photos into Mum's old handbag, along with her wedding ring and brooch. It wasn't possible to save everything you valued, though. In the end you were left with little more than what you stood up in, but alive.

Mrs Downs came to the door as soon as Sally knocked.

'Come in, Sal. What can I do fer yer?'

Sally was surprised at how clean the house was, despite what had happened. 'I was wondering if yer was thinking of sending Connie away?'

'We was talking about it, but I ain't sending 'er back ter Worthing. What yer doing wiv your two?'

'I dunno. I don't think they should stay 'ere now. I remember yer saying you 'ad a relation in Wiltshire.'

'That's right, me sister.'

'Babs was talking about it the other day. You thinking o' sending Connie there?'

'I dunno. I don't fink she'd be that pleased ter see Connie.' She bent her head closer. 'We don't really git on. She married some sort o' posh bloke.'

'Why don't yer write and ask 'er if she knows of someone? Maybe they'll 'ave 'er, and Babs and Johnny as well. It might be better if they was all together.'

'I s'pose I could drop 'er a line. She can only say no.'

'Thanks. I know Babs would be 'appy with Connie.'

'I'll let yer know as soon as I 'ear. You orf ter work then?'

'I'm going ter see if the factory's still there.'

'It's a bad business.' Mrs Downs looked round and whispered, 'Can't talk too loud now a lot o' the plaster's orf these walls, but I reckon the bugs from Tanners' next door 'ave got 'eadache.'

Sally laughed. 'As long as they don't all come marching through in ter 'ere.'

'They'll git me shoe on their 'eads if they do,' smiled Mrs Downs.

'I'd better be going,' said Sally.

'Take care, love.'

Mrs Downs had made Sally feel better, and her spirits were further restored to see the factory was still standing.

'Bit of a mess in 'ere, Sal,' said Peggy, the girl she worked near. 'Old 'Arry ain't that pleased.'

Sally put on her overall. 'Why's that?' And she added in a whisper, ''E ain't lost somebody, 'as 'e?'

'Don't fink so. Your lot all right?'

'Yes, and yours?'

'Yeah, fank Gawd. Mind you, me place is in a bit of a state. Still it's a good excuse not ter do any bloody 'ousework, and at least this place is still 'ere so we can still earn a few bob and not 'ave ter go in anovver factory.'

Nellie, another of the work force, came up to Sally and Peggy. ''Ere, d'yer wonner good laugh?'

'Dunno what yer find ter laugh about,' said Peggy.

'Me winder cleaner. Guess what?' She stopped to make sure her audience was giving her their full attention. Sally could see a grin already spreading across Peggy's face.

''E done me winders in the week and when 'e come round fer 'is money I told 'im ter sod orf. Well, by the time 'e come round, all me winders 'ad bin blown out, not a bit o' glass left. 'E was hopping mad. I told 'im I ain't gonner pay fer sumfink wot ain't there.'

'Poor bugger,' said Peggy, smiling. 'I bet there's a lot o' winder cleaning rounds going cheap now.'

'Yeah,' said Nellie. 'It's just the sort o' job my lazy old man's looking for, a winder cleaning round wiv no winders.'

Sally and Peggy were still laughing when Harry, the foreman, came along the line.

'Glad yer can find somefink ter laugh about.'

'Well, we're still 'ere, ain't we, 'Arry?' said Peggy. 'That's gotter be worth a laugh.'

'S'pose it is. Well, yer can git on wiv some work. Just do the best yer can, gels. They've put the gas on, so we can still carry on. We've got blokes coming ter board up the winders later.'

'Yer don't want a winder cleaner, do yer?' yelled Nellie.

'What's she on about?' asked Harry, nodding his head in Nellie's direction.

''Er old man's looking fer a job,' said Peggy.

'Silly cow,' was Harry's remark as he walked away.

'Good fing it ain't winter ovverwise we'd freeze ter death.'

'I'm gonner git meself some trousers,' said Peggy. 'I 'eard they've got some cheap in Cheesemans.'

'I reckon we'll need 'em in the winter,' said Sally.

'I reckon we'll need 'em in the shelter,' said Peggy.

'Come on, gels, less of the old chat,' said Harry, coming up to them again. 'We've gotter git on. Our boys are waiting fer these.'

Sally laughed. 'But what they for?' All the months they'd been soldering wires on to a metal plate, but nobody knew why.

'Top secret,' said Harry. 'Now git on wiv it, gels. 'Itler might be over later.'

'Then what?' shouted Peggy.

'Then it's down the shelter.'

'Then what?' someone shouted.

'Wait and see,' said Harry.

'Is that a promise then, 'Arry?' another voice shouted out. A few of the women laughed.

Sally suddenly realised that the bombing wasn't going to get people down. They were going to carry on just the same.

Chapter 15

When Sally arrived home from work feeling tired and dirty, she was pleased to see her father back already.

'The kids got the water. They've gorn and put a standpipe at the end of the Grove fer now till they repair the mains. It's outside the Nag's.'

'That should be a good excuse fer some of 'em ter drop in fer a quick one,' said Sally, taking off her hat.

Her father quickly took a breath. He looked drawn, as if in pain.

'You all right, Dad?'

He laughed, but Sally thought it sounded false. 'Course. I've made a cuppa. Jess managed ter git us a bit o' scrag end and she's made us a stew.'

'The butcher's still there then?'

'Yeah. She said it was in a bit of a mess. She found a baker's open and got us a loaf as well, so we've got a bit a tea.'

'Good old Jess,' said Sally, wearily sitting at the table. 'Didn't fancy tinned stuff again,'

'Factory all right then?'

'Not too bad. Not got any windows. Where's Pete?'

'Over 'is mum's.' He sat at the table. 'They've made a bloody fine mess o' the docks. All those big sheds 'ave bin buckled wiv the heat – those what's still standing, that is. Couldn't git very close, it's still smouldering. Don't suppose they'll ever see a ship in there again.' He played with the spoon in his saucer. 'Sal, there's talk we might 'ave ter work away.'

Sally put her cup back down. 'D'yer know where?'

'No. It could be only over the water. They didn't git it as bad there as the Surrey.'

'Will the ships still be able ter get up the Thames?'

'Dunno.'

'Where's Johnny and Babs? I didn't see 'em out playing.'

'I fink they're round Tamar Street, playing on the bomb site.'

'Well, we'd better 'ave our tea then get ready ter go in the shelter.' Sally sighed. 'I suppose this is 'ow it's gonner be from now on.'

'It won't last. 'E ain't got that many bombers, and the way our lads are blasting 'em out the sky, 'e's gotter stop soon.'

Although Sally smiled, she wasn't convinced. 'I'll go and get Pete and the kids.'

When Sally turned into Tamar Street she was surprised to see a police car and a Black Maria parked there, and a number of policemen milling about. Fear gripped her. 'What's 'appened,' she asked the nearest constable.

'Looters,' came the brisk reply. They've been 'aving some o' the kids as lookouts.'

Panic filled Sally. She hurried on. They'd been told looters could be shot. She felt sick. The kids were playing round here. What if the police mistook them for the lookouts?

To her relief she saw Babs and Johnny with a group of

children standing looking at the bombed houses. She called them and they turned and came running.

'Guess what?' shouted Johnny. 'Some bloke's in there and the police are after 'im. 'E's bin pinching a lot o' stuff.'

'We saw one come out wiv a fur coat,' said Babs. ''Is mate 'ad a suitcase so full o' stuff, 'e could 'ardly lift it. Then the police come up. 'E's in the nick by now.'

'They didn't ask yer ter keep a lookout fer the cops, did they?'

'Na,' laughed Johnny.

''E 'ad 'is mate ter do that,' said Babs.

'It ain't 'alf exciting, ain't it?' said Johnny, jumping up and down.

Sally looked at them. So many things were changing, the kids included. They were streetwise, and in a gang. Perhaps they were getting too unruly. Today Sally realised their father looked old, a worried frown permanently etched on his brow. The whole family was in danger of bombs and the bombing had changed the way they now had to live. This morning at the factory she'd thought the war wouldn't change people after all, but she'd been wrong. She put her arms round the kids' shoulders.

'Go on home. Dad's got the tea ready.'

The kids sent safely on their way, Sally then went to Pete's old house. She was greeted by a very angry Granny Brent, who started to tell Sally that some of Gwen's mother's stuff hat been pinched.

'I'd like ter cut their bloody 'ands orf. Thieving swines. It's bad enough being bombed and losing yer 'ome, wivout some sod pinching the clothes orf yer back. By the way, Gwen's gonner stay 'ere wiv us while the boys are away. She don't fancy being alone in that poky little flat.'

Sally thought of last night and how cramped it had been with all of them in the shelter. 'You coming over ternight?' she asked.

'Yeah, be over after tea.'

Over the next few weeks, everybody tried to carry on as usual. One Sunday morning, after a particularly bad raid, when Pete came back from checking his car, he told Sally that more and more families were sleeping under the arches.

'What, in yours?'

'Na, next door.'

'I don't think I'd like sleeping in there,' said Sally.

'Those arches are bloody strong – not that I'd fancy sleeping under 'em, either. At least me car's safe there. There's a bit o' dust on the old girl, though. Better give 'er a bit of a polish,' he said, taking the cleaning things.

Sally just tutted.

Every night the family would go to the shelter, Granny Brent, Gwen and Vera joining them, and every night they had no sleep as the bombers came over. The bombs and the loud crack of the anti-aircraft guns made them jumpy. The atmosphere, hot and claustrophobic, didn't help.

Sally woke with a start. Tonight it had been her turn to sleep on the bottom bunk. Babs was restless above her, and as she tossed and turned, Sally hoped she wouldn't wake Johnny, who shared the bunk with her. Sally raised her head and looked around the shelter. The dim light from the hurricane lamp was casting strange shadows. Granny Brent had her head back, leaning against the wall. Her mouth had dropped open – she grunted and it closed automatically. She didn't open her eyes.

Sally watched mesmerised as a long-legged spider slowly made its way down the far wall. It stopped and she could almost imagine it looking round before it went out under the door. She hated sleeping in here with all the creepy-crawlies that invaded every night. She shuddered to remember what happened to Peggy from work one night in their Anderson. Peggy had woken up to find something pinching her head. When she'd finally managed to untangle it from her hair, she'd discovered to her horror it was a large cockroach. She reckoned her screams could be heard for miles. Peggy said she now went to bed wearing a pale pink swimming cap. Sally smiled to herself – that must be quite a sight.

Gwen was sitting next to Granny Brent on an upright chair. Her head had fallen forward, her hands were resting on her stomach that showed there was a baby inside. Sally looked at her swollen ankles; Gwen never complained. Vera gave a sigh. Happy-go-lucky Vera was down-to-earth like Sally and they got on well together. She'd told Sally about the long letters she'd had from her boyfriend, Roy, in the air force. He had recently been promoted to sergeant. She was very fond of him, and looked forward to his coming home on leave. Perhaps they would get engaged? That would be nice for Vera.

'You all right Sal?' whispered Pete.

'Yes, thanks.'

'Can't yer sleep?'

'Shh. I'm all right. Go back ter sleep.'

'It's gone a bit quiet, I'll just pop out for a jimmy.'

Sally didn't hear Pete return, she had dropped off at last.

* * *

The following morning, while Pete took his mother home, Sally and her father were alone in the kitchen.

'Sal, I don't like ter say nuffink, but I reckon we'll 'ave ter try and do somefink about Pete's mum, 'is sister and Gwen staying 'ere night after night.'

'Pete did say they was thinking of going under the arches, but I don't think 'e's very 'appy about that. He don't reckon they'll get a lot o' sleep with them trains over'ead all night, and now they're running guns up and down the lines, 'e's worried that those tracks'll show up in the moonlight.'

'Well, we ain't gitting a lot o' sleep and we all 'ave ter go ter work just the same. It's getting bloody 'arder and 'arder ter git there, specially now we're working the other side of the water. Every morning, there's hose pipes ter fall over and craters and unexploded bombs making the buses take all kinds of diversions. Even gitting down the bloody underground's a work of art wiv 'aving ter step over all the people what sleeps down there.'

'Don't yer think I know what it's like?' Sally's voice rose in anger.

'Don't go gitting on yer 'igh 'orse wiv me, gel. I'm only saying.'

'Well, you tell Pete, you see 'im more than I do.' Sally felt tired and tetchy as she tied her scarf round her hair and tucked the ends into the turban. She bent down to look in the mirror, wedged against the wall, that now had a large crack running through it. There wasn't any point in putting it back on its hook. They'd been lucky when it fell off that it didn't smash completely. Sally remembered thinking that that could have brought them seven years' bad luck. Now she wondered if they had seven years left.

There were no ornaments or anything that could break left out. The dresser had been stripped and the windows boarded up, candles strategically placed for when the electric went off. Everywhere looked dark, dirty and desolate. Winter was coming and, to add to their troubles, there was a shortage of coal.

As Sally walked to work her thoughts were full. She felt guilty at being short with her father. They still hadn't got the kids away – Mrs Downs' sister hadn't proved very helpful – and there had been so many arguments with them saying they didn't want to go, and did Sal and Dad really want to send them away?

The schools were closed again because off the worsening conflict and Johnny was happy playing on bomb sites. He looked permanently scruffy. His collection of shrapnel, his pride and joy, was vast, and he could no longer carry it around in a tin box.

Babs was growing up. In January she would be fourteen and she wanted to go to work – but where? Sally didn't want her to go into a factory. Perhaps she could work in a shop. A lot still had 'Business as Usual' signs nailed to boards that covered their broken windows.

Sally felt miserable. If only they could go out, to the pictures or shopping. But it was too risky to go too far. She felt trapped and powerless, and the air-raid shelter was beginning to seem like a prison.

Chapter 16

By the beginning of November, everybody was taking the air raids in their stride. Large silver barrage balloons now floated overhead to deter low-flying enemy bombers, and during the day, if they had the odd raid, Sally and her work mates went to the factory shelter. They soon had a singsong going, accompanied with a round of dirty jokes. At night the scenario was less jolly. The drone of the planes and the terrifying noise of bombs exploding, mixed with the rat-a-tat from guns sited on backs of lorries, regularly ruined their sleep. It had turned cold and the Fullers and Pete sat in the shelter with blankets round them, nervy and miserable.

Now Granny Brent, Vera and Gwen went under the arches to sleep. Vera told Sally a good crowd sheltered there, and on Saturday nights they took in a few drinks and played cards. There was even talk of the Brents taking the piano in there. Sally almost envied them; her life was very dull at the moment. Playing games like ludo and snakes and ladders with Johnny and Babs was beginning to get very boring.

There was a downbeat sameness to the mornings after, too. The Fullers would emerge from their shelter tired and weary. Sally, her father and Pete would go off to work, never knowing what they would find, leaving Babs and Johnny to their own devices.

At the end of the month something odd happened.

Sally woke in the shelter with a start. In the dim light from the hurricane lamp she looked at the alarm clock. The hands were pointing at six o'clock. She put it to her ear to make sure it was still going. Pete was lying beside her on the mattress that almost filled the shelter's floor space. He grunted and turned over.

'Pete, it's six o'clock,' she whispered. 'It's morning.'

'What?' He sat up. 'We bin asleep all night?'

Sally nodded. 'We ain't 'ad a raid.'

'What's up?' asked her father wearily. He had been sleeping next to Pete.

'We ain't 'ad a raid,' said Pete.

Stan sat up. 'I don't Adam and Eve it.' He scratched his tousled head. 'I wonder what game 'e's got up 'is sleeve now.'

'I don't know and I don't care,' said Sally. 'I'm gonner make a cuppa.' She stood up, pulled down her jumper, and dusted the fluff from the trousers she slept in. She folded her blanket and put it on the chair with her pillow, just as she had done every morning for weeks. Gingerly, she stepped over Pete and her father, carefully made her way to the door and pushed it open. 'It's very quiet out here, and it's raining and cold.' She shuddered and slipped on her shoes over Pete's socks, which she wore at night. 'It's a bit eerie.'

Tiger came racing out of the lav when she pushed its door open. She picked him up. 'You're nice and dry. I bet yer 'ad a good night's sleep. Now I s'pose yer off-ter find yer lady friend.' She gave him a kiss and put him down.

Pete followed her into the kitchen. 'Ter fink, we've bin asleep all night.'

'And we've still got water and gas,' Sally shouted from the scullery. She felt elated. 'I feel like running round shouting.'

'Yer better not. Folks round 'ere won't fank yer. After all, it's the first decent night's kip they've 'ad in months. I'll put the wireless on. We might find out what—' He stopped. The announcer was telling them that Coventry had been last night's target. The bombing had been devastating, the city flattened. Stan came to join them and they listened in silence till the end of the bulletin.

Sally sat at the table. 'I don't wonner sound selfish, but it makes a change fer someone else ter get it,' she sighed.

'Yeah, but how long will 'e leave London alone?' asked Pete.

For two weeks nothing happened in London. Every night they settled in the shelter expecting a raid, but it didn't come.

'Can't we sleep in our own beds ternight?' asked Babs one evening. 'It's ever so cold in that shelter.'

Sally looked at her father. 'What d'yer think, Dad?'

'I dunno.'

'Please,' pleaded Babs. 'I won't git undressed.'

'I wouldn't mind gitting me 'ead down in a proper bed,' said Pete. He gave Sally a wink, making her blush.

'Connie and 'er mum and dad 'ave bin sleeping downstairs under the kitchen table,' said Babs.

'Couldn't we do that?' asked Johnny eagerly. 'It sounds real good.'

'The kids could stay downstairs if yer think that's safer,' said Pete. 'What d'yer say, Pop?'

'We could give it a try.'

That night Pete and Sally went upstairs to bed. They lay quietly after making love.

'I didn't think this would ever 'appen again,' whispered Sally, snuggling close to him.

Pete blew his cigarette smoke into the air. 'Same 'ere. Can't say I ever fancied doing it with yer father laying next ter me.'

'Peggy at work was telling me she saw a couple at it when she got caught down the underground one night.'

'Blimey, that ain't very private.' Pete stubbed his cigarette out. 'Now come on, love, turn over and let's git some shut-eye. We don't know 'ow long this reprieve is gonner last.'

Sally sighed with pleasure. It was like heaven to be in a soft warm bed again with Pete's arms around her.

Without the raids to worry them, people were now thinking about Christmas.

'Florrie in the grocer's was telling me that Lord Wootton said we're gonner 'ave a bit o' extra tea and sugar fer Christmas,' said Jessie, plonking her shopping basket on Sally's kitchen table.

'I s'pose that's better than nothing,' said Sally.

''Ope we gits a bit extra meat. Funny, ain't it, before it was rationed yer always got more than yer asked fer – now it's yer dead one an' tuppence worth,' said Jessie putting a packet of mince on the table.

'That looks nice. I'm really grateful ter you getting our

meat ration fer us,' said Sally, getting a small plate from the cupboard.

'Mind you, I 'ad a bit of a go at the butcher terday. I wanted ter know why we don't see any kidneys or liver now. I asked 'im if the farmers was breeding 'em wivout any innards. Yer should 'ave seen 'is face.'

Sally laughed. 'What did 'e say?'

'Told me I was a saucy cow. Still, it caused a laugh. By the way, I saw Tommy Tanner, and 'e reckons 'e can git us a chicken fer Christmas. D'yer want one?'

'I should say so. 'E didn't say how much?'

'Na, yer know Tommy.'

'Still, it'll be nice anyway.'

'Me mum'll clean it fer yer, but you'll 'ave ter pluck it yerself 'cos the fevvers gits up 'er nose.'

'That's fine.'

'You sleeping upstairs now?' asked Jessie, lighting up a cigarette.

'Just me and Pete and Dad. The kids are down 'ere. What about you?'

'I'm downstairs wiv the kids, just in case. It'll take me too long ter git 'em down the stairs when 'e starts again. But it's nice ter be indoors. That shelter's a bloody cold draughty 'ole. 'Ere, d'yer fancy going to the pictures Sunday?'

'Wouldn't mind,' said Sally. 'Seems ages since we went.'

'We'll go up the Red Lion, ter the first 'ouse, then we can be 'ome 'fore it gits dark, just in case. Mum won't mind 'aving the kids.'

'That'll be smashing. D'yer know what's on?'

'Na, but it'll be good ter git out for a change. What yer doing fer Christmas?'

'Dunno, ain't really thought about it. Mind you, I'll miss the parties they used to 'ave over the Brents'.'

'Be nice if Reg got 'ome.'

'Pete thinks 'im and Danny might be sent overseas soon.'

'Blimey, that'll break the old girl's 'eart. Where's Lena now?'

'Up in Scotland somewhere. She should be getting some leave soon. At least Granny Brent'll be cheered up by that. Maybe we can have a night out with Lena when she's back – try ter make it just like old times?'

'Ain't Vera's bloke up Scotland way?'

'I think so, but Scotland's a big place, and she didn't say where Lena was, or if she was near 'im.'

'Saw Gwen in Florrie's. She's gitting a size.'

'She's 'aving trouble with 'er feet.'

'So she said. I'd rather 'er than me,' said Jessie. 'It ain't funny waddling round like a whale.'

Sally laughed. 'Still it don't last for ever. Babs was saying she thinks Connie's sisters might be 'ome fer Christmas. Joyce ain't too far away. Saw a picture of 'er – she don't 'alf look good in 'er uniform.'

'She still got that long blonde 'air?'

'She wears it tucked in a roll now, it looks ever ser smart.'

'Good job Reg ain't 'ome then, she might find 'e fancies 'er. They like 'em in uniform.'

'Well 'e 'ad the opportunity, she wanted to write to 'im but 'e turned 'er down.'

'No. Why was that?' asked Jessie wide-eyed.

'Reckoned 'e wasn't any good at letter writing.'

'Silly sod. Mind you I wouldn't like ter be 'er sister Doreen and working on the land.'

'And those baggy khaki breeches don't do a lot fer yer,' laughed Sally.

'Yer needs somefink like that, I reckon, when yer being chased by a cow.'

Sally looked surprised. 'What d'yer mean?'

'Well, if yer shits yerself . . .' Jessie grinned.

Sally tutted. 'Trust you to think of somethink like that.'

On Sunday, over tea, Sally was excitedly telling them about the film she'd seen, and Babs was moaning because she hadn't taken her.

Pete suddenly asked, 'How d'yer fancy a day out next Sunday?'

'Great,' said Johnny. 'Where to?'

'Pete didn't ask you,' said Babs sulkily.

''Ave yer got enough petrol?' asked Sally

'Yeah, might as well use it up before they take it away altergevver, and I reckon we should make the most o' this lull in the air raids.'

'Wouldn't mind going to the seaside,' said Sally.

'Blimey, that's a long way, and a bit cold,' said her father.

'We can wrap up. 'Sides, we could do wiv a nice breath o' fresh air,' said Pete. 'Well, I fink it's a good idea. We'll go ter Brighton.'

Sally leapt up and hugged Pete round the neck.

'Can we come?' asked Babs.

'Course.'

'I'll bring me boat,' said Johnny.

The day of the outing was cold and bright, and they were up early, eager to be off. Sally was surprised at all the bomb damage they passed, and all the detours they had to take to get out of London.

'Look at that – just a great empty space and a pile of rubble. What used ter be there, Dad?' she asked.

'Dunno,' said her father, sadly. 'I lorst me bearings a while back. Everyfink looks ser different.'

'We've been lucky in Sefton so far—' said Pete.

'Quick, touch wood,' interrupted Sally.

At Brighton, they strolled along the front.

'Look at all that barbed wire,' said Babs, pointing to the spiky rolls stretched out along the beach.

'I wanted ter go and sail me boat,' said Johnny. 'Why they done that? It wasn't like that at Worthing.'

'I expect it is now,' said Sally.

'It's in case the Jerries try to invade,' said Pete, putting his arm round Johnny's shoulders.

'Will we 'ave ter fight 'em if they come 'ere?' asked Johnny, his eyes lighting up with anticipation.

'That's what we got the 'Ome Guard for,' said their father.

'Wish I was old enough ter fight,' said Johnny, kicking a stone. 'Pete, is Reg and Danny gonner fight 'em?'

'Dunno. Can't say I want 'em to.'

'If they gits killed, will they 'ave a funeral like Mum's?'

'Johnny!' shouted Sally. 'That ain't a nice thing ter say.'

'I only asked.'

Babs was picking up a few stones at the edge of the beach. 'Can I take some o' these 'ome ter prove ter Connie that we've been ter the seaside.'

'Course,' said Sally.

'Can we go in a café and 'ave a cuppa?' asked their father, banging his hands at his side.

'Why not? It's a bit fresh out 'ere,' said Pete.

'Well, yer said yer wanted a bit o' fresh air,' laughed Sally.

'There's fresh and there's bloody perishing.' Pete put his arm round her waist and pulled her close, pretending to shiver. 'We'll just 'ave this tea, then we'd better start making tracks. Don't like being out after dark, not wiv the blackout and all the diversions.'

In the warm café Sally looked at her father. 'You all right, Dad?'

'Yeah, course.'

'Yer look a bit pale.'

'It's that bloody wind. Still it'll keep the fog away.'

She smiled, but she was worried. Over the months he had grown to look old and sad, almost as if he was keeping something from her. Perhaps the war and the sleepless nights had been getting him down, she thought.

With Christmas only a week away, Jessie came racing in as soon as Sally got home from work.

'Guess what,' she said, waving an envelope. 'I've 'ad a Christmas card from me old man. Look.' She thrust a snow scene with robins into Sally's hand. 'And 'e's sent the kids some money.'

'No! What's 'e after? It's very pretty.'

'Dunno. Still it's nice of 'im, ain't it?'

Sally smiled. 'You still got a soft spot fer 'im?'

'Yeah, s'pose I ave.'

'D'yer know where 'e's stationed?'

Jess nodded. 'Up north somewhere.'

Sally smiled. 'You didn't write ter 'im when yer got that last letter, did yer?'

'Na, Mum didn't want me to. But 'e must fink about us.'

'Would yer fancy seeing 'im again?'

'Wouldn't mind.' Jess sat at the table, looking serious. 'It would be nice ter 'ave someone ter cuddle up to at nights.'

Sally laughed. 'You'd be very popular in the barracks with all the other blokes.'

'Yer know what I mean. I still miss 'aving a bit of – yer know . . .'

'Why don't you drop 'im a line and tell 'im about the kids. You never know, 'e might 'ave a nice 'ouse tucked away somewhere be now.'

'That'd be nice. After all, 'e was always good at 'is job. I could send 'im a Christmas card and fank 'im fer the kids' money.'

Jessie had a dreamy faraway look in her eyes. Sally smiled. She hoped her friend wasn't going to raise her hopes too high. Still, everyone needed their dreams – more than ever these days.

Chapter 17

On Christmas Eve afternoon, Sally wandered round the market trying to buy a few last-minute odds and ends. There weren't many men serving on the barrows nowadays, as most of them had been called up. Some traders had tried to make their stalls look Christmassy by draping tinsel and paper chains over them. The decorations from past years looked faded and tarnished, but at least they were festive. The market had to shut down early as the traders weren't allowed to light their lamps after dark because of the blackout.

One man, too old to be called up, was wearing a paper hat and trying to bring a bit of Christmas spirit to the crowds. He ran the greengrocer's stall and was singing, 'Yes, We Have no Bananas,' at the top of his voice.

Sally smiled and pulled her scarf tighter at her throat. The air was damp, and the fog beginning to thicken. She wondered when they would see a banana or an orange again. Her thoughts went to past Christmases – the thrill of feeling the stocking hanging at the bottom of the bed, the lumps and bumps that you tried to identify in the dark and the orange, always stuffed down the toe. She sighed and hurried home. That all seemed a lifetime ago. She felt guilty at the few things that she managed to get everybody.

If only there were more goods in the shops. It had come to something when even your Christmas dinner had to be bought on the black market.

After tea, and despite Babs' and Johnny's protests, their father, Pete and Sally decided to go up the Nag's.

'What if we 'ave a raid?' asked Johnny, sitting on the bed watching Sally put on her make-up. 'We could be dead, blown ter bits, before yer got back 'ere. Then yer'd be sorry.'

'Johnny, it's only a couple o' doors away,' said Sally, pressing her lips together to blot her lipstick and peering in the dressing table mirror, one of the few in the house that remained intact. 'We can be back 'ere before the siren's finished. 'Sides, we've only 'ad false alarms just lately.'

'Well, I don't fink yer should go,' said Babs, who'd been listening at the door.

'Well, I reckon Dad could do with a night out. 'E don't look well,' Sally replied, patting her hair.

''E's always 'aving a night out. 'Im and Pete go up the pub every Friday night.'

'Don't be difficult, Johnny, or I'll get yer sent away.'

'You always say that.' He hung his head.

'Come on, let's go downstairs. Remember, Father Christmas will be 'ere ternight.'

'Don't talk daft. We know it's you. 'Sides, if 'e really is true, 'e might git bombed, or blown out the sky by one o' the fighters while 'e's flying around up there, or 'is reindeers might git caught up in the barrage balloons.'

Sally ruffled her brother's hair.

'Don't,' he yelled, smoothing it down.

'Well, I don't fink it's fair,' said Babs, pouting, 'you lot going out and leaving us.'

'Don't you start,' said Sally, pushing them into the kitchen. 'We're going and that's that. Yer can listen to the wireless. It's usually good on Christmas Eve.'

Pete looked up and grinned when they came into the room. 'Remember who's gonner come down the chimney ternight, kids.'

'Don't talk rot,' said Babs. 'We know it's you.'

'Hark at Miss 'Igh and Mighty,' said Pete.

'Babs, don't talk ter Pete like that. Yer still not too old ter git a swipe, yer know,' said her father.

It was Sally's turn to grin. She knew their dad would never lay a hand on any of them. 'Right, that's enough, we're off.' She picked up her handbag.

'Well, just don't git too drunk,' said Babs. 'In case yer gits our presents mixed up.'

Stan laughed. 'Give us a kiss, gel. Don't worry, we won't be late.' He held Babs close.

'And don't put any more coal on the fire, we ain't got much left,' Sally said at the door.

'I've banked it up wiv the potato peelings, so don't go poking at it,' said their father. 'Left alone it should last all evening.'

'See yer later, kids,' said Pete as they left the room.

When they walked in the Nag's they were surprised at the number of people there. It had a party atmosphere. Wally, being a typical rosy round-faced well-built landlord, had put up some paper chains and was wearing a red crepe paper hat. Unusually his wife, Pat, was also behind the bar. Quiet, shy, mousy, she was a complete contrast to Wally in every way.

'Pity Reg and Danny ain't 'ome,' sniffed Granny Brent when Sally and Pete joined her. 'Looks like you'll 'ave ter tickle the ivories ternight, Pete.'

Sally squeezed along the window seat beside Vera. 'All right then?' she said to Gwen, who was sitting next to her.

Gwen smiled weakly. 'Not too bad. I only 'ope Danny don't go abroad till after the baby's born. Be nice if 'e could see it before 'e goes.'

Pete put a port and lemon on the table for Sally. 'You ain't 'alf a size, Gwen. Let's 'ope yer don't 'ave ter run 'ome.'

'How much longer yer got?' asked Sally.

'A couple o' weeks, so the doctor reckons.'

'Is Roy coming 'ome?' Sally asked Vera.

'I fought 'e was, but it don't look like 'e can git any leave.' Vera looked sad. 'I'm really upset about it.'

'P'raps 'e'll git 'ome next week. Then we can all go out on New Year's Eve,' said Sally.

'Yeah, that'll be nice.'

'Is Lena coming 'ome?' Sally asked Vera quietly. Vera looked across at her mother who was busy talking to Gwen. 'Dunno. Mum's really worried about 'er. She ought ter write now and again, just ter let 'er know she's all right.'

'Don't suppose they get a lot of time.'

'No, but then she never 'ad a lot o' time for any of us. Reckon she'll be gadding about wiv 'alf the camp, if I know Lena.'

It upset Sally to see Vera so down, and was about to say so when Sadie Tanner began yoo-hooing and giving them a wave.

'I bet she's gonner 'ave a full table this Christmas,' said Granny Brent, nodding towards Sadie. 'It seems 'er old man and young Tommy can git 'old of anyfink, at a price.' She straightened her shoulders. 'Looks like she's been on the gin again. Bloody 'ell, she's coming over.'

''Allo then. All right?' Sadie stood hovering over them, her face flushed and her large black hat with the squashed rose slightly askew. ''Ope that bastard keeps away over Christmas. Those raids 'ave bin gitting on me nerves. Upsets me somefink rotten, they do.'

'They don't do the poor buggers what gets killed or loses their 'omes a lot o' good,' said Granny Brent. 'You gonner git on that piano then, young Pete?'

'Just going, Ma.'

'Your Reg or Danny coming 'ome?' asked Sadie.

'No,' said Granny Brent curtly.

'Wot about your Lena? Ain't seen nuffink of 'er since she joined up.'

'She's too busy,' snapped Granny Brent.

'Wot she doing then?'

'Dunno, it's top secret.'

Sally and Vera grinned at that remark.

'My Teddy can't get 'ome. I don't 'alf miss 'im.' Sadie sniffed and took an off-white handkerchief from her tatty coat pocket.

'Come on, old gel,' said Mr Tanner, taking her arm. 'Yer got a few gins on the table ter sup yet. Gin always makes 'er tearful,' he said over his shoulder as he led her away.

'Dunno why she said she misses Ted,' said Granny Brent when they were out of earshot. ''E was always in the nick.'

Mrs Downs came across to their little group. 'Nice ter git out fer a change. Doreen's 'ome from the country so we can leave Connie wiv 'er.'

'Is Joyce coming 'ome?' asked Sally.

'No. She 'opes ter git some leave next week, but it won't be the same. Still, it'll be nice ter see 'er. Did yer git one o' Tommy's chickens?'

'Fink the whole Grove got one,' said Granny Brent. 'Mind you, they don't look bad birds.'

'I wonder where Tommy got 'em from,' said Sally.

'Don't know, but I can't say I'm sorry ter see the back of 'em. Yer know, 'e kept 'em in the air-raid shelter this last week?' said Mrs Downs.

'No! said Granny Brent, wide-eyed.

'Yer should've 'eard old Sadie screaming at 'em. Gawd knows how many times they got out – every time she went ter feed 'em, I fink. The bloody racket they made when she chased 'em round the yard. There was them squawking and flapping their wings, and 'er screaming and flapping 'er 'ands, and bleeding fevvers flying about all over the place.'

'Fank Gawd they wasn't cockerels,' chuckled Granny Brent. 'Ovverwise yer'd 'ave 'em crowing at the bleeding crack o' dawn.'

'How long they 'ad 'em there?' asked Vera in amazement.

'Only the week. Still the poor little buggers won't be squawking no more. The old man was nearly all day yesterday wringing their necks. I couldn't look.'

Everybody was laughing and Mrs Downs dabbed her eyes.

'Can't say I'd fancy sleeping in their shelter with all that chicken shit,' said Pete.

'Can't say I'd fancy sleeping in 'er shelter anyway,' said Granny Brent. 'Bet it's full o' bugs.'

'Good job young Tommy don't keep 'orses,' laughed Gwen, holding her stomach.

'Don't reckon they'd even smell the difference,' said Mrs Downs.

'Pete, git on that piano,' said Vera, 'ovverwise Wally'll be calling time soon.'

When Pete started playing, and everyone was singing, Sally went over to have a word with Mr Slater.

''Allo, gel, yer look very nice ternight,' said Mr Slater, raising his voice above the din as Sally sat at his table.

'Thank you. How's yer sister? 'Allo, Bess,' said Sally, rubbing the top of the dog's head.

'Not too bad, love. This break old Hitler's giving us is a chance ter recharge our batteries.'

'How's Fred, don't see much of 'im these days.'

'Looking really well. 'E's in charge of 'is post now, yer know?'

'No, I didn't. Looks like another drink's been put on the table so I'd better get back. Merry Christmas ter you and yer sister,' said Sally.

'And ter you, love,' said Mr Slater.

When Wally called time Pete started to play a knees-up. Sadie leapt to her feet and dragged her husband and Mr Slater with her. Bess faithfully followed although her legs were as unstable as his.

'Poor old bugger,' said Granny Brent. 'Why can't Sadie leave 'im alone, and look at 'er showing 'er pink Celanese drawers again – dirty cow.'

'Come on, Vera,' said Sally, jumping up. 'Let's make the most of it.'

Wally finally threw them all out. Pete and Stan staggered home, and after all the good nights Sally was having a job to hold them both up.

'Shh, the pair o' yer. You'll wake the Grove.'

'Sorry, Sal,' said Pete, a broad grin filling his face.

They leant against the door while she fished through the letter box for the key.

''E won't be over ternight,' said her father, looking up at the sky. 'It's too cloudy.'

'Be quiet, and watch the blackout,' she whispered loudly as Pete switched on the light while her father was still caught up in the curtain that hung in front of the door.

'Sorry, Sal,' said Pete again.

She wanted to laugh but decided against it as that would only encourage them to be silly.

'And don't wake the kids.'

'Sal, the kids' presents, 'ave yer got 'em?'

'Yes, Dad. You go on up and I'll put them in the front room.' She couldn't go into the kitchen as that's where her brother and sister were sleeping.

'See yer both in the morning,' said her father as he very carefully made his way up the stairs.

'D'yer want me ter 'elp yer, Sal?' asked Pete.

'No, you go on up.'

The front room was cold as they couldn't waste precious coal on a fire in here now. Sally sat on the brown Rexine settee with the presents round her. Even trying to find suitable paper to wrap them in had been difficult. There was no Christmas tree this year, though they had put a few paper chains up in the kitchen. She looked at the space where her mother's photo had always been before her father had tucked it safely in his policy bag to go into the shelter with them. There were no pictures on the walls, only large cracks with the lathes showing through. The windows were boarded up and the room looked sad and sorry with its war wounds showing.

'Good job you can't see it, Mum. I can't keep it clean now.' Tears ran down Sally's cheek. 'I wonder what sort of Christmas we'll have next year – that's if we're all still here.' She wiped her eyes and quietly closed the door as she left.

Upstairs, she wasn't surprised to see Pete lying on his back fast asleep. His mouth was open and he was gently snoring. She snuggled against him, he didn't wake, but he held her close. Sally drifted off to sleep quickly, the comfort of a real bed still a novelty after the shelter.

On Christmas day, Babs and Johnny were pleased with the few presents Sally had managed to get them.

'That chicken was lovely,' said Pete, smacking his lips after they finished dinner. 'Reckon some poor farmer's going be wondering where 'is birds 'ave flown to.'

'And I reckon there's enough left over fer a pie termorrer,' said Sally.

'That's good,' said Johnny. 'Now wot about the pudding?'

Sally looked apprehensive. 'Don't know what it's like, mind. Florrie let us 'ave a bit of dried fruit, but she 'ad ter ration it out evenly.'

'Well, I fink yer done wonders, Sal,' said her father. 'Smovver it in custard, and we won't notice if a few a currants are missing.'

Sally didn't have the heart to tell them it was made from a government food fact recipe and had carrots in it.

For the first time that Sally could remember, Christmas night was quiet. She held on to Pete's arm, strolling back across the road after spending a few hours with Granny Brent. 'I wonder if we'll ever 'ave the old Christmases back again?'

'Dunno, love. It ain't the same with Danny, Reg and Lena away. The place seems empty without 'em.'

'Good job in some ways Gwen's moved in with yer mum. At least she's got the baby ter look forward to. Gwen looks well, Don't she?'

'Yeah.'

Sally took a deep breath. 'Pete, I'd like to 'ave a baby.' She'd been biding her time for many weeks and now she'd said it.

He stopped in the middle of the road. 'Be sensible, Sal. You know what I said when Gwen was first expecting. I don't fink it's right to 'ave kids in war time.'

Sally bent her head. Deep down she knew Pete was being sensible. How could Gwen and the baby manage if something happened to Danny? 'I suppose you're right. Vera seemed a bit down last night,' she said, changing the subject.

'It's hard for one twin when the other's away, 'specially at a time like this. And she was 'oping 'er young man, Roy, would be 'ome. He said a few weeks ago 'e was getting leave, but 'e didn't turn up. I told 'er they can't pick and choose when they want ter come 'ome.'

'No, I suppose not.' Sally stopped at the front door. 'Pete, I'm worried about Dad. Is 'e all right?'

'I fink so. Why?'

'I don't know, can't put me finger on it.'

'Mind you, I don't fink 'e's been doing a lot a work. I'll 'ave a word with 'im.'

Sally reached up and kissed his cheek. 'I love you, Pete Brent.'

Pete put his arms round her waist and pulled her close. 'And I love you, Mrs Brent, and lets 'ope the New Year brings an end ter all this,' he whispered, kissing her mouth hard.

As Sally melted into his arms she too wished the war would end soon; then she could have her baby.

Chapter 18

On Saturday Sally came home wearily from work and slumped into the chair.

'Been busy then, gel?' asked her father.

She nodded. 'Lifting those heavy boxes of these wire things all morning takes it out of yer.'

'Who collects 'em?'

'The lorries. I think they've been taken over by the army, but they don't send ser many blokes now so we 'ave ter help.'

'Ain't yer got any men left in the factory now?'

'No, only a couple o' boys and the foreman. I think 'e's exempt.'

'Pete's over 'is mum's, been trying ter take that printing machine ter pieces. 'E's gonner take it under the arches ter try and stop it from going rusty.'

'So 'e said. This is a nice fire. It's freezing in that factory.'

'I was lucky, I managed ter git a bag of coal.'

Sally slid down in the chair, the warmth from the fire was making her drowsy and her lids began to get heavy.

'I'll git the tea,' said her father.

The kitchen door slamming made Sally jump, quickly bringing her back.

'Joyce is 'ome,' shouted Babs, rushing into the room.

'And guess what, she's gonner take me and Connie ter the pictures termorrer.'

'That's nice of her.' Sally sat up and smoothed down her hair. 'Where's Johnny?'

'Just coming. Joyce looks ever so smart in 'er uniform. Sal, how old d'yer 'ave ter be ter join up?'

'Eighteen, I think. Why?'

'I'd like ter go in the army or sumfink like that. Don't know I'd fancy being a land gel like Doreen, though.'

'Well, yer ain't old enough, and Babs, don't let Dad 'ear yer talk about that 'cos 'e'll go mad.'

Babs sat next to Sally. 'If this war's still on when I'm eighteen then I'll join up and Dad won't be able ter stop me.'

'Christ, I 'ope this ain't gonner go on fer another four years.'

'Sal, wouldn't yer like ter go in the army or sumfink?'

'No I wouldn't.'

'Joyce said it's ever so good. She's got lots of friends and they 'ave lots o' dances and shows.'

'And who would look after you lot if I went off and joined the army?'

Babs grinned. 'Yeah, p'raps it's best if yer stay. Me and Connie was talking about looking for a job next week.'

'Any idea where yer want ter work?'

'Don't wonner go in a factory.' Babs screwed up her nose. 'I quite fancy working in a shop.'

'That could be nice. We'll go out next Saturday and make a few enquiries.'

Babs was becoming a nice-looking young woman. Her hair had grown and she was filling out. Soon she would be a woman in every sense.

'Good, we'll go down Rovver'ive New Road,' said Babs eagerly. 'There's a couple of shops that sells nice frocks. I quite fancy that.'

'Oh yes, and what d'yer fancy?' asked their father, walking into the kitchen carrying the teapot.

'Me and Sal's going out next Sat'day ter see about gitting me a job.'

'Our little Babs starting work. Yer mum would be that proud of yer, love. D'yer fink there's much work about?'

'Dunno. I want ter work in a shop.'

'I reckon she stands a good chance,' said Sally. 'A lot of girls 'ave joined up and I don't think it'll be long before the rest of 'em gets called up.'

'Gawd 'elp us, don't say that, gel,' said her father.

'Well, that's got some of the stuff that's worth saving safely put away under the arches,' said Pete, walking into the kitchen. 'Mind you, I dunno how long it'll stay safe, not with Tommy Tanner and 'is old man sniffing around.'

'They wouldn't pinch any of it, would they?' asked Sally.

'They would if they 'ad a market for it.'

'When we gonner take these down?' asked Sally the next day, looking up at the drooping Christmas paper chains looped across the ceiling.

'It ain't twelf night yet,' said her father. 'Leave it till after New Year. Don't wonner upset our luck.'

Sally smiled. 'OK, we'll do it next week. After all we need all the luck we can get.'

When Babs came home from the pictures she was full of it.

'Don't keep on about it, Babs,' said Johnny.

'Well 'er an' Jess don't take me,' she pouted.

'Joyce Downs don't see 'er sister day in and day out like I do so it's a bit of a novelty fer 'er ter take 'er out,' said Sally, as she busied herself laying the table.

After tea, Sally, her dad and Pete were getting ready to go out to the pub when the air-raid warning started.

'Sod it,' said Stan.

'I thought we'd finished with this lot,' said Sally.

'Well, we knew it wouldn't last for ever,' said Pete. 'Come on, you git settled in the shelter while I pop over ter Mum just ter make sure they're all right.'

'They'll go ter the arches, won't they?' asked Sally, busy collecting bedclothes.

'Yeah, but they might need 'and.'

'Kids quick, 'elp yer sister,' said their father.

They raced outside clutching their bundles of bedding.

Johnny stopped to look up at the searchlights swooping across the black sky, lighting up the silver barrage balloons. 'Well, we ain't got a bomber's moon ternight. It's a bit cloudy,' he said, knowledgeable.

Pete was back in the shelter and it was a while before they heard the familiar drone of enemy planes overhead.

'Fought this was gonner be anovver false alarm,' said Pete.

The deep booming of the guns was suddenly mixed with the high-pitched scream from bombs. The shelter's floor tossed and heaved. Dirt and dust filled the cramped space and everyone's nose and throat. Nobody could speak as the ear-shattering blasts took their breath away. The sound of falling masonry was louder than they'd ever heard before. They crouched on the floor with their hands over their ears, expecting every second to be their last.

'What's that smell?' asked Sally.

'Smells like burning oil,' said Pete.

Her father looked up. 'I read somewhere 'e's got bombs filled with oil. I reckon 'e's trying ter set us alight this time.'

Sally shuddered. The thought of being burned alive filled her with horror.

The smell of burning oil and smoke seeped through the ill-fitting door, and the noise from small explosions sounded very near.

One loud crash shook the shelter hard, and with the sound of walls collapsing Sally thought the shelter would cave in. She was terrified they would all be buried alive under it.

'That was close,' said her father, his face ashen.

'D'you think the house 'as gone?' she asked.

'Dunno. Christ, this is a bad one ternight,' whispered Pete.

Suddenly they could hear a woman screaming. Everyone in the shelter sat up.

'Sounds like someone's in trouble,' said Pete, scrambling to his feet. 'I'm going out ter look.'

'No, Pete!' cried Sally, hanging on to him. 'Don't, please don't go.'

Her father was also on his feet. 'We must, Sal. Someone might want 'elp.'

In the few seconds the door was open for them to get out, Sally could see outside bright with the glow of fires all around them.

Babs sat on the floor crying as more bombs rained down. 'We're all gonner die,' she sobbed.

'No we ain't,' said Sally, wiping her dirty face.

'But Dad and Pete will if they stay out there,' said Johnny tearfully.

'They'll be careful, and they'll be back soon,' Sally said, all the while silently praying.

The sound of bells ringing frantically from the fire engines and ambulances was very near, almost as if they were in Sefton Grove. Tears filled Sally's eyes. Please don't let it be anyone we know, she murmured.

After a while the bombing eased, and the gunfire was now in the distance, as this wave of planes finished their deadly destruction and headed for home.

'I'm going out to look for Dad and Pete,' said Sally, struggling to her feet. Grit and dirt filled her mouth.

'Don't leave us!' cried Babs.

'Please, Sal, don't go.' Johnny hung on to her arm.

'I must. What if they're in trouble?'

'Sal,' Babs was crying, her dirty face streaked with tears, 'we've only got us, and if you go . . .' She couldn't finish the sentence.

Sally threw her arms round her young sister and they rocked gently together. Johnny pushed his way between them and they stood locked in a tight little knot, all gently sobbing. They could hear men shouting and the crashing of tiles and glass.

It was a while before Sally could broach the subject again. 'Look, it's gone all quiet now. I've got ter go and find out what's 'appening.' She gently pushed open the shelter door. She put her hand to her mouth as a long loud gasp escaped from her lips. Babs and Johnny were at her side. Fires were burning all around them – the sky was lit up like daylight. The roof of Silly Billy's house was alight. Sally's thoughts went to his mother: was she in the shelter?

The Fullers' house looked still intact, so did Jessie's, but how long before the fire spread from Billy's along the roof to theirs? She could hear a lot of men shouting from the street.

Sally moved cautiously into the yard, jumping back when the light cold spray from the firemen's hose that was playing on Silly Billy's house caught her. She looked up. The back of her own house had lost part of its roof. Babs and Johnny were close behind her. 'I'm going ter try and git through the 'ouse, you two stay 'ere.'

'I ain't staying,' said Babs.

'I ain't gonner stay 'ere on me own,' sniffed Johnny. He wiped his nose with his sleeve, leaving a clean streak across his face.

Sally knew she couldn't leave them. 'Well, stay close, and be careful.'

Holding hands, they slowly and carefully picked their way across the debris-strewn yard. The lavatory door was hanging at a drunken angle. Sally was filled with alarm when she found she couldn't push the scullery door open, and began to panic. 'What we gonner do? It's stuck.'

'How we gonner git out the yard?' cried Babs.

Sally took a deep breath. 'We'll have ter try and stay calm. P'raps if we push together.'

''Ow did Dad and Pete git out?' asked Johnny.

'I don't know. P'raps this lot fell down after they got through. Don't ask stupid questions,' Sally shouted angrily. 'Now push.'

With their combined efforts the door moved slightly.

'There's a lot o' stuff fallen behind it, blocking it,' said Sally with her shoulder against the door. 'We'll 'ave ter keep pushing.'

Gradually they opened it wide enough to enable them to squeeze through into the scullery. All the wood that had been blocking the windows all these months was thrown across the room. They carefully moved on towards the kitchen, crunching on what had been the ceiling. Sally looked up, she could see the sky. A few of the paper chains still hung limp and sad. Others were torn and moved gently in the slight breeze. One of the legs of her father's bed was hanging precariously through the ceiling. She moved her brother and sister quickly on, terrified it would fall.

Finally they got out of the front door. They stood in the middle of the road staring in amazement at all the activity, damage and destruction around them. Wreckage spewed over the road, blocking the paths. The Grove was full of people. Men were running around shouting orders. Fires were burning and firemen were dragging long hoses from the fire engines.

Babs shook Sally's hand and pointed to a crowd of busy men who seemed to be around Connie Downs' house. 'D'yer fink Connie's all right?'

'Dunno,' was the only answer she could give.

From where they were standing they could see Mr Slater's house was on fire. Flames were coming through the windows and front door. It was well alight and in the flames it looked as if all the back had gone.

Sally caught sight of Silly Billy and his mother sitting on the kerb, looking forlorn and cold. She rushed over to them. 'You all right?' she asked anxiously.

The warden who was comforting them said, 'What you kids doing out 'ere? Git back in the shelter 'fore the next lot comes over.'

Sally had almost forgotten the raid was still on. 'I'm

looking for me dad and 'usband. D'yer want ter try and git into our shelter?' she asked Billy and his mum.

'No ta,' said Billy. 'Mum fills safer out 'ere, we fought we'd be buried alive when the roof went up.'

'But it's freezing, and—'

'Yer better git those kids orf the street, gel.' As the warden finished the sentence the long clear note of the all clear filled the air. He took off his tin hat, scratched his wet hair and cast his eyes to the sky. 'Fank Gawd fer that. I wonder what's made 'im stop now.'

'Is there anythink we can do ter 'elp?' asked Sally.

'Could do wiv a drink,' said Billy.

'A cuppa would be nice,' said his mother, pulling the blanket she had round her shoulders tighter. She tried hard to raise a smile. 'Me bedroom's in a bit of a state.'

Sally managed to return the look. 'I wonder if Wally in the pub's got some water ter make a cuppa.'

'I'll go and ask 'im if yer like, Sal,' volunteered Babs eagerly.

'All right, but be careful, and, Johnny, you'd better go with 'er.' As soon as they were out of earshot she asked, ''As anybody in Sefton been killed?'

''Fraid so, love,' said the warden. 'Mostly down that end.' He nodded in the direction of the Slaters'.

Tears filled Sally's eyes. 'When me brother and sister gets back tell 'em ter wait 'ere fer me. I'm gonner see if I can find me dad, and if 'e want's any 'elp.'

'Be careful, gel, and don't git in the way,' yelled the warden after her.

Sally walked down the road, stumbling over firemen's hoses and rubble. Granny Brent's house was still standing. It was those up the far end by Brigg Street that seemed to have got it worse. Where was Pete? Granny Brent? Perhaps Pete had gone round there to look for her. Sally suddenly felt sick with worry. She must try to get to the arches to see if she, Gwen and Vera were all right. The smell of dirt, burning oil and fires got up her nose. There was a great gap at the end of the Grove where last night there had been houses. Some small fires were being left to burn themselves out while others were being attacked viciously with stirrup pumps by the occupants. She was angry; Sefton Grove had been her home for all her life and now it was scarred and battered. And what about the people – people she had known all her life. A loud sob filled her with despair.

Suddenly she was aware of the heat from the fire, someone shouting at her.

'Keep back, gel. Where d'yer fink yer going?' A fireman whose face was thick with grime grabbed hold of her arm.

'I'm looking for me dad and 'usband.'

'Well, yer can't go near there, it's dangerous. That bloody lot could fall any minute.'

'But me dad and 'usband—'

'Was they in there?' He nodded towards what was left of Mr Slater's house.

'I dunno. They ran out of our shelter when the 'eard some woman screaming.'

'Where d'yer live?'

'Down there.' She pointed behind her.

'Well, go on back. Yer can't do much up 'ere.'

'But me dad and 'usband—' repeated Sally.

'They could be round the back in the next street. It'll be easier ter git ter 'em that way.' He patted her shoulder. 'I expect they're all right.'

‘’As anybody been . . . ?’ Sally knew the answer to that question before she’d finished asking as, out of the corner of her eye, she saw a body shrouded in a piece of floral curtain.

‘’Fraid so.’ His voice softened. ‘And they’re still gitting ’em out, so go on back, love.’

‘Do you know who it is?’

‘Sorry, love, I don’t know.’

‘Can I get to the arches? Me mum-in-law sleeps in there.’

‘Not at the moment yer can’t. Go on ’ome, love, it’ll be light soon.’

‘But me ’usband . . .’ Sally’s eyes filled with tears.

‘I’m sure they’re all right. There’s a lot o’ blokes round the back.’

Sally slowly turned. Who had been killed? The Slaters, Downses and Sadie’s family all lived next door to one another, and now all that was left would be a pile of rubble. It began to rain, and the drizzle mixed with tears stinging Sally’s eyes.

Chapter 19

Sally was deep in thought as she walked back to her brother and sister.

'Wally's took Billy and 'is mum in ter the pub and made 'em a cuppa,' said Babs, adding almost excitedly, ''E's gonner make a lot more so we can give the firemen and the wardens some.'

It was at that moment Jessie and her family joined most of the Grove who had come out to stare at the damage and the fires.

Jessie ran up to Sally, crying. 'Ain't it awful, Sal?' She was holding Pat and threw her free arm round Sally's neck and wept. 'I've never bin ser frightened in the whole o' me life,' she sobbed.

'You all all right?' asked Sally to Jessie's mum and dad.

'Yeah. See poor Billy's place caught it bad. What's your place like?' Mrs Walters was having a job to keep hold of Harry's hand.

'It looks a bit dangerous. We've lost part of the roof and ceiling,' said Sally.

'Seemed ter miss us. Keep still,' she said to her grandson. 'I ain't letting yer run orf. Yer could fall down a bloody great 'ole or sumfink and end up breaking yer neck.'

'I wish I knew was what 'appening down there.' Sally nodded towards the end of the road.

'We 'eard a woman screaming. Any idea who it was?' asked Mrs Walters.

'No. Dad and Pete went running out, but I ain't seen 'em. I 'ope they're all right.' Sally wiped the rain and tears from her face. 'There's a body up there.' She nodded her head towards the end of the road, but I don't know who it is.'

'Oh my Gawd,' Mrs Walters quickly put her hand to her mouth.

Babs suddenly began crying. 'D'yer fink it could be Connie?'

Sally put her arm round her shoulders. 'I don't know.'

'I couldn't bear it if Connie was—'

'Let's wait and see. When Dad gets back 'e'll be able to tell us more.' Sally pulled Babs close as her young sister's tears flowed.

'Sal, why don't yer all come in our place? It's a bit of a mess but better than standing out 'ere in the rain.' Mrs Walters gently took hold of her arm. 'Can't make yer a cuppa tea, though.'

'We could go up the Nag's,' said Johnny, 'Wally'd make yer a cup.'

'That sounds like a good idea,' sniffed Jessie, pulling at the blanket she had wrapped round Pat.

As they made their way to the Nag's, Sally heard her name being called.

'Vera!' she screamed out and ran back to embrace her and Granny Brent. Gwen was puffing behind them.

'You all right, love?' panted Granny Brent in Sally's ear as they stood hugging each other.

Sally could only nod.

'Yer soaking wet,' she said as they broke away. 'Where's Pete?'

'I think 'e's 'elping.'

'It looks bad. Saw two bodies when we come past, but they wouldn't tell us who they was.'

'I don't suppose they know,' said Vera.

'There's a lot o' fires round Silver Street. I'm glad I ain't living there now.' Gwen looked tired.

'The Nag's got water and Wally's making everyone a cuppa,' said Sally as they slowly made their way along Sefton.

'I fink I'll go indoors first, if yer don't mind, Sal, just ter make sure nuffink's alight. Mustn't let the place burn down. Gotter 'ave somewhere fer this new baby ter call 'ome.'

Sally hugged her mother-in-law again. 'I'll bring yer a cup down.'

In the Nag's everyone was sitting around quietly talking, looking tired and dirty. Most were sitting in damp clothes, and the smell of warm, wet cloth mingled with those of burning, soot and dirt.

A cup of tea was put into Sally's hand as soon as she walked in.

'When yer finished yer tea why don't yer pop 'ome and get those wet fings orf, Sal?' said Mrs Walters. 'Yer soaked frough – you'll catch yer death if yer ain't careful.'

'Well, one good fing,' said Wally. 'This rain'll 'elp put the fires out.'

Sally shuddered. She suddenly felt cold and her wet clothes were sticking to her. 'Yer better come along as well,' she said to Babs and Johnny.

Her brother ran his fingers through his normally tousled hair now stuck flat against his head.

'What about your clothes?' she asked Billy's mother. 'Can I bring yer back somethink?'

'It's all right, Sal,' said Wally. 'Me Missis is sorting sumfink out fer 'em both.' He put his head closer and added in a whisper, 'I fink all their stuff's got burnt. It's a bit of a state in there by all accounts.'

When she had finished her tea, Jessie's mum stood up. 'I fink we'd better go 'ome and try ter clear up some o' the mess.'

'Me dad's bed leg's 'anging from the ceiling,' said Johnny, giving everyone a slight grin.

'No!' said Mrs Walters. 'Is it safe ter go in?'

'It don't look like it,' replied Sally.

'Well, just you be careful, love, and if we can do anyfink ter 'elp yer only 'ave ter ask.'

'Sal, if yer want some dry fings I can let yer 'ave 'em,' said Jess.

'Thanks, but I think we'll be all right, we'll go now as well.'

It was getting light as the trio made their way back to number sixty-eight Sefton. Sally pushed open the front door and began to realize the full extent of the damage to their house. She didn't want to venture upstairs in case the floor gave way. Fortunately, they kept some clothes downstairs. She looked into the front room. It appeared safe enough. 'Look, go in there,' she said, holding the door open for Johnny and Babs, 'and find some dry clothes, but don't touch anythink in case somethink falls on yer – and be quick.'

'Where're you going?' asked Babs. 'Don't leave us.'

'Course I won't. I'll just put some dry things on, then we'll go back to the Nag's. It's a lot safer than in 'ere.'

The warmth from the pub's fire made Sally feel very drowsy. Johnny and Babs were curled up beside her on the bench seat, fast asleep.

'It's been a rough night, ain't it, love?' Wally sat on a chair opposite her.

'What's gonner 'appen ter Billy and 'is mum?'

'They're gonner take 'em somewhere safe, so the warden was saying. Seems they've got places all ready fer this.'

''Ave yer found out who's dead yet?' whispered Sally.

'Na.' Wally looked quickly from side to side. 'They asleep?' He indicated to Babs and Johnny.

Sally nodded.

Wally leant forward. ''E was saying that one body – 'e finks it was female – badly burnt. She was running down the road all alight, screaming.'

'That must 'ave been who we 'eard.' A tear slowly ran down Sally's cheek.

'We'll know who soon enough when yer dad and Pete gits back. That warden was saying they've got hundreds of cardboard coffins stacked up, waiting. Bloody awful fought, ain't it? Always fancied a nice padded oak box with brass 'andles meself. I only 'ope it's strong cardboard. Wiv my weight I'd 'ate ter fall frough the bottom when they was taking me out.'

Sally tried to raise a smile.

'It's been a bloody awful night. We won't be able ter take too many of these.' Wally stood up. 'Better go and see if anyone else wants a cuppa. Fank Gawd we filled up a few bottles wiv water last night. Mind you, the tea could taste o' beer, but I don't s'pose anyone'll complain.'

As Wally walked away Sally wondered what the day and tonight would have in store for them. Wally was right, they couldn't stand too many like last night. She closed her eyes, her thoughts going back to the bodies lying out in the cold and rain, she gave a deep sob.

She opened her eyes to find Vera standing over her. 'Sorry Sal, did I wake yer?'

She sat on the bench next to Sally.

'What's your place like?' Sally asked, wiping her eyes.

'Inside's not too bad, the shed's gorn. An incendiary must o' landed right on top of it. It's burnt ter the ground. Mind you, was only a pile o' rubbish after the last time.'

'Good job Pete got the machine out then. Our place is in a bit of a state. Part of the back of the roof's gone, and some of dad's bedroom floor.'

'Still, yer alive, that's the main fing. Ain't Pete or yer dad back yet?'

'No, I 'ope they're all right.'

'Me too. 'Ere's Wally wiv me tea. Sal, why don't you and the kids come down ter our place?'

'I'm waiting fer news.'

'Well blimey, everybody knows where yer'll be. Come on. Yer looks done in.'

'OK, we'll be down later.'

It seemed to Sally that she had been sitting in the Nag's for hours, too frightened to go home to the unstable house. People were coming and going, all bringing with them bits of news. When the bottled water ran out a warden told Wally there was a burst water main in Tamar Street, and they were putting a stand pipe up there. Johnny and Babs helped with the slow process of collecting water, and the tea making began again.

'Just seen yer dad,' said Wally, returning from one of his trips laden down with buckets of water. 'I told 'im yer was in 'ere. 'Im and Pete 'ope ter be back soon.'

A wave of relief washed over Sally. At least Dad was safe.

'You should see the state of 'im, Sal. 'E's filfy dirty,' said Johnny.

'I asked 'im if Connie was all right, but 'e walked away. 'E wouldn't answer me.' Tears filled Babs' eyes and plopped on to Sally's arm.

'P'raps 'e don't know. She might 'ave been taken somewhere safe before Dad got there. Did 'e tell yer anythink else?' Sally asked Wally. She knew she didn't have to spell it out.

'Na. There's still a lot going on, and the tea wagon's up there now.'

'I'll go up and see if I can 'ave a word with 'im.'

'I wouldn't if I was you, love. They're very busy.'

'I'll tell 'im we'll be in Pete's mum's.'

'Well, wrap up. At least the rain's stopped, but it's still perishing.'

''Ave they taken the . . .' she hesitated. 'Yer, know, away?'

'Yeah.'

'Did you find out . . . ?' Sally's voice trembled.

'I didn't like ter ask.'

Granny Brent threw her warm, fat, wobbly arms round Sally when she walked into the kitchen.

'Come and sit yerself down, love. Gwen's upstairs 'aving a lay down.'

'Everythink's all right then,' said Sally, looking round Granny Brent's kitchen.

'Yeah. The paint, wot there was of it, on the back winder's bin burnt orf, but we mustn't grumble. Sorry I can't make yer a cuppa. Got no water again.'

'I wish Pete and Dad would come back.' It still worried her that no one had seen Pete.

'They wouldn't leave if they still fought they could be useful.' Granny Brent sat at the table next to her.

'Sal, can I go out the back?' asked Johnny. 'I might find the bomb case.'

'If yer want, but don't make too much noise, yer might wake Gwen.'

Babs was still looking very tearful.

'Come upstairs with me, Babs,' said Vera kindly. 'I might be able ter find yer a scarf or jumper I don't need.'

'All right.'

It was just after that that Pete and her father walked in. Sally looked at them in disbelief; their faces were streaked with dirt, the front of her father's grey wiry hair had been singed. They looked tired and drawn. Their clothes were wet and almost white with dust. She threw her arms round Pete's neck.

'Steady on there, love.'

Sally cried tears of joy and relief. 'I've been so worried about yer.'

Stan took his tobacco tin from his pocket, wincing.

'Dad, who's been . . . ?'

Her father appeared to be having difficulty as he slowly and silently rolled a cigarette. He ran his tongue along the gummed edge of the paper and studied it a while before lighting it. 'That woman we 'eard screaming was young

Joyce Downs.' He stopped and swallowed hard. 'It seems an oil bomb 'it the corner of Slater's shelter and she run out ter 'elp 'im and 'is sister, and . . . the oil . . . All that lovely 'air of 'ers caught light.' His voice was faltering. 'She was running down the road all alight.'

'Is she . . . ?' asked Granny Brent.

Pete nodded.

'What's these oil bombs then, son?'

'It seems these bombs are full of oil and when they explode all the burning oil goes everywhere.'

'What's 'e gonner fink of next, the wicked sod?' said Granny Brent, her voice full of hate. 'Poor Joyce. She was a lovely gel. What a dreadful way ter go,' she sniffed, and hurriedly blew her nose.

Sally felt her warm tears dropping on to her hands. All that was going through her mind was Joyce, poor Joyce. She couldn't speak.

Pete cleared his throat. 'We've bin 'elping round the back, 'elping ter git Mr Slater and 'is sister out—'

'Are they . . . ?' interrupted Granny Brent softly.

Again Pete only nodded.

'It's a bloody shame,' said Granny Brent, shaking her head.

They hadn't heard Vera and Babs come down the stairs. They were standing at the open door.

Babs suddenly burst out. 'What about Connie? Wot's 'appened to 'er?'

'Sit down love,' said her father. 'She's all right.'

Babs began laughing; it was a loud hysterical laugh that mixed with her tears. 'That's good, where is she?'

'She's in 'ospital.'

'But you said . . .'

'Let Dad finish, Babs,' said Sally.

'How many's gorn then, Stan?' asked Granny Brent, her voice trembling.

He took a deep breath. 'The Slaters, and young Joyce. The rest of the Downses are in 'ospital wiv cuts and burns and shock, and they took the Tanners as well, but I fink they're all right, but shocked, mind. We 'eard the old man's got a broken leg.'

'A lot of this is only what we've bin told,' said Pete.

'But I saw . . .' Sally couldn't finish the sentence.

'We do know who's bin killed, though.' Pete stopped, his voice dropped. 'We identified 'em.' His eyes were full of tears.

Granny Brent went to pat his hand, but he quickly drew them away.

'What's wrong, son? Show me yer 'ands.'

Like a small boy he sheepishly put his hands on the table, they were black and blistered.

'We was trying to put Joyce . . .' His voice broke, and his tears fell.

Sally rushed to his side and held him close.

'Oh my Gawd,' said his mother. 'Babs, go and git Johnny ter run up the Nag's fer some water. These 'ave got ter be bathed and some Germolene put on 'em. Show us yours Stan.'

He too did as he was told. The scars of this terrible night would not be forgotten for a long time.

Chapter 20

'Our place is in a bit of a state,' said Sally as they crossed the road.

'Don't worry, we'll soon git it right.' Her father tenderly put his bandaged hand on her shoulder.

'There's plenty round 'ere who'll give us an 'and if we can't manage,' said Pete.

Sally opened the front door. 'Be careful. I dunno what's really 'appened, just that Dad's bed's leg's 'anging through the kitchen ceiling.' She suddenly wanted to laugh at the situation.

'You kids wait 'ere while I go and 'ave a look,' said Stan, picking his way along the passage and pushing open the kitchen door.

Sally was almost expecting to hear a great crash, but it remained quiet. ''Ow did you two get in? We didn't 'alf 'ave a job opening the scullery door with so much stuff wedged behind it,' she said to Pete.

'That must o' come down after we left,' he said, following her father.

Sally could hear them talking but couldn't make out what they were saying as Johnny was busy telling her about his latest great find.

'A whole incendiary case. I don't reckon many of me

gang's got one o' these, not like this.' He lovingly stroked it. 'Me mate Tony's gonner be ever so jealous.'

'It's not still alive, is it?' asked Babs anxiously.

'Course not, daft. Look, yer can see where it's burnt frough.' He shoved the burnt-out shell under his sister's nose.

'Don't!' she yelled.

'Be quiet,' said Sally crossly. 'I'm trying to 'ear what Dad and Pete's saying.'

They both came along the passage towards her.

'Looks like a bit of the chimney's come frough the roof and finished up in the kitchen,' said her father. 'We was lucky, it must o' bin the incendiary what finished up in Billy's roof what 'it it.'

'I'm going up ter Wally ter see if 'e's got a ladder,' said Pete, 'so's I can make the tiles safe. Then we'll see about the bedroom floor. You kids better go over ter me mum's.'

Babs and Johnny turned to go.

'And don't git in the way, and don't worry 'em,' yelled their father after them.

'What can I do?' asked Sally.

'Just clear up this end. Don't go in the kitchen till we've made it safe,' said Pete, going out of the door.

All morning the banging and shouting went on in many of the houses in Sefton Grove, as broken tiles were thrown to the ground, glass was shovelled up and dumped in the road, and repairs were started. The fires had been put out and the fire engines left the street, and the great burnt-out hole that was once the Slaters' house. Mr Walters and Wally came and gave Pete and Stan a hand to fix the roof, and to pull the bed back up. That was accompanied by another fall of the kitchen ceiling, and Sally yelling at them to be careful. They then set about making the floor safe.

'Everyfink will 'ave ter be brought down,' said Sally's father.

'We can bring yer bed and bits of furniture into the front room,' said Sally. 'Good job all yer bedding's in the shelter otherwise it would 'ave got wet with the rain.'

'We'll put some boards over the hole in the ceiling so the rain don't come frough inter the kitchen,' said Pete.

'One good fing – the joist's still sound. So yer can still go up – but don't jump about, mind.' Her father grinned. 'Bloody turn up fer the book, ain't it? 'Ere, Sal, you should see yer face. It ain't 'alf dirty.'

'Yer don't look exactly clean and well dressed yerself.'

'I s'pose we'd better start on the kitchen,' said Pete. 'It's a bloody mess in there now.'

'I ain't dare open the door,' said Sally.

'There's a lot o' soot in there now, as well as the bricks from the chimney. Sal, go up the Nag's and git some more tea. This is thirsty work.'

'OK, Dad.'

When she returned with the tea the kitchen door was wide open and she could see her father and Pete standing looking at the floor.

'What is it? What's wrong?'

Pete stood to one side.

Sally gasped and fell to her knees. 'Is 'e . . .?'

''Fraid so, love,' said her father.

'What will Babs say? It'll be a terrible blow on top o' Connie's finishing up in hospital.'

'It was quick,' said Pete. ''E must 'ave 'ad an 'eart attack.'

'Poor old Tiger,' sniffed Sally. 'Babs'll go mad. 'E's nearly as old as 'er.'

'We'll wrap 'im up and see if we can bury 'im in the yard.'

'We'll 'ave ter tell 'er,' said Sally.

'Leave it till she comes back,' said Pete. 'No point in upsetting 'er any more.'

'No,' said Sally. 'She's still not convinced Connie's still alive.'

'We didn't say anyfink before, but old Bess 'as gorn as well,' said Stan.

'Oh no! She was a lovely dog.' Sally angrily swept her hand across the table, raising the dust as she brushed some of the debris on to the floor. 'It ain't fair.' She banged the dirt from a chair and plonked down on it. 'Bloody war.'

Pete put his arm round her heaving shoulders. 'Come on, love. Yer a bit upset, that's all. Yer bin frough a lot terday.'

She shrugged his arm away. 'That's it. Babs and Johnny's going away.' She looked up at Pete. 'Can't *we* go away? Can't we get away from all this?'

'Where would we go love?'

'I dunno.'

'What about me mum and Vera? I couldn't leave 'em.'

Sally didn't answer.

''Sides, what would we live on? And if I leave the docks I'll git called up – and where would we go?' Pete asked again.

Sally looked across at her father. 'Would yer come with me, Dad?'

'I wouldn't wonner leave 'ere, love. This 'as bin me and yer mother's 'ome all the while we've bin married.'

Sally stood up. 'How can yer call this 'ome, this bloody great pile of rubbish. Look at it.' She waved her arms round the sad-looking kitchen. 'Good job Mum's not 'ere. She'd go mad at all this mess.' Tears ran down her face. 'Can't even see the hearth fer bloody soot,' she sobbed.

'I know, love, but I ain't letting no bumped-up little paper 'anger send me orf wiv me tail between me legs, no, I'm gonner stay, but I fink yer right about the kids, though,' said her father. 'I'll find out if they can be evacuated again.'

Sally looked at Pete's sad face. Deep down she knew she couldn't really leave. This was her home.

'Come on, Sal, let's git started,' said Pete.

'What's the point? We could all be dead by morning.'

'Now come on, gel, we mustn't talk like that,' said her father. 'Remember, where there's life, there's 'ope.'

Sally gave him a weak smile, at the moment she didn't have a lot of hope. She gathered up the tablecloth. 'I'll wash this out,' she said, reluctantly walking into the scullery. Then: 'Sod it, sod it, sod it!' she shouted.

Pete and her father came rushing after her together.

'What is it?' asked Pete, his face full of anguish.

'I forgot. We ain't got no water.'

Pete laughed. 'Sorry, Sal, but it's funny ter 'ear yer leading off like.'

'Well, I don't think it's very funny.'

'Come on, love,' said her father, grinning. 'You ain't gonner let a little fing like this git yer down, now are yer?'

Sally half smiled back. 'No. I s'pose not.'

'That's me gel.'

All day they worked clearing up, the dust, dirt and soot getting down their throats and clogging their nostrils. Granny Brent had sent Vera over with some food, and

Wally brought in a couple of bottles of beer. The afternoon was drawing to a close when Sally said it was time for Babs and Johnny to come back and get ready to go in the shelter.

Johnny returned, full of his latest finds, while Babs was wearing a new jumper and scarf.

'That's nice,' said Sally.

'Yeah, Vera give it to me.' She held out her hands. 'Look, she let me paint me nails!'

'She's lucky she's still got some nail varnish left. Dad's got somethink ter tell yer, so sit yerselves down.' Sally looked away, she couldn't face them.

They both had a puzzled look on their faces.

'I'm gonner send yer away, yer gonner be evacuated again.'

Babs stood up. 'Well, I ain't going. I'm gonner start work soon.'

'Sit down,' shouted her father. 'And if I say yer going yer going, and that's that.'

'No I ain't, and yer can't make me.' Babs walked over to the kitchen door.

'Oh yes I can, young lady.'

'Well then, I'd run away.' Babs slammed the door as she stomped out of the room.

'Don't slam the door,' shouted her father after her. 'And come back 'ere, yer little cow.'

The room was filled with apprehension, nobody spoke, then Johnny said quietly. 'If Babs ain't going, nor am I.'

Stan came to stand in front of Johnny. 'And I say you are—'

'I ain't, I ain't. I ain't gonner miss the war. What if yer all got killed. I ain't going and you can't make me – so there,' he cried, his voice high and quavering.

Sally couldn't believe what she was hearing, Johnny never answered his father back.

'What did you say, son?'

Sally cringed, silently begging him to apologise.

'I ain't going away. I'll run away like Babs said. Then yer'll be sorry.'

'Don't yer talk ter me like that.' His father's voice was rising. 'Don't yer dare answer me back.' He raised his dirty bandaged hand and hit Johnny round the head.

Johnny stood motionless. His eyes filled with tears and very slowly they ran down his cheek and fell on to the floor. Sally was speechless, she knew her eyes were wide open. Pete left the table and walked into the scullery.

'I know you don't love me,' sobbed Johnny. He ran to Sally and buried his head in her jumper.

Stan sat down, his face pale. With trembling, fumbling hands he took his tobacco tin from his jacket pocket.

'So yer don't fink I love yer,' he whispered. 'All I want is fer you three ter 'ave a life, a good life, not spend it trapped round 'ere, never knowing if . . .' His voice trailed off.

Sally didn't know what to say. She had never known her father hit any of them. Suddenly, he began pulling the bandages off his hand, wincing as he did so.

'Dad, don't,' said Sally, gently pushing Johnny to one side.

'I can't roll a bloody fag wiv this lot on me fingers,' he said angrily.

'Pete, Pete,' she called out. 'Give Dad a fag. Johnny, go and tell Babs to come back 'ere. We might as well get all the bad things over at once.'

Johnny looked surprised. 'What bad fings?'

'Just go and get Babs.'

Babs was in the room almost at once. Her face pale, and her eyes red through crying. 'What other bad fing yer got ter tell me? Is it Connie?'

Sally sat at the table and shook her head. 'It's Tiger.'

'Tiger? Where is 'e? Tiger,' she called, looking round the wrecked room.

'I'm sorry, Babs,' said Pete.

Her big brown eyes opened wide. They filled with tears. 'Is 'e . . . ?'

Sally nodded.

'What yer done wiv 'im?'

'Would yer like us to bury 'im in the yard?' asked Pete.

'Is 'e all squashed?' asked Johnny, intrigued, and quickly forgetting his anger.

'No, I fink 'e musta died o' fright. D'yer wonner see 'im?' asked Pete.

Babs nodded. ''E's not all, nasty – is 'e?' she sniffed.

'No. 'E's out back.'

Ceremoniously they all trooped out into the yard. There wrapped in a cloth was Tiger.

'E's all stiff,' said Johnny.

'So would you be if yer been dead fer hours,' said Pete.

Babs crouched down and gently stroked his back. 'I loved yer, Tiger,' she whispered. 'I'll make yer a cross and come and see yer every day.' She looked up at her father. 'I ain't ever gonner leave 'im yer know.'

Without answering, Stan turned and walked away.

'Pete'll see to Tiger,' said Sally, watching her father. 'I won't be long.'

She found him sitting in his armchair, his face buried in his hands, and she knew by his heaving shoulders he was quietly weeping.

'Dad.' She knelt down and threw her arms round his neck. His warm tears fell on to her face. 'Dad, don't.'

He put his arm round her shoulders. 'Sorry, love,' he croaked. 'I only want what's best fer the kids.'

'Course yer do.'

'I didn't mean ter 'it Johnny.'

'I know yer didn't. We're all a bit upset, we've bin through a lot terday. Wait till termorrer, then I'll 'ave a quiet word with 'em. P'raps I can make 'em see sense.'

'That's if we 'ave a termorrer.' He wiped his eyes.

'Don't say things like that. Let's 'ope the New Year brings us somethink better. Come on, we'll get this little ceremony over.'

They went into the yard in time to see Babs put a piece of wood into a small mound of earth.

'Don't worry, Tiger. I'll make yer a proper cross later,' she said to the ground.

During the following week, although the raids continued, Sefton Grove was spared. To avoid any more arguments, Sally and her father gave up the idea of sending Babs and Johnny away for the moment.

The Tanners' house had been badly damaged and they moved further up the Grove into an empty one. Everybody helped with the moving, and it was the talk of the Grove.

'Fank Gawd the bugs and fleas 'ad left,' laughed Wally that evening when most of the Grove assembled in the Nag's. 'Me missis made me fumigate meself when I got in.'

'Under all that muck yer couldn't see what was old rubbish and what was new,' said Pete.

'It was the rats I was worried about. Can't stand rats,' said Mr Walters.

''Er old man's a crafty sod,' said Stan. 'Did yer see 'im sitting on 'is arse giving 'er orders.'

'Oh Dad, be fair. 'E 'as got a broken leg,' laughed Sally. 'It was Sadie going on about that 'at that made me laugh. She thought someone 'ad pinched it. I ask yer, who'd pinch a thing like that?'

'D'yer know she wanted ter take a bunch o' dead flowers with 'er?' said Pete.

'No,' said Granny Brent. 'Silly cow.'

'Mind you,' said Pete, 'I was a bit surprised at some o' the very nice bits they've got in there.'

'Yeah, it makes yer wonder what poor sod they pinched it orf,' said Mr Walters.

'Well, yer 'as ter make sure everyfink's screwed down when young Tommy brings yer in somefink,' said Wally.

At the end of the week the funerals of Joyce Downs and the Slaters took place. They were very sad affairs. The Slaters' was first and Florrie in the grocer's had seen to their arrangements. Fred looked smart in his warden's uniform, but Sally could see his eyes were clouded with tears. As the cortege walked slowly past the shell of the Slaters' house, everyone knew the ruin would be a constant reminder of that dreadful night, and the dear friends they had all lost.

Jessie was still crying on the way back from the church. 'How many more?'

'It ain't over yet,' said Sally, holding her arm. 'We've got Joyce's tomorrer. You thought any more about going away?'

'No, I ain't got nowhere ter go. 'Sides, I don't wonner leave Mum, but I gotter fink about the kids. Sal, I dunno what ter do,' she sobbed. 'I fink I'd better write ter me old man and tell 'im what's 'appened, just in case. I'd 'ate for the kids ter be left on their own.'

Sally patted her friend's hand. She couldn't think of any comforting words.

Mr and Mrs Downs had been allowed out of hospital for Joyce's funeral. They were suffering from burns and shock. A friend of Mrs Downs who lived in the next road had seen to all the arrangements. Connie was too ill to leave the hospital and Babs was very upset. She hung on to Sally's arm and cried continually.

'Why can't I go and see Connie?' pleaded Babs.

Sally swallowed hard. Mrs Downs had told her Connie wasn't to have visitors, and she was in a bad way. 'You know they ain't coming back ter Sefton,' Sally told Babs after the funeral. 'They're going to a farm in Devon, near where Doreen works. She's trying to find 'em an 'ouse.'

'I ain't 'alf gonner miss Connie, she was me best mate,' Babs sobbed.

'I know.'

'Still, she's still alive, that's the important thing,' she said bravely. 'I expect she'll write to me soon, then perhaps one day I can go and visit 'er.'

Sally gave Babs gave a weak smile. 'That'll be nice.'

But it wasn't to be. A week later Connie died from her injuries. Babs was in a state of shock, and couldn't be consoled, walking about in a daze all day. First Mum, now Connie, thought Sally. It was more than a child of her age should have to face.

[illegible]

[illegible] because [illegible] there [illegible].

[illegible]

[illegible] together.

'Good.'

[illegible]

[illegible]

Chapter 21

Although the raids continued every night they weren't as ferocious as on that terrible night, and everybody in Sefton Grove was convinced they'd had their share of tragedy.

The following week Sally was pleased when Babs had a letter telling her she had got the job she'd been after. It was in a small, family-run dress shop, and they wanted her to start right away. Since Connie's death Babs had looked miserable and Sally noticed she wasn't eating properly. She hoped going to work would help her little sister take her mind off losing Connie.

'You'll have to cheer up you know, you can't carry on like this in the shop,' said Sally gently after reading the letter. 'Try and buck up, love. I know it ain't easy for you, but life 'as to go on.'

Babs smiled. 'I'll try. But I dunno what I'm gonner do without Connie to talk to.'

'Pr'aps you'll find someone at work.'

'There's only Mr Silverman and 'is daughter.'

Sally felt very apprehensive for Babs when she watched her leave for her first day at work, and she thought about her all day. But she needn't have worried. That evening Babs was full of it, and thrilled at working with clothes, and with Rachel, the shop-owner's daughter.

Babs' cheering up made Sally feel more relaxed, and now that some of the schools were open, Johnny was happy with his mates. To them the war was the most exciting thing to have happened to them, and they seemed to spend all their spare time scrabbling about on bomb sites. Any hopes Sally and her father had had about sending him away were now quashed.

Just two weeks after the funerals, Reg and Danny came home on embarkation leave. They were greeted with lots of hugs, kisses and handshakes. They looked well and much fitter this time, and seemed to have lost the pallor most Londoners had. They even appeared taller.

'Look at yer 'air,' yelled Reg's mother. 'Looks like they got the shears ter that lot.'

Reg grinned and ran his fingers through his short dark hair which now stuck up like a brush.

'Mind you, yer look very nice the pair o' yer in yer uniforms.' Granny Brent smiled, her face flushed with pride. 'Pity our Lena ain't 'ere.' She dabbed at her eyes.

'Looks like all that fresh air and square-bashing suits yer,' said Pete.

Danny was admiring Gwen's size, continually patting her large stomach. 'I can't believe I might be 'ere when 'e's born.'

'How long leave yer got then?' asked Sally.

'Only a week.'

'Looks like yer'll 'ave ter git a move on then, gel,' said Granny Brent, giving Gwen a nudge.

'Where d'yer think you'll be sent to then, Reg?' asked Pete.

'We reckon it could be somewhere warm from the kit we've been issued wiv.'

Danny laughed. 'But knowing the army we could finish up in the arctic.'

'Get bloody cold knees if we do,' said Reg.

'Shh,' laughed Sally putting her finger to her lips. 'Remember what the posters say. Careless talk costs lives.'

Granny Brent grinned and tutted.

'How's Lena, mum?' asked Reg.

'She's all right, up north somewhere. You know Lena, she don't write that often.'

'Ain't she 'ad any leave yet?'

'Dunno. If she 'as she ain't come 'ome for it.' Granny Brent looked angry.

'How's that bloke of yours, Vera?' asked Danny.

Granny Brent pulled a face at him behind Vera's back.

'Dunno. 'E don't write ser often now. 'E said 'e'd be 'ome at Christmas but 'e didn't turn up,' Vera replied quietly.

'Well, there is a war on yer know, and we can't do as we like.'

'No, I know.' With that Vera left the room.

Granny Brent looked towards the closed door, and said in a low voice, 'Wouldn't be surprised if 'e ain't got anovver gel.'

'Why? What makes you say that?' asked Sally.

'Dunno. Just feels it in me water.'

'And we all know about your water, Ma,' laughed Pete.

Reg said solemnly. 'Looks like yer've had it bad round 'ere. Slaters' 'ouse is in a bit of a mess, what's left of it. Is the old boy all right?'

Pete shook his head. 'They got the Slaters, and Joyce and Connie Downs.'

'Joyce Downs?' repeated Reg. 'Fought you said she was in the army, Ma?'

'She was,' said Sally. 'But she was 'ome on leave then.'

'Yeah. It was very sad,' said Granny Brent.

'Always 'ad a bit of a soft spot fer Joyce. Bloody shame.' Reg stood up and took his packet of cigarettes off the mantelpiece. 'I should 'ave dropped 'er a line.'

'That wouldn't 'ave saved 'er,' said his mother.

'No, I know.' Reg lit his cigarette and blew the smoke high in the air. He tapped the end of his cigarette into the ash tray. 'Silly Billy's place is in a bit o' a mess. They all right?'

'Yeah. Been taken ter some place in the country so Wally was saying,' said Pete.

'Glad ter see the Nag's still standing,' Reg said, quickly changing the subject. 'What say we all go up there this evening?'

'Only for a little while then, Reg, just in case the sirens go,' said his mother.

'Don't worry, Ma.' He kissed her cheek. 'I'm 'ere ter protect yer now.'

'Old Wally's 'aving a bit of a job keeping the beer flowing, though,' said Pete. 'Can't get the deliveries. It's you blokes in the army what's supping it all.'

Reg laughed. 'Gotter make the most of it. Dunno where we're gonner finish up – could be dry.'

'Mind you, I'm sure that Wally waters 'is beer down,' said Granny Brent.

'What makes yer say that, ma?'

'Well, when we ain't got any water, 'e's always got bottles full.' She sniffed and straightened her shoulders. 'So it makes yer fink, don't it?'

Reg laughed. 'Well I'll let yer know later.'

It was early evening when Reg and Danny walked in the Nag's, and after all the back slapping and handshakes the pub was soon ringing with the sound of Reg thumping away on the piano. All the pints he'd been bought were jumping up and down on top of the piano. He drank the top off each first, 'Just in case I spills any,' he said cheerfully.

The Tanners, Mr Tanner with his leg in plaster, were in their favourite corner and they lustily joined in the singsong.

Sally, sitting next to Vera, bent her head closer to make herself heard. 'What's up, Vera? Yer don't look very 'appy.'

'I'm giving up me job.'

'What?'

'Shh, keep yer voice down.'

'What yer gonner do?'

'I wanted ter go in the forces, but you know Ma – we've 'ad some terrible rows over it. But I feel I wonner do me bit, Sal.'

'But yer do in the factory.'

'It ain't the same, and I s'pose I'm not like Lena, I can't just go orf and leave Ma.'

'Yer will if they make it compulsory.'

'That's what I told 'er. Anyway I've decided ter go on the buses.'

Sally laughed. 'I'm sorry, Vera, but I can just see you running up and down the stairs yelling, "Fares, please."'

A broad grin slowly spread across Vera's sad face. 'Yeah, it could be quite a laugh, and Gawd knows I could do wiv a few of 'em.'

Reg burst out with a knees-up, and they all jumped to their feet.

'You all right, Gwen?' asked Granny Brent when Gwen jumped up.

She laughed. 'Yeah, I better 'ave a dance. It might make 'im git a move on.' She pointed to her large stomach.

Danny looked worried as he held on to her arm. 'D'yer fink yer should be doing this?'

'Yeah, it might like doing a knees-up.'

Everybody was laughing and singing. It was a far cry from a fortnight ago when they'd sat in here drinking tea, and Sally couldn't believe how completely the atmosphere could change.

'Look, why don't we git a few bottles and take 'em under the arches ternight?' Reg said to Pete as he closed the piano lid. 'Yer don't 'ave ter go ter work termorrer – do yer?'

'No, but . . . What about you, Pop?' Pete asked his father-in-law.

'I couldn't leave the kids.'

'Bring 'em along,' said Reg.

'Na, fanks all the same, but I try ter get all the sleep I can these days.'

Pete looked at Sally. 'What about you, love?'

'I can't leave . . .'

'Go on, gel. Don't worry about me,' said her father. 'You go orf and enjoy yerself. 'Sides, yer deserve a break.'

'That's settled then. Wally, let's 'ave a few bottles ter take away,' said Reg.

'Yer sure yer don't mind?' Sally asked her father quietly as they shuffled through the door, noticing again how tired and old he looked.

'Course not. I fink yer better be making a move,' he said, looking up at the night sky. ''E could be over soon.'

It was almost as soon as they settled themselves under the arches that the siren started. Sally looked around, amazed at how cosy the people had made it. There were beds, tables and chairs. She could see why a lot of people preferred it to being shut up in a poky shelter. Sally remembered Vera had told her they were trying to get hold of a piano and she could imagine what fun it would be here then. Suddenly she was filled with guilt. What if anything happened to her dad and the kids tonight? She wanted to run home now. She didn't want any of them to be separated. Pete was talking to Reg, but she had to tell him how she felt. She had to go home.

''Allo, Sal. Ain't seen you up 'ere before.'

Sally looked up surprised. It was Tommy Tanner. 'Do you and yer mum come up 'ere then?' she asked.

'Na, only me. They've got a card school going every Sat'day night in next door, and I always fancied meself as a card sharp.' He ran his fingers over his slicked-down hair. 'Yer managing all right then?'

'Yes, thanks.'

'Well, don't forgit if yer ever short of anyfink, just give us a shout.' He looked about him sheepishly. 'I can usually git me 'ands on most fings.'

'I won't forget,' said Sally, her thoughts still on her dad.

She confessed her fears to Pete but he only told her to settle down and stop worrying. Then he announced that he was going next door with Reg to the card school.

Sally was angry. Pete had wanted her to come here and now he'd left her. She sat talking to Vera and Granny Brent till they decided to settle down and try to get some sleep.

Danny and Gwen sat in the corner and Sally envied the way they held hands and cuddled. If only Pete was romantic like his brother . . .

Gradually her lids became heavy and she drifted off into a light sleep. She was dreaming of dancing on a big liner. A handsome man was asking her to go for a walk. He held her in his arms and was kissing her . . .

'Sal, Sal!' Someone was shouting at her. She opened her eyes. Danny was standing over her, shaking her.

'What is it? What's 'appened?' She was disorientated. She could see Granny Brent and Vera huddled together in the corner and hear the loud crack of the guns as they ran along the railway track above them, firing at the enemy planes.

'Sal, d'yer fink yer could go next door and git Pete?' Danny looked pale and worried. 'It's Gwen, she's started.'

'Oh no.' She looked surprised. 'But what can Pete do?'

''E still got 'is car 'ere, ain't 'e?'

'Yes, but I don't think 'e's got any petrol.'

''E must 'ave a drop. We want 'im ter run Gwen ter the 'ospital.'

''E can't do that, not in an air raid. Can't we phone for an ambulance?'

'Don't fink they'll come even if we could find a phone that works, and Ma reckons Gwen should be in 'ospital. She reckons there could be complications.' Tears welled up in Danny's eyes.

Gwen's muffled groans came from the corner.

Danny looked round anxiously. 'I've got ter get back to 'er. Please, Sal, see what yer can do.'

Sally looked bewildered. She would have to go outside. Pete was only next door, but there was a raid on. She knew

Pete had some petrol, but was it enough? And where could he get any from at this time of night? And did she want him to drive to the hospital in an air raid?

'Sal, fer Christ's sake git next door and git Pete.' Granny Brent's voice was loud and angry.

Vera came over. 'Mum's very worried about 'er,' she said. 'She's losing a lot of blood.'

Sally quickly pulled on her shoes and coat. Why did Gwen have to have her baby now? She shouldn't have done that dancing. Sally fought and fumbled her way through the blackout curtain and door, and was suddenly outside. She stood looking up at the sky for a few moments, mesmerised. Searchlights swept back and forth, catching in their beams the large silver barrage balloons, serene and elegant as they slowly and gracefully turned in the breeze.

The noise from the guns, and flashes of bright light as they let off their salvos were quickly followed by loud bursts of exploding shells. Sally had never been outside in a raid before. It was fascinating, if it wasn't so frightening, almost like a giant firework display.

She quickly made her way along to the next arch and banged on the door with her fists. What if they were all asleep? Would she be able to make anyone hear? She banged again, much louder this time, and called Pete's name. At last the door was opened.

Pete dragged her inside. 'Christ, Sal, what yer doing out there at this time a night?'

Before she could answer the men sitting round the table laughed and swigged down their drink.

''Allo, Sal. We fought yer was the police,' said Tommy Tanner. 'We couldn't git the table cleared away quick enough.'

Reg wiped the beer froth from his mouth with the back of his hand and laughed. 'That'll be a right turn up fer the books if I'd got nicked fer gambling just 'fore they sent me overseas.'

'Pete, yer gotter come next door,' gasped Sally. 'It's Gwen, she's started.'

'So, what d'yer want me ter do, 'old 'er 'and?' he laughed and looked round for support. 'It ain't nuffink ter do wiv me.'

'That's what she's got an old man fer,' said Reg. ''E started it, so let 'im finish it. 'Sides, Ma's in there.'

They all laughed.

'I'm just going out ter 'ave a jimmy,' said Tommy Tanner, gathering up his cards, 'and I'm taking these wiv me, so yer can't look at 'em.'

'Just ser long as yer don't piddle all over 'em and make 'em stick tergevver,' shouted a red-faced man Sally didn't know.

Sally was getting angry. How could she make this pathetic lot of drunks see sense? 'Pete, listen to me.' Her voice was serious. 'Danny wants yer ter take Gwen to the 'ospital in yer car.'

'What? I ain't gitting the car out in a raid. What if me little Betsy gits damaged?'

'Pete,' yelled Sally, 'stop being so bloody stupid and come next door.'

He straightened up.

'The little lady's gitting a bit mad, Pete me boy,' said Reg. 'Better do as she says.'

'And you'd better come along as well,' shouted Sally.

'Me? What can I do?'

'You can look after yer mother and brother.'

Tommy Tanner came back. 'We gonner carry on then? I'm on a winning streak ternight,' he said to Sally.

'Sorry, mate,' said Pete. 'Looks like we've got ter be off.'

'Duty calls,' said Reg, standing up and adjusting his forage cap.

Tommy threw his cards on the table. 'I knew it. I bloody well knew it. Fanks a bunch, Sal. I'll remember this when yer wants sumfink,' he said angrily.

'About time too,' said Granny Brent, when they got back. 'Where's the car?'

'Pete's just gorn ter git it,' said Reg. 'Is she all right?' He looked across at the small gathering in the corner.

'No she ain't.'

'Is there anyfink . . . ?'

'Give Danny a drop o' this brandy.' Granny Brent thrust a small bottle into Reg's hand. 'And you can keep yer eyes orf it. I keeps it fer emergencies.'

'I'll go with Danny and Gwen if yer like,' said Sally to Granny Brent.

'Better not, love, just in case sumfink 'appens ter yer. I wouldn't be able ter face yer dad then.'

Sally wanted to shout at her, 'But what about Pete?' But she knew it was no use arguing with Granny Brent. Her word was always law.

Chapter 22

Sally slowly opened her eyes. She could hear people bustling all around her. Quickly she sat up.

‘’Allo, love. All right then?’ Pete was sitting next to her.

‘Pete, you’re back. Why didn’t yer wake me?’

‘Ain’t bin back that long.’ He smiled. ‘’Sides, yer was sleeping like a baby so I didn’t like ter wake yer.’

‘Is Gwen . . .’

‘She’s in safe ’ands. Danny’s still wiv ’er. ’Ere’s Vera with a cuppa fer yer.’

‘Thanks, Vera. Is the raid over?’ she asked, getting to her feet.

‘Bin over quite a while now,’ said Pete. ‘The all clear went just after we got ter the ’ospital. Mind you, it didn’t ’alf take us a time ter git there wiv all the diversions. I was dead worried she was gonner ’ave it in me car.’

Sally held the cup to her lips. ‘I hope Gwen’s gonner be all right,’ she whispered.

‘Course she is,’ Pete smiled. ‘Remember she’s a Brent now, so that makes ’er tough.’

Sally smiled back at him. ‘It’s nice Danny’s ’ome ter see the baby.’

'Yeah.'

They said their goodbyes to everyone under the arches and walked slowly home.

'Sorry about last night, Sal.'

'That's all right.'

'Na, I shouldn't 'ave left yer.' They stood at the top of Sefton, and he put his arm fondly round her waist.

'Well, everythink's still 'ere,' Sally said with relief in her voice. 'I was dead worried about Dad and the kids.'

'I know yer was. Saw some pretty rotten fings at that 'ospital last night. I fink it frightened Danny. 'E was saying they ain't 'ad any raids where they've been, and 'e's worried about leaving Gwen and the baby.'

'Will 'e try and get 'em away?'

''E ain't got a lot o' time. 'Sides, I don't fink she'll go.'

'We've all got ter try and stick it out. It can't last for ever. Ain't 'e worried about yer mum?'

'Course, but let's face it, yer wife's different, she means . . . Well she's different, that's all.'

Sally smiled up at him. This was Pete's way of being romantic. 'Funny them not 'aving any raids. No wonder Lena don't want ter come down 'ere if she's 'ad any leave. Yer mum's getting very annoyed with 'er.'

'Yeah, I know, but I told 'er, Lena can't do what she likes, not now.'

'Pete, you don't think she's got a feller up there do yer, and she won't let on?'

'Dunno. Why d'yer say that?'

'It's funny she's not been 'ome. I would 'ave thought she couldn't wait to show off 'er uniform, and 'er new bloke if she 'ad one; after all, you know Lena.'

'Yeah, we all know Lena.'

Sally knew from his tone that he wasn't interested. They walked on together in silence.

That afternoon, Sally was over the Brents', telling Vera about Babs' job.

'She loves it, she's working for this Jewish bloke. 'Is daughter works in the shop as well. She's a bit older than Babs, and from what I can gather she's a bit of a girl, but they get on all right, and 'ave lots of laughs. She was telling me the shop ain't got any windows, so ter get people in 'e's painted great big red arrows on the wooden boards telling people ter follow 'em fer a surprise. When they gets 'em inside, well, yer know 'ow they try ter sell yer things, and Babs said it nearly always works. She's amazed at the stock 'e can get 'old of, so don't forget, if yer want a new frock or coat see Babs about it.'

'I expect most o' the time I'll be in me uniform.'

'D'yer think yer gonner like the job?'

'Yeah. Wish I'd done it monfs ago.'

It was late in the afternoon when Danny came bursting into the house shouting that Gwen had had a baby girl.

He stood in the passage bursting with pride. 'Yer should see 'er. She's lovely. Got lots o' black 'air and blue eyes.'

'What's all the bloody noise going on down 'ere, I'm trying ter—' Granny Brent reached the bottom stair and Danny grabbed her and twirled her round.

'I'm a dad! I'm a dad!'

'Silly sod,' she gasped. 'Put me down.'

Pete and Reg, who'd been salvaging type from what was left of the shed in the yard, walked into the kitchen wiping their hands.

'What's going on?' asked Pete.

'I'm a dad,' grinned Danny rushing up to hug his two brothers.

The house was ringing with laughter.

'You really are Granny Brent now,' said Sally.

'So I am.' A beaming smile filled her round face. 'Is Gwen all right?' she asked.

'Yeah. Mum, just yer wait till yer see this baby – 'er tiny toes and fingers. She's perfect.'

Pete grinned when Reg said, ''Ark at 'im. Always said 'e was the daft one in the family.'

'When can we go and see 'er?' asked Vera.

'In the afternoons. She'll be in fer nine days.'

'Nine days? Yer knows that'll cost yer? Hummh, when I 'ad my lot I was lucky if I could stay in bed fer the rest of the day.'

'Yeah, well fings is different now, Ma.'

'Looks like we'll 'ave ter wet the baby's 'ead ternight then, don't it?' said Reg.

'I should say so,' agreed Pete. 'You going up the 'ospital ternight, Dan?'

'No, they like ter git 'em settled in the shelter 'fore the raids.'

'And I like ter be in the shelter 'fore the raids an all,' said Sally, giving Pete one of her looks.

There were many tears as Reg and Danny said goodbye at the end of their leave. As Sally held them both tight, she knew everyone's thoughts were the same as hers. The only bright spot in those dark weeks was Gwen's baby, Dorothy. Everything about her was to be recorded in a notebook for Danny.

Sally was telling Florrie in the grocer's about the small christening party they were going to have for Dorothy when Sadie Tanner walked in.

Outside, Sadie took Sally to one side, and said quietly, 'Yer don't 'ave ter worry too much about saving yer rations fer yer christening party. Yer knows Tommy and me old man can git 'old o' most fings.'

'Don't yer worry about 'em getting caught?' asked Sally.

'Na. Most o' the coppers round 'ere 'ave bits and pieces orf 'em anyway.'

When Sally got home she could see Jessie hanging out her washing in the yard, and she went out to tell her what Sadie had said.

Jessie looked agitated, and didn't seem very interested in what Sally was talking about. She glanced over her shoulder at the house and came closer to Sally. 'I've 'ad another letter from Vic. 'E want's me ter take the kids ter see 'im.'

'Where is 'e?'

'In the country. 'E's worried about the bombing and the kids, and 'e reckons I should move near 'im.'

Sally laughed. 'What? After all the grief 'e's caused you in the past? What's yer mum got ter say about it?'

Jessie quickly glanced at the house. 'Keep yer voice down. I ain't told 'er. I was finking of going ter see 'im and then p'raps I could make up me mind then.'

''Ow yer gonner do that without yer mum knowing?'

'Dunno.'

Sally was getting cross with Jessie. 'You've been on about this fer months. Why don't yer just tell yer mum yer going and leave it at that? 'Sides, why's 'e ser keen on seeing you and the kids again after all this time?'

'From what I can gather, sumfink 'appened ter one of 'is mates' family and I fink 'e feels guilty about us.'

'Well, I'd go and find out all I can. Ain't no point staying 'ere if 'e can find yer a nice 'ouse.'

'I've still got Mum and Dad ter worry about.'

'Yeah,' said Sally wistfully, 's'pose yer 'ave.' Although she was fed up with hearing about Jessie's problem, she knew Jessie only had her to tell her troubles to. Still, it made her cheerless company and Sally was more likely to seek out Vera for a chat these days.

Vera was now working on the buses, and loving every moment of it. She often told her family about the bombing and diversions they had to take. Some of the drivers didn't know where they were, and one got into a lot of trouble when his bus got stuck under a railway arch. The girl passengers would fall asleep on their way to work, having been up most of the night fire watching through the raids, though they still had to go to work next day. After a while, when Vera got to know them, she would wake them when they got to their stops. She got very upset when any of her regulars didn't turn up, wondering if they were alive or dead.

It was March when Gwen came running breathlessly across to Sally and Pete. 'Yer better come over quick,' she said. 'Yer mum's 'ad some bad news.'

Sally put her hand to her mouth and gasped. 'It ain't Reg, is it?'

Everyone lived in fear of the telegram boy cycling up to their door.

'No, it's Lena.'

'Lena?' cried Pete, as they ran across the road.

Gwen pushed open the door and Granny Brent rushed towards Pete, her eyes blazing with anger.

'Mum, what's up, I thought Gwen—'

'The bloody cow's gonner git married at Easter and she's 'ad the bloody cheek ter ask us all to it,' she raged, waving the letter under Pete's nose. 'Well, I ain't gonner allow it.'

'Now calm down, Ma. When? Who to?'

'Yer better read the letter, Pete,' said Gwen.

When Pete finished the short letter he handed it to Sally. 'Crafty sods,' he said. 'Where's Vera?'

'Upstairs.'

He raced up them two at a time.

'I don't believe it,' said Sally. 'Vera's Roy and Lena, 'er own twin sister, carrying on tergether all this time. Poor Vera. How's she taking it?'

'Broken 'earted, ain't she? I'll kill that Lena, and 'im if they ever 'ave the gall ter come back 'ere.' Granny Brent's face was full of fury.

'Fancy 'im not writing and telling Vera 'e'd met Lena.' Sally sat at the table. 'Or Lena saying she's met 'im.'

'I reckon that's why they didn't come 'ere at Christmas. They must o' bin swanning around tergevver,' Gwen said.

'D'yer think there was somethink between 'em 'fore they got posted together?' asked Sally.

'Dunno,' said Gwen.

'Wait till Danny and Reg 'ear about this. They'll soon sort 'im out – and 'er,' said Granny Brent. 'I'll put the kettle on.' She waddled out into the scullery.

Gwen leant forward and whispered to Sally, 'I ain't gonner tell Danny. I don't want 'im upset. 'E's got enough on 'is plate what wiv the war, me and the baby.'

'I won't let Pete tell Reg – not that 'e writes to 'im that much – but we can't stop Ma from telling 'em,' said Sally.

'I'll take Vera and Pete up a cuppa if yer like, Ma,' said Gwen when the tea was brewed.

'All right, love.' Granny Brent sat at the table. 'Always knew that Lena would bring me 'eartache one day.' She blew her nose. 'Good job two of me boys found good gels. I only 'ope Vera gits over this.'

Sally swallowed hard. 'Poor Vera,' she said out loud.

Jessie was very sympathetic over what had happened to Vera. She told Sally she was going to meet her husband in the West End at the end of the month as he'd got some leave. Sally was glad she'd made up her mind to do something positive at last. The heavy raids on London continued, and everybody was hoping the spring would bring them some respite, although the nights in the shelters had become such a part of their lives that Sally's family happily played cards as the bombs fell around them now.

'Glad it ain't my turn fer fire watching ternight,' said her father one weekend. He coughed, and Sally was aware he'd been having difficulty breathing lately, although he said it was just a cold.

'I don't like it when I 'ave ter go out,' said Sally.

'Yer don't 'alf look funny in that tin 'at, Sal,' said Johnny. 'It looks like a pimple on a pie crust.'

'Well, yer wouldn't catch me wearing it or going out if I didn't 'ave to.'

'I fink it's all wrong making young women stand around looking ter see if a fire's started,' said her father.

'I fink some of 'em are 'aving a good time from what I've 'eard goes on down the wardens' posts.' Pete grinned.

'I can tell yer, nothink like that goes on at our place. 'Sides, they're all too old fer me,' laughed Sally.

'When I'm eighteen will I be able ter do fire watching?' asked Babs.

'Christ, I 'ope this lot's all over by then,' said Pete.

'Mr Silverman said the Germans do terrible fings ter the Jews, and 'e'll kill 'imself and 'is wife and Rachel if they ever got 'ere.'

'What does Rachel 'ave ter say about that?' asked Sally.

'She agrees with 'er dad.'

'Well, let's 'ope they don't git 'ere then,' laughed Pete, 'ovverwise you'll be out of a job.'

'Oh you,' said Babs indignantly. 'That ain't a nice fing ter say.'

Sally smiled at her sister. Babs thought her boss, Mr Silverman, and his daughter were wonderful.

Long after they'd settled down, Sally lay awake listening. Her father's breathing didn't sound right. Gradually, her eyes closed.

Sally woke with a start. She wasn't sure how long she'd slept but now her father was making funny noises. 'Pete, Pete,' she whispered, shaking him. 'What's wrong with Dad?'

Pete rolled over. 'Christ,' he said, quickly sitting up. 'Pop. Pop.' He shook him, but to no effect.

Sally hastily climbed over Pete and was at her father's side. 'Dad!' She tried to wake him, her tears falling. 'Pete, what's wrong with 'im?'

'Dunno, love. 'E's gone a terrible colour.'

'What's the matter?' asked Babs sleepily.

'It's yer dad,' said Pete.

Johnny jumped down from his bunk. 'What's wrong wiv 'im?'

'We don't know,' said Sally irritably.

'Is 'e—'

'No, 'e ain't, stupid,' said Babs, pushing him away. 'Look, yer can see 'im breathing.'

'Stop it! Stop it, you two!' yelled Sally. 'We've got ter get 'im to a doctor.'

'How we gonner do that?' asked Pete.

'Dunno.' Sally became flustered. 'Pete, can yer take 'im ter the 'ospital in the car?'

'I dunno. What if I go ter the wardens' post first and ask them fer 'elp?'

'What can they do?' She was relieved to see her father was breathing a little easier now.

Pete scratched his head. 'They could phone fer an ambulance.'

'D'yer think they'd come?'

'I dunno, Sal. I honestly dunno.'

'Is the raid still on?' asked Johnny.

'I think so,' replied Sally. 'But it's very quiet. Pete, could yer take 'im ter the 'ospital in the car?' she asked again.

'I suppose so. We ain't got much choice, 'ave we. What about the kids?'

'We'll come wiv yer,' said Babs.

'No, I'll ask Jessie if they'll let yer go in there with them.'

Sally carefully opened the shelter door. 'It seems quiet enough,' she said over her shoulder. 'I won't be long.'

The fence between the houses had long gone and she was back in a flash.

'Come on, you two. Take yer blankets and pillows, and we'll see yer as soon as we can.'

'I'll go and git the car,' said Pete.

Johnny began to cry. 'I don't want Dad ter die,' he said, burying his head in Sally's jumper.

''E'll be all right once we get 'im ter 'ospital,' she said, trying to sound convincing.

Babs bent down and kissed her father's cheek. Then she put her arms round Johnny's heaving shoulders. 'Don't let Dad 'ear yer,' she said gently, moving him towards the door. 'Sal and Pete'll look after 'im.'

In the car, Sally sat with her father's head cradled in her lap. He was still unconscious and she gently rocked him back and forth, letting her tears fall on to his face. His colour had gone and he looked grey and very ill. She took her handkerchief and ran it soothingly across his forehead to wipe away the tears that had gathered in the deep furrows of weather-beaten face. He didn't move.

Chapter 23

Sally sat nervously holding Pete's hand, waiting for the doctor to return. All through what had seemed to Sally an endless journey, they had been silent. She'd held her father close, and winced for him every time the car bumped over hose pipes and potholes as Pete struggled to negotiate the bomb-damaged roads.

'What d'yer think's wrong with 'im?' whispered Sally as they sat in the white-walled room.

'Dunno, love.'

She gazed at the blacked out window. 'Yer wasn't 'alf a time getting the car,' she suddenly said.

''Ad ter git some petrol. Good job it was Sat'day and Tommy was up there playing cards.'

A nurse came into the room and Sally held her breath.

'Mrs Brent? The doctor would like to see you.'

The nurse pushed open the doctor's office door and Sally knew by the grave expression on his face that something was very wrong.

'I'm sorry. I'm afraid . . . It was his heart.'

Sally heard herself moan. Then breaking down in tears, she buried her head in Pete's rough coat. Above her sobs she could hear Pete talking. He lifted her head and slowly her sobs subsided.

'Come on, Sal. Yer got ter go and see yer dad,' he said softly. Taking her arm, he held on to her firmly as they followed the nurse.

In a cold clinical room, her father lay with his eyes closed. He looked very peaceful. Sally gently kissed his already cooling cheek. She wanted to throw her arms round him and take him away – run away with him. She desperately wanted to give him back his life.

She could hear Pete making some arrangements, but she still couldn't believe this was happening. She couldn't think straight. 'What . . . ? How . . . ?' The words tumbled out. ''E was a stevedore, 'e was strong.' Sally could hear herself talking.

'I'm afraid that sometimes happens. Would you both like a cup of tea?'

'Ta, that'll be nice,' said Pete. After the nurse left the room, Pete took Sally's arm again. 'Come on, love,' he said sadly. 'Let's leave 'im. There's nuffink yer can do fer 'im now. At least it was quick.'

Sally was filled with anger, and she brushed his arm away. ''E shouldn't 'ave gone at all.' She wanted to hit Pete. How could he say something like that?

As they made their way home daylight was just beginning to lighten the sky. Sally sat silently staring out of the car window. The dark, weird and unusual shapes of bombed buildings stood defiant, ready to meet a new day.

'What's Babs and Johnny gonner say?' she finally whispered.

'It's gonner be 'ard fer 'em.'

'First Mum, now Dad. Suppose 'e didn't suffer like some o' those that lived there.' She inclined her head towards the piles of rubble and burnt-out buildings they passed.

'Sod it,' said Pete angrily. 'There's another copper telling us we can't go down this road.' He slowed down and wound down his window as the policeman came up to him.

'Sorry, mate, this road's blocked. Yer'll have ter turn round.'

Pete banged the steering wheel with frustration. 'We've been up all night and we wonner git 'ome ter git some sleep. Ain't there any way we can git through? It's an 'ell of a long way round fer us.'

'Sorry, sir.' The policeman leant forward. 'Been out on the tiles all night, 'ave we then?' Before Pete could answer he added gruffly, 'Get out the car. Now where did yer get the petrol from fer all yer gadding about?'

'We ain't been gadding—'

'I ain't talking to you, miss,' he interrupted, looking into the car. 'Show me your identity cards.'

Sally froze. She remembered Pete saying he'd got the petrol from Tommy Tanner, and that could only mean it was black market, and pink. If he was found out he could face a heavy fine, or even prison. She hurried out of the car. 'Please,' she said to the policeman as tears ran down her face, 'we've been at the 'ospital all night. Me dad's just died.' For her this was the last straw. Everything was getting on top of her and her nerves were at breaking point. She sat on the running board and with her head in her hands, let the tears flow.

The policeman crouched down beside her. 'I'm sorry, miss, but I 'ave ter make sure yer not using the car fer just gadding about. It's me job, yer know.'

Sally nodded.

'Come on, love, get back in,' said Pete. He turned to the policeman. 'It's been a shock fer 'er.'

The policeman looked round. 'I understand, mate, but yer know 'ow it is? I 'ave me orders.' He handed them back their identity cards.

'Can we go now?'

'Yeah, but yer'll still 'ave ter go round. This road's got a bloody great crater in it.'

'That's all right, officer,' said Pete, quickly. 'Come on, Sal. Jump in and let's git 'ome.' He started the car and gave the policeman a wave. When he'd turned the car round he sighed and wiped the sweat from his top lip. 'That was bloody close, and that's the last time I'll git petrol off of Tanner.'

'Is it pink?' Sally sobbed.

'Yeah.'

'That's all we needed,' she said miserably.

Sally stayed in the kitchen while Pete went next door to collect Babs and Johnny because she couldn't face Jess and her parents just yet. When the kids walked in, the look on their faces told her they knew. They rushed to her and together, in a tight little knot, they cried.

Everybody in Sefton was shocked at the news, and offered help. Granny Brent took Sally to one side and told her she would be willing to look after Johnny through the day, and make sure he went to school all the while the school was still standing.

'It'll be nice ter 'ave a little'n around again.'

Sally didn't think Johnny would enjoy being called a little'n, but he did like Granny Brent's cooking.

Once again, Sally found herself standing in the church to which over the last few years she'd paid too many sad visits. It, like the rest of them, was showing its war wounds. The stained-glass windows had gone, and all the silver had been put in a safe place. She felt guilty that she didn't come to church for anything other than weddings, christenings and funerals. As a child she had attended the Sunday school, but like most children round here, the Fullers were only sent to get them out of the way while their father had an afternoon nap. Like her parents, Sally had been married here – Gwen and Danny also, and their baby, Dorothy, christened here. They were the happy times. They had been here for her mother's funeral, and because of the war, Joyce and Connie Downs' and the Slaters'. Now it was her father's. Sally looked at his simple coffin standing in front of the altar. How many more? Her eyes stung as her tears fell and she tried to comfort her brother and sister.

After Jess had seen her husband, Vic, she was full of it, telling Sally how handsome he looked in his uniform and how sorry he was for leaving her. 'D'yer know, 'e's really changed,' said Jessie dreamily. 'And 'e wants ter see the kids.'

'That's nice,' said Sally, but she couldn't really work up any enthusiasm at her friend's news.

At Easter nobody sent Lena any congratulations on her marriage to Roy, and her name was never mentioned in front of Granny Brent. Vera appeared to be happy working on the buses, but she'd told Sally she would never trust another man, and would never speak to her sister again. Fortunately, Gwen's new baby brought a lot of joy to the Brents, but Sally was still very unhappy. The death of her father had affected her deeply, and she didn't seem to have anything to look forward to. Her life seemed to be all work and no play. The only bright spot was seeing the enjoyment

Dorothy brought Gwen. One day she was showing Pete the Easter bunny she had managed to get for the little girl.

'I know it's a bit late, but Peggy at work couldn't get the stuffing for it in time for Easter, but Gwen don't mind waiting. It's smashing ain't it?'

Pete looked up from his newspaper. 'Yeah, it's all right.'

'I think it's lovely.' Sally sat cuddling the brown furry rabbit. 'She's been making 'em out of her mum's old fur coat. Well, Dorothy'll love it.' Sally sat back. 'Pete, could we think about 'aving a baby?'

'Don't start on that again. 'Ow can you even fink of it when yer see what's bin 'appening round 'ere. What if we got killed, who'd look after it then?'

Sally couldn't look at him for she had no answer. 'Gwen don't think like that,' she said quietly.

'Gwen and Danny ain't got no bloody sense, that's why. Look 'ow he got 'imself in a state when she was 'aving it. 'E told me they shouldn't be 'aving one with all this trouble, it only gives 'im more grief and worry.'

'But Gwen don't mind, she loves Dorothy.'

'Course she does. But yer must admit Gwen can be a bit of a silly cow at times.' He paused. 'You're upset over yer dad going, it's only natural yer needs someone ter fuss over.'

Sally put the rabbit back in a bag.

'Come 'ere.' He held out his arms. 'Come on Sal,' he said gently. 'Just fink how we'd feel if anyfink 'appened to our kid. Be sensible.'

How could she make him see she didn't want to be sensible? Although deep down she knew he was right, that didn't stop her from wanting something exciting to look forward to for a change.

As she cuddled close he whispered, 'We will one day, love. But let's wait till fings get a bit better, and we can sleep safe in our beds again. After all a damp shelter ain't the best place for a baby, now is it?'

Sally held back the tears. 'No,' she croaked. She knew he was right.

Spring came and filled everybody with optimism. Although the raids still continued, most nights they weren't so heavy and everybody was taking them in their stride. Babs and Johnny slept in the kitchen under the table, and Pete and Sally were now downstairs in the front room. She was thrilled the nights they made love, and angry when their lovemaking was interrupted by the siren. Sometimes the bombers left London for other cities, leaving sleep and privacy undisturbed.

It was the beginning of May when Jessie raced into Sally's waving a letter.

'Vic's got some leave and 'e wants me ter take the kids ter see 'im.'

'You going?' asked Sally.

'Yeah. Me and Mum 'ave 'ad a bit of a bull and a cow about it, but I told 'er I'm going and that's that.' She lit a cigarette, blowing the smoke high in the air.

Sally smiled. She'd never heard Jess be defiant before. 'When yer going?'

'Two weeks' time. 'E's even sent me the fare.' Her face was wreathed in smiles. 'I'll 'ave ter try and git somefink new ter wear. I ain't got time ter make meself sumfink. 'Sides, they ain't got much down the market now that old Jack's gorn. 'E used ter git hold of a nice bit o' material.'

'Go along ter Silverman's. Babs says they can always get stock.'

'That's a good idea. Babs was telling me 'er and the old man's daughter, Rachel, sometimes go up West ter the pictures.'

'Yeah, I'm glad she's found someone ter go out with. After Connie died she was in a bit of a state. Rachel's only a couple o' years older than Babs, but a lot more grown up, and they seem ter get on really well together.'

'That was a shame about Connie and Joyce.'

Sally didn't answer. It went without saying.

The second Saturday in May Jessie and the kids looked very smart as they waved goodbye.

Mrs Walters stood with Sally watching them go. 'Don't she look nice?' she said.

Sally nodded, noting Jessie's mum seemed to have come round to the idea of her visiting Vic. 'They get some smart frocks in Silverman's. I only 'ope she ain't gonner finish up miles from anywhere, not in those high heels.'

Mrs Walters grinned. 'Can't see 'er walking frough the cow pats in them shoes. But 'er and the kids do look nice. Only 'ope 'e appreciates it.'

'Jessie said you 'ad a bit of a row about 'er going.'

'Yeah, but it's only 'cos I worry about 'er. I 'ope 'e ain't 'aving 'er on again.'

''E sounds as if 'e's changed.'

'Yeah, but if 'e puts 'er up the creek again I'll bloody well 'ave 'is balls on a plate.'

Sally laughed. She knew how much Jessie was looking forward to this week, and all the loving that she'd been without for such a long while. In many ways she envied Jess. She was going to have a week of loving, and hopefully not be disturbed by air raids.

'Me and the old man's going out ternight,' said Mrs Walters smugly.

'That's good. Anywhere nice?'

'Ter see 'is sister. She lives over the water. It was 'er birfday last week. Don't see much of 'er these days. She ain't got no time fer Jess, so we fought we'd go while Jess is away.'

Sally knew all about that aunt, who hadn't approved of Jess having to get married. 'She 'aving a party?'

'Na, but I expect we'll go up the pub fer a few.'

'Yer staying overnight?'

'Na, don't like being away from me 'ome too long.'

Sally smiled. 'Well 'ave a good time, and don't get too drunk. See yer termorrer.'

'Git drunk? Christ, chance'll be a fine fing if their landlord waters the beer down like what Wally does,' said Mrs Walters over her shoulder as she went in her house.

The following morning Sally listened out for the Walters.

'Pete, I'm a bit worried about Jess's mum and dad. I ain't 'eard 'em about.'

'I reckon they 'ad a skinful and missed the last bus.'

Sally nodded half-heartedly. 'But she said they wasn't staying the night.'

'Yeah, but if the old man got too drunk there's no way she could bring 'im 'ome.'

'Yeah, I s'pose yer right.'

All through the day Sally listened for her neighbours' doors slamming, or the lavatory chain being pulled, but it remained quiet.

Sunday evening was drawing to a close. Pete had been outside to the lav, and he looked worried when he came in the kitchen. 'Sal.' He beckoned for her to follow him.

'What is it? They 'ome?' she asked when they were in the yard.

'No. I ain't 'eard 'em. Look, Sal, it's ever such a bright night. Look at that moon.'

She laughed and nudged his elbow. 'Yeah, it's really lovely.' She looked up at the clear sky. ''Ere, you ain't getting all romantic, are yer?'

He looked surprised. 'No, yer silly cow. It's what they call a bomber's moon. It means they could be over ternight. I fink we ought ter sleep in the shelter.'

Sally felt foolish and, moving away, said, 'All right. I'll tell the kids ter get ready.'

Pete grabbed her and spun her round – he was grinning. 'Yeah, I guess it is romantic, and I could do fings ter you when yer looks so sad and rejected.' He kissed her full mouth long and hard.

She responded, suddenly wanting him to make love to her. 'Don't let's go in the shelter, let's go to bed now,' she whispered breathlessly as his hand ran down her thigh.

Pete kissed her with more urgency. 'I love yer, Sal. I don't ever want ter lose yer.'

'Pete, I want yer to—' Her voice was silenced by his kisses and then the wailing sound of the siren. 'Don't let's go in the shelter,' she said, breaking away. 'I'll tell the kids we'll be in later.'

Babs and Johnny rushed into the yard.

'Cor, that's a bomber's moon right enough,' said Johnny, looking up at the darkening sky. 'I reckon they'll be over in force ternight.'

'I'll get me bedding,' said Babs quickly.

In the far distance they could hear the familiar deep

throbbing of the enemy planes' engines. The put-put of anti-aircraft guns got louder as the planes came nearer.

'Right everybody, in the shelter,' said Pete, pushing them forward. 'I'll get the bedding.'

'Don't forget the policy bag,' yelled Sally after him.

All night the bombs fell as wave after wave of planes came over, their ear-shattering explosions, mixed with loud thunderous cracks of the anti-aircraft guns, filled the air with noise, smoke and dust.

''Ope 'e drops most of 'em somewhere else ternight,' said Pete apprehensively.

'Even if 'e does, I s'pose we'll still 'ave more mess ter clear up in the morning,' said Sally despondently.

Johnny looked at his sister, his face full of fear. 'We gonner die?'

'Course not, silly.' Babs bent her head and appeared to carry on reading her magazine. 'Yer should be used ter all this by now,' she suddenly added.

'Don't reckon you'll git as much shrapnel this time, Johnny,' said Pete. 'Don't sound like 'e's going fer this side of the water ternight.'

'So far,' said Sally under her breath.

All night the raid continued, the shelter rocked and the ground heaved, but after the all clear they emerged safe once again.

The following morning, after the usual clearing up, most people tried to get to work. The factory was still standing. Peggy, Sally's work mate, said she'd heard it was the West End that got the worst of it.

Nellie arrived very late and told everybody the trams and buses were all over the place. Sally wondered how Pete had managed to get to work. Babs was within walking distance so she wouldn't have any trouble – that's if the shop was still standing.

At the end of the day, as Sally made her way home, her thoughts were again of Mr and Mrs Walters. She was worried that everybody seemed to think the worst of the raid was over the other side of the Thames, where Mr Walters' sister lived. She knocked on their door, but there was no reply. She felt increasingly anxious and helpless to do anything.

It was soon after that Pete got home. He looked tired and dirty.

'Did yer 'ave a job getting ter the docks?' Sally plumped up the cushion on the armchair. 'Sit yerself down, tea's made.'

'It's a bloody mess over there, Sal,' he said, slipping into the armchair and lighting his cigarette. 'I ain't bin ter work. I've bin 'elping ter git some of 'em out.' He looked up at Sally. 'It tears yer 'eart out ter see grown men sitting in the road crying over a kid's dead body.' He hunched his shoulders and, leaning forward, drew long and hard on his cigarette. 'Fought I'd seen it all after Joyce Downs.' His voice was barely above a whisper.

'When's it all gonner end?' Sally said sadly. 'And Pete, Jessie's mum and dad ain't 'ome yet.'

'They might be 'aving a bit o' trouble. The roads're in a right state. A lot o' trams can't move 'cos the tracks are all twisted and buckled. I tell yer, Sal, people can't stand too much o' this.'

All evening Sally sat straining her ears, listening for any sound that would announce her next-door neighbours were safe at home, but their house remained empty.

The sun was shining as Sally walked home from work the following day. Gwen was hovering over Dorothy's pram outside Granny Brent's.

'Sal,' she called. 'Ma wants ter see yer.'

Sally crossed the road. Straight away her thoughts went to Johnny. If he'd been climbing over the bomb sites and torn his trousers again, she'd give him what for.

'Yoo-hoo,' shouted Sally as she walked down the passage. 'It's me.'

'Come and sit yerself down, love,' said Granny Brent in a quiet tone. 'I've got the kettle on.'

Sally was beginning to get worried. 'What is it?'

'We've 'ad the police 'ere.'

Sally gasped and her hand flew to her mouth. ''Ere? What about?'

'Well, over the road really. They've bin looking fer young Jessie.'

Sally felt sick. 'Is it 'er mum and dad?'

Granny Brent nodded. 'They're in 'ospital, pretty bad by all accounts.'

Sally felt tears stinging her eyes. She'd known them all her life. And what about Jessie?

'D'yer know where Jessie is?' asked her mother-in-law, as if reading her thoughts.

Sally shook her head.

'The police want 'er back 'ere as soon as possible.'

Poor Jess. She was happy somewhere enjoying herself, not knowing. 'I don't know where she's gone, but she won't be 'ome till Sat'day.'

'That's what I told 'em, but the police don't fink they'll last that long.'

'Did they tell yer what 'ospital?'

'Guy's.'

'I'll 'ave ter get over there.'

'You'll 'ave a job.'

'But I must see 'em. What can I tell Jess if I don't . . . ?' Sally let her tears fall.

'Ain't yer even got an inkling?'

Again Sally only shook her head.

'Don't worry, love, she'll understand.' Granny Brent patted her hand. 'Kettle's boiling. I'll just go and fill the pot.'

Gwen walked in with Dorothy over her shoulder. 'It's a bad business, ain't it? Those kids'll miss their gran and granddad. Lived with 'em all their lives, ain't they?'

'Yes,' whispered Sally. 'I'm only just accepting Dad going, now this. When's it all gonner stop, Gwen?'

'I wish I knew.' She gently kissed her baby's cheek. 'I only wish I knew.'

Pete was equally shocked and upset at the news when he got in. 'Look, let's go in next door and see if we can find one of Vic's letters.'

'We can't do that.' Sally was horrified that Pete would even suggest such a thing.

'If we found one at least we could tell the police roughly where she was.'

Sally knew he was right, and although she had been in the house, and Jessie's room many times, as they made their way up the stairs she felt full of guilt. She opened the drawers of her dressing table, knowing exactly where Jessie would keep her letters.

'I've got 'em.' Sally carefully took a letter out of an envelope. 'This address is Gloucestershire. I remember she said somethink about 'im taking the kids to see a church, or somethink, but I wasn't really listening.'

'Write it down, and I'll go and use Wally's phone. The police'll know what ter do. They'll send someone round to tell 'er.'

'Poor Jessie,' whispered Sally, wishing she could be there to comfort her friend when she heard the news.

Chapter 24

Late on Wednesday night, someone came banging on the shelter door.

'Who the bloody 'ell is it?' yelled Pete.

'It's me, Jess.'

Pete flung open the door and Jessie rushed in through the small doorway, clutching her daughter Pat to her. Behind her came Vic, carrying Harry, fast asleep, over his shoulder.

Sally began to cry with joy as she threw her arms round Jessie and Pat. Jessie too was crying. Through her tears Sally looked over Jessie's shoulder at Vic. He was just as she remembered him, tall and good looking. He had brought Jessie back and she would need him more than ever now. She hoped he'd stay with her this time.

'How? Where?' Sally was full of questions.

Jessie sat down. 'The police went ter Vic's camp. It was 'is mate's place we was staying at, so 'e told 'em, and they come and told me about Mum and Dad.' She stopped to blow her nose.

'Jess, I 'ope yer didn't mind me going through yer things. I 'ad ter find out where yer was.'

Jessie shook her head.

'I didn't read any of yer letters, honestly.'

'S'all right.'

'Vic, put 'Arry up there on the bunk.' Pete pulled the covers back for him. 'We've got a flask o' tea if yer fancy one.'

'That'll be great, fanks. It's been a long day.'

''Ave yer bin ter the 'ospital?' asked Pete.

Jessie nodded. 'Sal, they've gorn.' Tears ran down her mascara-streaked face. 'What am I gonner do, Sal? I didn't even get a chance ter say goodbye. I ain't ever 'ad ter . . .' She couldn't finish.

Babs looked sad and took a whimpering and bewildered Pat from Jessie. They sat on the bottom bunk and Babs began playing with her.

Sally held her friend tight. Jessie buried her head in Sally's shoulder and her sobs filled the shelter.

'We'll 'elp yer, yer know that,' said Pete, pouring out the tea.

'Thanks, Pete,' said Vic. 'It's a bloody shame. We was 'aving such a good time.' He stopped and swallowed hard. 'I've got a couple o' real smashing kids.' He ruffled Pat's fair hair, and brought a smile to her pretty elfin face.

'Do yer know why yer mum and dad didn't come 'ome on Sat'day or Sunday after seeing yer aunt?' asked Sally.

'I saw me cousin in the 'ospital. 'E ain't too badly injured, fank Gawd, and 'e said they stayed 'cos me aunt wasn't too well.' Jess sniffed hard. 'They didn't wonner leave 'er.'

'What about yer aunt?' whispered Sally.

'She's gorn.'

Johnny looked up. 'You're an orphan like us now then, Jess.'

Both Sally and Jessie couldn't control their sobs any longer.

'Yer better stay in 'ere fer the night,' said Pete. 'Mind you, the raids ain't bin ser bad since that last lot.'

'Yer certainly 'ad it rough round 'ere,' said Vic.

Pete half laughed. 'Yeah, I fink yer could say that.'

'If yer don't mind, I'd rather go 'ome,' said Jessie quietly. 'All the kids toys're in the shelter, and the poor little buggers don't know what's 'it 'em yet.'

'What about yer bedding? It'll be all damp,' said Sally.

'Me and the kids stuff's indoors. We'll be all right. They ain't 'alf gonner miss Mum and Dad.' Jess wiped her eyes. 'Bin there wiv 'em all their lives, they 'ave – wiping their noses and—'

Vic gave an embarrassed cough.

'Look,' said Pete awkwardly. 'I know me and Sal are at work, but if there's anyfink we can do, just let us know.'

'Thanks, Pete,' said Vic quickly. 'I've got the rest of the week off, and I'll request compassionate leave. After all, it's still family.'

Sally noted that Jessie gave him a weak smile. 'I'm sure that if yer don't wonner cart the kids round with yer termorrer, Granny Brent and Gwen will look after them fer yer.'

'Thanks, Sal. I'll probably do that.' Jessie kissed her cheek. 'See yer termorrer.'

After they left, Johnny and Babs soon settled down, but Sally lay wide awake for hours. She knew Pete was also awake but they didn't speak. They each had their own thoughts.

Sally wasn't surprised when after Jessie's parents' funerals

Jessie told her she was moving near to Vic. He'd found them a house, and Sally was helping her pack. 'Yer sure yer doing the right thing, Jess?'

Jessie nodded. 'I can't stay 'ere.' She was holding one of her mother's hats, looking at it and slowly turning it over. 'Ain't got nuffink ter stay 'ere fer now. 'Sides, it's gotter be safer fer the kids.'

'Yeah. But going off with Vic . . .'

'I can't git over the way 'e's changed. 'E's ever so kind and considerate now, not a bit like the toerag I married.' Jessie put the hat in a cardboard box along with other items of her mother's clothes.

Sally sat on the bed. 'I'd never thought I'd 'ere yer talk like that about 'im after all yer said in the past. D'yer know what made 'im change?'

Jess sat next to Sally and offered her a cigarette. She shook her head. Jess lit up and puffed smoke in the air. 'It seems when 'e went orf with that tart, she frew 'erself at 'im, yer know. Well, she didn't do anyfink fer 'im. 'E even 'ad ter do 'is own washing.' A sad little smile played around Jessie's mouth. 'That's when 'e said 'e found out how much 'e missed me.'

Sally wanted to smile at that, but thought better of it.

'Anyway, when the war started 'e joined up straight away. 'E was only living in digs so 'e 'adn't much ter lose. Then it seems 'is best mate's wife and kids got killed and it made 'im realise what a fool 'e'd bin.'

'Why ain't 'e bin sent abroad?'

''E's somefink ter do wiv intelligence, so 'e 'ad ter stay 'ere.' Jessie smiled. ''E's still got those come-ter-bed eyes ain't 'e? And 'e's still good at it. Christ, I didn't know how much I missed a bloke's 'ands all over me till now. What about you; still gitting yer share?'

'It's a bit awkward in a shelter with the kids.'

'Yeah, s'pose it is.'

'Come on,' said Sally, getting to her feet. 'We'd better git a move on otherwise Vic will be 'ere ter take you away and we won't be ready. Where yer taking yer mum and dad's things?'

'The Salvation Army said they'd like 'em. Seems there's a lot o' people what's bin bombed out wiv only what they stand up in.' Jessie turned away, and with a catch in her voice said, 'I'll write, Sal, I promise.'

'I know yer will.' As Sally helped Jessie pack, she knew it would be a long, long while before she would see her friend again.

One day not long after Jessie had gone, Babs came home full of the party Rachel was going to have for her eighteenth birthday.

'She's bin telling me about the big 'ouse they've got, and she's got all the latest records. She's bin teaching me ter dance in our lunch break, and there's gonner be lots o' food there as well.'

'Where do these people get it from with everythink on ration?' asked Sally.

'Same old story, love,' said Pete. 'Money talks.'

'Will boys be there?' asked Johnny.

'I expect so,' said Babs, casually.

'Cor, can I come?' said Johnny. 'I fancy a lot o' food.'

'No yer can't, 'cos I'm gonner stay all night.'

'Oh yes, and who said so?' said Sally.

Babs looked at her sister in amazement. 'What?'

'I ain't said yer can go yet,' said Sally.

'Yer wouldn't stop me, would yer?'

Sally grinned. 'Course not. But behave yerself with all those boys around.'

She tossed her head. 'I ain't a baby, yer know.'

'I know, that's what I'm afraid of.'

Babs gave Sally one of her defiant looks. 'That's it, start going off.'

'I'm only saying. 'Sides, what yer gonner do if there's an air raid?'

'Don't worry. They've got one o' those table shelters – Morrison, I fink she called it,' she added with a smile.

'I bet Babs is enjoying 'erself. Let's 'ope we don't 'ave a raid ternight,' said Sally, as she and Pete were listening to the wireless that Saturday.

'Babs said they 'ad a Morrison shelter,' said Pete, looking up from his paper. 'Christ knows 'ow they'd all get under that.'

'It could be cosy,' laughed Sally.

'It's good ter see yer laugh, Sal,' said Pete, folding his newspaper.

'Ain't 'ad a lot ter laugh about just lately, 'ave we?' She sighed a long deep sigh.

'P'raps now Hitler's started on Russia fings might git a bit better fer us,' said Pete.

'D'yer think so?'

'I'm 'oping so.'

'That bloody washer going in the washing up bowl was the last straw terday,' said Sally. 'All me washing up water ran away, and the tea towel's got a rusty iron mark on it now. Dunno how I'm gonner git it out.'

'Yer could try rubbing a lemon on it.'

'Don't talk daft, Pete. We'd like ter see a lemon.'

'I'll try and find a new washer fer yer bowl.'

'Wouldn't it be nice if we could just go out and buy a new enamel bowl, or a lemon. I gets a bit fed up with keep 'aving ter make do.' Sally suddenly felt very low.

'Cheer up, Sal. It ain't like you ter let fings git yer down.'

'Well, we ain't got nothing ter look forward to, 'ave we?' She took a deep breath. 'Pete, couldn't we talk about a baby?'

'Blimey, Sal, if yer can't get this and that, how d'yer reckon yer gonner manage wiv a baby?' His voice softened. 'No, let's wait till we know fings are getting better.'

She gave him a weak smile. 'I know yer right. It's just that I think everythink's passing us by. Life seems only about not 'aving things. I don't want ter put off the baby for ever.'

'Sal,' Pete paused. 'I've got somefink ter tell yer, and I'd better git it over before Johnny comes back.' He sat forward.

''E's only gorn round the corner to 'is mate's 'ouse.'

'I know.'

Sally became worried. 'What is it, Pete?'

'I'm being sent to Cardiff next Wednesday.'

She was stunned. 'What? When did yer know?'

'Yesterday.'

'How long for?'

'Dunno. All the while they get the ships, I s'pose.'

'Why didn't yer say somethink?' She felt her world was falling apart.

'Didn't know how to. I'll write, love,' he said, kneeling down in front of her.

'But why you?'

'There's a few of us going. There ain't many boats coming up the Thames now since that last lot. They're all being sent ter other ports, and I 'ave ter go where they send me.' He kissed her forehead.

'Everybody's leaving me,' Sally sobbed. 'First Dad, then Jess, and now you.'

'Don't cry, love. Look, I'll tell yer what, when I gits settled, and if it's safe, yer could come down fer a week. I'll try and git some time off and we could 'ave a second honeymoon.' He grinned. 'What d'yer fink of that?'

She tried hard to smile through her tears. 'That'd be nice. I'd like that.'

'After all, Cardiff might not be such a bad place,' said Pete, scrambling to his feet as Johnny slammed the front door.

Sally could feel anger welling up inside her. So what if Cardiff wasn't such a bad place? London was bloody awful and now she was to be left to cope with it all by herself. Mum, Dad, Jessie, Pete – most of the people she'd ever been close to were dead or gone away, leaving little to look forward to. No husband, no baby, just rationing and nights cowering in the air-raid shelter – Sally saw her bleak future stretching ahead.

In June 1941 clothes were rationed, but Babs told Sally not to worry as she would be able to wangle anything her sister wanted. Sally admired how well dressed Babs was now. Most of her wages went on clothes, and she spent a lot of time with Rachel Silverman, coming home late and wearing a lot of make-up. Sally worried about her when there was a daylight raid, but Babs took it all in her stride, going down the Underground if they were up the West End, or even staying in the cinema after they had been told an air raid was in progress. Sally was horrified about that, but Babs said by the time they got out and into a public shelter it was all over and then they missed half the film. In the last six months Babs had really grown up, and was gradually getting over losing her best friend.

Pete wrote regularly from Cardiff. He said his digs weren't too bad and his landlady, a big round woman called Megan, was a good cook. The docks had plenty of work and he always sent Sally money.

For Sally the summer was dragging. She was restless, her evenings often spent alone if there wasn't a raid on, and it wasn't till the end of August that she finally managed to get away. Babs was thrilled when the Silvermans said she could stay with them for the week, and after leaving Johnny with Granny Brent, with instructions to behave himself, she finally got on the train to Cardiff.

The corridor was packed, mostly with servicemen and women, and all their equipment. Sally envied the way they were laughing and chatting together, as if it were some big outing for them, but perhaps it was just bravado. She suspected most of them were going off into the unknown.

After picking her way over kitbags and rifles she was lucky enough to find an empty seat in the corner of a no smoking compartment. She gave the woman opposite a smile, put her suitcase on the rack and settled down. As the train slowly pulled out of war-torn London she stared out of the window. Not really seeing, she sat back and let her thoughts wander. Jessie's last letter had said how happy she and Vic were in their new house. Sally had seen for herself how much the war had changed him, and was pleased he was now caring and loving, and a great comforter to Jessie after her loss. Her thoughts wandered to the empty house next door in Sefton Grove. The street was sad and empty-looking now, showing its war wounds. So many people had deserted their houses. The great hole that had been the Slaters' house had been sprouting pretty wild flowers all summer.

Sally tried to doze but there was too much noise coming from the corridor. Men's loud voices mingled with girls' high-pitched laughter caused the woman opposite to look up from her book and tut loudly.

At long last the train pulled into the station. Sally looked about her, bewildered, wondering if Pete would be here to meet her. She rushed along the platform when she heard her name being called, and fell into his open arms.

'I ain't 'alf missed yer,' he said. Lifting her off the ground and twirling her round, he buried his head in her neck.

'I must say yer look well,' she said, standing back to admire him after the hugs and kisses. 'Yer a bit fatter – must be all of Megan's good food.'

'Yer don't look ser well,' said Pete, drawing her close again. ''As it bin bad?'

'Not really,' she said cheerfully. No point in saying it was awful. That wouldn't help.

Pete picked up her case. 'Come on, we've got ter catch the bus.'

'Is it far?'

'Na, only a couple o' stops.'

'Yer mum, Vera and Gwen all send their love.'

'How is Vera these days?'

'Not bad at all. She's lost a bit o' weight. Must be all that running up and down the stairs on the bus.'

'I'll never forgive that bloke Roy, or Lena, fer upsetting 'er like that.'

'Nor will Vera or yer mum, but it's all in the past now, and it's a good job she found out what 'e was like before she married 'im.'

'Yeah, s'pose so.'

'Gwen's baby's lovely.' Pete didn't reply. 'Pete,' Sally said, cuddling up to him, 'I do miss yer. How long d'you think you'll be 'ere?'

'Dunno.'

'I could come down to live, too.'

'And what about Johnny and Babs? She wouldn't fank yer fer dragging her ter this place.'

Sally wanted to shout out, And what about me? Why don't people think about me? But she thought better of it. She wasn't going to let anything stop her from enjoying this week with Pete.

Megan welcomed Sally with open arms. 'You're right, boy,' she said to Pete. 'She is a lovely lass.'

Sally blushed.

'Go on up and unpack. I'll leave a pot o' tea in the dining room.' Megan gave them a smile. 'I'll put the cosy over it,' she said, shuffling out of the room.

Upstairs Pete took Sally in his arms and kissed her long and passionately. He gently pushed her back on the bed.

'No, Pete. Megan will 'ear . . .'

He silenced her with a kiss. 'The kitchen's a way away, and Megan's no fool. She knows we won't be down fer tea fer a while.'

So Sally lay back and let her love for Pete surround her. There weren't going to be any lonely nights for a whole week.

* * *

Sally had known Pete would only be able to have the weekend off, as the ships had to have a quick turn around, but she didn't mind. For a whole week she was sleeping in his bed, and their loving was undisturbed. For the first time for months, she felt relaxed and happy, then all too soon it was time for her to leave. It was a very tearful goodbye at the station, and as she sat on the train she wondered when she would see him again, and the thought of having a baby was once again on her mind. If only she could make Pete see things her way.

Throughout autumn everybody who was able was doing war work, or fire watching. Railings had been taken away for scrap iron, and rationing was getting harsher, with lots of goods scarce. As Babs now spent every Saturday evening with the Silvermans, Sally and Johnny went along to the arches with Granny Brent. The one they used held a few vans, and Pete's car was sheeted over in the corner, a reminder to Sally of the good times they had had. She recalled that day in Brighton. Dad was still alive then. It all seemed so long ago.

A piano had been installed, and after a few bottles of beer the atmosphere was happy and relaxed. As on most Saturdays, everybody was singing, but it suddenly went very quiet when the vicar walked in. Sally wanted to laugh at the tin hat perched squarely on his head, a cross painted on the front of it.

'Silly bugger,' said Granny Brent, after he had left. 'Does 'e reckon that's gonner save 'im?'

'I was more worried about 'im seeing all the empties,' said Mr Roach from Silver Street.

'I saw yer trying ter push the crate behind that van wiv

yer foot while 'e was saying a prayer over yer,' said Granny Brent. 'I fought it was 'cos yer didn't want ter give 'im a drink.'

'That an' all,' he said with a smile. Mr Roach liked his beer and by the end of the evening he usually finished up in the corner, drunk. They all still laughed at the night he went out for a jimmy, and wasn't missed for over an hour. There was a raid on at the time, and when they realised he was missing, his companions went looking for him and found him lying in the road, unconscious. Fearing the worse, they carried him in, only to find that in the blackout he'd walked into a van and knocked himself out.

Tommy Tanner and his father still played cards next door. Tommy was now into selling clothes without coupons, but that didn't interest Sally, as Babs could always get her something if she wanted it. The only time she went out now was to the pictures with Gwen or Vera, and so dressing up wasn't important to her.

December started cold and miserable, with Sally hoping for the letter from Pete that said he would be home for Christmas. It would be better not to feel sour and lonely at what should be such a happy time. On Sunday the seventh, she was busy washing out her stockings when the music on the wireless was interrupted. She stopped singing along with it and listened. The announcer was saying the Japs had bombed Pearl Harbor. Sally didn't know where that was but it sounded important. He went on to say a large number of American ships had been sunk. She sat at the table. This was awful, the Americans weren't at war; Pete was always having a go about them for wanting to remain neutral. Would this mean they would have to join in now? If they did, would this make any difference to Britain? With luck it could be all over soon.

Sally thought about the Americans she saw at the pictures, and all her heroes. She picked at the chenille table cloth and smiled. Just think, Tyrone Power and Clark Gable might come over. If they did, would she get a chance to see them? That thought brought a wide grin to her face, and it could bring a bit of excitement into her life.

Chapter 25

At Christmas, they'd pooled their resources with Granny Brent's and everyone tried to have a good time despite the rationing. It wasn't like the old days, but they knew those Christmases had gone for ever. Sally's thoughts were of her father. This was the first Christmas without him. Pete had managed to get home and Sally was pleased that most nights they could sleep in their beds, but she felt distanced from him. She saw the way he looked at the shabbiness of Sefton Grove and she suspected he would be glad to get away from the memories and back to Cardiff. She felt indignant but kept quiet. In any case they had little to say to each other now. She wasn't entirely sorry when he went back.

In January 1942, on Babs' sixteenth birthday, Mr Silverman invited Sally and Johnny over for tea. Babs was thrilled with the lovely pale blue frock they'd given her, and excitedly discussed with Rachel where she would wear it.

'That's very nice of you, Mr Silverman,' said Sally as they sat in the dining room after they'd finished tea. Babs, Johnny, and Rachel were in the lounge, as they called it, playing records.

'Think nothing of it. We think the world of Babs, don't we, Mother?'

His wife nodded. 'She's been such a tonic for Rachel.' She bent her head closer. 'I like them to go out together. Babs is such a steadying influence on Rachel.'

Sally couldn't begin to imagine what Rachel had been like before Babs came on the scene. Sally liked the Silvermans and their daughter, and when Rachel asked Sally to go along with them to the West End to see the latest films, Sally agreed to go the following week. Babs wasn't that pleased about her big sister going with them, though.

When Sally met them outside the Odeon Leicester Square she was a bit apprehensive, but soon found herself laughing and giggling along with the younger girls. After, she told Granny Brent and Gwen how much she'd enjoyed herself, and was looking forward to going out with them again, but she was worried about leaving Johnny.

''E want's ter stay with 'is mate round the corner, but I dunno.'

'Leave 'im wiv us,' said Gwen. ''E ain't no trouble.'

Granny Brent gave Sally one of her looks. 'Just ser long as yer remember yer married, and don't start acting like some of these 'ere flighty bits.' She straightened her shoulders, 'We've 'ad enough wiv one carrying on, we don't want any more disgrace brought on the family.'

'Christ, Mum, she's only going to the pictures wiv 'er young sister and 'er workmate,' said Gwen, looking across at Sally and raising her eyes to the ceiling.

'Yeah, I know, but there's a lot o' young men looking fer a pretty gel ter take advantage of, and what about all these foreigners over 'ere? Don't trust 'em, any of 'em.'

Sally smiled. 'I'll let yer know if I'm gonner turn out to be a scarlet woman.'

'Opportunity would be a fine fing, wouldn't it, Sal?' laughed Gwen.

Granny Brent tutted. 'I can't 'elp it if I worry about yer.'

Sally kissed her cheek. 'We know that.'

Before long, Saturday night at the pictures became a weekly event eagerly anticipated by Sally. She was amazed at the amount of people sleeping down the Underground, and some nights on their way home they'd join in the singing and dancing if there'd been a wedding or birthday to celebrate. Rachel was good fun to be with, and the years' difference between Sally and Babs seemed almost to disappear.

The war had changed the way women and girls dressed. Everything had to be practical now. Hemlines were up, clothes were unpicked and turned inside out to make new, and with so many shortages everyone was beginning to get very inventive. Sally and Babs would spend evenings melting down odd scraps of lipstick to make new ones, as lipsticks were impossible to get. Even the Silvermans and Tommy Tanner couldn't get silk stockings now, so when they went out, Sally and Babs used gravy browning to colour their legs, fake seams carefully drawn in with eyebrow pencil. Women wore bright colourful snoods over their hair, and trousers were now normal for factory work and the shelter. The street fashions all added to the air of independence so many women now felt.

'It's Sally's birthday next Saturday,' said Babs, putting her arm through Rachel's as they came out of the cinema.

It was a warm pleasant June evening, and still light. Despite the occasional air raid, the West End still attracted a lot of people. Men and women wearing uniforms from different nations, walked and talked together.

'How old will you be Sally?' asked Rachel as they made their way to the Underground.

'An old woman of twenty-three,' replied Sally with a grin.

'I'm surprised you haven't been called up,' said Rachel.

'I had to register, but for one thing I'm married.'

'But you haven't any kids,' said Rachel.

'No.'

'She does want 'em, though,' interrupted Babs. 'But, Pete, 'er 'usband, don't fink it's a good idea yet.'

Sally didn't like her private life discussed. 'And another thing,' Sally continued, going back to the original subject, 'I'm doing essential war work.'

'Don't ask 'er what it is,' said Babs, laughing. 'She's bin doing it fer years but she still don't know what it's for.'

'I reckon I might have to go soon if they start calling up eighteen-year-olds,' said Rachel. 'I don't want to, but—'

'We know, there's a war on,' said Babs angrily. 'Well, it ain't 'appened yet. 'Sides, I don't want yer ter go.'

'Can't your dad help?' asked Sally.

'Don't know. We'll have to wait and see. Anyway, what we going to do about your birthday, Sal?'

'I dunno, hadn't thought about it. Babs behave yourself,' said Sally quickly when two American soldiers passed them and gave them a long low wolf whistle.

'I love these Yanks,' said Babs, looking back at them.

'You watch out,' said Sally.

'They've got smashing uniforms.'

'Babs, about your sister's birthday.'

'Well, I reckon we should all go ter a dance fer a change,' said Babs, still looking behind.

'Sally – what d'you think?'

'I dunno. I ain't bin ter a dance fer years,' said Sally.

'I fink it would be great,' said Babs. 'Shall we go ter the Palais?'

'It would be a nice change,' said Rachel. 'And I think these American bands are just groovy.'

Sally smiled. 'Yes, it would be a nice change. I'll 'ave ter find out if my mother-in-law will 'ave Johnny all night though.'

All the way home, Sally wondered if she should tell Granny Brent she was going to a dance. She knew she didn't mind her going to the pictures, but a dance – she would be out much later, and even dancing with men. It was only a one-off for her birthday, but would Granny Brent approve? What excuse could she give her for getting home late? Johnny was always saying he wanted to stay with his friend Tony, but Sally couldn't suddenly send him round there to sleep. Besides, Granny Brent might not like it.

The following evening Sally was walking home from work when she saw Gwen in front of her. She called out.

''Allo, Sal,' said Gwen, stopping and turning round. 'Just finished? You on fire-watching ternight?'

Sally could have kissed Gwen, this was the excuse she'd been looking for. 'No, no not ternight, but I might 'ave ter do it Sat'day.'

'That's a shame. That's yer night out wiv Babs, ain't it?'

Sally nodded.

'Can't yer git someone ter swop?'

Sally felt her face flush; she hated telling lies. 'No, I don't think so.'

'That's a shame. It's yer birfday as well, ain't it?'

Sally nodded.

'Don't worry, we'll 'ave Johnny as usual. Pity yer can't go out on yer birfday, though. Bloody war.'

Sally half smiled. It would only be the once, just for her birthday. 'Thanks, Gwen,' she finally said.

'Yer don't look very 'appy,' said Babs, walking in and throwing her hat on the chair. 'It's bin a bit warm terday, ain't it?'

'Babs, about Saturday.'

Babs sat at the table. 'I'm really looking forward ter that. Dunno what I'm gonner wear, though.'

'Babs, I've told Gwen I'm fire watching.'

'What? Why?'

'Well, Granny Brent's a funny old dear and I don't think she'd 'ave Johnny if she knew I was going ter a dance.'

'But it's yer birfday.'

'I know. She don't mind 'aving 'im if I'm fire watching, or going ter the pictures, but a dance – she thinks I'll be after the men and—'

'Silly old cow,' interrupted Babs.

'Don't swear.'

'Well, she is.' Babs laughed. ''Ere, yer going ter tell Pete?'

'No. Why should I?'

'Dunno.'

'I'm sorry I said I'd go, all the fuss it's causing.'

'Don't talk daft. 'Sides, yer deserve a nice night out.' Babs kissed Sally's cheek.

Sally looked at her in surprise. 'What made yer do that?' she asked, gently touching her cheek.

'Dunno,' said Babs flippantly. 'Yer ain't a bad sister. Now how we gonner git yer out of yer siren-suit and tin 'at on Sat'day and inter yer dance frock?'

Sally laughed. 'Couldn't I go in that?'

'Don't think yer'd git many dances.'

Sally put on her tin hat and looked in the mirror, now back on the wall since the raids eased off. 'Oh, I dunno. I think I look rather fetching.'

When Babs told Rachel about the difficulties, she had the solution. They would go to the Silvermans' to get ready. Babs would take their clothes to work, and Sally would meet them there later.

All week Sally felt guilty when she saw Granny Brent. She and Babs had decided not to tell Johnny in case he blurted it out.

'What if we have a raid and get stranded?' Sally asked.

'We don't get that many now,' said Babs as she painted her fingernails.

'What if they meet someone from the factory and ask if I'm fire watching?'

'Now who do they know at the factory?'

Sally shrugged her shoulders.

'Stop worrying. This so-called stocking repairer makes good varnish, don't yer fink?' Babs waved her hand in front of Sally. 'D'yer like the colour?'

'It's all right.'

'Fancy making it red. Would 'ave fought it would o' bin colourless. They must o' known we'd be using it as varnish.'

'It's just a way of getting round regulations, calling it somethink else.'

On Saturday Sally was thrilled when she got home from work to find a long loving letter and birthday card from Pete. Before putting the card on the mantelpiece along with the others, she took it over to show Granny Brent.

'What time yer got ter go back ter work ternight?' asked Granny Brent.

'I'll go along about seven.'

'That's a bit early, ain't it?'

Sally felt her face flush, and she pushed her pipe cleaner curlers further under her turban. 'Me and a couple o' the girls are going fer a drink first. Is that all right?'

'Course, love. Pity Pete ain't 'ere ter take yer out.'

Sally wasn't sure it was a pity. The prospect of the dance was more exciting than anything she could remember.

Chapter 26

Sally couldn't believe her eyes when she walked into the dance hall. It was full of people locked together in each other's arms, a mass of colours moving round the floor in one direction.

Babs, who was looking far older than her sixteen years, was shaking Sally's arm. 'Look at all them uniforms.'

Rachel was smiling. 'Just listen to that music.'

'Wow, am I gonner 'ave a good time ternight,' said Babs, moving forward to make herself seen. Almost at once she was being whisked round the dance floor by a young man in a blue air force uniform.

Sally smiled and sat on a empty seat that ran along the wall. This was so different from the dances Solly used to have. The music was much better and she couldn't see this lot doing a knees-up or the Lambeth Walk.

'Would you like this dance?' a young man wearing army uniform asked her in broken English.

She stood up, and taking her hand he led her into the milling throng. He wasn't a very good dancer, and Sally smiled through her pain every time he stepped on her toes with his large army boots.

'Sorry, don't do a lot of this type of dancing in Poland,'

he said, his brown eyes shining. 'Would you rather have a drink?'

'That would be nice,' replied Sally.

The band began playing a jitterbug and Sally stood watching the girls being thrown over the Americans' shoulders. She was amazed at some of the antics – she'd seen it at the pictures, but this was real life . . . Her toes were tapping and she could hardly contain her excitement.

Babs came towards her, her face flushed to a pretty pink, her eyes bright. She was smiling and dragging an American behind her. 'This is my sister, Sally,' she announced. 'This is Chuck.'

'Hi,' he said casually. 'I'm looking for my buddy.' He raised his hand. 'There he is. Joe. Joe, over here.'

When Joey Power came towards them, Sally felt her heart stop. If he hadn't had a crew cut, he could have been the dead image of Tyrone Power.

The Polish man was standing with two drinks in his hand. 'Did you want this shandy?' he asked.

'Thanks, that's just what I could do with,' said Babs, taking the drink from him.

'Care to dance?' Joey asked Sally.

She nodded, unable to stop staring at his deep brown eyes. He put his arm round her waist and gently eased her through the crowd and on to the dance floor.

All evening they laughed and danced. Sally felt like Cinderella, and knew the time must come soon when they would have to leave. Never in her life had she had so much fun. Rachel had joined Babs and Chuck, and they were busy discussing the sounds of the big American bands. Rachel, to Chuck's delight, was very knowledgeable. Sally could see Babs was a bit put out.

'Say, when can we see you girls again?' asked Chuck.

'When are you in town again?' asked Rachel.

'We could try and get up here, say, next Saturday. It ain't too far away,' said Chuck eagerly.

'But Berkshire's miles away,' said Rachel.

'Not compared to the States,' said Joey. 'Can you make it, Sally?'

'I don't think so,' she said coyly. 'I've got me young brother ter think about.'

'Oh yeah, Johnny. You told me about him.'

'But don't let me stop you two,' Sally said quickly to Babs and Rachel. 'Yer don't need me around. Look, I don't want ter be a spoilsport, but I really think we'd better be off.'

'We'll walk you to the subway,' said Joey.

Sally smiled. 'We call it the Underground.'

'Yeah, and what about all those people sleeping down there? We couldn't believe it when we saw it on the newsreels, could we, Chuck?'

'It's very safe,' said Sally.

Chuck had his arms round Babs and Rachel's shoulders. 'I reckon we should try and get up here next Saturday, Joe. Say, give me your father's phone number, Rachel. I'll give you a ring and we'll make some arrangements.'

'Sure,' said Rachel. 'We can talk some more about big bands.'

'And I'll teach you how to jitterbug.'

She laughed. 'I'd like that.'

Sally could see Babs pouting, and she was very quiet all the way home.

'That was certainly a night,' said Rachel. 'I think that Joe fancied you, Sal. Didn't he look like Tyrone Power with short hair?'

''E said 'is surname's Power,' said Sally.

'Yeah, and I bet 'e told yer 'e lives in Hollywood,' said Babs sullenly.

'He didn't say where he lived,' said Sally.

'Chuck said they live near New York, quite close to each other, I think. He said they were buddies before they joined up. Both worked in some sort of office to do with finance.'

'Yer found out a lot about 'im in a short time,' said Babs to Rachel.

'He does like to talk,' she smiled.

That night, lying in bed, Sally couldn't stop thinking about Joe. He was nice and considerate, and he looked like her hero, Tyrone Power. When she saw films about America, it always seemed so romantic, and so far away. She would love to go out with him next Saturday, but... She twisted her wedding ring round. She was married to Pete, and they had been through a lot together. She turned over, wondering what would happen on her next birthday and resolving to go down to see Pete soon, but the idea of a visit felt like a duty. She cuddled her pillow for comfort. Six months without love was a long while.

The following Saturday Babs and Rachel were going to meet Chuck and Joe.

'Why ain't yer going ter the pictures wiv yer sister ternight?' asked Granny Brent.

'They don't want me. They've got themselves a date,' said Sally.

'Oh?' Granny Brent sat forward. 'And where'd they find 'em?'

'At a dance, I think.'

The old lady straightened her shoulders. 'Just as well yer was fire watching then last weekend, wasn't it?'

Sally grinned. 'Yeah.'

It wasn't till Sunday morning that Sally saw Babs. ''Ave a good time last night?'

'No.'

'Why was that?'

'Rachel and Chuck didn't stop talking and dancing, and that Joe's such a bore. 'E's more interested in you than me, kept asking me all about yer. I told 'im yer married, and yer 'usband's a big beefy docker.'

Sally laughed. 'Who? Pete?'

'Well, 'e got on me nerves.'

Sally put her arm round Babs' shoulder. 'Never mind, there's plenty more out there.'

'Plenty more what?' asked Johnny as he walked into the kitchen half asleep.

'Yanks,' said Sally.

Babs brushed Sally's arm away.

'You going out wiv a Yank?' Johnny's eyes lit up. 'Cor, can 'e git some chewing gum and chocolate and—'

''Ang on, 'ang on. I ain't going out wiv 'im any more.'

'Why?' asked Sally.

''Cos 'e ain't interested in me, I told yer.'

Sally looked at Babs and shook her head. She was worried she would say something about her.

'Well, that ain't very nice, is it, Sis?' said Johnny. 'Why don't yer fink about us fer a change. We could 'ave all sorts o' goodies. D'yer know they can git anyfink, they ain't rationed.'

'Well, if yer fink I'm going out wiv someone just ter git

you chewing gum, yer got another fink coming.' With that little speech she slammed out of the room.

Sally looked at Johnny and shrugged her shoulders.

Over the following weeks Rachel saw Chuck, but Babs didn't go out with Joe again, so just she and Sally went to the pictures. Johnny was now thirteen, and after a lot of pleading, on Saturday nights he stayed with his friend Tony. They'd got themselves a part-time job doing deliveries for the greengrocer. Johnny was thrilled that he was allowed to ride the large delivery bike.

'When I leave school I'm gonner work there all the time.'

'Knowing you, you'll probably change yer mind before then,' said Babs.

It wasn't till August that Sally managed to get a week with Pete again. She was happy in Cardiff, and when she got home she was more miserable than ever. Apart from Pete, something else was missing in her life. Would a baby bring her happiness? But Pete was still against having a baby while the war was on. Perhaps at Christmas, when he came home and saw for himself how quiet things were, she might be able to change his mind.

It was late on Saturday night when Babs came home. Sally was waiting up for her. 'Everything all right?' she asked when she walked in. 'Been out with Rachel?'

'Yeah bin to a dance, did yer 'ave a nice time?'

'Yes thanks, but Cardiff ain't like, well . . .'

'Guess what. Chuck and Joe brought a mate wiv 'em ternight. 'Is name's Benny and 'e's ever ser nice. I'm gonner see 'im next week.'

Sally smiled.

'That Joe keeps asking about yer. I told 'im yer was away wiv yer 'usband.'

Sally tried not to feel too smug about the fact that somebody might be interested in her, nor too irritated that that person knew she'd been away seeing her husband. 'Johnny been all right?' she asked casually.

'Yeah, I fink so. Don't see much of 'im.'

'I'm going up now. We'll 'ave a chat in the morning. Night, Babs.' Sally kissed her sister's cheek.

Sally lay wide awake, thinking. What would Dad have said about Babs going out with an American? Still, it should please Johnny. And what about Johnny wanting to work at the greengrocer's – what would Dad have said about that? Johnny hadn't had much of a chance with his education, though, with schools shut and sitting in the air-raid shelter for hours. Everybody was waiting for the second front to start. They'd all had enough of war. If the Allies did invade, Pete said he and Sally could think about a baby. Every time Sally saw Gwen's Dorothy, she knew that's what she wanted more than anything else in the world.

Two weeks later, when Sally got home from work, there was a note on the table. It was from Granny Brent asking her to come over. Sally froze. Why wasn't she standing at the door like she always did if she wanted to see her? And why wasn't Gwen walking up the road to meet her like she did if there was any letters or news from . . . ?

Sally quickly ran across the road and pushed open the kitchen door. She knew something was wrong.

'Sal.' Gwen jumped to her feet, her eyes were red, and her face wet with tears. 'Oh Sal, what am I gonner do?'

Sally quickly looked round for Granny Brent. 'What's happened? Where's . . . ?'

'She's upstairs.' Gwen sat at the table. 'Sal, both Reg and Danny 'ave bin taken prisoners,' she sobbed.

Sally sunk into a chair. 'Not both of 'em?'

'I love my Danny ser much, I don't want 'im ter . . .'

'Oh Gwen, I'm so sorry.' She put her arms round her sister-in-law and held her close. Gwen's sobs filled Sally's ears. 'D'yer know if they're all right?'

'The Red Cross'll let us know as soon as they can.'

Sally looked at Dorothy playing on the floor, happy and completely oblivious to her father's plight. Perhaps Pete is right after all, she thought to herself. A baby should have both parents.

'Poor Ma,' Sally whispered. 'Shall I go up?'

'Give 'er a little while.' Gwen wiped her eyes on the bottom of her floral apron. 'I'll make a cup o' tea and yer can take it up ter 'er. What we gonner do?'

'Pray they're being well looked after. Does Vera know?'

'No, not yet, she don't finish 'er shift till eight.'

Granny Brent had her eyes closed when Sally walked into the bedroom. Although a big woman, she now looked sad and vulnerable. She had a photograph in her hand Sally knew well. It was the family, taken nearly thirty years ago by the Red Cross who sent it to Granny's husband in the first war. The Brents were all smiling, but they looked so poor.

'I've got yer a cuppa,' whispered Sally, not really wanting to wake her.

'It's all right, love, I ain't asleep, just laying 'ere wiv me eyes closed remembering the good times when we was all tergevver.'

Sally sat on the edge of the bed and took the photo from her hand. How could she call this the good times? 'I'm ever so sorry about Reg and Danny,' she said, looking at the three little boys, Danny just a baby.

'I only 'ope them there Germans look after 'em, not like in the last lot.' She slowly pulled herself up. 'I tell yer, gel, if I lose any more I'll do meself in.'

'Oh don't talk like that Ma. 'Sides, what would little Dorothy do without 'er favourite gran?'

A slight smile lifted her mouth. 'She's lovely, ain't she? When's that Pete gonner make me a gran again?'

'I wish I knew. I keep on about it, but yer know Pete. 'E don't like ter be rushed into anythink.'

'Just ser long as yer don't leave it too long and I ain't 'ere ter see it.' She carefully swung her legs over the side of the bed. 'I'd better go down. Shouldn't 'ave left Gwen like that, but well, after losing me old man, and that Lena going orf, and now this, it all got a bit much.'

Sally patted the back of her hand. 'She understands.'

Sally felt she had to write to Pete telling him about his brothers straight away, although their letters had been less frequent recently. It would be Christmas before she saw him again, but she'd got used to being by herself.

Babs never stopped talking about Benny. Sally sometimes worried about her when she was very late home, but if she mentioned her fears, Babs would fly off the handle, yelling that Sally didn't trust her, but it wasn't Babs she didn't trust. Babs' eyes had a sparkle, especially on Saturdays when she and Benny went with Chuck and Rachel dancing, or to the pictures.

'Dunno why yer don't bring yer Yank 'ome,' said Johnny.

'I ain't gonner parade 'im round fer everyone ter see.'

'Can 'e git me an 'at badge?'

'I dunno, I ain't asked 'im.'

'What about some chocolate?'

'I eats it.'

'Yer mean cow.'

'Stop swearing, Johnny.'

'Well it's 'er.'

'Stop it, the pair of you.'

'Yer wonner ask yer big sister ter find 'erself a Yank,' said Babs, walking out of the kitchen.

'Yeah, why don't yer, Sal? 'E'd be a lot more fun than boring old Pete.'

'Pete ain't boring.' Sally felt she had to leap to Pete's defence.

It was weeks later that Babs asked Sally if she could bring Benny home on the Sunday to tea as he had a weekend pass.

'Where's he staying Saturday night?' asked Sally, almost dreading the answer.

''E's going to the American club,' she smiled. 'Don't worry I ain't jumping inter 'is bed.'

Sally looked at her young sister and swallowed hard. Babs had grown into a lovely-looking girl who took a lot of pride in her appearance. Mum and Dad would have been proud of her.

All Sunday afternoon Sally and Babs had been fussing around laying the table and trying to make tea look a lot more than it was. They had got shrimps and winkles, and

Babs sat patiently taking all the winkles out of the shells and putting them in vinegar.

'No good giving 'im a pin. 'E wouldn't know 'ow ter git 'em out,' laughed Babs when Johnny asked her what she was doing.

'And you, young man, can go and smarten yerself up, and comb yer 'air,' yelled Sally after him.

Sally and Babs tried to stifle their laughter when Johnny walked back into the kitchen, his hair was parted on one side and stuck flat against his head with water. 'This all right?' He was still trying to smooth it down with his hands.

'You look very smart,' said Sally.

'Well, it all better be worf it. If I don't git an 'at badge I'll ruffle it all up again.'

Sally had to go into the scullery and bury her head in the towel behind the door to suppress her giggles.

This was the first time Sally had met Benny, and he appeared to be a very pleasant young man. Johnny was over the moon with his badge, chocolates and gum, and told him he could come again.

Benny told them he lived just out of New York, and his father was a businessman. He showed them photographs of his parents.

'This is a lovely house,' said Sally. 'Is it yours?'

'Yeah,' he smiled. 'I was born there. I'm the only boy. Got an older sister, she's married. It almost broke Ma's heart when I volunteered for the army.'

'Why did yer?' asked Sally, holding the photo.

'Felt it was the right thing to do.'

'Do that Chuck and Joe live near you?' she asked tentatively. 'Chuck said they live in New York.'

'No, there's a lot o' people live in that city.'

'Oh.'

'Why, you interested in them?' Benny grinned, showing his white even teeth. He was very good-looking.

'No, course not,' laughed Sally. 'I only just wondered. America always seems such an exciting place ter live.'

'It can be.'

'More tea?' asked Babs.

'No thanks. The bombing must have been hell. How did you guys put up with it?'

'We 'ad to,' said Babs. 'Me and 'im was evacuated at the very beginning o' the war, but we come back when the old lady started putting 'im in a cupboard.'

'No!' Benny's pale blue eyes widened. 'What for?'

'She just did,' said Johnny quickly.

Babs whispered in Benny's ear, and Johnny went bright red. 'I was only a kid at the time,' he said, picking up his badge and polishing it on his coat sleeve.

All too soon it was time for Benny to leave. Babs said she'd walk with him to the tram stop.

'I like 'im, Sal,' said Johnny after they'd gone.

'So do I,' said Sally wistfully.

On Monday, on her way home from work, Sally decided to call on Granny Brent first. The door was on the latch and as she walked down the passage she could hear her talking to Gwen.

'Well, I fink it's all wrong. She's only a slip of a kid. And I blame that Sally fer letting 'er sister go out wiv a Yank, parading 'im up the Grove like 'e was some sort o' film star.'

Sally knew they were talking about Babs. Trust Granny Brent to be looking out of her window when Benny went past. She was angry and wanted to run in and defend her sister, but thought better of it. She quietly turned and went out.

Chapter 27

Pete was very upset that his brothers had been taken prisoners of war, and he worried about the effect it might have on his mother. Sally had tried hard to reassure him in her letters that Granny Brent was well, and as far as they knew his brothers were safe. Gwen and his mother had been told by the Red Cross they could be hearing from them quite soon. Before, when she'd seen on the newsreels the soldiers fighting in North Africa, Sally had always eagerly looked for Danny and Reg. Many times she had imagined she saw Danny's cheeky face grinning at her from the screen. Now the scenes from North Africa upset her.

Although Babs saw Benny almost every weekend, when she got her first letter from him she sat and read it over and over again.

'Yer do like 'im, don't yer?' she asked Sally for the tenth time.

'Yes I do.'

'I think 'e's really dreamy.' Babs held his letter close to her heart.

'Oh Babs, yer like a lovesick schoolgirl.'

'No I ain't.' She quickly put the letter to one side.

There was a touch of winter in the air now and, walking

home from work, Sally was not looking forward to the long, dark, dreary lonely nights ahead. She missed having Pete's arms wrapped round her, keeping her warm, and contented, although in other ways she didn't miss him at all. She wished she had Jessie to talk to. She sighed and, pushing open the front door, was pleased to see on the mat a letter for her. Much to her surprise it was from Joey.

Dear Sally,

I hope you don't mind me writing to you. I got your address from Benny. He seems really stuck on Babs. He's always talking about her. I know you're married and your husband is working away, but I was wondering as Chuck goes out with Rachel, and Benny with Babs, if perhaps we could go to a movie one Saturday? Just as friends, of course. It gets very lonely here on camp even with all these guys around. I'll understand if you don't think it's right, but I can assure you it will be strictly platonic.

Yours gratefully,

Joey Power.

Sally read it over again, and was tickled pink to think someone actually wanted to take her out. But should she go? She sat at the table and read the letter again, grinning. It couldn't come to any harm just going to the pictures with him, could it – just two lonely people sitting in a cinema together? After all, she hadn't hid the fact that she was married. But what would Pete say, or Granny Brent?

Sally quickly put the letter in her coat pocket when Johnny walked in behind her. There was no point in telling him.

That evening, when Johnny was in bed and Babs was standing in front of the mirror putting her hair in curlers, Sally said casually, 'I had a letter from Joey today.'

Babs spun round. 'What?'

Sally took the letter from the pocket of her coat that hung behind the kitchen door, and handed it to her.

When Babs finished reading it she looked up. 'Well, what yer gonner do?'

'Don't know.'

'Yer know it won't do any 'arm.'

'But I couldn't go, could I?'

'Why not? Who's ter know?'

Sally grinned. 'Mind you, I could always say I was going with you.'

'You little devil, Mrs Brent.'

'If I did go, you wouldn't think it wrong, would yer?' Sally was full of concern.

'Na. 'Sides, if I asked Benny we could go tergevver.'

'Could you? Would 'e mind?' asked Sally eagerly.

'Course not. Gives yer somethink ter fink about, don't it?'

Sally nodded.

'I'm off up. Goodnight.'

Babs left Sally to her thoughts. She sat for a while, trying to weigh it all up. Half of her wanted to go out with someone, but deep down she didn't want to deceive Pete. But after all, it was only to the pictures, and anyway, if she went on her own she could find herself sitting next to an American. That thought convinced her.

On Saturday, Sally wasn't sure what to wear. She didn't want to be over-dressed, nor did she want to look dowdy.

She finally settled on her grey suit. She had taken extra care with her hair and make-up. Looking in the mirror for the fourth time, she giggled. 'You're acting like a silly schoolgirl now,' she said out loud to her reflection, patting her hair.

As she closed the front door she looked up and down the Grove, making sure nobody was about, pleased the nights were drawing in so that with the blackout curtains drawn, Granny Brent wouldn't see her going out. She would be sure to comment about her being a bit done up just to be going to the pictures with Babs.

Johnny was no problem now. He was staying the night with Tony when they finished work. Sally's heart was thumping as she tottered along in her high heels. She was meeting them outside the cinema, and felt like a young girl going on her first date. As she boarded the bus it suddenly occurred to her that this was her first ever date. She and Pete had just drifted into love and marriage. She sat upstairs on the bus and, lighting a cigarette, hoped nobody she knew would see her. Thankfully, the bus windows were covered with green anti-splinter mesh, and the lights were very dim. She felt excited, nervous, and very guilty.

Joey's broad smile melted her fears. He produced a box of chocolates. 'Don't worry, we get plenty of candy,' he told her in his soft modulated drawl. 'We don't have rationing on camp.'

Inside the cosy dark cinema, Babs and Benny sat next to them. Benny had his arm round Babs, but to Sally's relief Joey made no attempt to do that.

At the end of the film they decided to go to Lyons Corner House. Joey had very good manners, pulling out Sally's chair, lighting her cigarette for her. She had never been treated like this before. Over their cup of tea she laughed and relaxed, but all too soon it was time for her to go.

'If I can get away, could we do the same next week?' Joey asked as they walked slowly to the bus stop.

'I suppose so,' said Sally coyly. 'Come on, Babs,' she called over her shoulder to her sister, who was locked in Benny's arms.

'I'll let Rachel know,' said Joey, as Babs and Sally climbed on the bus.

The following morning Sally was singing along with the wireless when Granny Brent walked into the kitchen. 'You sound 'appy.'

Sally held her heart. 'Yer frightened the life out o' me.'

'Did yer go ter the pictures last night?' she asked, sitting herself at the table. 'Vera come over ter see if yer wanted ter 'ave a game o' cards, but you was out.'

Sally was taken off guard. 'Yes, I went with Babs,' she said quickly.

'What about 'er boyfriend? She packed 'im in already?'

'No, 'e was at camp.' Sally was flustered.

'Oh.'

Sally hated being deceitful.

'I've only come ter say that I've 'eard on the grapevine the coalman might be round this way termorrer, and if I see 'im, d'yer want a bag?'

'Yes, please. D'you want a cuppa tea?'

'No fanks, love. See yer termorrer.' She left as silently as she had come.

As Sally closed the door behind Granny Brent she wondered whether she'd seen her go out last night. Why would she come over just to ask about coal? She knew they would have it. Granny Brent was a forceful woman, and

Sally wondered if she'd be on the look out for her going out next Saturday. Sally smiled to herself. I'll tell her I'm going with Babs again, she decided. But what would she say if she knew I was going with a Yank? Sally sat at the table and pulled at the tablecloth's loose chenille threads. What about Pete? Once more she was filled with guilt, although it was strictly as a friend that she would be seeing Joey again, and at the moment she desperately needed a friend.

After that, every Saturday Joey could manage they went to the pictures. Babs and Benny didn't always go with them. Sally enjoyed Joey's company. They laughed a lot and she found they liked the same things. He was so different from Pete, happy-go-lucky, perhaps because he didn't know where he would finish up and there was no point worrying. Many Americans were being sent to Europe and Asia, and it upset Sally to see the fighting in the papers and on the newsreels.

One evening at the end of November Joey announced that next week was his birthday. Babs had already told Sally that she and Benny, and Rachel and Chuck were going to a dance, then on to a club, and they wanted Joey and Sally to join them. Sally said she would think about it.

This evening, Sally and Joey walked to the bus stop alone, discussing the dance. Benny was on duty so Babs wasn't with them.

'Oh come on, honey,' said Joey. 'It should be good fun.'

Sally hesitated. 'I don't know.'

'After all, it is my birthday.'

'Oh all right.' She smiled broadly, something she found she was doing a lot lately.

'Great.' Joey grabbed hold of her and kissed her on the

mouth. 'Sorry,' he said quickly. 'I promised myself I wouldn't do that.'

'That's all right,' said Sally softly.

They continued walking in silence.

'See you next week,' said Sally, when the bus came, standing on the platform and waving.

As she sat in her seat the conductress came down the stairs. 'Fares, please,' she called.

It was Vera. Sally wanted to curl up and die.

''Allo, Sal. You look a bit tarted up. What yer doing out round this way?'

'Been ter the pictures.'

'What, on yer own?'

'No.' She couldn't say she was with Babs as Babs would have been on the bus as well. 'I went with Rachel,' she said quickly. 'Yer know, the girl Babs works with.' Had Vera seen her at the bus stop with Joey? Sally's head was spinning.

'Oh yeah?' Vera reached up and rang the bell. 'Good film was it? What d'yer see?' she asked brusquely.

Sally was sure Vera didn't believe her. 'The new Betty Grable film. It was very good.' Well, at least that bit was true.

'Yer lipstick's smudged.'

Sally dived into her handbag and took out a mirror and a handkerchief. 'Must o' bin when I 'ad a little cry over the newsreel. It showed some of the prisoners of war, and I can't 'elp thinking about Reg and Danny.' Again, that was true.

'That always makes me a bit weepy as well. Gotter go. Some o' these'll try and jump off wivout paying if I ain't quick enough.'

Sally breathed a sigh of relief. She would have to stop seeing Joey. She couldn't stand this way of carrying on.

'But yer promised 'im,' said Babs angrily the following morning when Sally told her she wasn't going to the dance.

'I know, but I got on Vera's bus last night and I know she suspects something by the way she looked at me, and 'e'd smudged me lipstick.'

Babs laughed. 'So 'e kissed yer then?'

'Shut up.' Sally's thoughts were in a turmoil.

'It ain't doing any 'arm. 'Sides, they could all go off and get killed soon,' said Babs flippantly.

'Don't say things like that,' said Sally, genuinely concerned.

'It's true though – then yer'd be sorry.'

Babs was right: what harm did it do? And Sally did like being in Joey's company. Well, she had all week to think about it.

Sally was pleased Joey wasn't like a lot of the brash Americans, and at the dance, when he held her close and she felt his warm breath on her neck, it seemed she was floating on air. He smiled down at her and she could imagine she really was dancing with Tyrone Power. She never dreamt she could enjoy herself so much – the music, the company, it all seemed unreal. Over coffee he told her about his family. She sat listening, enthralled at his soft, slow drawl. There was nothing loud about Joey. He told her he came from a small town and that his parents owned a farm.

'Is it very big?'

He laughed. 'Not to our standards, but I guess to you guys over here it is.'

Sally suddenly sat up. 'But Chuck told Rachel you were both from New York.'

'I'm afraid Chuck tends to shoot his mouth off. He likes to impress people.'

'What about Benny?' asked Sally, worried that Babs had also been told a tale.

'You don't have ter worry about him. He really does come from New York, and his family have plenty of dough.'

Sally smiled. 'I don't want to see Babs hurt.'

'Benny's all right. What about you?' Joey took her hand.

She shivered with excitement, but, feeling guilty, quickly pulled her hand away. 'I'm all right.'

'This Pete must be quite a guy. I'd sure like to meet him sometime.'

'I don't think that would be a very good idea.'

'Sally, that's a pretty name, goes with a pretty girl.'

Sally blushed. 'Don't talk daft.'

'Sally, could I see you again, not just at the movies? Could we go somewhere quiet? Perhaps in the country for the day?'

Sally felt embarrassed. She took her compact from her handbag and peered in the mirror. 'Don't know,' she said, running her little finger over her lips. 'It's a bit cold in the country this time of year.'

'I'd like to see a little of the real English countryside before it's too late.' He toyed with his cigarette.

She snapped the compact shut. 'Why?'

'We may be moving on soon.'

'D'yer know when?' she asked softly.

'The sarge reckons it could be just after Christmas. A lot o' guys have got a seven-day furlough over the holiday.'

''Ave you?'

He nodded. 'But mine's not till after Christmas.' He tapped his cigarette into the ashtray.

'Do you know where you might be sent?' asked Sally.

'He can't tell us, but we don't think we'll be staying in England.'

Sally suddenly felt sad. 'I wish you hadn't told me that,' she said. 'I was enjoying myself up till now.'

Joey smiled and shook his head. 'I don't believe this. You care? Really care?'

Sally was taken off guard. She did like him, but had to bluff this out. 'Course I do, you're a nice bloke. Come on, they're playing "In the Mood".' She leapt to her feet and pulled him up. At least this wasn't a slow dance and he wouldn't hold her so close.

For the rest of the evening she tried to keep it light-hearted. When they went on to the club Benny and Babs were getting a little drunk and spent all the time in each other's arms. Sally was worried about her sister. She knew Babs adored him and would do anything he asked. Sally was determined to stay sober and keep an eye on her.

'Sal?' Babs peered in the mirror in the club's ladies' room. 'I ain't coming 'ome ternight. Me and Benny's going to an 'otel.'

'What?'

'Shh, keep yer voice down. Don't want everyone ter come wiv us.' She looked round the room grinning.

'But, Babs, yer only sixteen . . .'

'Sal,' her voice became serious, 'I know what I'm doing. I love Benny and want ter be wiv 'im.'

Sally suddenly realized her little sister was growing up. 'But Babs, what if yer finish up wiv a baby?'

'I'll 'ave ter go ter America then, won't I?' She leant forward and said softly, 'Sal, I really do love 'im, and as they're going away I want 'im ter be the first.'

Sally looked at her. What could she say? Would this be happening if their father was still alive? 'Babs, there ain't no answer to that. But, Babs . . . be careful.'

Babs kissed her cheek and said cheerfully, 'Well, yer know what they say: if yer can't be good be careful.'

Sally looked sad and added almost to herself, 'And if yer can't be careful name the first one after me.'

Babs threw her head back and laughed. 'Come on. Let's go and sing 'appy birthday ter Joey before 'is birthday's all over.' She pulled Sally up from the stool.

It was well past midnight when Sally realised she might have missed the last bus. 'What am I gonner do?' she asked as they queued to collect their coats from the cloakroom.

'Come ter the hotel wiv us,' said Babs.

'How can I? What if Granny Brent comes over in the morning?'

'I dunno why yer worry about that old woman.'

'It's because she's my mother-in-law, that's why.'

Babs raised her well-defined eyebrows. 'Is that the only reason you won't come with us?'

Sally didn't answer and quickly looked away, pretending she hadn't heard her.

Outside, Sally decided to try the Underground. It meant a long walk the other end, and Joey wanted to see her all the way home but she declined. Sefton Grove was the last place she wanted to be seen with him, but there was no way she was going to stay out with him all night. Well, not tonight anyway.

As they walked towards the station he put his arm round her waist and she didn't pull away. She felt contented, she knew she could easily fall in love with him. It would be very different from the kind of love that she had for Pete – that was a steady dependable love. With Joey it would be for now, full of laughter and fun. When the train arrived he kissed her goodnight and, as they went their separate ways, deep down Sally knew she wanted to be with him, but didn't have the guts to say so.

It was Sunday afternoon when Babs got home. Sally had had a bad night worrying about her, and all day she'd been anxious, so she greeted her with open arms when Babs finally walked in.

Babs looked embarrassed. 'What's this in aid of?' she asked, pushing Sally away.

'I've been worried about yer.'

'I'm all right.'

'Is that all yer got ter say?'

Babs grinned. 'Why? D'yer want me ter go inter all the grimy details?'

It was Sally's turn to be embarrassed. 'Course not.'

Sally picked up the kettle and shook it. 'I'll get some water and make a cuppa tea.'

'Sal, me and Benny want ter git married.'

Sally sat down at the table wide-eyed. 'But yer only known 'im a few months.'

'I know. But I do love 'im, and 'e loves me.'

'Are yer sure it's not just because 'e's lonely and a long way from 'ome?'

'No.'

'But, Babs, you're so young, and 'ow old is Benny?'

'Twenty. We've made up our minds, Sal.'

'What can I say?'

'Yer could say you'll give us yer consent.'

'Will yer go ter America?' Sally's voice was soft.

'I expect so, one day.'

Tears rolled down Sally's face.

'Oh come on.' Babs held her tight. 'Don't start crying.'

Sally wiped her eyes on the bottom of her pinny. 'I can't 'elp it. My little sister getting married and going off ter America. Everybody's leaving me.'

Babs held her tight. 'I didn't fink it would upset yer like this.' She, too, was crying.

Sally felt Babs' warm tears against her cheek. She knew she mustn't stop her sister's happiness.

The week before Christmas a letter arrived from Pete, saying he would be coming home for Christmas.

Sally sat thinking of the past. There were so few friends around now. Even the odd times on birthdays she'd been in the Nag's with Granny Brent, it seemed empty and quiet. This was the second Christmas without their father and they still all missed him. Johnny said very little about his dad, and Sally was pleased he had Tony to talk to and go around with – more so since Pete was away.

Sally envied Jessie when she wrote and told her about the wonderful Christmas she was going to have with Vic. She wished she had Jessie to confide in, especially about Benny and Babs.

Babs was thrilled when she received a letter and card from Benny's sister in New York.

''E's told 'er all about me,' she said as she read the letter.

'That's nice. Did she mention anythink about 'im getting married?'

'Course not. We've only just talked about it ourselves. She writes a nice letter, though, look.'

Sally was pleased Benny did really love Babs and not just think of her as a one off.

'She's asked me ter write back.'

Benny would be spending Christmas with them and was thrilled to be invited to celebrate in an English home. Sally had warned him not to get too excited as things were very scarce, but he told her not to worry, he'd bring his rations. Sally had discreetly asked him to say nothing about Joey in front of Pete. Chuck was also on leave and spending Christmas with Rachel. Although the Silvermans were Jews, they still had a good spread.

Joey was on duty over Christmas, and Sally felt sad that he would be on his own.

She looked up at the few paper chains she'd managed to get hold of. She was determined to have a good time and do the best they could. Even Johnny was going to get some fruit from his boss. They had saved their meat ration and were all going over to Granny Brent's for dinner, although there wasn't any sign of Tommy Tanner's chickens again this year.

Chapter 28

Pete was home on Christmas Eve. Sally hung dutifully on to his arm as they walked into the smoke-filled pub. After everybody had finished patting him on the back and greeting him warmly, the customers asked him to play the piano. He wasn't as skilled as Reg, but soon it was like old times, people buying him drinks as he banged out all the old tunes. Sally realised how happy she was, surrounded by people she loved and who loved her.

Benny's presence caused a lot of whispered interest. He and Babs sat at Granny Brent's table along with Sally and Vera. Granny Brent had given him the once over earlier.

'Yer don't mind Benny coming over fer dinner termorrow, do yer?' asked Sally, trying to make herself heard above the singing.

'Course not.' Granny Brent gave him a big smile. 'All that stuff 'e's brought's gonner give us a bloody fine Christmas. Ain't seen ser many luxuries fer years. Mind you, I don't like that peanut butter stuff – makes the jam taste funny.'

Benny laughed.

Sally had also been amazed at the food Benny had brought them, including things they'd never even heard of.

Sadie Tanner came waddling over. 'Don't see ser much of yer now,' she said, talking to Granny Brent but all the while studying Benny.

'Ain't got nobody ter bring me out much now, 'ave I?' said Granny Brent brusquely.

'My Tommy couldn't git any chickens again this year. 'E could only git us a duck.' She gave Benny a broad grin.

'Where'd 'e git that from?' asked Granny Brent.

Sadie pulled her coat round her. 'I don't ask.'

Sally wanted to laugh. She could just imagine Tommy in the park chasing a duck round the pond.

'I'd rather 'ave chicken,' said Granny Brent.

Sadie moved closer. 'Not ser keen on duck meself. It's a bit greasy.' She patted her big black hat, not taking her eyes off Benny all the while she was talking. 'But beggers can't be choosers, can they son?'

Granny Brent looked annoyed. 'Well I 'ope fer your sake it ain't tough,' she said, straightening her shoulders. 'Ovverwise yer might break yer false teef.'

'Mum,' said Vera, giving her a look.

'S'all right, gel. I'm used ter yer muvver's sharp tongue after all these years. Don't see anyfink o' your Lena now. She's in the air force, ain't she?'

'She was last time we 'eard,' said Vera quickly.

'She ain't 'ad no leave at all, 'as she? She found 'erself a fancy man then, or somebody else's?' Sadie threw her head back and laughed.

Sally was worried, she could see Granny Brent was beginning to get rattled.

'Dunno, it ain't none of my business.'

'Since when?' asked Sadie, swaying uneasily.

Granny Brent's look was forbidding. Turning away, she tutted loudly.

Sally gave Babs a nod.

'Ben, Sally want's anovver drink,' said Babs, also noting the danger signals.

'Sure, hon.'

Sadie sidled up to Ben. 'See yer got yerself one of our gels already. You spending Christmas wiv 'em?'

Ben smiled. 'I sure am.'

'You'll be 'aving plenty on yer table then,' she said to Sally. Then turning back to Ben said sweetly. 'Yer gits 'old of plenty o' nice fings, so I've 'eard.'

Sally couldn't believe the silly look Sadie was giving Benny, but was pleased they'd changed the subject.

'We do all right,' said Benny. 'Can I get you a drink?'

'Ta ever so, I'm on gin as well ternight,' she said looking at the table. 'Got ter make the most of it ain't we gel, when Wally's got a few bottles in,' she said, looking at Granny Brent who was still ignoring her.

Nobody moved up to give Sadie a seat, and Benny put the drink in her hand.

'Ta.' She smiled up in his face, her eyes glassy. 'My Ted's in the jungle. The poor sod's 'aving a bad time.'

Granny Brent visibly bristled. 'And what about my poor boys, I bet they ain't 'aving a good time stuck in some godforsaken prison camp.'

Tommy came swaggering over to them. He put his arm round Sadie's shoulders. 'There's a drink on the table for yer, Ma.'

She looked up at him, then at Benny. 'This 'ere's me boy, 'e's a good lad.'

Sally wanted to laugh at that.

‘’Allo mate,’ said Tommy, giving Benny a nod. ‘I’ll ’ave ter ’ave a word with yer sometime. ’Eard yer can get ’old of some good gear.’

Benny looked puzzled.

Sally stood up. ‘I think Mr Tanner’s calling you, Sadie.’

‘Oh yeah, ’e’s got me anovver drink. Merry Christmas all.’

Granny Brent picked up her glass and watched Sadie and Tommy Tanner weave their way back, knocking into a few tables as they went. ‘Look at that. The silly cow’s gone an’ spilt that bloke’s drink. Serve ’em right if ’e upped ’em one. I would ’ave give ’er one if she’d stayed ’ere much longer,’ she said, quickly knocking back her gin.

‘What did her boy wanner see me about?’ asked Benny.

‘Probably ter find out if yer can get anythink fer ’im ter sell on the black market,’ said Sally.

‘Don’t yer ’ave anyfink ter do wiv ’im, lad,’ said Granny Brent. ‘A bad lot, those Tanners.’

Benny grinned.

After a few more drinks Granny Brent sat back and started to reminisce. Benny thought she was wonderful and hung on to her every word. She told him how she lived in the old days and, of course, her boys.

Babs was getting a little impatient with him, and tried hard to pull him away.

‘Hang on, honey,’ he said, taking her arm from his. ‘Granny Brent sure has a tale to tell.’

‘’E’s a nice lad,’ she said when he bought her another drink. ‘Looking forward ter Christmas then, son?’

‘I sure am.’

'What about yer mum and dad?'

'They've got my sister, and they'll have a lot o' friends over.' He looked a little sad.

Sally was pleased Pete started to play a knees-up. She hadn't told Granny Brent about him and Babs getting married. 'Come on, Ben, we've got ter teach yer ter do this.' She dragged him to his feet. She didn't want anyone to be sad this year, but her thoughts briefly went to Joey. Would he be sad on his own?

Christmas morning, everybody eagerly opened their presents which, as usual, Sally had spent hours searching the shops for. But it was Benny's presents that brought forth the most ohhs and ahhs. Sally had some nylon stockings. She had heard about them, but never seen them before. She couldn't believe how fine they were, and unconsciously, unable to suppress her excitement, kissed Benny's cheek.

'Hey,' he rubbed his cheek.

Babs laughed. 'Watch it. 'E ain't Joe, yer know.'

Sally froze. Had Pete heard her?

'Oh yeah, and who's this Joe then?' Pete asked casually, looking up from his presents.

'A friend o' mine,' volunteered Benny quickly.

'You bin out wiv 'im then, Sal?' Pete's voice was low and even.

She felt her face flush. 'I went with a crowd of 'em when it was 'is birthday.'

'Yer didn't tell me.'

'Wasn't anythink ter tell. Right, let's get this paper cleared away, then I'll pop over ter Ma's ter see if she needs 'and.'

'You'd better see Babs' present first,' said Benny, handing Babs a brightly coloured box.

Her face went scarlet when she opened it. 'Oh Ben, Ben!' She threw her arms round his neck and kissed his face all over.

'Dunno what 'e's given 'er, but it must be pretty good,' said Pete, looking amused.

'Let me see it,' Sally asked Babs. She knew it was an engagement ring. Benny had already told her, but she hadn't said anything to Pete about them getting married, and she was pleased it took away the tension there might have been over the mention of Joe. 'It's lovely,' she enthused.

'What's this then?' asked Pete as Babs held out her hand with the ring on her finger.

'Me and Benny's gonner git married.'

'What?' Pete quickly looked at Sally. 'Did yer know about this?'

She nodded.

'And yer gonner let 'er?'

'Yes, if that's what she wants.'

Benny put his arm round Babs' waist. 'Don't you approve then, Pete?'

'Dunno. It's a bit sudden.'

''Fraid we don't have a lot of time these days for too many formalities. You of all people should know that.'

Pete didn't answer Benny but turned to Babs. 'You're a bit young, Babs. If yer dad was still 'ere, 'e wouldn't 'ave approved.'

'Well 'e ain't, and fer all we know we may not be 'ere fer much longer, so we're gonner grab all the 'appiness we can.' She rushed into the scullery.

Sally knew she was crying and quickly followed her.

'I'm sorry, Babs. Don't take any notice of Pete. Yer know what 'e's like.'

'You don't mind though, do yer?' sobbed Babs.

'Course I don't. If Benny's gonner make you 'appy, then that's all I worry about.'

''E will. I know 'e will.'

Sally wondered what Pete's reaction would be if he knew Babs and Benny had spent the night in a hotel together.

'Come on, dry those tears. Let's enjoy this Christmas.' Sally put a comforting arm round her sister's shoulders. 'Who knows where yer'll be this time next year. Yer could be in America.'

A smile lifted Babs' face. 'Yeah. I'm really gonner read all about America. I'll make Benny a good wife.'

''Ave yer decided when you'll get married?'

'No. There's a lot of forms and fings 'e's gotter fill in and 'e reckons if we start now by the time they git back from wherever they're sent overseas, we should be able ter git married right away.'

Sally cuddled her sister close. She couldn't believe this was her little Babs. She thought of the time she was evacuated. She had looked so lost and vulnerable then. Now she was talking about getting married. How the years had flown. Would this war ever be over?

Sally couldn't look at Babs. What if Benny never . . . ?

'Right, now wipe yer face,' she said suddenly, 'and come back in the kitchen.'

Pete looked glum when Sally returned. 'Come on, cheer up. You coming over ter Mum's with me?'

'Yeah, I'll just git me coat.'

Outside Sally turned on him. 'Look, Pete, I know yer

mean well, but I think we should let Babs make up 'er own mind.'

'But a Yank? What she wonner git 'erself mixed up wiv a Yank fer?'

''E is nice, and she loves 'im.'

'Huh. Loves? She don't know the meaning of the word.'

Sally almost said, do you? But held her tongue.

'She's still only a kid. What is it about these blokes? Is it their flash uniforms? I reckon what they say about 'em's true: over 'ere, overpaid and oversexed. Good job yer dad ain't 'ere. 'E'd 'ave somethink ter say about all this.'

'Well 'e ain't, so don't go poking yer nose in where it ain't wanted.' Sally was angry with Pete but more angry with herself for reacting like this. This wasn't how she wanted this Christmas to be.

'Does Ma know?' he asked, pushing open the front door.

'No.'

'Yer gonner tell 'er?'

'I'll let Babs do that.'

'You'll let Babs do what?' asked Vera, coming down the stairs.

'She'll tell yer later,' said Pete.

'Well, whatever it is, Pete, it ain't made yer very 'appy by the look on yer face.'

Sally laughed. 'Come on, let's give Ma 'and.'

Gwen had taken Dorothy to her mother's this year. Sally felt the number of people spending Christmas with them was shrinking, and knew Christmases would never be the same till Reg and Danny came home. She was pleased to have Benny with them, but secretly worried as to where Babs might be next year.

'Very nice,' said Granny Brent at the ring Babs proudly displayed, though Sally noted that when Babs turned away Granny Brent gave her a look of disapproval, but said nothing.

After dinner they sat round the fire and talked about the old days. Benny couldn't believe it when earlier Sally got Pete to carry a bag of coal across the road to his mother's.

'It's in very short supply,' she told Benny. 'We won't be 'aving a fire in 'er ternight, so Pete's ma can 'ave a fire in the front room as well. We all 'ave ter help out.'

After tea they went into the front room and Pete played the piano. They sang all the latest, and a lot of the old songs, then, all too quickly, once again Christmas was over.

It was quiet in the camp as most of the guys were on furlough. Joey lay on his bed, hands behind his head. Rumours were flying around all the time but they still didn't know for certain where they were being sent. Benny and Chuck were lucky to be spending Christmas with families. Joey thought about his own family. It seemed a lifetime since he had seen them. This life was so different to the farm, but he was seeing the world. He would never have come to England, or met Sally, if he hadn't joined the army. He smiled. Sally was such fun to be with, not silly and giggly like a lot of girls he'd met. If only she wasn't married. He wanted to tell her he loved her, but knew she loved her husband. Benny was a lucky son of a gun, having money, looks and Babs. He would be part of Sally's family one day.

Joey knew he had to see Sally again before they moved

on. He'd tried hard not to tell her how he felt, it wouldn't be fair, but if anything happened to Pete . . . How can I tell her I love her? How can I make her love me? He turned over, he loved her, and at this moment he ached for her, and wanted her warm sweet smelling body next to his.

Vera was working Saturday night, so Sally and Pete had taken Granny Brent to the Nag's. It had been a noisy, lively evening, and despite the fact that Pete had to go back to Cardiff the following morning, they had enjoyed themselves.

Pete, with one arm round Sally, lay on his back, the end of his cigarette glowing in the dark.

She felt so happy, there hadn't been any raids over Christmas so they'd been sleeping in their bed and made love every night. She didn't want this to end, she didn't want him to go away. She cuddled up to him, but suddenly her thoughts went to Joey, was he thinking of her? He was going away. She couldn't ever let herself be tempted to spend a night with him. She'd finish up with nothing if Pete ever found out . . . She shuddered.

'Cold, love?' asked Pete pulling her closer.

She had to think about her own future. 'Pete, now that things are quietening down can we think about a baby?'

He blew smoke into the air. 'D'yer know love, I've bin toying with the same idea.'

'You 'ave? Oh Pete.' She smothered his face with kisses.

''Ere, steady on gel.'

'I'm coming to Cardiff at Easter.'

Pete leaned over and stubbed out his cigarette. 'That'll be nice.' He paused. 'Sal. About Babs and this Yank.'

Sally bristled, why did he have to spoil things, and why

couldn't he call him Benny? 'I know you don't approve, but this is war time and . . .'

He raised himself up on his elbow. 'Ma reckons she's far too young ter fink about gitting married.'

Sally sat up. 'D'yer honestly think they will get married? 'E's going abroad. What if 'e gets killed?' Her voice was rising in anger. 'Don't you of all people think she deserves somethink ter look forward to? Christ, she lost 'er mum and dad in a short time, besides almost being killed in air raids. Let 'er 'ave some happiness. Beside, it ain't none of yer mother's business.'

'Shh. Keep yer voice down.'

Sally was angry, very angry. Joey wouldn't think like this. She got out of bed and went to the window, and pulled back the blackout curtains. 'We all need somethink to look forward to,' she whispered, staring out at the dark night.

Pete sat up. 'Are yer going out with any Yanks?'

She felt stunned and held on to the window sill. 'Course not. What made yer ask that?'

'Ma reckons yer going out a lot lately.'

Sally bit her lip. 'I told you, I go ter the pictures wiv Babs and Rachel . . .'

'Yeah, but what about when they go wiv their Yanks.' Pete spat the words out. 'Who d'yer go wiv?'

Sally felt trapped. What had Granny Brent told him? Why hadn't he said anything before? Why did he have to wait till now? Had Vera told him she'd seen her on her bus? All these questions were racing round her head. 'I told yer, I went ter a dance with 'em once. Yer don't begrudge me that, do you?'

'Was that wiv this Joey bloke?'

Sally was taken aback. He'd remembered his name. She

had to bluff this out. 'I think that was Benny's mate's name.'

Pete threw himself back on the bed. 'Christ Sal, yer ought ter bloody well know 'is name if yer was wiv 'im all night.'

'I wasn't with 'im all night, I just 'ad a few dances with 'im, that's all.'

'Gwen's husband's away, but yer don't see 'er gadding about wiv Yanks.'

'I ain't been gadding about with Yanks. Gwen's got a baby ter . . .' She stopped. She wasn't going to make excuses, or commit herself. She liked Joey, he was good company and although she often thought about him, she was married to Pete.

'So this is what this is all about?'

'No.' Sally sat on the bed. 'Pete, I love you very much, and I miss you. I've got nobody ter go out with, only Babs.' She felt tears rolling down her cheeks. 'I get so lonely. It's all right fer you, yer can go up the pub with your mates and have a drink and play cards, but I can't.' She sniffed. 'I ain't even got Jessie ter go out with now. This bloody war's getting me down, I ain't got nothink to look forward to, not even a baby.'

'I'm sorry love, but I couldn't bear ter think of yer out wiv someone else. Come on, wipe yer eyes.'

Sally did as she was told.

'Now, git back in bed. Yer freezing.' He put his arms round her. 'Christ, yer feet's like blocks of ice.'

She cuddled up and he kissed her long and hard. 'It really is about time we started finking about a baby.'

'You do mean it don't yer, but why all of a sudden?' She turned away. 'It ain't ter try and keep me in, is it?'

He laughed. 'Course not.' He turned her back to face him. 'I want us ter start a family 'cos fings are getting better. They're pressing for a second front, and that could make a lot of difference.'

'Yer sure that's the real reason?'

He kissed her neck. 'Yeah. I love yer, Sal, and I want ter make yer 'appy, I know yer wants a baby, and after seeing little Dorothy, well I reckon our Danny's a lucky bloke, well 'e was till 'e got captured, but it must give 'im somethink ter look forward to.'

'But you've always bin . . .'

'I know. But we've got ter start finking about us, and our future.'

'D'you think the war could be over soon?'

'Humm. Don't let's talk about that,' he whispered, his hand slowly travelling over her body.

She felt warm and relaxed. 'Pete, when shall we . . .'

'How about now . . . ?'

Sally melted against him. This is what she wanted – him, and to be loved.

Chapter 29

After Christmas Pete had gone back to Cardiff, and Benny was back at camp.

'I ain't 'alf gonner miss 'im, Sal.' said Babs. 'I really do love 'im. D'yer feel like that about Pete?'

'Course I do.'

'Well, yer don't show it.'

'We can't all moon around like lovesick calves. We going to the pictures Sat'day?' asked Sally, quickly changing the subject.

'Dunno. Don't feel like going out much without Benny. They've stopped a lot of weekend passes. 'E said they're really tightening up at camp.'

'Babs, you ain't married yet so don't start spending yer life moping around.'

'I ain't moping. What about Joey? Benny said 'e's got some leave due, why don't yer go out wiv 'im?'

Sally stood up. 'I'll make some cocoa.' She hadn't told Babs about the conversation she'd had with Pete about Joey, and it didn't matter how much she enjoyed his company, there was no way she was going to give Pete, or Granny Brent, any reason to suspect that she'd been out with him.

Babs had gone to bed and Sally sat at the table slowly

stirring her cocoa. The weather had turned. All day it had been cold and damp with the threat of snow hanging heavy in the grey sky. She was feeling fed up at the thought of another long lonely winter ahead of them. If only the war would come to an end, then Pete would be home. She knew being away had made him think differently, but was still surprised at him talking about a baby. That would be wonderful. Then they really would all have something to look forward to.

On Saturday, as Sally made her way home from work, the sleet was stinging her eyes, making her put her head down against the cold blustery wind. Turning into Sefton Grove she almost bumped into an American soldier. 'I'm sorry,' she said, looking up. She suddenly felt the colour drain from her face. 'What you doing 'ere?' she said angrily.

'I'm on furlough and feeling a bit low, and I didn't have anywhere to go so I thought I'd come and see my favourite girl.' Joey had a broad grin.

'You shouldn't be 'ere. You're drunk,' she said, pushing him to one side when she caught the smell of his breath.

The grin was still there. 'I ain't drunk, honey, just had one or two to give me Dutch courage.'

Sally looked round anxiously. 'What d'yer want courage fer?'

'To come and ask you out. Please, Sally. We're all being shipped out soon, and I'd like to take you out again.'

'Yer could 'ave phoned Rachel, or written. Yer didn't 'ave ter come 'ere.'

'I'm sorry, but I wanted to see you this weekend. Do you want me to go down on my knees?'

She laughed; she couldn't be angry with him for long. 'Don't talk daft.'

'Please, Sally. This'll be the last time.'

'The last time?' she whispered. The sudden realisation that he could be gone out of her life very soon hit her.

'Yeah, we're off soon.'

'Well, all right then, I'll meet you outside the tube station tonight. Now go before someone sees you talking ter me.'

'Can I kiss you?'

She wanted to say 'Yes, please', and hold him close, but instead said softly, 'No yer can't. Now be off.'

'What time?'

'About seven. Now please go.'

'OK, promise me, then.'

'I promise,' said Sally, grinning.

'I'm very fond of you, Sally.' He saluted. 'Right ma'am.' He walked smartly away. At the corner of Brigg Street he turned and clicked his heels.

Sally stood and laughed. She wanted to tell him she was fond of him as well. 'You are good fun, Joey, and I do like your company,' she said to herself. She loved Pete, but right now she needed someone like Joey to cheer her up. She hurried home to get ready.

She was just putting on her lipstick when someone banged on the front door. She looked at her watch – six o'clock – and checked the seams of her precious nylons before going downstairs. Who the hell would be banging like that? Everybody she knew used the key hanging on the string behind the door. Panic suddenly filled her. Joey hadn't come back here for her, had he? She rushed down the stairs and flung open the door, ready to give him a right ticking off. 'What the 'ell . . . ?'

It was Tony, Johnny's friend. 'Tony? What's wrong?'

His face was ashen. 'Johnny's bin knocked down by a car.' He ran the back of his hand under his nose.

Sally felt her legs giving way. 'Where is 'e?' She held on to the wall.

'They took 'im ter 'ospital in an ambulance. Mr Booker told me ter come and tell yer.' He nervously rolled his cap round and round in his hands.

'Is 'e badly hurt?'

'Dunno. 'Is 'ead's all covered wiv blood, and 'e didn't open 'is eyes, and 'e wasn't moving.'

Sally took a deep breath to steady herself. 'What 'ospital's 'e in?'

'I fink they was gonner take 'im ter St Olave's.'

'I'll just get me handbag.'

'Was yer going out, Sal?'

'Yes, yes I was. Look, I've got ter go over and tell Granny Brent. Thanks fer coming, Tony.' She ran up the stairs and collected her handbag.

Tony was just wheeling his bike out into the road. He looked up when Sally shut the front door. 'Shall I tell Mr Booker yer gorn ter the 'ospital?'

'Please.'

'Yer'll let us know 'ow 'e is, won't yer?'

'Course.' She ran across the road and rushed into Granny Brent's.

'Christ, Sal, you're in a bloody 'urry,' said Granny Brent when Sally burst into the kitchen. 'What's up? Yer look like yer seen a ghost under all that make-up yer got plastered all over yer face. Orf out somewhere then? Yer done up like a dog's dinner.' There was definitely a note of disapproval in her voice.

'Ma, Johnny's in 'ospital. 'E's been run over by a car,' she said quickly.

'What? When?'

'I don't know, I'm just going up ter St Olave's ter try and find out. Could yer tell Babs when she gets in?'

Granny Brent gave her a quick look. 'Ain't yer meeting 'er then?' she asked, surprised.

'No.'

'Oh I see.' Granny Brent straightened her shoulders.

'I'll let yer know how 'e is as soon as I can.' Sally left as fast as she'd come in.

The journey to the hospital seemed to take for ever, and when she finally arrived the nurse at the reception desk wasn't particularly helpful.

'What name?' she asked.

'John Fuller.'

'Do you know what happened?'

''Is mate told me 'e's bin knocked down by a car, that's all I know.'

The nurse studied some notes and looking up said, 'Wait here.'

Sally sat on a seat and looked around the white-tiled walls. This is where she had sat with Pete while they waited for the doctor when her dad . . . Tears filled her eyes. Please, don't let anything happened ter Johnny. I couldn't bear ter lose another, she prayed silently. People were coming and going, and Sally thought she'd scream if somebody didn't come soon to tell her what had happened to her brother.

She looked at her watch. Babs should be at home now. Panic filled her; she hadn't left a note. Babs didn't even know she was going out tonight. She wouldn't go over to

Granny Brent's, so would they go over and tell her? And Joey. He would think she'd stood him up. But she couldn't worry about him. Johnny was the one that needed her now. Her head was spinning with unanswered questions. She looked anxiously at the door, hoping Babs would walk in.

'Mrs Brent, you can see your brother now, but you mustn't stay too long.'

'Nurse, my sister should be 'ere soon, would yer—'

'Don't worry, I'll tell her.'

Sally followed the nurse down the corridor. Sally's high heels echoed loudly on the tiled floor, and she tried walking on tiptoes to deaden the sound.

The nurse pushed open the door to the ward and walked purposefully down the middle. Sally's eyes took a few seconds to become accustomed to the darkened room. At the far end, the nurse pulled back the curtain that surrounded a bed. Sally quickly drew a deep breath when she looked down on the small bandaged head of her brother. Johnny's eyes were closed, and his breathing laboured.

Sally kissed his bruised cheek. 'Will 'e be all right?' she asked the nurse.

'I'll let you speak to Sister.'

Sally let her tears run unheeded down her face and fall on to Johnny.

'You can sit with him for a while. Would you like a cup of tea?'

'Yes, please.'

The nurse swiftly and silently moved away.

Sally took hold of Johnny's hand and held it against her cheek. 'Please, open your eyes. Just tell me you're all right.'

There was no movement.

The nurse brought Sally a cup of tea. 'Sister will have a word with you when you've finished your tea. Her office is at the end of the corridor.'

'Thank you,' whispered Sally.

She finished her tea and made her way to the sister's office. The door was open and the sister beckoned her in.

'Come in, Mrs Brent. Take a seat.'

Sally did as she was told, as if in a trance. She couldn't believe this was happening.

'I'm afraid your brother is badly injured. The X-rays show a broken bone in his left leg, and we think there is some damage to his spine. We don't think there is a lot of damage to his head. It's mainly superficial.'

Sally sat listening, but not really taking it all in. 'Will 'e be all right?' she finally asked.

'It's much too early to say. I'm afraid we shall just have to wait and see. I suggest you go home.'

'But what if 'e wakes up?' asked Sally in alarm.

'He won't wake up tonight. He's been given a sedative.' The sister stood up. 'Come back in the morning. I know it isn't proper visiting times, but we may have some news for you then.'

There were so many questions Sally wanted to ask, but the words wouldn't come. She stood up, and at the door asked, 'Can I go and say goodnight to him?'

Sister smiled. 'Of course.'

Once again Sally kissed her brother's cheek, but there was still no movement. 'See yer termorrow, Johnny,' she whispered.

Outside the hospital she sat on the wall and lit a cigarette.

It was pitch black, and ghostly figures, huddled against the cold night air, were quickly coming and going. They couldn't see her tears falling. She wished Pete was here as he had been over her dad. She missed him and needed him now. He would be strong and ask all the right questions. She wanted him to hold her and comfort her, she felt so alone and vulnerable. The snow was beginning to settle, the flakes lightly brushed against her face, but she didn't feel the cold – she didn't feel anything. She was numb. If only they had let her stay with him . . . She felt so helpless – she couldn't stay but she didn't want to go home.

What about Babs? She should be here soon if Granny Brent had told her. The silence wrapped itself round Sally and in the far distance she could hear an air-raid siren wailing. Her eyes went back to the hospital. She couldn't see them in the dark but she knew sandbags were piled high in front of all the downstairs windows. How would they get Johnny into the shelter if the raid got this far?

There were muffled footsteps behind her and Sally quickly put out her cigarette. She didn't want a warden shouting at her for showing a light.

'Sal, Sal, is that you?' It was Babs.

Sally threw her arms round her sister and they cried long and bitter tears.

'What's wrong wiv 'im?' sobbed Babs. 'Granny Brent only said 'e was in 'ospital.'

''E's been knocked down by a car.' Sally stopped. She suddenly caught sight of a soldier standing a way back. 'Joey?' she called out, almost in disbelief.

'I'm sorry, hon, I don't want to intrude, but I saw Babs at the subway station and she told me what had happened. Is he badly hurt?'

'Yes.'

'You're shivering. Look, you're freezing. Let's find a bar and you can both have a brandy.' He didn't wait for an answer, but took their arms and marched them along the street.

They didn't argue, and silently walked beside him. Sally didn't notice the snow coming over her shoes. When they pushed open the door of the first pub they came to, the heat was so overbearing, Sally thought she would pass out.

'You all right Miss?' shouted the barman, as Joey helped her into a chair.

'Have you any brandy?' Joey asked him anxiously.

He looked around sheepishly, then leaning over the counter asked, 'Depends. What's wrong wiv 'er?'

'She's had a shock. Her young brother's in hospital.'

'Well, all right, but don't let these ovvers see it.' He touched the side of his nose. 'This lot can sniff out spirits at fifty paces.'

Joey looked round, amused. He could see through the partition that most of the customers were in the other bar, and so busy playing cards and dominoes and shouting so loud, that they couldn't possibly see or hear what was happening on this side.

'This is purely medicinal, yer understand.' The barman furtively ducked down behind the bar and came up with two large glasses, both with a very small amount of amber-coloured liquid in them. 'Can only spare yer two, one each fer the ladies. And fer Gawd's sake don't let me regulars find out ovverwise they'll skin me alive. Like gold dust brandy is now. But I always keeps a drop fer medicinal purposes, understand?'

'Yeah,' said Joey. 'Anyway, I'd rather have a beer.'

The man grinned. 'A feller after me own 'eart.' He plonked the beer on the counter. 'Can't stand all these spirits – makes me bad.'

All the while Joey was up at the bar, Babs was rubbing Sally's hands. 'Yer freezing. 'Ow long yer bin sitting out there?'

'Don't know.'

'Does Johnny look bad?'

Sally nodded.

Joey put the drinks on the table.

Sally looked up and gave him a slight smile. ''E's unconscious, and 'e's got a broken leg, but it's 'is spine they're worried about.'

Joey played with his glass. 'Look, I'll just finish this drink, then I'll leave you both. You'll be all right, won't you?'

Sally touched his hand. 'No, stay, Joey. We need someone to talk to.'

He gently patted her hand. 'If you're sure that's what you want.'

'When can we go and see 'im?' asked Babs.

'Not till the morning.'

Tears ran down Babs' face. 'I wish Benny was 'ere.'

'Do you think the bartender will let me borrow his phone?' asked Joey. 'I might be able to get Benny to talk to you.'

A smile lifted Babs' mascara-streaked face. 'Could yer? I'd like that.'

'I'll have a word.' Joey left the table, but was back very quickly.

'It's OK. Come on, Babs, it's out the back. You'll be all right here for a while?' he asked Sally.

She nodded. 'You go on. It'll be nice for 'er to talk to Benny.'

Babs was smiling when she returned. 'I've phoned Rachel and told her, 'cos Benny said 'e'll be able to phone me there. She said we can stay if we want.'

'I don't think I want to go there . . .'

'But, Sal, I've told Benny and—'

'You go. I'll be all right. I'll walk ter the Underground with you.'

Babs kissed her cheek. 'I'll only go if yer really sure yer'll be all right.'

Sally turned to Joey. 'You wouldn't think she was me younger sister the way she talks ter me sometimes.'

'Don't worry,' he said to Babs. 'I'll walk you both to the subway.'

Outside, the cold air struck them, making Sally shiver. The snow was settling fast and walking against the wind was proving difficult.

Waiting on the platform for Babs' train, they were warm in the Surrey Docks Underground station. The train arrived and, after kissing her sister, Sally waved her goodbye.

'It's lovely and warm down 'ere. Don't think I fancy going out in the cold again,' said Sally as they picked their way over the people who were settling down for the night.

'Would you like another drink?' asked Joey. 'I can't guarantee it'll be brandy again.'

'I wouldn't mind finding a café and 'aving a cuppa tea.'

'You English and your tea. OK, let's see what we can find.'

'Up West's our best bet.' Sally didn't like to tell him she

didn't want to go home alone. 'I'm sorry, Joey, about our date.'

'Don't worry. I only wish there was more I could do. Benny said Johnny's a great little feller.'

'Yes, yes 'e is. This train'll do,' said Sally.

Once in the cold of the West End the first place they came to was a small restaurant.

Sally sat with her hands round her cup. 'I wish I could 'ave stayed with Johnny.'

'He's in the best place, and I'm sure when you go in tomorrow he'll be awake and full of questions.'

'But what if 'e can't ever walk again?'

'I'm sure the doctor's are doing all they can.'

'I 'ope so.' She put her cup down.

Joey wrapped his fingers round hers. 'Sally, you know how I feel about you, don't you?'

She half smiled. 'It's only 'cos you're away from 'ome. You'll meet plenty o' other girls . . .'

He gently kissed her fingers. 'I've met other girls, but none of them are like you. You're pretty, and warm and you enjoy life.'

As much as she loved to hear this, Sally had to be on her guard. Her family came first, before any feelings she had for him. She pulled her hand away. 'Don't, Joey. You know I'm married, and I love Pete.'

'And I love you.'

She sat back staring at him. She suddenly laughed.

He looked hurt. 'Please don't laugh. I love you, Sally, and want to marry you.'

'But, Joey, I'm married.'

'You can get a divorce.'

'What?' She was shocked and confused that he would say

something like that. 'This ain't America, you know. Our kind o' people don't get divorced. We don't do things like that.'

'Is that all that would stop you?'

'No, no course not. I love Pete.'

'But you like me, don't you?'

'Yes.' Her mind was spinning with bewilderment, brandy and the shock of what had happened to Johnny.

'We're good together, aren't we?'

'Yes.'

'We have lots of laughs, don't we?'

She couldn't deny that. 'But, Joey, I do love Pete, and when you're back 'ome you'll forget all about me and meet some nice girl and marry 'er.'

He sat back and lit a cigarette. 'I don't think so.'

'We'd better be going soon.'

'Do you want another?' He pointed to her empty cup.

'Wouldn't mind.'

The restaurant door opened and a man stood and brushed the snow from his coat. He stamped his feet hard. 'All the buses have stopped,' he said to all and sundry. 'Got any spare rooms, Phil?'

'Only the usual couple,' answered the proprietor.

'Well, I'll have one.' The man turned to Sally and Joey. 'And if I were you I'd book the other. It's really bad out there now.'

'What about the tube?' Sally asked.

'That's still all right,' he replied. 'Pot of tea, please, Phil.'

Joey looked apprehensive. 'Sally, you have a long walk from the station. I'll come with you.'

'You can't, you won't be able ter get back.'

'I won't let you go on your own. Besides, look at your shoes.'

When Sally looked down, she could have cried. Her lovely shoes were wet and going out of shape. 'Seven clothing coupons they cost me. I ain't got any more coupons left.'

Joey stubbed his cigarette out hard in the ashtray. 'We could stay here the night,' he said suddenly.

'What?'

'Well, you heard what that feller said.'

'Yes, but I couldn't . . . unless 'e's got another room.'

'I'll ask.' Joey went to the counter.

Sally saw Phil shake his head. They both looked in her direction. What should she do? She had to get back to the hospital first thing in the morning, so she'd be wise to stay near an Underground station. But if she had to spend the night in the same room as Joey, she would have to be on her guard. She trusted him, but did she trust herself?

Chapter 30

Sally was thankful the air raid didn't reach them, and before they went upstairs Joey had bought her another brandy to help her sleep. She'd felt embarrassed at the thought of sleeping in the same room as him, and when he turned out the light, quickly took off her frock, jumped into bed and got under the bedclothes. She shivered with cold and her head felt muzzy. She wasn't used to brandy and two in one evening on an empty stomach were taking effect.

Joey pulled back the blackout curtains and the reflection from the snow lightened the room. When he banged his shin on the bedpost, Sally laughed nervously, and buried her head in the pillow. After a while she hoisted herself up on one elbow, and looked down at him lying on the floor beside her, and started to giggle. What would Granny Brent have to say about this situation? Sally put her hand over her mouth to stifle her laugh; the brandy was going to her head. 'You all right down there?' she asked.

'It's a bit hard, but at least Phil found me a pillow and a blanket.'

'It must be a lot better than sleeping down the Underground.'

'Yeah, I suppose so.'

This was something they had discussed earlier, but Joey thought Sally needed to get her wet shoes and stockings off. His concern had warmed her.

'Turn over and go to sleep.'

'I can't.' Her mood quickly changed, and she felt sad. 'I keep thinking about Johnny. I'm so worried about 'im. What if 'e can't walk?' Her tears began to fall, slowly at first, then in floods, and the sound of her sobs filled the room.

Joey sat on the bed beside her. He took her into his arms and gently rocked her. 'Shh, my poor love. I'm sure he's going to be just fine.'

Sally wept uncontrollably in the comfort of his arms. 'I love me brother. We've bin through such a lot together.'

Joey held her tight. 'I know.' Her tears were wetting his bare shoulder. He lightly kissed her cheek, she raised her head and he held her tear-stained face in his hand. Suddenly his lips were on hers, softly at first, then with great ardour and passion. She didn't pull away. At this moment she needed love and affection so very much.

He kissed her mouth, face and neck, all the while whispering how much he loved her. He gently pushed her back on to the pillow and, lying beside her, ran his hand down her neck. He calmly slipped the thin straps of her petticoat from her shoulders, and moved his hand slowly over her breasts. Nothing was hurried.

Sally caught her breath. She knew this was wrong, but she didn't stop him. He fondled and kissed her breasts, running his tongue over her taut nipples, very slowly and deliberately. Sally thought she was going to explode with desire. He was caring and loving, and all the while whispering tender words. Feelings were going through her she had never felt before. Now Joey's hand was sliding over her slip. He pulled it above her waist and caressed her thighs. She wanted to scream out with pleasure. Then his warm hand was on her flat stomach. It wasn't demanding or rushed. She felt like dying in a sea of ecstasy.

'Sally, I want you so much,' he murmured.

She couldn't answer.

'May I?'

She wanted to cry out, 'Please, please, please . . .'

Then suddenly the thought of Pete filled her mind, how he had been so loving before he went back to Cardiff just the other day, and how he had agreed they could have a baby at last . . . She pushed Joey's hand away. 'I'm sorry, Joey. I shouldn't 'ave let yer . . .'

He grabbed her hand. 'Please, Sally. Don't try and stop me, not now.'

'No, Joey! We mustn't.' She sat up and self-consciously straightened her slip. 'I can't!'

He sat up and ran his hands through his cropped black hair. 'Why? I thought you liked me.'

'I do. But I don't love you.'

'You don't have to love . . . What if I go away and get killed?'

'Joey, don't say things like that. Don't try and blackmail me. It won't work.' She reached over to the bedside table, picked up the packet of cigarettes and offered him one. 'I'm very fond of you, and I like your company, but you know I love Pete, and I'd never do anythink ter 'urt 'im.'

'Lucky old Pete,' said Joey sarcastically. He stood up and lit his cigarette.

'Please, don't be angry with me. I'm sorry, it's my fault, I shouldn't 'ave let it get so far.' Sally felt very guilty. Her thoughts were in a turmoil.

He shrugged, and got back down on the floor.

Sally lay back. Deep down she knew she had wanted him to make love to her, but all her life she had been bound by unwritten laws and conventions. She was married to Pete, and she loved him, and she wasn't going to spoil her future with him for what could only be a one-night stand. She was fond of Joey and, at one stage, even thought she loved him. What if she had let him get closer to her and left Pete for him? Would it have been worth it? She dreaded to think how upset Pete would be. No, she loved good old dependable Pete, and the thought of starting a new life didn't appeal to her, even if he did look like Tyrone Power. A slight smile lifted her mouth. Besides, one GI bride in the family was enough. And what about Johnny? She was suddenly full of fear. He would need her more than ever now. She turned over and longed for the morning. 'Good night, Joey,' she whispered.

'Good night, Sally.'

Joey drew hard on his cigarette. He was annoyed with himself. This wasn't the way he wanted it to happen. He loved Sally. He knew he would have to wait for her, even if it meant till after the war. Perhaps then she would see that he really did care and meant what he'd said. She was wonderful and brave, and he loved her deeply.

Sally woke with a start. Her head was pounding. Where was she? Someone was knocking on the door. She sat up and looked at the floor – he'd gone. The knocking continued. 'Come in,' she called, pulling the sheet around herself.

'Good morning.' Joey, with a tray in his hand, looked fresh and wide awake.

Sally smiled. 'Tea in bed. This is a luxury I never ever get.'

He grinned. 'I could change all that.'

She didn't comment, but asked, 'What's the weather doing?'

'Not too bad. It's stopped snowing, and is beginning to thaw a little.'

'Thank goodness. Now if you don't mind I'd like ter get dressed.'

'Phil's doing breakfast when you're ready. It's only dried egg scrambled on toast, but it smells good.' He turned to go.

'Joey.'

He stopped in the doorway.

'I'm sorry about last night.'

He waved his hand dismissively.

'No, I mean it. I'm very fond of you, and I'm really grateful that you've been looking after me.'

'Think nothing of it. Now come on down. Then we can go along to the hospital.'

There was no sign of Babs when Sally and Joey arrived at the hospital.

'She's got a way to come,' said Sally as they mounted the steps. She stood at the door. 'I'm frightened to go in. What if 'e ain't no better. What if . . . They wouldn't know where I was last night. They wouldn't be able to tell me if—' Panic filled her.

'Now come on. I'm sure he's fine, but you can't expect miracles overnight,' said Joey, taking her arm and leading her through the door

At the reception Sally saw a different nurse from the one the day before, who told her Johnny was still in the same ward, and that she could go along to see him.

'I'll wait here,' said Joey.

'Tell Babs where I am, won't yer?'

'Course.'

There was a little more life in the ward this morning. A few of the patients were sitting up, and one or two of them even gave her a smile. As she made her way to the far end, she prayed he would be awake.

The curtains were still drawn round Johnny's bed, and she hesitated before gently easing them to one side. He was still in the same position, lying on his back with his eyes closed. Blood had seeped through the bandage round his head, his face was swollen and the bruises had changed colour. Tears filled Sally's eyes. She pulled the chair closer to his bed, never taking her eyes off his face. She held his hand and kissed it. 'It's me, Johnny, Sally. Can you 'ear me?'

She was sure that under his closed, swollen eyelids she could see movement. 'Johnny. Wake up.' She kissed his hand again. 'Please wake up. Tell me yer feel all right.' Even as she said it she thought to herself what a stupid thing it was to say. She could hear voices the other side of the curtain, and recognised that one belonged to Babs. The curtain was pulled aside and Babs stood transfixed, her face drained of colour.

'Don't sit on the bed,' said the nurse. 'It might distress him. I'll get you another chair.'

'Yer didn't tell me 'e was this bad,' Babs whispered, as her tears fell.

''E looks worse today.'

''As 'e woke up yet?' asked Babs as she eased herself round the bed.

Sally shook her head.

The nurse returned with the chair. 'You can only stay for a little while as all his dressings have to be changed.'

'Nurse, I think 'is eyes are moving,' said Sally.

'They will do. He's still semi-conscious.' The nurse smiled and walked away.

Babs sat the other side of the bed from Sally and held his other hand. 'Wake up, Johnny. Please,' she begged. She turned to her sister. 'Sal, what we gonner do?'

'Keep coming back till 'e's better.' There was a long pause, then Sally asked, 'Did Benny phone?'

Babs nodded.

'How is 'e?'

''E's ever so upset. 'E only wishes 'e could be with me.'

'That's nice,' said Sally not taking her eyes off Johnny.

'Rachel's mum and dad was upset as well.'

'That's nice,' repeated Sally.

'What's Joey doing 'ere?'

'I'll tell you later.'

Babs looked at Sally. 'Ain't yer bin 'ome?'

'No.'

It was hard to keep up a conversation, and despite the fact that they didn't want to leave him, when the nurse ushered them out, both Babs and Sally almost uttered sighs of relief.

The snow had turned to slush when they got outside.

'How is he?' asked Joey.

'About the same. At least we'll be able to get 'ome now the buses are running,' said Sally, pulling on her gloves.

''Ave yer bin 'ere all night?' Babs looked from one to the other.

'Sally couldn't get home. The buses had stopped, and she was wet through so we stayed in a small hotel.'

'Oh?' said Babs suspiciously. 'She could 'ave walked 'ome from the station.'

'We went up West,' said Sally.

'So?' said Babs.

'It's not what you think,' said Joey, holding up both his hands. 'It was all above board and proper.'

'What yer going to do today, Joey?' asked Sally, changing the subject.

'Don't know. I might go to the movies this afternoon. Do you want to come?'

'No thanks. When's your leave up?'

'Not till Wednesday. I expect you'll be here every day, so I know where to find you if I'm at a loose end.'

'OK. This is our bus. Thanks again, Joey.' Sally kissed his cheek.

'Bye, Joey,' said Babs as they climbed on to the platform.

Sally was dreading being alone with Babs as she knew the questions would be coming thick and fast, and she wasn't wrong. As soon as they sat down Babs started.

'Why didn't yer go 'ome?'

'I didn't want ter be alone. I wanted some company so we went for a cuppa, and when we found out the buses 'ad stopped we stayed up West. The snow was very thick and I didn't want ter walk from the station.'

'Where d'yer stay?'

''E told yer, in a small hotel.'

'Was yer in the same room?'

'No, course not,' lied Sally.

'The buses was running when I went ter Rachel's.'

'I told yer we went fer a cuppa tea first, and it was after that they stopped.' Sally stared at the green mesh on the bus windows. The thought uppermost in her mind was: I 'ope Joey don't tell Benny that we slept in the same room, as 'e would be sure ter tell Babs.

As soon as Sally and Babs walked pass Granny Brent's, Gwen was banging on the front room window, and two seconds later she was at the front door. ''Ow is 'e?' she called out.

Sally crossed the road, she didn't want to shout it out. 'Go on and put the kettle on, Babs. I'll be in later.'

'Come in,' said Gwen. 'Ma's in the kitchen.'

Sally followed her along the passage, fearful of what they would ask.

''Allo, Sal,' said Vera when they walked into the kitchen. 'Christ, yer look a mess. Look at yer shoes. Yer bin out all night?'

'Thanks.' Sally ignored Vera's last sentence, she knew she looked a mess, and didn't need Vera to remind her.

'Well, 'ow is 'e?' asked Granny Brent.

''E's still unconscious. 'E's badly bruised and got a broken leg, but it's 'is spine they're worried about,' said Sally, sitting herself at the table.

'Did 'e talk ter yer?' asked Granny Brent.

'Don't talk daft, Ma. 'Ow could 'e if 'e's unconscious.'

'Who you calling daft? Just yer watch yer tongue, me gel. Yer still ain't too old ter get a swipe, yer know.'

Vera tutted and raised her eyes to the ceiling.

'Did yer stay up there all night?' asked Gwen.

'Yes, by the time I got out the 'ospital all the buses 'ad stopped running, and I didn't fancy walking from the station. Me shoes were wet through. They said we could go back in this morning.'

'Don't tell me about it,' said Vera. 'That snow caused a right rumpus I can tell yer. There's buses left all over the place.'

'Where d'yer stay?' asked Granny Brent.

Sally panicked. She could feel her face burning. What could she say? She couldn't think quick enough. 'I stayed down the Underground,' she lied.

'Was Babs wiv yer?'

'No, I mean yes.'

'Babs didn't know yer was going out when Gwen went over and told 'er about Johnny.' Granny Brent looked at Sally suspiciously.

'No I know.' Sally dropped her head.

'I fought yer might 'ave gorn wiv the gel she works with, but Babs didn't fink so – Rachel, is that 'er name?'

Sally nodded, and lit a cigarette.

'Babs said Rachel 'adn't said so. Mind you yer looked very nice when yer went out. Fought yer'd got yerself a fancy man.'

Sally wanted to get away from all this questioning. Did they suspect? Did they know? She knew she had to try and bluff it out. She nervously tapped the end of the cigarette into the ashtray. 'I was going ter go up West with a girl I used ter work with. She's getting married next week, and a few of us was going fer a drink.'

'Bit sudden, wasn't it?' Granny Brent asked. 'Not letting yer sister know.'

'She met us outside work yesterday, and told us. I didn't 'ave time ter tell Babs, and I was just about ter leave 'er a note when Tony arrived.'

'Oh.'

Sally was pleased Granny Brent seemed satisfied with that explanation. 'I must go, we're going back to the 'ospital later on.'

'All right, love.' Granny Brent's voice softened. 'Let's know if we can do anyfink ter 'elp.'

Sally kissed her mother-in-law's cheek. 'Thanks.'

Outside she took a deep breath. The cold air filled her lungs, and cleared her head. She felt relieved. She never wanted to go through that kind of third degree again. Although she liked Joey's company very much, she would keep well clear of him from now on. She had to think of Johnny now; her life was here, in Sefton Grove.

She hurried home. She had to tell Babs to back up her story that she was down the Underground station with her last night, and all night.

Chapter 31

It was early evening when Sally and Babs walked in the hospital once again.

'Mrs Brent,' called a nurse, as they approached the ward. 'Sister would like to see you right away.'

Sally froze, and Babs clutched at her hand. 'D'yer know what about?' croaked Sally.

'I'm afraid not.'

'I'm frightened, Sal,' said Babs, her grip tightening.

'Come on, the sister's office is this way.'

'Sit down,' said the sister when they entered her room. She stood up and walked round to the front of her desk, perching herself on the edge and putting her hands together. 'I'm sorry, but I have some bad news for you.'

'Is 'e dead?' asked Babs, starting to cry.

Sally's head was swimming. She could hear herself asking what had happened to him, but to her, no words seemed to be leaving her lips.

'No.' The sister looked surprised. 'He has regained consciousness,' she went on, 'but I'm afraid at the moment there isn't any movement in his legs.'

'Will 'e be a cripple?' whispered Sally.

'He is at the moment.'

'Will 'e always be one?'

'We don't know. Time will tell.' She walked back round the desk, sat in her seat and picked up a pen.

There were so many questions Sally wanted to ask, but her brain wouldn't function. All she could think about was Johnny, poor Johnny, not being able to walk. Silent tears ran down her face.

'We shall keep him here for a while,' said the sister. 'Then perhaps after a period in a convalescent home, you can have him home. Do you live in a house?'

Sally nodded.

'Do you have a bathroom?'

Sally shook her head.

'What about a toilet?'

'We've got an outside lav.'

'That's good, that's very good.' All the while the sister was writing. 'He won't be able to climb stairs. Could he sleep downstairs?'

Sally nodded.

'Do you have a husband?'

'Yes.'

'Is he in the forces?'

'No.'

'Good. If there are any steps perhaps he could make a ramp for Johnny's wheelchair. Don't worry too much, these young lads very quickly adapt. We will show you how to look after him, give him baths and make sure he doesn't get bed sores. They can be very painful.'

Sally sat as if in a dream: wheelchair, ramps, baths, bed sores. She knew she was answering questions, but really didn't know what she was saying, or being asked to do.

'This is far too much for you to take in in one go, so every time you come to see Johnny, we will talk a little and then it will get easier for you.' Sister stood up and opened the door. 'I'm sure you both want to go and see him now. Don't forget, I'm always here to help.'

Outside the room Babs burst into tears. Sally held her close, as much for her own comfort as for Babs'.

'Now come on,' said a nurse. 'You must put on a brave face. Dry those tears.'

They did as they were told.

'Now let's see a smile. We can't have you visiting Johnny with sad faces, can we?'

But smile was something Sally knew she couldn't do.

There was a big change in Johnny when they finally saw him. He was still lying flat on his back, but he had a fresh clean bandage round his head, and some of the swelling on his face had gone down.

''Allo, you two,' he said, opening his eyes and giving them a weak smile. 'Didn't fink anybody was gonner come and see me.' He spoke very softly and slowly.

Sally leant on the bed to kiss him and he winced. 'Me back's a bit sore. I reckon I didn't 'alf go a cannon. What yer crying fer, Babs?'

Babs sat on the chair. 'I love yer, Johnny, I really do.'

Sally too had tears in her eyes, but she tried hard to keep them under control. 'I'm glad yer awake. We've bin ter see Sister,' she told him.

'Oh yeah? When am I coming 'ome?' He didn't move, and he looked exhausted.

Sally gave Babs a quick glance. 'She didn't say. 'Ave they told yer what's wrong?'

'I've got a broken leg, and some cuts ter me 'ead, and some bruising on me back.' Johnny was fighting to keep his eyes open.

'Is that all?' Sally tried to make it sound light-hearted.

'What else they told yer?' asked Babs.

'Why? What else d'yer want me ter 'ave?' His eyes closed again. 'I feel ever ser tired. I fink I'll 'ave a little kip.' There was a long pause. 'Will yer tell Mr Booker I'll be away fer a few days, just till me leg gits better?'

'Course,' said Sally, as the bell for visitors to leave rang. 'We'll be in ter see yer tomorrer.'

'I'll be 'ere.' He didn't open his eyes when they gently kissed him goodbye.

Outside they sat on the wall and cried.

''E don't know,' sobbed Babs.

'Poor Johnny. Who's gonner tell 'im?' whispered Sally.

'The doctor, I s'pose.'

'Why didn't the sister tell us 'e don't know? We might 'ave blurted it out.'

'I dunno. Sal, what we gonner do?'

'What can we do? I've got ter write and tell Pete. I wonder 'ow long 'e'll be in 'ospital?'

'Dunno, it could be a long while.' Babs shivered.

'Come on, let's get 'ome and light the fire. At least it's dark. I don't want ter go and see Granny Brent any more today. I couldn't stand any more questions.'

'She might be looking out 'er window.'

'I 'ope not. Come on, 'ere comes our bus.'

Monday night when they went to the hospital Johnny turned his head away from them as they approached his bed.

'Mr Booker sent yer two apples,' said Babs eagerly.

'And look,' said Sally, careful placing a brown paper bag on his locker, ''ere's me week's egg ration. So tomorrer yer'll be able ter 'ave a proper boiled egg fer breakfast. We only got one each this week, and Babs 'as already 'ad 'ers.'

Johnny still had his head turned away. Sally walked round to the other side of the bed. 'What is it, Johnny? You still tired?'

'Yer know, don't yer?' Tears were trickling down into his ears. 'Yer both know. Why didn't yer tell me last night?'

Sally tried to hold his hand, but he pulled it away. 'I ain't lorst the use o' me 'ands, only me legs.'

Sally felt helpless standing there.

Babs couldn't speak. She put her handkerchief to her face.

'Don't, Babs,' said Sally sternly, walking back to her chair. 'Yes, we know, and we're all gonner do the best we can.'

'You might, but I might as well be dead. Go on, go away. I don't wonner talk ter yer.'

'Johnny,' sobbed Babs, 'we ain't ever gonner leave yer.'

He turned his head and faced them, more tears spilling from his sad eyes. Sally wanted to throw her arms round his neck and hold him tight. He looked so afraid, frail and small.

'What about when yer goes to America? You'll leave me then. And what about when Pete comes back? 'E won't want me crashing about.'

'Don't talk daft,' said Sally.

'I ain't talking daft, I've bin finking about it all day, ain't I? Got nuffink else ter do, 'ave I?' He turned his head away from them again.

Sally was heartbroken. What could she say?

'Johnny, it might not be for ever,' said Babs. 'They don't know yet.'

He didn't answer.

'It's a shock,' said Sally to his back.

'We'll be able to manage,' said Babs.

Again no response.

'I'll go and 'ave a word with the sister,' said Sally.

She needed an excuse to get away. They all needed time to get over the shock.

'You was quick,' said Babs, when she returned.

'The sister wasn't there.' Sally sat down, and once more the conversation ceased.

Every evening over the following week Babs and Sally went to the hospital, and the conversation with Johnny was always the same. He told them he didn't want to see them, and lay with his head turned away, his eyes closed. After being at work all day it was tiring and miserable talking to the back of his head. Sally began to think she would scream at him if he didn't answer their questions.

'Well 'e's 'ad a big shock,' said Granny Brent, when Sally went over and told her the latest developments.

'I know, but surely he could . . .' She burst into tears.

'There, there, love.' Granny Brent put her arm round Sally's shoulders. 'What they told yer?'

'Not a lot. We don't know when 'e'll be 'ome. The nurse was saying they'll probably send 'im to a convalescent 'ome first, ter get 'im used ter being in a wheelchair.'

'Poor little sod. Bin frough all that trouble when 'e was evacuated, then the bombing, and now finished up like this. It ain't fair.' Granny Brent sat at the table. 'Did they ever find the sod what knocked 'im down?'

'No. Trouble is, it was dark, and what with the blackout—'

'What's Pete gonner say about it?'

'Dunno. I should be getting a letter from 'im soon.'

At the weekend Johnny's friend Tony came round and asked if he could visit him. Babs and Sally were pleased at that, and took him along on Sunday, Sally and Babs taking turns to wait in the corridor so as not to be more than the regulation two. Seeing Tony really made a difference to Johnny, who put on a brave face and attempted to be cheerful.

'Yer really cheered 'im up,' said Babs, as they waited for the bus.

'Yeah, can I come again?'

'Course,' said Sally.

'I'll tell Mr Booker. 'E said 'e'd like ter see 'im as well, but 'e's worried 'cos they only let two round the bed and visiting's only fer 'alf-hour.'

'That's all right. If yer both come together that'll give me and Babs a night in ter wash our 'air.'

'OK, I'll tell 'im.'

Sally was thrilled to get a letter from Pete the following week and one from Joey. Babs had one from Benny.

Sally had tears in her eyes when she read them. Pete was so upset, and was going to try to get home. He thought Sally needed him to be with her. It was a warm and loving letter.

Joey's letter was also warm. He said how sorry he was about Johnny, and how much he missed her. They had been moved north, and he asked her to write if she felt she could. He promised he would never be demanding, but he would always be there if she needed him, and he would always love her.

Babs had tears streaming down her face when she read

Benny's letter. 'They've gorn up north somewhere – 'e mustn't tell me where,' she whispered. ''E's ever so sorry about Johnny, and 'e's gonner send 'im a parcel.' She looked up. 'Ain't that kind of 'im?' She sniffed and after wiping her nose, folded her letter. 'Sal, I'm gonner tell Benny I can't marry 'im.'

'What? Why?'

'It's Johnny. I've bin finking about it, and I can't go off and leave yer ter look after 'im on yer own.'

Sally sat in her father's armchair. 'Don't talk daft. You can't give Benny up. You don't want ter end up an old maid like poor Miss Slater was, do you? 'Sides, you love Benny.'

'I know, but I've bin giving it a lot o' fought. You'll 'ave ter give up work ter look after 'im, and yer gonner miss yer money coming in, and yer can't expect Pete to keep footing the bills, so I feel I should do me bit.'

Sally didn't interrupt. She could see this speech had been carefully prepared, yet she couldn't believe little Babs was saying she was willing to give up all her future happiness to stay and help look after their brother. Sally jumped up and threw her arms round her neck. 'Oh Babs, Babs. I couldn't let you do that.'

'Why not? You're going to.'

'But I'm married, and I'll 'ave Pete ter 'elp me.'

'But yer wants a baby.'

'Yeah, that's something I do want.'

'Well then, when yer fall yer won't be able ter lift Johnny, will yer?'

'It's got ter 'appen first. Even then I expect we'll manage.' Sally couldn't believe this was Babs being so practical. 'You've certainly been giving this a lot o' thought.'

Babs sat at the table and pulled at the chenille tablecloth's loose threads. 'Yeah, well, you've looked after all of us since Mum died, and never fought about yerself, so perhaps it's about time we fought about you.'

'Babs, I'm not going ter stop you marrying Benny whatever happens. The war could be over soon and then Pete will be back, and—'

Babs smiled. 'I s'pose I could always ask Benny ter settle down over 'ere.'

'That'll be nice, but I can't see that 'appening, can you?'

Babs shook her head.

'Please, Babs, don't say anythink ter Benny. Give it time. I'm sure we can work this thing out. Besides, I want ter 'ave a pen pal in America.

'Daft 'apporth,' was Babs' reply.

At the end of February the hospital told Babs and Sally that Johnny was being moved to Devon at the end of the week.

'Mr Silverman said I could 'ave some time off ter visit if I want. 'E's bin ever ser kind about 'im, ain't 'e?' said Babs.

Sally smiled. So many people had been kind. The Nag's had a collection and bought him some books, and a lot of people had given up their egg rations to him. Somehow Mr Silverman had got hold of some chocolates, and Benny's parcel really brought a smile to Johnny's face.

'I'm just going out for a wee,' Sally said, getting up quickly.

She leant against the lavatory wall. This was the second morning she'd been sick. This couldn't be true. Was she really going to have a baby? She wiped her mouth and pushed back her damp hair before returning to the kitchen.

'Are yer all right?' asked Babs when Sally walked in.

'Course.'

'Yer was gorn a while.'

'Just bin checking the shelter. These daylight raids 'ave bin getting ter be a nuisance. I'll 'ave ter get Pete ter make sure we can get Johnny in through that little door.'

'Yer look ever ser pale. Yer sure yer all right?'

Sally sat at the table. 'Babs, I think I'm gonner 'ave a baby.'

'What? You sure?'

'I've bin sick.'

'Well, that don't mean . . .' She gave Sally a suspicious look. 'Sal, is it Joey's?'

Sally's head shot up. 'What? Course it ain't. What made yer say that?'

'What about that night yer stayed up West wiv Joey?'

Sally felt her face go hot. 'I told yer . . . we didn't do anythink.'

'What yer blushing fer then?'

'Babs, yer gotter believe me. It is Pete's.'

'But Pete's bin so against a baby.'

'At Christmas we talked about it, and 'e reckoned it would be all right now the war is going a bit better, but I didn't think I'd fall right away. Ain't yer pleased?'

'Dunno. I s'pose so.'

'I thought yer'd be . . .' Sally got up.

Babs put her arm round Sally's shoulders. 'Course I'm pleased. It's just a bit of a shock, that's all. I'll be Auntie Babs. Come on, Mum,' she laughed. 'We'd better be going if we're gonner see Johnny.'

'Babs, don't say anythink ter Johnny about the baby just yet.'

'Why? 'E'll be tickled pink ter be an uncle.'

Sally laughed, but it wasn't a real laugh. 'I ain't really sure meself yet. I've only missed once. Besides, I'd like Pete ter know first.'

Babs gave her a funny look. 'Christ, this is turning out ter be a year, what wiv you and Johnny. Looks like I'll be the only healthy one left.'

'I ain't ill.'

'I know, but yer should see yer face.'

As they made their way to the bus stop, Sally's thoughts were on her baby. What if she and Joey had made love that night? She wouldn't have been sure whose baby it was. She shuddered. What if Pete hadn't stopped taking precautions, and . . .? That would have been the one thing Pete would never have forgiven her for, and the Brents were such a close-knit lot, she would never had been able to face them. She pulled the scarf at her neck tighter. Thank God that hadn't happened and she could hold her head up and face everybody with a clear conscience. That was a worry she needn't have, but instead she'd got Johnny to worry over, and he was really going to need her.

Babs was right, this is certainly turning out to be a year they'd never ever forget.

Chapter 32

Joey sat looking at Benny. 'You writing another letter to Babs?'

'Sure. I bet you're wishing you had Sally waiting for you.'

Joey lay back on his bunk. 'Yeah,' he drawled. 'Send my regards.' He wanted to say send Sally my love, but he'd promised her he wouldn't do anything like that.

Chuck came into the tent. 'These flies are driving me mad. I dunno how you can sit there looking so cool, Ben.' He wiped the sweat from his forehead and neck with a damp piece of cloth. 'Christ, it's hot.'

'Just sit down and think nice thoughts,' Benny laughed. 'Mind you, a lot of my thoughts when I'm writing ter Babs makes me sweat.'

'Those Fuller gals certainly got a hold o' you two,' said Chuck.'

Joey's thoughts went to Sally. He thought about the letter he kept in his wallet, sent in reply to the one he'd written to her after his furlough. In it she said she was fond of him, but that was all. He had told her how he felt, and that after the war he would write again. If she didn't want to answer, he would understand. She said she wouldn't write any more as it wouldn't be fair for him to hold out false hopes. He thought about her caring for her young brother for the rest of her life. How many young, pretty girls would do that? And what about Pete? God, did he know what a lucky guy he was?

'I'm going for a drink. Coming, Joe?' said Chuck.

'Sure.'

'Wouldn't mind if it was something a bit stronger than lemonade,' said Chuck, following Joey out of the tent.

The blazing sun struck the backs of their necks as they started to make their way to the mess tent, the ceaseless boom of guns an accompaniment to this and every activity.

'Rommel would sure like it if we were all falling about drunk,' said Joey.

Joey often wondered why they were fighting over a desert – bright yellow sand that got in your food, your eyes, up your nose and in your ears, and other places if you weren't careful. He had never heard of this godforsaken place before. Over the past month the company had been pushed back. Now they were gaining ground again. All the lives that had been lost seemed so pointless.

Someone was hitting the large metal triangle.

'It's the mail,' said Benny, rushing out behind them.

Joey saw no point in joining the rush. He wasn't expecting any mail. He'd had a letter from his Ma only last week, and nobody else wrote to him.

Benny came in grinning like the Cheshire Cat. 'I've got three letters from Babs,' he said, waving them in the air. He then sat on his bunk and retreated into his own private world.

Outside the sound of the tanks and lorries trundling along meant they would be on the move again very soon.

Sally sat reading the latest letter from Jessie. Her letters were getting fewer now. Jessie was thrilled about the baby, and was very sad to hear about Johnny. She was obviously happy, and Sally often wished she could see her again. If only they could have a night out together. They used to have lots of laughs. Since Johnny's accident and Joey going away, Sally hadn't had many laughs at all. She smiled to herself: what would Jessie have thought about Joey?

Pete was coming home at Easter. He hadn't been able to get away before as the docks were very busy. In his letters he'd said how thrilled he was about the baby, and couldn't wait to see Sally, and he would do all he could to help Johnny. Sally was looking forward to his homecoming far more than she ever had before.

Granny Brent, Vera, and Gwen were also pleased about the forthcoming baby, but Sally was sure Vera gave her a funny look when she told them, and they all queried the fact that Pete didn't want kids just yet. Sally was glad she could look them in the eye and tell them the truth.

Sally and Babs were very apprehensive about Johnny coming home. They hadn't seen him for over a month, and on Easter Saturday they were going to Devon to collect him.

Before Johnny had left the hospital he had seemed a little better. His head and back were healing, and he was getting used to getting in and out of the wheelchair. While he was away his letters had been very short, but he did say he was looking forward to coming home. Sally and Babs had decided to wait for Pete to help them go to Devon to collect Johnny.

On Thursday night, Pete walked in. He put his arms round Sally and kissed her tenderly. 'Yer ain't got much of a lump there yet, love.'

Sally laughed. 'It's good to see you again, Pete. You'll be pleased to know I've stopped being sick.'

Babs kissed Pete's cheek. 'You really missed somethink there – you should 'ave 'eard 'er.'

'We won't go into details now,' said Sally.

'How's Johnny?' Pete asked.

'A lot better now. 'E still can't walk, but at least 'e was talking to us.'

'And writing letters,' added Babs.

'That was awful when 'e wouldn't speak to us. We'd sit there all the 'alf-hour, and 'e wouldn't say a word.'

'We'd come out the 'ospital and 'ave a good cry,' said Babs.

'How's that bloke o' yours?' Pete looked across at Sally, who gave him a filthy look. 'Benny,' he added quickly.

'I ain't 'eard from 'im fer a while. I think 'e's in Africa.'

'That's where Reg and Danny got taken . . .' Again Pete took note of Sally's look. 'We're pushing old Rommel back over there now.'

'I'll put the kettle on,' said Babs.

'I expect you're dying for a cuppa,' said Sally.

He nodded.

'Pete,' whispered Sally when Babs went out the room, 'she ain't 'eard from 'im for a while, so watch what you say.'

'OK.' He raised his voice: 'It's good ter see yer looking so well, Sal.' Then added quietly, 'I've bin really worried about you.'

She smiled and gently touched his cheek. 'It's gonner be good to 'ave you and Johnny 'ome, like old times.'

'It will never be like old times again, not wiv Johnny in a wheelchair.'

'No, I know, but it'll still be nice to 'ave 'im 'ome.' She

was still smiling but in her heart she knew Pete was right. Things would never be the same.

They had been busy getting the front room ready for Johnny.

'How wide's this 'ere wheelchair?' called Pete from the passage.

'The 'ospital said we could get it through the door,' answered Sally.

'I only 'ope they're right.'

'Well, we'll see tomorrer,' said Sally, walking up the passage, wiping her hands on a cloth. 'What did you want to know for?'

'This is gonner be a tight turn fer 'im,' said Pete, standing looking at the doorway.

Sally looked too. 'We'll just 'ave ter 'ope it's wide enough,' she whispered.

'Sit down, love. You've bin doing far too much.'

'I'm all right.'

'You look tired.'

Sally smiled. 'I'm a bit on edge, that's all. But I'll be all right tomorrer, you'll see.'

Pete kissed her. 'I do love you, Sal.'

On Saturday they left home very early. Sally gazed out of the train windows, worried at how Johnny would be towards them.

They walked up a long gravel drive, towards a large white house set in luscious green lawns, and were surprised to see so many men and boys in wheelchairs. Some were laughing in groups, while others were by themselves reading. Nurses were hovering around the grounds.

'Ain't this a lovely place?' said Sally, looking around.

One of the nurses spotted them and hurried over.

'You must be Johnny's family?'

Sally nodded. 'Is 'e all right?'

'He's fine. I think he's in the back garden with his friends. I'll show you the way.'

Sally found it difficult not to stare at the men and boy's who'd lost one or both of their legs.

'Johnny,' called the nurse. 'Your family's here.'

The change in Johnny in such a short time was almost unbelievable. He looked tanned and well.

'You've put on a bit o' weight,' said Sally, bending down and kissing his cheek.

'It's all this sitting around,' he said cheerfully. 'If yer get me fings we'd better be off. I'll just say cheerio ter me mates.'

Sally, Pete, and Babs stood looking in amazement as Johnny sped along the path.

'The old dears in Sefton better watch out,' said Pete. 'When young Johnny goes downhill in that thing, 'e'll run 'em all over.'

Sally had tears in her eyes. ''E looks so 'appy, and so grown up.'

Pete put his arm round her waist. 'Now come on, love, no tears.

'Let's go and collect 'is fings,' said Babs, walking on.

Pete lifted Johnny up in his arms like a baby, and sat him in the train.

'I've put the wheelchair in the guard's van,' said Babs, sitting next to them.

Sally smiled at Johnny. She was thrilled that at long last they were having him home, but she was worried about how she would manage to lift him when Pete was away.

As if reading her mind he said, 'I can do a lot fer meself, yer know. They make yer back there.' He jerked his thumb behind him and laughed. 'I can even take meself ter the lav.'

'Thank Gawd fer that,' said Babs, screwing up her nose. 'Didn't fancy 'olding yer 'and out there.'

They laughed.

As soon as they turned into Sefton, Granny Brent came out of her house, quickly followed by Gwen.

'Yer look ever so well, lad,' said Granny Brent.

'Now don't fergit, Sal, if there's anyfink we can do, yer've only got ter come across.'

'Thanks, Gwen. I won't forget.'

Babs opened the front door, and they all stood to one side while Pete carefully manoeuvred the wheelchair into the passage.

'Well, that's the first hurdle over,' said Pete. 'Now we've got ter see if yer go through the front room door.'

Again Sally held her breath.

'This room looks great,' said Johnny, when he was inside. 'Cor, look at that plane. Where did yer git that from?'

Sally couldn't help the tears. 'Pete got a man where 'e works ter make it for you.'

Johnny shot across the room, banging the bottom of the bed. 'Sorry,' he said. 'I fergits.'

'That's all right,' said Sally quickly. 'Look what Babs got you.'

Babs brought in a box. 'Go on, open it,' she urged.

'Wow. Lead soldiers. Cor, fanks Babs! Where d'yer get 'em from?'

'Mr Silverman's friend.'

'I'll put the kettle on,' said Sally.

In the kitchen she leant against the door. Her tears fell. Johnny was home. At the moment everything was fine, but how would they manage?

'You all right, love?' asked Pete, walking in behind her.

She nodded and wiped her eyes on the multicoloured towel that hung on a nail behind the back door.

'It's gonner take a bit o' getting used ter, and it's a pity I ain't 'ere ter give yer 'and, but yer'll cope.' He kissed her neck as she filled the kettle.

Sally suddenly felt sorry for herself. Since her mum died, she'd always had to cope – through the evacuation, the bombing, her dad going – yes, she knew she had to cope with whatever life threw at her. But Johnny and Pete were home, and she wasn't going to let her feelings get in the way of this week of happiness.

All week visitors came and went, and Sally was pleased that Tony dropped round at every opportunity. She was surprised at how agile Johnny was. Pete made him a ramp to get into the yard, and he didn't need help to get to the lav, as he could move himself in and out of his chair. They tried to push him into the shelter, but the chair was too wide, so they had to let him drag himself through on his bottom. To Sally's amazement he laughed a lot and seemed to have accepted his handicap.

The night before Pete went back to Cardiff, they were all sitting listening to the wireless when Johnny asked, 'Ain't yer going up the pub, Pete?'

'Na, don't feel like it.'

'You lot ain't bin out since I've bin 'ome.'

'Don't worry, we will,' said Babs. ''Sides, since Benny's bin gorn I ain't got nobody ter go wiv.'

'What about yer mate Rachel?'

'Oh yeah, well there ain't bin that much on at the pictures lately.'

'Look, why don't we all go up the Nag's?' said Sally.

'I ain't old enough,' said Johnny, 'and I ain't sitting outside. You and Pete go. I'll stay 'ere and look after me sister.'

'Why, yer cheeky—'

'OK,' said Sally immediately. 'We won't be long.'

'You was a bit quick off the mark in there,' said Pete as they walked along the road.

'I feel like going out.'

''Ere, I 'ope yer ain't gonner get a craving fer the 'ard stuff.'

Sally laughed. 'No chance o' that.'

She was pleased it was quiet in the Nag's, and when Pete returned with the drinks, asked, 'Pete, you are pleased about the baby?'

'Course I am. Ma's tickled pink. She didn't fink I'd got it in me, but I told 'er, I was waiting till the time was right.'

Sally half smiled, as she too had been the subject of Granny Brent's questions, and sometimes wondered if the Brents thought the baby wasn't Pete's.

'Sal, I'm thinking of coming back ter London.'

Sally's heart gave a great leap of joy. That would make such a difference.

'But what about work?'

'I reckon there's plenty about. I've 'eard they're looking fer builders.'

'But you ain't a builder.'

'No, but I'm a quick learner, and there's a lot o' building ter be done round 'ere.'

Sally sat back. 'Won't yer get called up?'

'Building is gonner be exempt, so I've 'eard. Mind you, I don't know if it's true or not, but then I'll worry about that if and when it 'appens.'

'I can't believe this. Oh Pete, it'll be lovely ter 'ave yer around all the time.'

'I think yer really gonner need me, more so now Johnny's 'ome.'

'Pete. Why d'yer think 'e's ser cheerful?'

'I reckon those nurses told 'im off. That or 'e knows yer 'aving a baby and 'e don't wonner upset yer.'

'I suppose that could be it.' But Sally was worried that this might be the calm before the storm.

As spring slipped into summer, everybody was hoping the second front would begin soon. The war was definitely turning and that had given people renewed faith. Sally was getting larger, but felt fine, she had been told the baby was due at the end of September.

It was a warm evening and most of the few residents that were left in Sefton were sitting out on their window sills. Johnny had gone out with Tony, who'd become quite an expert with the wheelchair, and Babs was painting her fingernails.

'Sal, I'm getting ever ser worried about Benny. I ain't 'ad a letter from 'im fer months now.'

'I know. I don't suppose 'e gets a lot o' time to write if 'e's in the fighting. You didn't tell 'im you wasn't gonner marry 'im, did you?'

'Na, I couldn't bring meself ter do it.' She smiled. 'I

really do want ter marry 'im, and I'm really worried about 'im.' She blew on her nails. 'If anyfink 'appened ter 'im d'yer think 'is sister would tell me?'

'I would think so. She does write ter yer.'

'Yeah. 'Is family sound ever ser nice. They was really sorry when they knew about Johnny.'

'That was nice of Benny ter tell 'em.'

'Sal, d'yer ever fink about Joey?'

'Sometimes.'

''E really loved yer, yer know.'

Sally laughed nervously. ''E wouldn't now, not with this lump.' She patted her stomach.

It seemed as if Benny had heard Babs, as the following week she had a letter from him. At first tears filled her eyes, then her mouth fell open as she read it. She looked up at Sally and cried.

'What's wrong? Is 'e all right?'

Babs slowly shook her head. 'No. 'E's bin injured.'

Sally sat down. 'Does 'e say how bad?'

'No, but it must be bad as 'e finks – 'e's gonner be shipped back to America.'

'Does 'e say where 'e is now?'

'No.' She looked at the address. 'It's just a number. Sal, if 'e goes back that means I won't be getting . . .' Babs couldn't finish the sentence.

'Oh Babs, I'm so sorry, but it don't mean you won't get married. 'E loves you, and I'm sure 'e'll come back for you.' Sally knew she was clutching at straws. 'Does 'e say anythink about any of the others?' she asked quietly.

Babs looked up from her letter. 'No.'

Sally thought about Joey. What if he was injured, or . . .? This was something she might never know.

Chapter 33

After the first excitement of Johnny being home, Babs seemed to go into her shell. Every day she waited for the post, hoping for a letter from Benny. The waiting was making her miserable, and as the weeks went on, Sally was getting cross with her moping about all the time.

'You going ter get up?' she shouted angrily up the stairs one morning.

'No.'

'What about yer job?'

'I don't feel like going in terday.'

Sally walked into Babs' room and sat on the bed. 'You'll 'ave Mr Silverman find someone else. Look Babs, I'm sure you'll hear from Benny again soon.'

'But what if 'e's dead?' Babs turned away.

Sally couldn't answer that. 'But 'e wrote to you, and I'm sure 'is mum or sister will write and tell you how 'e is as soon as they know. Babs, you're young and pretty – don't waste your life moping about.'

'I ain't moping about. I just don't feel like going ter work, so leave me alone.'

Sally stood up, her temper rising. 'What about me? I don't always feel like work, but I've got ter do it.

Remember when you said you wasn't gonner marry Benny, you was gonner stay 'ere and 'elp me with Johnny?'

Babs didn't answer.

'What 'appened ter that promise, I'd like ter know?' said Sally as she went downstairs.

June had started hot and sticky, and Sally wasn't looking forward to endless warm days. She put her hands in the small of her back to ease the drag. She was weary, her face damp with sweat. If only Pete could come home. In the last letter she had had from him he'd said it was more difficult than he'd thought to get out of the docks, but he was still trying.

'You all right, Sal?' asked Johnny as she walked into the kitchen.

'Not too bad.'

'It's 'er, ain't it?' He cocked his head towards the door.

'We mustn't be too 'ard on 'er. She's going through a rough patch.'

'Ain't we all.'

Sally smiled. Johnny was growing up fast. She often heard him telling Babs to help. A while back, when they were sitting quietly together she'd asked him why he was a lot happier now, despite his disability. He'd told her that at the convalescent home there were pilots and soldiers who'd lost their legs, and they were happy just to be alive. These men were his heroes. There were kids as well, who'd got some nasty injuries, and it made Johnny realise that he too could have lost his legs in the bombing and it wouldn't do any good hating the world. Sally had thrown her arms round his neck and cried.

Johnny was struggling hard to help himself, and when he banged his wheelchair into the furniture Sally tried not to shout at him. He'd look up and say, 'Sorry, I ain't a very good driver yet, am I?' and give her one of his cheeky grins. He told her he was going to walk again, and Sally would sit massaging his legs, trying to make the muscles strong. They all laughed together if he tried to do too much and fell over. After he'd been out with Tony they would often come back laughing and sweating because Johnny would try to race the tram Tony was on.

Babs too was beginning to come to terms with her lot – the fact she might not hear from Benny again. Then unexpectedly a letter arrived from America.

'Who's it from? 'Is sister?' asked Sally eagerly as Babs tore at the envelope.

'No. It's from Benny,' she said, excitedly scanning the pages.

'How is 'e? Is 'e all right?'

''Ang on.' She sat at the table. 'Sal, 'e's at 'ome. 'E says 'e's not too bad. There's a note from 'is sister as well.' Babs was grinning and began to read her other letter. 'She says 'e'll get well a lot quicker with a lot o' love and care.' She looked up. 'Ain't that nice of 'er?'

Sally was watching Babs' face, pleased to see her smiling again.

'Do they say what's wrong with 'im?'

''E's got shrapnel wounds, but . . .' She stopped, her eyes were open wide, and full of amazement. 'Sal. They want me ter go ter America,' she said slowly.

'What? Why?' asked Sally.

'Benny's coming out the army, and they want me ter go over there.'

'What, ter get married?'

'Yes.'

'Yer can't afford that.' Sally felt deflated. She didn't want Babs to go.

'They're sending me a boat ticket.'

'Is 'e still in New York?' asked Johnny.

Babs nodded.

'That's good. I fancy going ter New York, and if yer living over there I'll 'ave somewhere ter stay.'

'But I can't go. I can't leave you two.'

'What? You must,' said Sally, suddenly realising this was Babs' future. 'Yer'll never get this opportunity again. Yer got ter go. Yer said yer want ter marry Benny – well, now's yer chance.'

'Yeah, but what about you, and the baby, and Johnny?'

'Don't even think about it.'

'If yer don't go, yer could end up being an old maid, and looking after me fer the rest of yer life,' Johnny laughed.

'Yuck!' Babs put out her tongue. 'That's it. That's made up me mind.'

Sally hugged her sister, tears stinging her eyes.

'Yer better send us some wedding cake,' said Johnny, smiling, but he too had tears in his eyes.

'Don't worry, I'll send yer lots and lots o' parcels.'

Over the next few weeks, as plans were made, many letters arrived for Babs, including the boat ticket. She waved it in the air. 'I can't believe it – me going on a big ship.'

Sally was pleased to get a letter from Benny's parents telling her not to worry, and how much they were looking forward to seeing Babs, as Benny didn't stop talking about her. They enclosed photos of him when he was a boy.

'That shows what nice people they are, don't yer think?' said Sally when she showed Granny Brent the letter and the photos.

'Well I 'ope so, fer 'er sake. It's a long way away, and she can't come running back just like that.'

Sally didn't pursue that any more.

The next job was to start turning out Babs' clothes.

'Come on, Babs, we've got a lot to do,' said Sally.

'Good fing the Silvermans are 'elping me get some new stuff. Thanks fer giving me yer clothing coupons.'

'Well, I can't wear any new things yet, so yer might as well 'ave 'em.'

'That was nice of 'em all over at Granny Brent's ter give me some as well, wasn't it?'

'They ain't a bad lot, even if Granny Brent don't approve o' young girls going off ter live in strange countries.'

'Sal, you sure about me taking yer wedding dress?'

'Don't let's go through all that again. I'm only too glad yer gonner be wearing it just as long as you send me lots of photos. Jess is tickled pink that the frock she made's going ter America.' Sally was sad she wouldn't see her sister married, but she wasn't going to let Babs see that. At least she'd know what she was wearing.

'I'm ever so excited. I 'ope I like it over there.' Babs sat on the bed.

'America's a big place.'

'Would you like ter go?'

'Course. It must be lovely ter see Hollywood and all the film stars.'

'Hollywood's a long way from New York. D'yer ever fink about Joey?'

'Sometimes.'

''E was nice, and 'e did look like Tyrone Power. I wonder if 'e's still alive?'

Sally often wondered that as well, but there was no way she would ever know. 'Now come on, stop dreaming. It's a pity Jessie ain't around now. She'd see you 'ad plenty o' new clothes ter take away with you.'

'Sal, I wish you 'ad someone ter take you out now,' said Babs with genuine sadness in her voice. There was always something sad about packing to go away that made you wistful.

'I'll be 'aving Pete and the baby soon.' Sally sat on the bed. She desperately wanted Babs to be happy. She knew Benny loved her, and wanted her near him, that was surely proof enough.

On Saturday night they were all in the Nag's at a party Sally had arranged to say farewell to Babs. Pete had come home for the weekend and Granny Brent and all those that were left in Sefton came to wish Babs a safe journey. Wally even let Johnny come in and sit in the corner.

'Cor, I've only ever bin in 'ere in the day, it looks different at night.'

'When did I let you in?' asked Wally.

'When we 'ad the big raid, remember?'

'Oh yeah,' said Wally. 'Christ, that was some night.'

Sally sat next to Johnny. As she looked round, her thoughts went to all those familiar faces that had gone, many for ever: her father, the Walters, Joyce and Connie Downs and the Slaters. Poor Miss Slater – they never really knew about her all the years she lived here. In her mind's eye Sally could still see Mr Slater being dragged up to dance by Sadie. The times he'd fallen breathless into his chair saying, 'There's many a good tune can still be played on a old fiddle, gel,' and with a twinkle in his eye, he'd smooth down his thin dapper moustache. He'd been such a nice man. And there'd been the times dear old Bess had had to be taken home in the wheelbarrow. Those days would never come again.

Everybody seemed to be moving on. They only saw Fred now and again. He had been promoted and was very important at the wardens' post. Sally thought about those that had just upped and left. What had happened to Silly Billy and his mother? Were they still alive? Then there was Jessie – she'd left Sefton and was happy – and the Downs', now settled in the country. And, of course, there were Reg and Danny, who hopefully would be back one day. And where was Lena? Nobody ever talked about Lena.

'Sal, Sal, you all right? I've bin talking ter yer.' Granny Brent was shaking her.

'Sorry, I must o'drifted off.'

'What, wiv all this bloody racket? Look at that Sadie Tanner dancing wiv yer sister. That Sadie's showing 'er drawers again.'

Sally smiled. Sadie always liked to show off her pink Celanese knickers so everybody knew she was having a good time.

'Yer gonner miss Babs,' said Vera, coming and sitting next to Sally.

'Yes, I am.'

'How yer keeping?'

'Not too bad.'

'I bet yer miss going out wiv Babs and Rachel?'

'A bit, but what with Johnny and the new baby I'll 'ave me work cut out.'

Vera moved closer. 'I've gotter say this, Sal, but a while back I was worried about yer. I fought at one time yer was playing the field.'

Sally was taken off guard. 'What d'yer mean?' she countered.

'I fought yer was going out wiv a Yank like Babs.'

Sally laughed. 'I am married ter yer brother, yer know?' But she was worried that Vera might have said something to Pete or her mother. She had to find out. ''Ere, I 'ope yer kept yer thoughts ter yerself and ain't bin saying things about me ter yer mum. Yer know what she's like – she'd 'ave me fer breakfast,' she said jokingly.

'Na, I wouldn't say anyfing like that. 'Sides, one black sheep in the family's enough, though I did worry fer a bit.'

'Well, I can assure yer I've bin a good girl. Never 'ad the chance. Guide's honour.'

Vera laughed. 'Yer wasn't a guide.'

'No, I know.' Sally breathed a sigh of relief.

'Mind you, didn't fink we'd be seeing young Babs going off to America.'

'A lot o' people 'ave left Sefton.'

'Yeah, I know. I still miss Lena in a funny sort o'way.'

Sally looked at her, surprised, but pleased she'd changed the subject. 'Do yer? But I would 'ave thought after—'

Vera quickly looked at her mother, who luckily was deep in conversation with Mr Roach, who used to go under the arches with them. 'It's 'im I feel sorry fer – Roy – 'cos if 'e don't come up ter scratch, she'll make 'is life 'ell.'

Sally laughed. 'It's a bit different between me and Babs.'

'What's different?' asked Babs as she fell into a chair.

'Nothink,' said Sally. 'Enjoying yerself?'

She kissed Sally's cheek. 'I'm gonner miss all this, and you.'

Sally choked back a tear. She would miss her, more now than she dare let on.

They walked home laughing and chatting loudly. Babs was pushing Johnny along in his wheelchair, and Pete had his arm round Sally's large waist. Pete had told her he hoped to be coming back for good at the end of the month. Sally felt a tear trickle down her cheek, this would be the last time they would all be together. She was anxious about Babs' journey, thinking it must be very dangerous with all the enemy submarines, but Pete had tried to reassure her that things were better now. After all, the American soldiers had come over safely to start with, and people crossed the Atlantic to America every day. But Sally was still worried. She was glad it was dark now and nobody could see her crying.

It was hot and dusty at the railway station, and the platforms seemed to be full of servicemen and women rushing about.

'Yer shouldn't 'ave come, Sal,' said Babs as they struggled with her bags and suitcase and made their way to the platform.

'Yer couldn't 'ave managed without me. 'Sides, I wouldn't let yer go all that way without seeing you off.'

'I know.' Babs put her case on the ground. 'I'll just get me breath back. I wish Johnny was 'ere,' she said, looking all around.

''E couldn't manage 'is chair up and down the steps.'

'No, course. Sal, do you fink I'm doing the right fing?'

'It's a bit late now.'

'No, it ain't.'

'You ain't got second thoughts – 'ave you?'

Babs shook her head. 'No, it's just . . .' She picked up her case. 'Come on.'

The train was standing at the platform and Babs threw her arms round Sally. 'I ain't 'alf gonner miss you,' she sobbed.

Sally held her close. She too had tears running down her face. 'And I'm gonner miss you. This reminds me of when you was evacuated.'

'I ain't got a label tied ter me coat now though,' she said, wiping her eyes.

'Let's 'ave no more tears. You're smudging your mascara. Think of Benny waiting for you.'

A faint smile lifted Babs' face. 'You do like 'im, don't yer?'

'Course I do.'

''Is mum sounds nice as well, don't she? I do love 'im, Sal.'

'Well 'e's a smashing bloke, and a good dancer. 'E taught me a few things.'

'That ain't everythink though, is it, Sal?'

'No. You just look after 'im and yerself.'

'P'raps when this war's over you and Pete can bring the little'n and come and see us.'

Sally laughed. 'I could just see Pete spending that sort o' money on a holiday.'

The train started to let off steam and the passengers were beginning to climb on board. People were shouting, children were crying, doors were slamming, windows were being pulled down and the gap quickly filled with people poking their heads out, waving and collecting those precious last-minute kisses.

Babs picked up her suitcase.

'You will write as soon as you can? Promise,' said Sally, holding on to Babs' arm.

Babs had tears streaming down her face. 'I promise, as soon as I can. Don't worry about me. You look after yerself for a change, and the baby, and Johnny.' She gave Sally a hug, and disappeared on to the train.

Sally frantically looked for her at the windows, but they were all full. Slowly the train began to move. Girls were running beside it, holding on to their loved ones' hands. Kids were waving wildly at the sea of faces that got smaller and smaller as the train gathered momentum. It wasn't till the train snaked out of sight that the people started to move away. Many were crying unashamedly.

Sally wiped her eyes. Babs had gone. All her life she had been there. Would she ever see her sister again? New York was such a long way away. As Sally pushed her way through the crowd, her thoughts wandered. His parents sounded nice people, and they must have money to be able to send Babs the fare to go over there. How they'd laughed at the photos of Benny when he was a boy . . .

She shuffled through the gates with the rest of those that had been left behind, touching her full stomach and smiling. She had plenty to look forward to. Pete would soon be working locally, and Johnny was happy enough, and who knew, he could be walking again? It was a shame Babs wouldn't be there to share the new baby with them, but she'd got a new life of her own, and she'd have a new husband. Sally prayed everything would work out fine for her.

At the bus stop Sally read the news vendors' lunchtime headlines. Italy had signed an armistice – that was good news. Perhaps the end was in sight now.

When Sally pushed open the front door, there was a letter on the mat simply addressed to 'Sally'. It had an American stamp.

'It must be from Benny's parents,' she said out loud. 'They don't know my married name.' She felt weary and put the letter in the pocket of her smock for a moment. It was Johnny's day to help Mr Booker. Once a week he went along to the shop to lend Tony a hand with the orders. It was good for him to feel useful.

Sally turned the wireless on and put her feet up, then sat back to enjoy her cup of tea. Only then did she remember the letter in her pocket.

She opened it, and took a quick breath.

Dear Sally,

I hope you don't mind me taking the liberty of writing to you, and calling you Sally, but we don't have a surname.

I found your letter in our son's belongings when they were sent to us from Africa. You see our dear boy Joey was killed over there. I know he was fond of you as he'd written and told us, but from what we can gather from your letter you didn't want to see him.

Perhaps you are married. I know Joey would have wanted you to know that he is no longer with us.

May God take care of you, and pray that perhaps one day we shall all be together.

Sincerely,

Mr and Mrs Power.

Sally sat looking at the letter, tears streaming from her eyes. Joey had gone, was never coming back. She thought of all the laughter, the dancing, and the fun she had had with him. She had been so fond of him and he'd been so good-looking – what if she'd gone off with him? What would her life have been? Deep down she knew she would never have done anything to upset her life with Pete. Pete would never be a romantic like Joey, but he was solid and reliable, and she really did love him, and he loved her, even if he didn't always show it in a way she would have liked. Poor Joey's parents, they must be devastated. To lose your child . . .

Despite the warmth of the day Sally shuddered. So many parents had lost their children, and so many children had lost their parents during these terrible years. She smiled through her tears when she felt her baby move.

'I 'ope you never 'ave to see the things we've seen,' she whispered, gently caressing her unborn baby.

The sound of the front door banging against the wall meant Johnny was home. His wheelchair trundled down the passage.

''Allo, Sal. Babs git off OK?' he said, pushing the kitchen door open.

Sally nodded.

''Ere, don't cry. She'll be all right.'

Sally blew her nose. 'I'll get the tea,' she said, disappearing into the scullery.

'I'll be glad when Pete's back,' shouted Johnny from the kitchen. 'We'll be able to go out tergevver then.'

Sally looked out of the scullery window at the air-raid shelter. So many people had gone out of her life and it seemed to be a monument for them, and all everyone had suffered.

Then she smiled. From the feel of it there was a new life coming into Sefton Grove very soon.